Praise

'Dramatic, mysterious and compelling ... it's easy to read this book in one sitting' *Vogue*

'Younger sister Nicola gives novelists Liane and Jaclyn Moriarty a serious run for the literary awards in this pacey, circle-of-friends thriller, which accelerates in its intensity and sheer originality with every page ... An Agatha Christie Mousetrap of a "who-wrote-it?" to solve' *Australian Women's Weekly*

'a delightful romp of a novel that will have you laughing on one page, crying at the next' *Better Reading*

'Readers ... will race to the end as a credit to Nicola's fine sense of pacing and suspense. An author to watch' *Booklist*

'A delightful, heartwarming exploration of the twists and turns of true friendship, *The Fifth Letter* was simply delicious from the very first page to the last ... Relatable characters, a fast-moving plot and just the right amount of mystery. I was hooked!' Rachael Johns, internationally bestselling author

'A brilliant and compelling novel where a twenty-year-old friendship is tested by the secrets they have been keeping. The plot is fascinating ... the author creates suspense and anticipation as truths — and lies — are spilled page after page' *Chicklit Club*

'Once you start you're not going to want to stop. Page turner indeed. Wow' *Sharpest Pencil*

Praise for *Those Other Women*

'This novel shows the same sharp eye for neat plotting that Nicola Moriarty revealed in *The Fifth Letter* ... Moriarty is fair-minded about this conflict, often manages to be funny about it, and deftly employs the features and uses of Facebook to kick along the plot' *Sydney Morning Herald*

'A firecracker of a novel' Liane Moriarty

'Nicola Moriarty instinctively knows what we want to read and gives it to us on a platter — juicy, topical, honestly raw and full of twists and turns that we never see coming, *Those Other Women* does everything right' Tess Woods, author of *Love at First Flight*

'Moriarty trains a spotlight on the pitfalls of social media and how quickly rumour is presented as fact' *Courier Mail*

'I devoured it, loved it and totally escaped into it ... Fun and topical' *Marian Keyes*

'A darkly droll page-turner ... a tasty divertissement' *Publishers Weekly*

Nicola Moriarty is a Sydney-based novelist, copywriter and mum to two small (but remarkably strong-willed) daughters. In between various career changes, becoming a mum and completing her Bachelor of Arts, she began to write. Now she can't seem to stop. Her previous works include the bestselling novels *The Fifth Letter* and *Those Other Women*.

nicolamoriarty.com.au
facebook.com/NicolaMoriartyAuthor
@NikkiM3 (Twitter)
@nicmoriarty (Instagram)

THE
EX

NICOLA MORIARTY

HarperCollins*Publishers*

HarperCollins_Publishers_

First published in Australia in 2019
by HarperCollins*Publishers* Australia Pty Limited
ABN 36 009 913 517
harpercollins.com.au

HarperCollins_Publishers_
Level 13, 201 Elizabeth Street, Sydney NSW 2000, Australia
Unit D1, 63 Apollo Drive, Rosedale, Auckland 0632, New Zealand
A 53, Sector 57, Noida, UP, India
1 London Bridge Street, London SE1 9GF, United Kingdom
Bay Adelaide Centre, East Tower, 22 Adelaide Street West, 41st floor, Toronto,
    Ontario M5H 4E3, Canada
195 Broadway, New York NY 10007, USA

A catalogue record for this book is available from the National Library of Australia

ISBN 978 1 4607 5663 8 (paperback)
ISBN 978 1 4607 1052 4 (ebook)
ISBN 978 1 4607 9069 4 (audio book)

Cover design by Hazel Lam, HarperCollins Design Studio
Cover images: Brunette woman by Marija Savic / stocksy.com / 1654898; redheaded woman by
Danil Nevsky / stocksy.com / 797901; all other images by shutterstock.com
Typeset in ITC New Baskerville by Kirby Jones
Author photograph by Sally Flegg
Printed and bound in Australia by McPherson's Printing Group
The papers used by HarperCollins in the manufacture of this book are a natural, recyclable product
made from wood grown in sustainable plantation forests. The fibre source and manufacturing
processes meet recognised international environmental standards, and carry certification.

For my two small girls, Maddie and Piper.
You're not allowed to read beyond this page
until you're older. Shall we say sixteen?
Sorry.

THE ELEVATOR

The door was almost closed when an arm was thrust through the crack, causing it to jolt to a stop and then slowly shudder its way open again. Georgia stepped back.

Whoever it is, just don't let it be Cadence, don't let it be Cadence. Please, please, don't let it be Cadence.

A woman stepped in, her eyes down, her face blotched with angry patches. Strawberry-blonde hair partly obscured her contorted features. But Georgia could still recognise her.

Cadence.

PART ONE

Georgia

CHAPTER ONE

'One of the other dolly birds tells me I won't be seeing you tonight.'

'Dolly birds,' Georgia repeated as she gently rolled her patient onto his side and lifted the dressing on his lower back. 'That's a new one I haven't heard before.'

'Who's going to tuck me in tonight?'

'I'm sure you'll do just fine with one of the other "dolly birds", Jerry.'

Georgia knew Jerry would be horrified if someone pointed out how inappropriate his comments could be at times. He was only acting this way because he was still frightened of complications post-surgery — even though he'd had a minor procedure and she'd reassured him many times there was next to zero chance of *any* complications. Dr Harris had wanted to send him back home immediately after the surgery, but Georgia had managed to convince him to let Jerry stay one night. For once they weren't over-extended and Georgia didn't see how it could hurt.

She examined the skin around Jerry's stitches. It was faintly yellow with bruising. No sign of the infection Jerry had insisted he could 'sense'.

She shifted slightly and her sneaker squeaked on the linoleum floor. Jerry made a face. 'Can't stand that sound.'

'Then you shouldn't spend so much time here.' She paused then added in a gentler tone, 'Healing up nicely round here, by the way. Textbook recovery.'

Jerry was a walking contradiction. He was nervous about being in hospital, yet he found reasons to get himself checked in as often as possible.

He gave a doubtful sounding huff. 'We'll see. Can't you do something about the constant beeping in here? Why is there always something beeping?'

'It's a hospital. Beeping sounds are a given. I find it soothing.'

She genuinely did. The constant beeps added a perpetual rhythm to her day as she did her obs. *Beep beep, take the blood pressure, beep beep, check temperature, beep, beep, heart rate low, oxygen saturation a concern, beep, beep, slipping into red zone …*

That rhythm meant she could handle emergency situations with a sense of calm. Other nurses who'd been at the job longer seemed to take it in their stride, but Georgia still needed to take a beat and prepare herself when things went south.

'I don't,' said Jerry. 'I find it bloody annoying.' His gruff tone failed to mask his nerves. 'So why are you abandoning me to leave early?'

'I'm not abandoning you,' she reassured him. 'And I'm not leaving early, either. I was on morning shift today. I have a date tonight.'

'A date! You're breaking my heart. I was going to get down on my good knee for you as soon as you let me out of this bed.' He shifted as he tried to turn his head and wink at Georgia.

'Hold still, I'm just going to re-dress this for you. What would Eileen say about you getting down on one knee anyway? Don't think she'd be too impressed. Especially after she brought you flowers.' Georgia nodded her head at the vase of sweet peas sitting by Jerry's bed. The floral scent was mingling with the familiar chemical smells of the hospital. 'From my own garden,' she'd told Georgia as she strode into the room in her pressed navy slacks and crisp white shirt, collar turned up; her perfectly set and dyed hair a blonde halo around her head. 'And this one is for you to take home,' she'd added, handing Georgia a small bunch of the pink and purple flowers, the stems wrapped up in damp paper towel and covered with twisted foil.

Jerry waved his hand as though to brush Georgia's concerns away. 'She'd enjoy the break from me. She's always said she likes the sound of a nice singles cruise with the girls.'

'Easy.' Georgia steadied him as he almost rolled onto his back. 'I'm not done here yet.'

She smoothed the new bandage and pulled his pyjama top back down, then eased him into a more comfortable position. He reached out for his comb and ran it through his thinning white hair. His sense of pride wouldn't allow him to sit with tousled hair for even a moment. The vulnerability in that one simple, self-conscious action gave Georgia's heart a sharp twist.

'So, who's this bloke you're going off on a date with tonight?'

'God, you're nosy,' she teased.

'Not nosy. Interested.'

He patted the side of the bed and she leaned against it, despite herself. She knew she didn't have the time, but she was looking forward to tonight and, if she was honest with herself, she was glad to have the opportunity to chat about it.

'All right, all right. His name is Brett and I met him through Tin — ah … through a dating app.'

'Swiped right on him, did you?' Jerry winked, clearly proud of himself for knowing about Tinder.

'Yes. He seems like a really nice guy. We've chatted back and forth for over a week and —'

'A week!' Jerry cut her off. 'You chatted *over* a week? Oh well, you've seen into each other's souls then. You're practically joined at the hip.' He shook his head. 'Jesus, Georgia, should you be meeting some bloke you met on the iPhone this soon?'

She laughed. 'You think I have time to wait around?'

'Young whippersnapper like you? Plenty of time.'

She was thirty-four, hardly a whippersnapper. Although as the youngest of her family, she did often feel like a baby. It didn't help that her older brothers still treated her like she was twelve, and when she was with them it felt natural to slip back into that role of baby sister, even if she didn't mean to. Three of them were married with kids. The fourth, Marcus, was getting married in a month. Soon she would be the last one standing. At least having several grandchildren meant her mother wasn't on at her to have kids of her own. In fact, she often made comments to Georgia about how children weren't a necessity to live a full and rewarding life. 'You could travel whenever you like,' she said, 'see the world.' She said this so much that Georgia sometimes wondered if her mother actually regretted having five kids. Her parents had taken off overseas the moment Georgia finished high school, and they'd been travelling on and off ever since.

The problem was, Georgia *did* want to have children. She wanted to meet someone. She wanted to settle down and get married and have the Cinder-fucking-ella happily ever after and screw it if that wasn't what women were supposed to want anymore. Obviously, she saw the problem with those sorts of innately sexist fairy-tale endings. She knew there was more to life than romantic relationships. She'd read books like *Eat Pray Love* and *Girlboss*; she knew the importance of independence and self-actualisation and career satisfaction. But she also didn't want to be alone any longer.

'See, I'm not so sure that I do have that much time, Jerry. Besides, until I meet him in person I'll never know if he is who he says he is.'

'Yes, but is it safe?'

'Very safe. I'm meeting him in a public place, plenty of people around. Now, I really have to go. I'll duck my head in and check on you again before I leave.'

'All right, but promise me I'll hear all about this date of yours tomorrow.'

'Deal.'

Georgia strode from the room before Jerry could protest. She knew she wasn't supposed to stop and chat when she was doing her rounds, but she loved getting to know her patients, and Jerry was a frequent flyer so it was hard not to get caught up chatting with him.

'Indulging Jerry again?' said a voice behind her as Georgia stepped out into the hall. She turned to see Amber leaning against the wall, arms folded. Her short hair was lilac and dead straight today. Interesting. Last week she'd been a brunette.

'What are you doing lurking there?'

'I'm not lurking. I was waiting for you. But I didn't want to come inside the hypochondriac's room and get stuck.'

Georgia elbowed her friend. 'Leave him alone, he's *fine*.'

'He's a time vortex.'

Georgia began heading for the nurses station, Amber following behind.

'Looking forward to tonight's date?' Amber asked.

'Yep. He's definitely the one.'

'Georgia!'

'I'm kidding. But seriously, I think it will be good. He does seem really nice. Not a single mention of wanting to send me a dick pic — serious improvement on the last two guys I matched with on Tinder.'

'Where are you meeting him?'

'The Crooked Tailor.'

'The cocktail bar in Castle Hill? Nice, I've been wanting to try that place out.'

Georgia had been wanting to try it out too. It was only a five-minute walk from her apartment, but every time she suggested it to the nurses at work after their shift or on a rare day more than three of them were off, they always ended up at the Bella Vista Hotel.

'You got anything on tonight?'

'It's my weekend with Violet; her dad is dropping her off later. I'm planning on a movie with popcorn at home.'

They stopped at the nurses station and Georgia leaned over the counter to swap her files over. 'That sounds nice.' She paused then added carefully, 'Do you miss her when she's with her dad?'

As usual, Amber's face shut down. 'Yep,' she said, her voice clipped. Despite being friends for more than two years now, Georgia still didn't know how Amber's eight-year-old daughter had ended up with the father almost full-time, while Amber only got to see her once every fortnight. It was clear that Amber found this tough, and Georgia desperately wished Amber trusted her enough to open up more. But she'd been down this road before and it had always resulted in Amber becoming more tight-lipped than ever. So, Georgia swiftly switched topics. 'Hey, I'm liking the purple hair. Did Denise say anything?'

Their boss was friendly enough but Denise was also very old-school in the way she ran her staff.

'She pursed her lips, like this,' said Amber, demonstrating. 'I've probably ruined my chance of getting that senior nurse role in intensive care.'

'Don't be silly. She can't overlook you because of purple hair. You're definitely the favourite for that position.'

'We'll see.'

'Hey, can you come with me to see that teenager we've got in bed fifteen? I think she was trying to play me for more pain meds she doesn't need.'

'Of course she was. She can tell you're a softie. Okay, I'll come with you and play bad cop if you promise me you'll wear your sexy red top on your date tonight.'

'Done.'

*

Georgia leaned one elbow on the bar and tapped out a message to Amber.

How's movie night going?

It was fun, but V's crashed out already. I'm doing the super creepy mum thing and watching her sleep because she's so damn beautiful. Hey, why are you texting me? Aren't you in middle of date?

So far, he's a no-show.

Shit. Sorry honey. That sucks. How late is he?

45 mins.

Why are you still there?!! Go home!

Yeah. Guess so. X

Georgia put her phone down and looked around the bar again. A small part of her was still hoping he might turn up. It didn't make any sense; they'd been getting along so well over the past few days. He was the one who'd suggested the date, and this venue as well. Why go to all that trouble only to stand her up? Was it possible he was here and they simply hadn't recognised one another? It *was* busy.

She'd strategically placed herself towards the end of the bar so that if she turned side-on she could see most of the pub as well as the main entrance. It was a great bar, part of the changing landscape of the Hills area where she'd grown up. There definitely wasn't anything like this around when she was in her early twenties and going out every night with her mates. Back then if you wanted funky little hole-in-the-wall wine bars you had to venture into the city.

That said, a night of drinks at the old Tavern when she was twenty had definitely been a hell of a lot cheaper than the two cocktails she'd had while waiting for her date. The atmosphere did make up for it though. The music was an eclectic mix of jazz and old-school hip hop. It was odd, but it worked. The couches were leather, the walls panelled with timber and the windows made of stained glass.

Brett had definitely said in his text that he'd meet her here at the bar. They'd agreed there would be no cheesy props — no 'I'll be the one with a yellow flower in my hair' or 'holding a copy of *Love in the Time of Cholera*', but Georgia was almost wishing they had done that. At least then she could be certain he wasn't sitting two metres away. Then again, she'd had to pretend she knew *Love in the Time of Cholera* when he'd made that joke. Had he brought it along, then he might have wanted to talk about it and she'd have to admit she didn't actually know anything about it, even though he'd spoken about it like it was a classic that everyone ought to have read.

The thing was, if he was here, surely he would have approached her by now to ask if she was his date. Plus, she would have been easy enough to recognise. The photo on her Tinder profile was a shot of her with her long, curly brown hair hanging in a plait over one shoulder, sunglasses propped up on her head, wearing a black singlet top. It was from last summer so her shoulders were browned from too much time spent in the sun. Tonight she'd worn a black top not too dissimilar to the one in her photo and styled her hair in the exact same way. She'd avoided adding any kind of filter to the shot because the last thing she needed was to have some guy start back-pedalling the minute he saw her face to face because she didn't look as good in real life.

It was probably about time Georgia admitted the truth. He really had stood her up.

She picked up her drink — The Burning Man, a concoction of bourbon, vanilla, turmeric and cinnamon — and swallowed the last mouthful. It burned the back of her throat but warmed her insides as it slid down towards her stomach.

She was about to hop off her stool when two guys appeared either side of her, one of them immediately invading her personal space by squeezing in between her seat and the wall at the end of the bar.

'Drinking alone?' asked the one on her right. 'That's a bit sad on a Friday night.' He was wearing a checked shirt with rolled-up sleeves that strained around his biceps and there was a powerful scent of spirits on his breath. The one on her left was in a similarly too-tight white T-shirt. But instead of showing off his biceps, it highlighted his paunch.

'Actually, I was just leaving.' Georgia tried to swing her legs out from under the bar but Checked Shirt moved in closer and blocked her.

''Scuse me,' she said. 'Can you move, please?'

'Only if you let us buy you a drink first.'

'I'm good, thanks.'

Even though the pub was packed, Georgia felt a panicked flutter in her stomach. She didn't like the way they'd positioned themselves either side of her, or the way he'd tried to patronise her.

The one on her left slung a heavy arm around her shoulders. 'Come on,' he breathed into her ear, 'don't be stuck up. Let us buy you a drink.'

On the word 'stuck', a tiny bit of spit hit her on the side of the cheek and she rubbed hard at her face with the sleeve of her shirt. An intense combination of fear and anger was rising up inside her. Once upon a time she would have brushed off their overt advances as the kind of shit that you had to put up with as a woman. She might have even laughed about it with her mates later on. *And can you believe, a bit of his spit landed on my face? So revolting!* But not anymore. Not since 'the incident' — as her parents called it. Besides, she didn't even have that many mates anymore. Just her friends from the hospital.

She was trying to figure out the best way to deal with them. Should she get physical? Jab them in the ribs with her elbows so she could make her escape — the same way she used to when she was young and her brothers were wrestling with her?

But then another voice intruded. 'Hey guys, how about you give her some space?'

Georgia twisted around and saw a third guy with blond hair standing behind them, taller than either of them, although he didn't look as well-built as Checked Shirt. If the three of them got into a fight, she wasn't sure how well he would fare. He gave her a quick smile before focusing his attention back on the two blokes and Georgia felt an unexpected jolt. She wanted to see that smile again.

'Get lost, mate, she's fine,' said the paunchier one.

'How about you let her speak for herself?'

Her confidence bolstered, Georgia spoke more firmly. 'Yeah, actually. What he said. I'd like you to give me some bloody space, thanks.'

A bartender appeared in front of them. 'Everything okay here?' He threw a tea towel over his shoulder and folded his arms as he looked between the four of them.

Her would-be saviour spoke up. 'It will be, once these two morons get the message they're not wanted here.'

'Gentlemen?' The bartender eyed them and then nodded his head towards the door, where a stocky security guard was stationed. The message was clear, and the two guys threw him a filthy look as they admitted defeat and headed for the door.

The bartender turned his attention to Georgia. 'Really sorry about that. I've been keeping an eye on those two all night but I got busy and didn't realise they'd started hassling you. It was Burning Man you were drinking, wasn't it? I'll grab you one on the house.'

Georgia was about to decline, but the thought of heading out alone straight after those two wasn't appealing. 'Okay, thanks,' she said.

The blond guy gave her a sympathetic look. 'You okay?' he asked.

'Fine,' she told him, but there was a slight wobble to her voice.

'Really?' His voice was soft and knowing, and Georgia gave in.

'Okay. I didn't love the fact that I had to be rescued just now.'

She was rewarded with another one of those quick smiles and she saw a deep dimple appear on his left cheek. Was that what made his smile so appealing?

'Nope,' he said. 'You didn't need rescuing. You looked like you were about to handle them yourself, but you were outnumbered so it was hardly fair.'

'Thank you, that was really kind of you. I'm Georgia, by the way.'

'Luke.'

Georgia offered her hand and it was enveloped in a warm, firm grip. 'Nice to meet you.'

'You too. I've seen those blokes hassling women here before,' he added. 'Hopefully they won't let them in again.'

'So, you just hang out here rescuing people?'

'Ha! Not exactly. I was here tonight with a few work mates and hung around for one more drink after they left — found myself people-watching.' He nodded his head at the stool next to Georgia. 'You mind?'

'All yours.' Georgia couldn't help noticing the movement of his biceps under his shirt as he sat down and leaned his elbows on the bar. Maybe she'd been wrong when she'd thought he wouldn't have been able to take on those other two idiots.

'Are you here alone?' Luke asked.

'Yes,' she said. 'I was meant to …' Georgia felt her cheeks warm slightly at having to admit she'd been stood up, but Luke jumped in for her.

'Don't tell me — some Tinder wanker stood you up?'

She couldn't help laughing. 'How did you know?'

'Because it's totally happened to me. And it sucks. Wow, what a shitty night for you.'

'Yeah, kinda has been.'

The bartender placed her cocktail in front of her. 'Right,' he said, 'just shout if you need me to get rid of this guy for you next.'

'Oi,' Luke protested.

Georgia laughed. 'Nah, he can stay.' She stirred her drink with her straw then picked it up and sipped it.

'So, who was he?' Luke asked.

'Who?'

'The guy you were meant to meet.'

'Oh right. His name was Brett.'

'Brett? Rubbish name. That was your first mistake.'

'Rubbish? What's rubbish about the name Brett?'

'The fact that he stood you up.' He grinned and the dimple returned, but this time she noticed that it was his eyes.

That was what made his smile so hot — his eyes crinkled and they were a pale grey-green and Georgia had to look away and clear her throat before she could respond.

'I don't think he stood me up because his name is Brett.'

'How do you know? It could be a character trait closely associated with the name.'

'All right, well, what was the name of the girl who stood you up then?'

'When?'

'I don't know when. You said it had happened to you.'

'Oh, no. No one's ever stood me up, I was just trying to make you feel better. You really think anyone's going to stand all of this up?' He motioned to himself and Georgia reached out to whack his arm with the back of her hand.

'Are you kidding me right now?'

He dodged her and laughed. 'Yes. I'm kidding. Her name was Laura.'

'Laura? Well there you go. Lauras definitely stand people up. Laura and Brett should probably get married.'

'Actually, I have a feeling Laura was a sixty-year-old man named Bruce. I did a reverse Google image search on her picture afterwards and it turned out to be a stock photo.'

'Hey, at least you didn't get conned into competing with fifty other guys for a date with Laura like that weird Tinder date in New York.'

'What? What happened?'

'I was reading about it on Facebook the other day. This model invited a whole heap of guys she'd connected with on Tinder to the same date, and then when they arrived she made them all compete "Hunger Games" style to go on the date with her. Apparently she had them doing push-ups and sprints.'

'Oh my God, that *is* weird.' He paused. 'Hey, you want another drink?'

Georgia looked down at her glass. She hadn't even realised she'd downed it so fast while they were chatting. 'Yeah, why not? But I'll buy, I owe you one.'

'No, you don't.'

'Yes, I do. You rescued me from a shitty, shitty night, so let me buy you a drink.'

They motioned to the bartender and ordered. Georgia managed to pay only by throwing out an arm to stop Luke from passing his card across. 'I told you, my shout,' she said crossly. 'What it is with men and their determination to pay for everything? You can buy the next round.'

'All right, all right. As long as you let me get the next one, then fine. Hey,' said Luke as they waited for their drinks, 'have I ever run into you here before? I'm suddenly thinking you look a bit familiar.' He stared right at her and Georgia felt herself warming under his gaze.

'Umm, I'm never actually been here before. My usual is the Bella Vista Hotel.'

'Ah well, maybe I've just spotted you there. Although ...' He stroked his chin thoughtfully.

'Although what?'

'Well, it seems wrong. See, if I had spotted you before I'm pretty sure I would have tried to hit on you. Hope you didn't shoot me down.'

'Oh my God, imagine if that had happened.' She gave Luke a smile. 'Although …'

'What?'

'I'm pretty sure I wouldn't have.'

Luke smiled back at her.

CHAPTER TWO

Georgia was feeling very 1990s Disney rom-com when she stepped inside her tiny one-bedroom apartment, the smile on her face making her cheeks hurt. Any minute now a small blue cartoon bird would land on her shoulder and she'd burst into song. Although her apartment wasn't really large enough or tidy enough for her to start spinning around in circles, singing about meeting Prince Charming. She'd probably trip over a basket of dirty washing and break a lamp.

They'd stayed at the pub chatting for a good two hours. She'd learned that Luke worked as a sales rep for an office supplies company, that his favourite music was R'n'B, and that he liked weightlifting and cycling. In response, she'd made him flex his biceps so she could see how genuine he was. It was an excellent excuse to touch his arms, and she'd conceded that he was, in fact, quite genuine. She liked that his muscles were lean like Ryan Reynolds' rather than bulging like The Rock's.

In return, she'd told Luke about her job as a nurse, that she loved getting to know her patients even though there wasn't usually the time, that she had four brothers, and also that she could recite every word to Salt-N-Pepa's 'Shoop'. Obviously, she had to back up her claim by immediately reciting the lyrics while Luke looked it up on his phone to check her accuracy.

When they'd eventually decided to call it a night, he'd walked her home and kissed her chastely on the cheek before calling an Uber for himself.

Stop it, she reprimanded herself now. *Do not get carried away.* She lifted her hands to her face to massage her cheeks and try to wipe the smile away. Just because tonight went well didn't mean he was going to end up being 'the one'. How many times before had she met a guy and thought they'd hit it off, only for him to ghost her out of nowhere? And why did they so often end up doing that after one, two or even three dates? Probably because she chased them away with her own fears and insecurities. *You have a shitty history with men, Georgia, never forget that. Luke might not even call.*

As if on cue she felt her phone buzz with a text message. She pulled it out to take a look.

Hey Georgia, this is Luke … from the pub … from tonight … from like, five minutes ago, actually. And now I'm saying that, I'm realising it's way too soon to text you, right? Oops.

Georgia couldn't help laughing out loud. She pushed away the nasty thoughts and took herself back to the place where she'd been when she first walked in the door. Blue cartoon birds of happiness. She kicked off her heels and walked over to her couch where she sat down with her legs tucked up underneath her before tapping out a reply:

Yep. You've blown it. Shown all your cards. Bugger. What are we going to do now?

Luke shot back:

Well clearly, you're going to have to show me some of your cards.

Georgia stared at her phone trying to think of a reply that was somehow witty and sexy and clever all at once. Did she keep the whole card analogy going? Did she turn 'showing him her cards' into a metaphor for something more explicit? God, flirting was hard sometimes.

Okay, I've got it. I'm going to have to even things out by asking you out for a drink before you ask me. Sound good? Puts us back on a level playing field.

Oh my God she's a genius. And I would love to … but how about we make it dinner?

Sold.

The smile was back. Georgia couldn't help it. It had been such a long time since she'd met a guy and it had been this much fun. And really, why shouldn't she feel optimistic about the potential for things to go well? *You'll meet someone when you least expect it.* That's what her mum always said when Georgia complained she was sick of being alone. Although this was often alternated with, *however, solitude really is a wonderful thing.*

That was kind of what had happened tonight, wasn't it? Well, she *was* expecting to meet someone; she'd just thought it would be Brett. She wasn't annoyed with him for standing her up anymore, she was glad. If he hadn't, she wouldn't have met Luke.

She lay back on the couch and stared up at the ceiling, then immediately realised the ceiling was swaying. She'd had way too many cocktails to lie flat on her back yet. She sat back up again, burped loudly and chuckled to herself. *Glad I didn't do that in front of him.*

She headed into the kitchen for a glass of water, which she forced herself to drink in one go before refilling it and taking it back to the couch where she picked up her phone again and texted Marcus. *You up?* A few seconds later, the phone was ringing.

'What's up?' he said. 'Everything okay?'

'Why do you assume there's a problem?' she asked. 'I just wanted to chat while I wait for the room to stop spinning enough that I can go to bed.'

'Ah, now I see. My little sister has gone and got herself scuttered. Georgia Fitzpatrick, tut, tut, tut.'

'Have not. Well, maybe a little. Well, maybe quite a bit. Is scuttered even a word anyway? I don't think it is. What's happening in your world?'

'Not much, you know, work, gym, the usual. Oh yeah, and that whole "I'm getting MARRIED in a month" thing.'

'Are you stressed? No cold feet, right?'

'Nope, I'm all good. Bianca's super organised so there's not really much that I have to do — apart from wear a nice suit and show up.'

'You typical bloody bloke. Man, I can't believe you're getting married and I haven't even met your future wife yet.'

'You've FaceTimed her.'

'Not the same as meeting in person. Anyway, she might have it all under control now, but make sure you're ready to help in case there's any last-minute panic. Remember Troy's wedding? Mum was meant to pick up the cake but she forgot and Chloe had a major meltdown.'

'All right, I'll make sure I'm ready to swoop in and save the day if needed. Room stopped spinning yet? I need to get to sleep, early start in the morning.'

'Yeah I'm good. Night.'

'Night, little Fitz.'

Georgia hung up the phone and was about to head to bed when she thought of something. She found a scrap of paper and a pen and scribbled down the words: *You might have met someone tonight!* Then she found her 'happiness jar' and pushed the note inside before replacing the lid. Once upon a time, she needed to find reasons to write notes for this jar as often as possible. Anything to help her believe that her life was good. But she'd actually forgotten about it these last few months. It was nice to add a new reason to be happy to the jar tonight.

*

Throughout the week, Luke messaged her the perfect number of times. Not so many that it felt over the top, considering they were only just about to have their first date. But he didn't go so quiet for her to worry he'd lost interest. Just the odd, 'looking forward to Friday' messages that made her skin tingle with anticipation.

As promised, she'd been in to see Jerry to tell him how the failed Tinder date had gone. He'd been so cross when he heard she'd been stood up that she was worried his blood pressure was going to spike. But when he heard about Luke's chivalrous actions he'd calmed down and listened quietly as she told him all about Luke.

'Sounding a bit smitten,' he said when she was done.

'Not smitten … yet,' she replied. 'Just hopeful.'

'Well, don't forget that it's fine to take these things slowly.'

'Trust me, with my track record, I'm all about taking it slow.' She'd meant for it to come out sounding light-hearted, but from the creased lines on Jerry's forehead, she realised she'd sounded more bitter than she'd intended. 'Sorry,' she said quickly, 'I just mean that … I umm, I've had my fair share of mistakes.'

'What happened?' Jerry asked.

'Oh, no, nothing in particular, I just mean the usual kind of dating stuff.'

'Georgia, respectfully, that sounds like bullshit.'

'Jerry!' Georgia laughed. 'Okay, okay, there's a story, but it's not something I'm all that fond of chatting about, so we'll leave it there.' She kept her tone firm so for once Jerry knew she meant business and didn't try to push her on it.

*

When Friday finally arrived, Georgia was the most nervous she'd been before a first date in a long time. Amber sat cross-legged on the bed while Georgia changed into black jeans and a silvery top. Her bed was the one indulgent thing she owned in her apartment. It was a king-sized four-poster, with sheer purple curtains, and it made her feel like a princess.

Her parents had bought it for her for her birthday four years ago. It was the most extravagant birthday gift they'd ever given to one of their children and Georgia knew full-well the purchase had been fuelled by pure guilt because they weren't there at a time when she most needed them. But that wasn't something Georgia liked to think about. The bed left little space for much else in her room but she didn't care, she adored it.

She and Amber had been out that afternoon for coffee and Amber had invited herself back to help her get ready.

'Amber, I'm a grown woman, I don't need "help" to get ready for a date,' Georgia had said as they'd left the coffee shop.

'But that's what the best friend always does in movies,' Amber had protested. 'And besides, I have nothing else to do because you're ditching me tonight.'

'I'm not ditching you. It's not like we had plans.'

'Well, it's more like a standing arrangement for Friday night drinks,' Amber grumbled.

'How can there be a standing arrangement for Friday drinks when half the time our shifts don't even line up?'

Amber often seemed needier on the weekends she didn't have Violet.

Now, as Georgia got down on her hands and knees to find her favourite heels at the back of her cupboard, Amber let out a huge yawn.

'Doesn't sound like you'd have been up for a big night out anyway,' Georgia said as she crawled back out of the cupboard with her shoes in one hand.

'I would have rallied. What are you doing with your hair? Up or down?'

'What do you think?' Georgia gathered her long curly hair up with one hand to demonstrate.

Amber twisted her face in thought. 'Drop it back down again.'

She complied.

'Now up.'

She gathered it back up again.

'Down … Up … Okay, now drop it again.'

'Oh my God, you're totally messing with me.' Georgia let go of her hair, grabbed one of her shoes and threw it at Amber.

Amber caught the shoe. 'You kept going with it way longer than I thought you would.'

'You are such a bitch.'

'And yet you love me anyway. Wear it down. I'd kill to have your curls.'

'Everyone always wants what they don't have.'

'I know, right? Oh hey, you know what I keep meaning to ask you? Did you ever hear from the dickhead who stood you up last weekend?'

'Brett? Yeah, I did actually, yesterday. He texted me out of the blue saying something like, "sorry I couldn't make it on Saturday, let's reschedule".' Georgia stood and walked over to retrieve her shoe from Amber.

'Are you fucking serious? So, there was no explanation as to why he didn't show up? Put the shoes on, I want to see what they look like with your outfit.'

'Nope. Nothing.' Georgia stepped into the shoes and took a few paces back so Amber could see the whole look.

'Shoes are perfect,' she declared. 'Who the hell does that? What did you say?'

Georgia sat down next to her. 'Nothing. I ignored it. He doesn't deserve a bloody reply.'

'Yeah, good call. Although I'd still want to tell him where to go. But I guess it isn't worth the energy.'

'Trust me, I know it isn't.' She lay back on the bed and sighed.

'Ooh, speaking from past experience?' Amber flopped back next to her.

'Huh? Oh, not really. I just mean … you know what men are like.'

Georgia realised she'd let her tone give herself away, the same way she had with Jerry. Amber had lifted herself up on one elbow and was looking at her with a quizzical expression. What was wrong with her lately? Why did her past seem to be getting to her so much? Infiltrating her mood, making her feel cynical about everything.

'I guess so,' Amber said slowly. 'But not all men are the stereotypical arsehole Bretts of the world. You know that, right?'

'Well, seeing as I'm about to go out with an absolute gentleman, yes, I think I do know that.' Georgia was sick of being in the hot seat. 'How about your ex? Violet's dad. What's he like? Good guy or no?'

Amber's eyes slid sideways. 'He's not my ex,' she said. 'We never dated. Anyway, I'm going to leave you to finish getting ready for your date.' She sat back up too quickly and gave Georgia a slightly forced smile before standing. 'Good luck, okay. I really hope it goes well.'

Georgia felt bad for asking. There was an unspoken rule between them that Violet and her dad were a subject they didn't broach apart from surface chatter. She wished she hadn't pushed it.

'Hey, thanks for coming around. It was nice.'

'Any time.'

*

Georgia hadn't exactly intended on inviting Luke back to her place — and more specifically, into her bedroom — after only one date. It wasn't like she had a rule, it was more that she usually liked to wait. Liked to get to know a guy better, liked to be sure, to feel … safe. But it was one of those dates where everything went so well that she didn't want it to end. So, suggesting they head back to her place for a drink after dinner seemed like the obvious progression. Because the thing was, she *did* feel safe with him.

Dinner had been at a restaurant overlooking Norwest Lake. They'd sat outside underneath the gas heaters, which had kept them toasty warm despite the chilly June night air. Luke had somehow snuck his credit card to the waiter at some point so there was no chance for her to argue over the bill, and while she would have been happy to split it, there was something quite sexy about the way he'd taken care of it.

Now they were sitting side by side on her couch, a bottle of open wine on the coffee table in front of them and glasses in hand. Both were turned slightly to face one another, allowing their body language to do most of the talking. Georgia had one leg folded underneath her and was playing with her hair, her elbow resting on the back of the couch. She'd switched on her two floor lamps and turned out the overhead lights to create a bit of atmosphere and also to hide the cobwebs in the corners of the ceiling. For added ambience, she'd also switched on the string of fairy lights she kept wound around the balustrade of the small balcony off her living room.

'So, there was something I kept meaning to talk with you about at dinner but I kept chickening out,' Luke said.

'Really? That sounds ominous.' Her body tensed.

'It does, doesn't it? I've made it worse by giving it an introduction like that, I should have just come right out and said it.'

'All right, best thing to do now is to say it, whatever it is. The longer you draw it out, the worse it'll get.'

'Here goes. I want to be upfront about my baggage. There's a reason I didn't invite you back to my place tonight … I have a problem ex and I still live with her.'

Georgia stopped playing with her hair. She took a large sip of wine before responding. 'You still live with your ex? As far as baggage goes, that's pretty much up there.' She took another sip and when she spoke again her voice was a note higher than she'd intended. 'I can see why you were nervous to bring that up.'

He still lived with his ex? God, she really did know how to pick them. Was tonight's date not heading where she'd thought after all?

'I know. It sounds ridiculous, doesn't it? The thing is, I thought it would be okay at first, that we could have a mature break-up but still live together until our lease was up, but it's turned really sour.'

'What exactly do you mean by sour?'

'I mean she's gone a bit "single white female" on me. Don't get me wrong — she's not the type that's going to start killing puppies or anything like that. I just mean she's sometimes really nasty to me. But then the next minute she'll be begging me to take her back, or sometimes even pretending we never actually split up.'

'And you're still living there?' She just stopped herself from adding, *are you kidding me*? This ex of his sounded obsessed. Was this something she wanted to get caught up in?

'I know, I know. Obviously, the plan is to move out now that she's got like this. The only thing holding me back is the finances. There's still a few months left on the lease and I know she can't afford it on her own. If I had enough money for two places, I'd get my own place to get away from her and pay so she could stay there till the end of the lease. As much as I can't stand the way she's acting right now, I still don't want her to end up on the street.'

'That's very sweet of you.'

'Thanks,' he said. 'I'm trying my best to do the right thing here, but it's hard. I'm sure the whole thing would be fine between us if we could just have that clean break that we need. Not see each other ever again.'

Georgia was slightly happier to hear that he sounded as though he was completely over her.

'Can you crash with friends or family until the lease is up?' she suggested.

'Unfortunately no. My family and all my best mates are back in Perth where I grew up.'

'Ah. What about sort of coordinating your schedules a bit so that you're home when she's not and vice versa?'

'I'd love to. Problem is she works from home, so she's there *all the time.*'

'Bugger. What does she do?'

'She's an artist.'

'An artist? That's pretty cool.'

'I suppose. But it can be really hard to support yourself as a full-time artist, so that's part of the reason she's not financially stable enough to afford a place on her own.'

'Ah, difficult.'

'I'm sorry, I've done exactly what I didn't mean to do.'

'What's that?'

'Talk about my ex on the first date. I knew I needed to tell you about my living situation with Cadence, but I didn't mean to start venting about her. I'm so sorry. If you want you can even the scales by telling me about your last ex?'

'Ha. Not bloody likely.' Georgia couldn't help allowing an image of Will, her last serious boyfriend, swim through her mind. She made an involuntary face of disgust. 'Let's talk about something else altogether.'

'What did you have in mind?'

'Anything!'

Luke reached out for the wine bottle and topped up both their glasses. He clinked his glass against Georgia's and then leaned in close and lowered his voice. 'Or … maybe we don't need to talk.' And then he kissed her gently on the lips before holding still, giving her the opportunity to pull away if she wanted.

She hesitated for a split second.

Everyone had baggage, right? How bad could one ex-girlfriend really be?

She kissed him back.

THE ELEVATOR

Georgia took another step back, until she was almost pressed against the back wall of the lift. Cadence hadn't seen her yet, she was facing the doors. Georgia's breathing rate increased, she was trying to keep quiet but her chest was heaving and she knew that Cadence was going to hear the sound of her ragged breathing.

She should never have come here.

CHAPTER THREE

When Georgia woke the next morning, rolling over with a smile on her face, her heart sank to discover the other side of the bed was empty. Luke had left without even saying goodbye: the trademark move of a fuck boy. How could she have been stupid enough to think this was anything more than a one-night stand? Why did she keep doing this — reading men wrong, convincing herself that she could still meet the right guy when, deep down, she knew she was damaged goods? She cringed at the way she'd snuggled into him after they'd had sex. Was he lying there all night just waiting for the chance to extract himself from her embrace?

She sat up, letting the covers fall down to her waist, revealing her naked breasts. That's when the door opened and Luke stepped into the room holding two cups of takeaway coffee. His eyes widened at the sight of her.

'Oh my God,' said Georgia, snatching at the covers to pull them back up.

'Now that is the best morning greeting ever,' said Luke, walking over to hand her one of the coffees.

Georgia kept one hand on the sheet as she took the coffee with the other. 'I thought you were gone!'

'Sorry, you were sound asleep so I thought I'd duck out for a quick jog and then I grabbed us a couple of coffees on the way back. I've got a killer headache after all that wine we had last night.'

She tried to hide the smile of relief that she hadn't misjudged him after all. He sat down on the side of the bed and touched the covers she'd pulled over herself. 'Umm, Georgia, you know I saw all of that last night when we … you know?'

'That's a hell of a lot different to copping a full frontal in the harsh light of day.'

Luke laughed. 'Yeah all right, fair enough. But just so you know, you look gorgeous in any light.'

'Hang on, did you just say you went for a jog, with a hangover?'

'Jogging clears my head. But the coffee definitely helps too.' He kissed her forehead and stood up. 'I'll give you some privacy to get dressed.'

Georgia hesitated for a split second then reached out to catch hold of his hand. 'Or … you *could* come back to bed.'

'Brilliant idea.'

*

It was well past midday when they finally surfaced from the bedroom, deciding to take a walk to a local cafe for brunch. Luke took her hand as they headed up the hill towards Old

Northern Road and Georgia loved how easily her fingers laced through his. How the rhythm of her step fell into line with his. She couldn't help thinking of Will, her ex who used to always be at least half a step in front of her, as though everywhere they went was a race to some imaginary finish line. Thinking of him turned her mind to Luke's ex.

'Hey,' she said, 'not to bring up exes again, but how's yours going to react to you staying out all night?'

Luke shrugged. 'Honestly, it's none of her business. But she already sent me a few texts asking about it.'

'Oh shit, really? What did she say?'

'They start out friendly enough. The first one came through late last night. It was something like, "Just making sure you're okay." Then they get a little … shall we say, hostile?'

'Bloody hell, no wonder you want to move out.'

'It's all good. Last night and this morning with you more than made up for copping a few nasty messages.' He squeezed her hand and grinned sideways at her.

*

Georgia looked up from her phone, bored of scrolling through her Twitter feed while she picked at her hospital cafeteria salad. Down the hall she could see a Catholic priest in full-length robes paying for his parking, while a woman in a burqa and a young man in a turban waited behind him. She smiled at the tableau of Western Sydney multiculturalism. An orderly walked by, pushing a woman in a bed with a blue disposable cap covering her hair. She wondered if the woman felt self-conscious about being trundled right through the hospital foyer and past the cafe while lying flat on her back in bed. She saw Amber approaching then and used her foot to push out the opposite chair for her. Amber caught the back of it and sat down. She pulled a sausage roll and small tomato sauce packet out of a brown paper bag and then bit the corner of the packet to open it before squeezing the sauce over the sausage roll. Their breaks didn't always line up, so Georgia was glad to see her friend.

'I am in the worst mood,' said Amber, speaking loudly enough to turn a few heads at the neighbouring tables.

'Fabulous. What's up?'

'Shocker of a date last night.' She picked up the sausage roll and took a huge bite, getting sauce on her chin as she did.

'Girl or guy?' Georgia tried to say it in a casual tone even though she still found it a little intimidating how progressive Amber was with her sexuality. It was funny, Amber was so cagey about her past, but when it came to her current escapades she was an open book, always keen to discuss her dates — both the success stories and the failures.

'Guy.' Amber spoke through her mouthful. 'I'm anti-girls at the moment.'

'Since when?'

'Since the Holly incident.'

'Ah yes. Holly. Didn't realise she'd deterred you long-term.'

'Yeah, well, maybe after last night I might switch back. Or maybe I need a breather from the lot of them for a while.'

Amber wiped the sauce from her chin with the back of hand and took another large bite. Now sauce dripped onto the front of her uniform.

'Amber, use a serviette for God's sake. So, what happened with this guy?'

Amber ignored the serviette comment and continued to eat as she spoke. 'We went for dinner at the Thai place on Lark Avenue. I suggested it, and you could tell he didn't like it the second we walked in. He kept making snide comments about the plastic tablecloths or whatever. Anyway, his phone must have rung at least five times throughout dinner and he answered it. Every. Single. Time. Twice I was mid-sentence and he held his hand up to silence me while he took the call.'

'That's so rude!'

'Right? I really regretted sleeping with him.'

'You still slept with him after *that*?'

'No! I was joking. You know I never sleep with people on the first date.'

'Bullshit.'

'Yeah, you got me. Holy shit. I haven't asked you how your date went on the weekend.'

'I know you didn't. I've been bloody waiting for you to.'

'Okay. So? Tell me!' She finished off the last bit of her lunch and licked her fingers.

Georgia hesitated then gave her a smile. 'It was awesome.'

'Really? Give me details.'

'Well … speaking of sleeping together on the first date …'

Amber slapped her hand down on the table. 'Georgia Anne Fitzpatrick! You didn't!'

Yet again people nearby looked pointedly at them and Georgia felt guilty when she saw that the husband of a teary-looking woman was eyeing them reproachfully. Sometimes it was easy to forget that while for them it was just their lunchbreak at work, for other people it was a break from watching a loved one reach the end of their life. She lowered her voice and leaned across the table. 'Yep. I did. And my middle name isn't Anne by the way.'

'Yeah well, I needed a middle name for impact and I didn't know what yours was.'

'It's Louise.'

'I don't care. So, how was he?'

'Really, really good. And even better the second time round in the morning.'

'He stayed the night?' Amber's voice was in danger of getting shrill again and Georgia flapped her hands at her.

'Shh! Yes, he did. And then we went out to brunch. And then we hung around for an afternoon coffee, and then a drink, and then dinner …'

'You're joking. How bloody long did this date last?'

'He went home late that night. So it was an epic, like, thirty-hour date. Best first date I've ever had.' She put a forkful of salad in her mouth and immediately regretted it. The lettuce had already wilted. She should have got a sausage roll like Amber. She pushed the salad to the side.

'You should have had a sausage roll; it was delicious,' Amber said. 'You weren't getting sick of him and going, *when is this guy going to leave?*'

'Not even a little bit.'

'Wow. Impressive. Let's hope he can back it up on the next date.'

'I reckon he will.'

'So when is it?'

'Wednesday night, because I'm working all this weekend.'

'Ooh, a mid-week date. You can't get drunk and stay out all night. That's the long-term relationship stage already.'

'No it's not!' Georgia paused and drummed her fingers on the table top, wondering if she should tell her the one worrying thing on her mind.

Amber was already onto her though. 'What is it?' she asked.

'Okay. There's one tiny, teeny hitch.'

'Oh no. What's the problem?'

'He has this obsessive ex who isn't over him yet, and umm … they still live together.'

'GEORGIA! NO!'

Rick, another nurse they often hung out with, wandered over with a coffee and sat down to join them. 'What's Amber screeching about?' he asked, leaning back in his chair and sipping his coffee.

'Georgia has a new boyfriend who still lives with an ex who isn't over him,' Amber replied.

Rick sucked in his breath through his teeth.

'Honestly, it's not a big deal,' Georgia argued. Her phone buzzed on the table and Amber reached across to snatch it up before Georgia could. 'Ooh, is this your new lover boy right now?'

'Oy, give it back.' Georgia held out her hand.

Amber relented and passed it over. Georgia unlocked her phone, unable to hide her smile, but then frowned. 'Oh.'

'What's up?' Rick asked.

'It's not him. It's this other guy. The one who actually stood me up the night I met Luke.'

'Brett?' said Amber. 'Why the hell is he still texting you?'

'I have no idea. I ignored the last one he sent me.'

'What's it say?'

'"Can you please give me another chance,"' Georgia read out.

'Tell him to go fuck himself,' Amber ordered.

Rick shook his head. 'Don't bother. Ignore, delete, block. Contrary to Amber's life philosophy, not everything needs to involve the F-word.'

'Prude,' said Amber.

'Potty mouth,' Rick retorted.

'Stop bickering, you two. I swear sometimes you act like an old married couple.'

'We do not!' Amber looked scandalised.

'If the shoe fits,' said Georgia, locking her phone. 'I gotta get back upstairs. Dr H is on; someone has to keep an eye on him and I don't trust Victor or Ally to say anything if they see him screw up.'

'I know,' Amber said. 'Victor stayed quiet yesterday when he tried to give Aspirin to a patient who was on ten milligrams of Warfarin. Thank God I was doing obs on the next bed over. I sidled over and was like, "Ah, you sure about that, doctor?" And Victor knew. He bloody knew. He's just too much of a soft cock to say anything.'

'Amber!'

'What? I say it like it is.'

'She's not wrong,' said Rick, running his fingers through his short dark hair and spiking it up. 'I've never heard her *not* say it like it is.'

'Anyway, I'm not having him send the old duck in 318 back downhill again,' Georgia said as she pushed her chair back and stood. 'She's only just starting to come out the other side after the complications she had with her pneumonia and she's desperate to get back home. She's really missing Leo and Fergie.'

'Her kids?'

'No, her cats.'

Amber rolled her eyes. 'Why do you know the names of this woman's cats?'

'Because I like to get to know my patients.'

'Yeah, all right. Go kick arse, lady. I'll see you up there soon.'

CHAPTER FOUR

'Muesli with berries and a big brekkie with scrambled.'

Georgia sat back as the waitress placed the muesli in front of her without waiting to hear who had what. She pointedly swapped it with the large plate of food that had been put in front of Luke.

'Waiters always do that,' she commented once the waitress had walked away.

'What?'

'They assume the bigger meal is for the guy.'

Luke shrugged. 'Take it as a compliment. They think you're too small to put away food the way you do.'

'That's not a compliment. That's patronising.'

'Maybe you're reading too much into it.' He smiled.

Georgia had been on night shifts for the last week and all she wanted to do Saturday was sleep, so Sunday brunch was the best option for their fifth date. They were seated outdoor at a cafe in Rouse Hill and despite the winter chill in the air, the sun was warm on Georgia's back.

'You want any bacon?'

'Too late.' Luke spooned in his first mouthful of muesli. 'Can't go back to bacon now.'

'All right,' she said, leaning back in her chair. 'The last few dates we've been on you've picked super healthy options, like the grilled chicken salad or the egg-white omelette or whatever. Is this a new health kick, or your normal state of being and you were hiding it from me before because you were too embarrassed to order a salad while I was ordering burgers and burritos?'

'A guy, pretending to be something he's not, to impress a girl? That's unheard of!'

Georgia laughed. 'No, seriously. I could tell on our first date that you were shocked when I powered my way through that massive T-bone steak and fries. Did you think then and there, *I've gotta keep up with this girl* or something like that?'

He shook his head. 'Not at all. I'm always going in and out of health kicks. You want to know a secret?' He leaned in and Georgia did the same. 'I was a fat kid.'

'You weren't!'

'I was. And I mean fat. My parents had to take me to the doctor and put me on a diet and buy me a treadmill so they could run me on it like I was a hamster.'

Georgia stopped smiling. 'Oh shit, I'm sorry. That sounds awful.'

'Don't be sorry. It's not like I'm traumatised or anything. It was what it was. I lost the weight, and I kept it off.'

'Well, you look pretty damn fit now.' Georgia paused then said carefully, 'You don't talk about your parents much.'

'No, I guess I don't.' He didn't elaborate and Georgia hesitated, wondering if she should push a little further. Even from the beginning, he'd always been so easy to chat to and she was loving getting to know him. He made her feel so comfortable, so confident. 'Did that affect your relationship with them, the way they dealt with your weight problems?'

'I don't know … I guess they were just looking out for my health.'

'Yeah, but it's the way you said they ran you like a hamster, it doesn't sound very … nice.'

'Are you psychoanalysing me?'

Georgia held up her hands. 'Me? No way, my medical expertise doesn't go beyond the body. Like I said, you don't really ever mention your family. What made you move to Sydney when your whole family is back in Perth?'

'To be honest, it was a bit of a whim. A job came up and it seemed like a good opportunity for a change. I love Sydney now though.'

'And have you seen them much since you came over?'

'Nope, not a lot.'

'How come?' Georgia wondered how she'd cope if she moved away from her family. Not very well, she decided.

'It's not really anything … I mean, we didn't have any big falling-out or anything like that, we're just not a close family.'

'I always thought my family was really close, but lately I'm not so sure. I don't really *know* my mum and dad anymore. Does that make sense? I mean they've changed so. much. And then my older brothers are in a different stage of life. They're married with kids and I don't get the kinds of things they're going through. The only one I'm close to is Marcus, but he's down in Melbourne.'

'That's tough.'

'Speaking of Marcus —' Georgia began, but Luke's phone started vibrating on the table. She stopped as he picked it up, glanced at the screen, frowned and declined the call.

'Who was that?'

Luke sighed. 'You don't want to know.'

'You know that makes me want to know more.'

'Fair point. It was Cadence.'

'Ah. So she's still hassling you?'

'Unfortunately, yes.'

'Does she know that you're ...' Georgia paused, unsure how to word it '... seeing someone?'

'Yep. I told her right away. It was difficult because I was trying not to upset her too much. But she could clearly tell how into you I am.'

Georgia felt her skin flush. She took a large sip of water.

'That mustn't have gone down too well then.' She was trying to feel bad for Cadence, but she couldn't help feeling secretly happy.

'You're right, it didn't go well at all. I didn't want to say anything, because I didn't want to worry you but ...' He stopped and chewed on his lip.

Georgia reached across the table and touched his hand. 'It's okay, you can tell me.'

'Truth is, she's got worse since I told her about you.'

'Oh no, I'm so sorry!'

'What? Why are *you* sorry? Trust me, none of this is your fault. Anyway, it's nothing I can't handle.' He laced his fingers through hers and squeezed her hand. 'This is her problem, not ours. What were you going to say before, something about Marcus?'

'Oh,' Georgia hesitated. She'd been about to say that Marcus's wedding was coming up, but she was very quickly losing her nerve. Surely it was far too early to invite him to a family wedding, wasn't it? 'It was nothing ...' she began, but they were both distracted then as a tall, wiry, bearded waiter stepped up to their table to offer them coffees.

'Long black, please,' said Georgia.

'Weak skim soy latte,' said Luke. Then he cringed. 'Shit,' he said as the waiter left, 'I can't believe I just ordered that in front of you.'

She laughed. 'You haven't asked for that any of the other times we've had coffee. Luke Kauffman, have you been hiding your coffee order from me all this time?'

'Yes! Of course I have. It's the most embarrassing thing ever. You're going to break up with me on the spot.'

Georgia leaned forward. 'Does that mean we're officially ... an item?'

Luke leaned forward too. 'Well ... let's see, how many dates have we been on?' He started counting on his fingers then stopped. 'Actually, I don't care, I just want to keep seeing you. So if that means we're official ... then yes, let's call it what it is. Unless, of course, my coffee order is unforgivable.'

'You know what? I reckon I could forgive it this once.'

CHAPTER FIVE

Georgia pulled up out the front of her parents' home and sat still in the car for a minute. Get-togethers with her large family could often be a bit overwhelming. She stared out the window at their house. It was such a contradiction to their personalities. A two-storey, sleek, contemporary home in Castle Hill with views of the Blue Mountains. If you were a door-to-door salesperson in the area and you knocked on their door, you'd probably expect to see an elegantly dressed middle-aged couple who looked just as slick as the house. Instead you'd be greeted by two barefoot hippies. They'd always had free-spirit type personalities but since all their children had grown up and left home, they'd really embraced their inner flower-children. Georgia was pretty sure that if they hadn't had grandchildren they wanted to spend time with, they'd have sold up their house and spent the rest of their lives travelling around Australia in a caravan.

The year after Georgia completed her Higher School Certificate and her parents took off to travel around Eastern Europe had been the beginning of a difficult stage in

Georgia's life. She knew they had every right to head off and do something for themselves for a change — they'd just got five kids through to adulthood. Her older brothers had all moved out and Georgia was going to live on campus while she started studying an Arts degree at university. So, it was the perfect opportunity for her parents to rent out their home and go exploring.

But Georgia hadn't anticipated how much she'd miss them. How hard it would be knowing she couldn't pop home on the weekends for a visit. And her brothers were all living on their own, getting caught up in new relationships or their jobs or running their own businesses. They had their own lives. It was Marcus moving away that had been the biggest shock though. He was only one year older than her and had always been her built-in best friend. So, when he announced he was moving down to Melbourne to be an apprentice chef, Georgia had felt abandoned.

Maybe if she'd sought help sooner it wouldn't have got as bad as it did. But her parents caught the travel bug and turned into fly-in, fly-out nomads, and with Marcus down in Melbourne there was no one around to really notice the change in her.

Georgia climbed out of the car and headed for the front door. As usual it was unlocked, because for some bizarre reason her parents seemed to think they lived in a sleepy little village rather than a Sydney suburb. She let herself in, kicked off her shoes and walked through to the kitchen and living area at the back. It was a hive of activity. Her three eldest brothers and their wives were all buzzing about, pouring drinks and chatting noisily while the kids darted between them playing a game of hide and seek. Her parents were gliding through the chaos like serene sailboats. Her mum, Susan, was wearing yoga pants that faded from orange to yellow and a turquoise top with silver and gold beads hanging from the sleeves. The clash of vibrant colours had quite an effect, and Georgia realised that her mum's hair — which had been auburn when she saw her just one week ago — was now silvery grey.

'Holy shit, Mum, what have you done to your hair?' she said as she dumped her bag on a couch and wandered over to give her a hug.

'I'm letting it go natural.'

'Is it different?' interrupted her eldest brother, Aaron, squinting and turning his head side-on.

'Seriously? It was red last week. Mum, silver's not natural.' Georgia pulled away from her mother and gave her dad a hug. Graham was wearing yoga pants as well, though his outfit wasn't quite so colourful. 'It's certainly a change,' he said quietly to Georgia as he gave her a kiss on the top of her head.

'It's natural, it's grey,' said her mum.

'You've clearly dyed it.'

'I'm embracing my senior years. Have a samosa.' Susan picked up a plate and held it out to Georgia.

'What's with the samosas?' Georgia said, taking one.

'Don't ask,' said Aaron.

'What do you mean, what's with the samosas?' asked Susan. 'This is our cuisine.'

Georgia leaned in to Aaron and his wife Kate, who were standing at the kitchen bench with their beers. 'What's she on about?'

'Apparently, it's a travesty that we never embraced Dad's Indian culture when we were growing up,' Aaron explained. 'Dinner tonight is an all-out Indian feast. Dad said Mum's been googling recipes all day.'

'But Dad's not Indian,' Georgia whispered back.

'Yes, but Grandad was Anglo-Indian. Look, just be happy Mum's not in a sari tonight. Apparently, she's thinking about wearing one to the wedding.'

Kate snorted and choked on her beer. 'Jesus, isn't that cultural appropriation or something?'

'Quite possibly,' said Georgia.

'Are we talking about Mum's new obsession?' asked Troy, wandering over to join them. 'She's actually done a pretty good job with the samosas.'

'They're frozen ones. I saw her stash the empty box,' Aaron said.

Troy laughed. 'Find out the brand. I want to buy them.'

Aaron shook his head. 'Don't ask her. She'll get all upset if she realises anyone knows they're not homemade.'

'I thought she didn't get upset about anything anymore. Part of her new ultra-calm Buddhist attitude. Wait, how does being Buddhist fit in with also being Hindu?' Georgia asked.

'Unsure,' said Aaron.

'Shit. Hattie has Max in a headlock again.' Troy strode away from them, his voice booming across the room as he approached his four-year-old daughter. 'What did I tell you about using the chokeslam on your cousins?'

'What's the deal with Hattie?' Georgia said to Aaron.

'Troy put her in a wrestling club; apparently she has some serious talent.'

'I can see that.'

'Watch Pete's face. He hates that Max is getting taken down by Hattie.'

'Oh my God, you're right. He's got the twitch happening under his right eye.'

Kate snorted yet again and Aaron passed her a tissue for the beer she'd spat out. 'She's so classy, my wife. You haven't got a drink yet, Georgie. You want a beer?'

'Yes, please.

A huge clang sounded, making them all jump. They turned around to see Susan holding a large mallet, which she'd just smashed against an oversized gong. 'Dinner!' she called happily.

'Who the hell bought that woman a gong?' Georgia asked.

'She bought it for herself,' said Aaron as he handed Georgia a beer from the fridge. 'Mum and Dad do morning meditation and they hit the gong every time they have an epiphany during their meditation.'

'Of course they do.'

*

Georgia had almost made it. Dinner was finished and cleared away. The butter chicken had been the favourite, with Susan clicking her tongue every time her family reached for the more unadventurous choice instead of the goat curry or dhokla she'd cooked. Luckily Hattie was like a small vacuum cleaner, hoovering up bowl after bowl of anything her parents put in front of her. Dessert was almost done and Georgia had flown under the radar the entire time, letting the conversation weave its way around the table, sliding past her and remaining on the edges as her brothers and sisters-in-law dealt with their kids and talked about which school Joshua was going to next year or how well Emma was sleeping through the night or how many trophies Hattie had already picked up at wrestling club. Sometimes it was easy to be invisible when you were in the middle of a table full of people.

And then the inevitable happened. 'So, are you bringing a date to the wedding, Georgia?' Pete's wife Aimee asked.

'Yeah, Mum said you're seeing some bloke you met through Tinder,' Troy added.

Georgia felt her cheeks redden. She hated the way her family discussed her love life. Always with this glint in their eyes, a slight smirk on their lips, as though just because she hadn't settled down yet her dating life was fodder for their entertainment.

'I didn't meet him through Tinder,' she said through gritted teeth.

'I thought Mum said it was a Tinder date,' said Pete.

Had her mum been telling *all* her brothers about Luke? She'd barely mentioned him when they'd spoken on the phone recently, but somehow her mother had picked up on the significance of this new guy in her life. She glared across at her mother, who smiled back serenely, oblivious.

'No, it's just that I was meant to be on a Tinder date when I did meet him.'

'What happened, Georgie, you get stood up or something?' Pete asked.

Georgia breathed out slowly through her nostrils. 'Can we talk about something else?'

She wished Marcus was here. It wasn't like there weren't times growing up that he picked on her or made fun of her, but he also knew when she'd had enough. If he was here right now, he'd pick up on her discomfort and say something funny to divert attention away from her. Instead, everyone was continuing to stare at her expectantly, ignoring her request to change the subject.

Thankfully, she was saved by Hattie, who stood up on her chair, leaned forward and vomited all over the table. There was instant chaos. Most people lurched backwards while Troy lunged forward, putting his hands out as though to catch it.

'Why did I do that?' he immediately wailed, realising his mistake, while his wife Chloe grabbed Hattie under the armpits, lifted her up and raced towards the bathroom, holding her out in front. Kate started snorting and they all watched in horror as Troy hovered over the table holding a handful of regurgitated goat curry. 'For fuck's sake, someone get me a bucket!'

Pete started gagging, and when Susan rushed to the kitchen to grab paper towel she knocked over the gong, causing a huge reverberating clang, which woke up Emma in her stroller and immediately added her distressed wails to the fray.

Georgia used the commotion to sneak out onto the back patio and call Marcus. Sure, she could help out, or she could let all the parents deal with the joy of having children and take advantage of the fact that right now, kids weren't something she had to deal with … even if she often wished she did.

'Georgie Porgie!' Marcus greeted her.

'Is there any world in which you might stop calling me that?'

'Hells no. What's up, littlest Fitz?'

Georgia sighed down the phone, taking her time to respond.

'Come on,' Marcus coaxed, 'tell me what's wrong.'

'I'm at Mum and Dad's,' she said eventually. 'Everyone was quizzing me on whether I'm bringing a date to your wedding.'

'Ah. You know they're just jealous 'cause your life is more exciting than theirs.'

'I don't think so. Hattie just threw up on the dinner table. I think their lives are exciting enough.'

Marcus started laughing. 'I love that kid, she's a classic.' He paused. 'So, are you?'

'Bringing a date?'

'Yep. You can if you want. We're doing cocktail-style so it doesn't matter to us.'

'I don't know. I mean there is this guy. And I really like him. But I don't know if it's too soon to do the whole invite to a family wedding thing.'

'Do you want to have him there?'

'Kind of. Maybe. I don't know!'

'Georgia? Come on. You know.'

'Okay. I want to invite him. But what if he's like, what the fuck? I'm not coming to Melbourne for a family wedding after only four or five dates.'

'If he says "what the fuck" to you then I'm flying up there to punch him in the face.'

Georgia laughed. 'Thank you, but I'd rather you didn't do that.'

'Listen, if coming to a wedding scares him off, then maybe he's not the guy for you. Or maybe it is too soon and that's okay. But if you want to ask him, then ask him.'

Georgia sighed again. 'Okay,' she said. 'I'll ask.'

'Good.'

'Oh hey, just a warning, Mum might be wearing a sari to your wedding.'

'Yeah, I'm all over that shit. She already called and asked if she could do a traditional Hindu blessing at the ceremony.'

'Of course she did. What did you say?'

'Well, Bianca was all good with it so I gave her the go-ahead. Look, it's just easier to give in to Mum on this shit.'

'Yeah, you're probably right. Okay, I better go back in. Thank you.'

'Any time. See you soon.'

Georgia hung up and turned around to head back in, but saw one of her other nieces had followed her outside.

'Hey sweetie, aren't you cold out here?' Georgia asked, crouching down in front of Gertie, Aaron's youngest, who was standing in front of her with a thumb in her mouth. Gertie sucked earnestly on her thumb and stared back at her. 'Or are you escaping the drama too?'

Gertie pulled her thumb out of her mouth, blew a raspberry at Georgia, then stuck it firmly back in again.

'I know exactly what you mean,' Georgia said, taking her by the other hand and guiding her inside.

*

Georgia was in the car and about to pull away from the kerb when she saw the edge of paper on her windscreen. Someone had shoved something under the wiper blade. It didn't look like a flyer; it looked like a handwritten note. She hesitated. Wasn't there some story doing the rounds on Facebook where you weren't supposed to get back out of your car if you spotted something on your window because a carjacker could lurch out of a bush nearby? But she was right outside her parents' house in the middle of Castle Hill. The street was quiet and empty. It seemed highly unlikely that there was a carjacker waiting to leap out at her. Maybe it was from one of her brothers; they'd all left before her tonight. It had been the kind of sudden mass exodus that always happened when everyone realised that the last person standing would have to help with the clean-up. The lot of them claimed they all needed to get small people home to bed, leaving Georgia behind to stack the dishwasher with her dad while her mum did her night-time goddess stretches.

Georgia took the keys back out of the ignition — just in case — hopped out of the car and walked around to the passenger side where she could reach the note. She unfolded it and read.

You're ugly as sin.

Georgia let out a bark of laughter. She looked around, half expecting to see someone watching her, waiting for her reaction. Maybe a couple of teenage kids who'd written the note as a nasty joke. In fact the back of her neck was prickling. *Was* there someone watching? She scrunched up the paper and shoved it into her pocket then called out to the street, 'No I'm not. I'm hot, you little dicks.'

Then she got back in her car and drove off, marvelling at her unexpected burst of self-confidence.

THE ELEVATOR

Cadence suddenly lurched towards the control panel and slammed her hand against the large red stop button. Georgia's head snapped up. What was she doing? What was about to happen? How far was she willing to go?

CHAPTER SIX

The previews had already started and they both ducked their heads low as they turned sideways and moved along the row of seats, trying not to step on toes or bang against knees. They found their seats and Georgia fell into hers before dumping her bag and jacket on the floor by her feet.

Luke leaned in and whispered in her ear, 'Hope we're in the right cinema; I didn't even look.'

'We're good, this is right.'

'Want me to run back out and get popcorn?'

'Thought you weren't fussed on popcorn?'

'I'm not, but I know you are.'

'Yeah, but you'll miss the start.'

'No, I won't. I'll be super speedy. Thirty seconds, in and out.'

Georgia laughed softly. 'Stay, I'll be fine without it.'

He looked sideways at her and then stood up decisively. 'Nah, I'm going back.'

Before she could stop him, he was squeezing his way back

down the row past several disgruntled patrons who all had to press themselves back into their seats out of his way.

Georgia remembered coming to the cinemas with Will once. As she'd grabbed popcorn and Maltesers from the candy bar, he'd raised his eyebrows and said, *Do you really think you need all of that?* She'd flushed red and put the Maltesers back on the shelf.

By the time Luke came back, the movie had already started. Luke sat down and passed over the popcorn along with a bag of Maltesers and a bottle of water, then leaned in and kissed her on the cheek.

She smiled and reached across to take his hand. 'You're the best,' she whispered.

*

Georgia shook out her jacket for the fifth time. The credits had almost finished rolling and Luke was on his hands and knees peering under their seats.

'It's not looking good,' he said. 'I can't see anything under here, apart from rubbish.'

'Shit,' said Georgia. 'Maybe I dropped them somewhere else?'

She'd been in such a good mood when the film finished. She loved happy endings. That was something she'd discovered when she'd finally started to work her way out the other side of her darkest time. If she was going to escape into a fictional world for a couple of hours she didn't want to emerge feeling raw and wrecked, she wanted to feel warm and refreshed.

And she'd been feeling pleasantly contented after making her way through the entire box of popcorn and bag of Maltesers, pretty much on her own too. But now her keys were missing. When she'd picked up her bag, she'd realised it had tipped sideways and half her stuff had fallen out. She'd gathered up her purse, phone, lipstick, and a few loose tampons and hair clips, before realising her keys were missing. She got down on her hands and knees for another look but Luke was right: they weren't anywhere.

'Could have fallen out of your bag in my car?' Luke suggested.

'Maybe. Lucky you drove, otherwise we'd be stranded.'

'Come on,' said Luke, standing and offering his hand to pull her up. 'Hopefully we'll find them in the car or on the way back to the carpark.'

Georgia didn't want to keep comparing him to her ex, but she couldn't help it. If this had happened with Will he'd be grumbling about how annoying it was that she hadn't kept a closer eye on her things.

On the way out they checked with the staff to make sure the keys hadn't somehow ended up in lost property, and when that didn't turn up anything, they walked slowly back to the carpark, eyes scanning as they went. A thorough search of Luke's car didn't offer any results either and eventually Georgia had to accept that she'd lost them.

'You definitely had them with you?' Luke asked on the drive home. 'You couldn't have left them inside your apartment?'

Georgia shook her head. 'Impossible, I lock the outside of the apartment door with the key as I walk out. One of my neighbours has a spare though, so at least I'll be able to get back inside. And I have a spare car key at home too.'

'That's good. Call the cinema tomorrow. Maybe the cleaner will have found them.'

'Hope so.'

They started chatting about the movie, discussing whether or not one of the main characters was actually British, or an American doing a British accent.

'You could tell,' Luke argued, 'by the way he said "aunt". He actually sounded like he was from Boston.'

There was a lull in their conversation, until Georgia found herself blurting out her invite. 'Doyouwannacome-toMarcus'swedding?'

'I'm sorry, what?' He laughed.

Georgia winced. 'Sorry … umm, would you like to come to my brother's wedding with me? Honestly, it's fine if you don't want to.'

'Ooh, wedding date. Serious stuff.'

'I know, I know. And it's a family wedding, so if you don't want to, honestly, just say no. I don't want to make you meet everyone so soon.'

'Georgia, I'd love to come.'

*

Georgia turned her bare feet outwards, lifted her heels and pushed the balls of her feet against the bar. She was lying flat on her back on a Pilates reformer bed, staring at the dark timber ceiling above and strongly regretting trusting Rick's advice, namely: 'You should come and do the advanced Pilates class with me, Georgia. You'll be fine without doing the beginner class first.'

'Breathe out as you release,' instructed the teacher from the front of the class. 'Drop back, bring your heels together, breathe in, tighten your core, draw your pelvic muscles up and in, curl your toes around the bar, heels together, push out, knees come apart.'

'How are you supposed to keep up with all of that?' Georgia hissed sideways at Rick.

'Focus,' he whispered back. 'It's easy.'

It bloody wasn't easy. It was impossible. Her muscles were quivering as she tried to hold the pose and she kept breathing out when she was meant to breathe in, or bending her knees only to look around and see that the rest of the class had their legs lengthened.

'Feel that stretch through your calves,' said the teacher. 'Isn't it yummy?'

That was the other thing. The teacher kept calling everything yummy. The pain in her hamstrings was yummy. The burning in her obliques was yummy. Georgia was pretty sure that wasn't the word she would use to describe her aching muscles right about now.

Oh, screw this.

She sat up as quietly as she could, lifted the panel on the end of the reformer bed and soundlessly unhooked the springs that provided the resistance for the exercises. Then she lay back down and got back in position. *Much better.* Now she could slide the bed back and forth with ease.

'We're shifting the focus now to your glutes and taking one foot off the bar. As you stretch out, lift your hips and push up towards the ceiling. Squeeze your buttocks together.'

Georgia pushed hard with one foot. With no resistance, the bed flew along the carriage, thrusting her backwards and she smacked her head against the bar on the other end. 'Ow!'

'Now really!' said the teacher.

'Sorry,' Georgia called out meekly.

An hour later she sat in the gym cafe opposite Rick, glaring at him over the top of her cappuccino.

'I swear to God I thought you'd be fine. It's not my fault you have the core strength of string cheese.'

'String cheese? Really? That's what you're going with?'

'I stand by that assessment. Come to a spin class with me next week, you'll like that better.'

'I really doubt that.'

'Hey, how's it going with the boyfriend who's not yet a boyfriend. Luke, was it?'

'Ah, actually … he kind of *is* a boyfriend now. We had the "conversation" recently.' Georgia held up her fingers to do air quotes.

'The "conversation"?' Rick treated the word with the same reverence. 'Big stuff.'

'Yep and he's coming to my brother's wedding down in Melbourne.'

'Jeez, you don't waste any time.'

'Yeah, well, who's got time to waste?'

'You'll have to bring him to drinks at the Bella Vista some time so we can all meet him.'

'Only if you promise to behave. Remember when I brought my ex Will to a nurses' get-together, and you all started talking blood and gore in front of him and he ended up being sick?'

'I'm ninety-nine per cent positive it was the Jägerbombs he was drinking and not our shop talk that did that.'

'Fair call.'

'All right, I need to take off. I'm on arvo shift. I'm booking you in for spin next week though. Your fitness game is weak, Georgia, *weak*.' He wrapped his knuckles on the table for extra emphasis as he stood up, slung his backpack over one shoulder, and left.

'Who says I even want to improve my fitness game?' Georgia called after him, but he just waved his hand in the air without turning around and she grumbled into her coffee. 'How did I let him talk me into joining this bloody gym?'

She pulled her phone out of her pocket and turned it back on — Rick had insisted it needed to be completely off for Pilates, not just on silent. 'Who ever turns their phone off these days?' she'd responded before giving in and doing as she was told.

The screen lit up and after a moment it dinged four times in a row as the messages she'd missed came through. The first was advising her she had a voicemail, and she listened to it and discovered that her keys had been found at the cinema. She was glad she'd left them her contact details. She'd have to go and pick them up later today.

The next one was from Luke:

How's your day going? Been thinking about you. Don't think I can wait until Saturday to see you again. Dinner tonight?

Georgia smiled and tapped out a reply.

Been thinking about you too. Just did a Pilates class at the gym. I'm 100% certain it was ten times harder than the weightlifting you do. HA! Huge yes to dinner tonight. Want to go out or come to mine?

She checked the last two messages. They were both from Brett.

Hey, can you please stop ignoring me? It's actually really rude.

The second message was two words.

Stupid slut.

Georgia felt her stomach plummet. *Slut?* He was calling her a slut? How dare he? She knew she shouldn't care, knew she shouldn't let the words of a virtual stranger affect her, but that word held so much power for Georgia. It made her skin crawl. And it brought back memories. Nasty memories.

She wished she'd listened to Rick the other day and blocked Brett's number right away. She did so now. Pressing 'block this caller' didn't feel quite as satisfying as slamming a door in his face would have, but at least he couldn't bother her anymore.

A moment later, Luke replied to her message:

Let me take you out. We can always end up back at your place afterwards. ;-)

The smile returned to her lips and the joyfulness, which had been knocked out of her when she'd read Brett's nasty messages, flooded her body again.

*

Dinner was at a Persian restaurant, which Georgia hadn't even known existed as it was tucked away on the ground floor of an office building and hidden from sight from the main road. It was the perfect choice for a cold wintery night, with the open wood fire and decorative rugs hanging on the walls adding to the cosiness. They shared lamb and chicken kebabs, and halfway through the mains, two belly dancers weaved their way through the tables, wriggling their hips and pulling people out of their seats to dance with them.

'This place is gorgeous,' Georgia said as their shared dessert was placed in front of them — homemade ice-cream with rosewater, saffron and pistachios, topped with Persian fairy floss.

'Yeah, and we have to try the hookah lounge afterwards as well.'

Georgia stopped with the spoon hovering in front of her mouth. 'I'm sorry, what?'

Luke grinned. 'Hookah … not hooker,' he clarified.

'Okay, I'm not hearing a difference.'

He laughed. 'It's hookah with an "h" on the end. It's this pipe that you smoke. You can get all these different flavours like apple or peach or strawberry, but it's minus the nicotine.'

Georgia raised her eyebrows. 'Interesting. And here I thought you were about to suggest a threesome.'

'Well, I mean, if that's on the table.'

Georgia laughed and popped the spoonful into her mouth. 'You wish!'

A waiter approached their table. 'Excuse me, sir, I have a message for you,' he said, passing Luke a small slip of folded paper.

Luke frowned. 'Thanks,' he said, opening it up.

'What is it?' Georgia asked, watching him read it.

'Fuck.' He scrunched the paper in his hand and then started looking around the restaurant, scanning the other tables.

Georgia was taken aback; she'd never seen him look so rattled. 'What? What's wrong?'

Luke handed the scrunched paper across to her. 'I'm so sorry about this,' he said.

Georgia opened the crumpled paper and read the message inside.

You can do much better than her.

Georgia handed the paper back. 'What the hell?'

'It's from Cadence.'

'Are you serious? She's here?'

'She must be. Or actually, I'm guessing she handed them the note and left. I don't see her anywhere.'

'Luke, how did she know we were here?'

'I have no idea … I didn't say anything about where I was going when I left the apartment tonight. I mean, I try to avoid talking to her at all. Oh my God, she must have followed me. I don't see how else.'

'Followed you? Shit. That's proper stalking stuff. That's creepy as hell.'

The feel of the restaurant shifted in an instant. It was no longer warm and cosy; instead it felt claustrophobic, stiflingly hot. The last mouthful of dessert seemed to be wedged in her throat. 'This is horrible. Why would she do this?'

'Because she's petty and awful. I really am so, so sorry.'

'Hang on, let me look at that note again.'

He passed it back across.

'Luke, I recognise this handwriting.'

'What do you mean?'

'I mean I already got a note like this.'

'What? When? Why didn't you tell me? I would have said something to her straightaway.'

'I didn't know it was her! It was left on my car. It said I was ugly. I thought it was some kid's idea of a prank.'

Luke's face paled. 'She said that to you? Where was your car when she left it?'

Georgia saw that his hands were shaking.

'Out the front of my parents' house. How is it even possible that she'd find me there? Is she following me too?'

'This is bad.'

'Can we … umm, can we please go? I don't want to be here anymore.'

'Of course.'

Georgia didn't even try to do their usual dance over whose turn it was to pay. She let Luke fix up the bill and stood waiting with her arms wrapped around herself. Her eyes were darting around as though at any moment a crazed woman might leap out at her from behind a pot plant. As she waited, she thought about that night she'd found the note on her car. How she'd been so blasé about it, how it had even made her *laugh*. How she had shouted out into the night that she was hot. It was humiliating. She wanted to reach back through time and slap herself. *Wake up, Georgia, Cadence is way more trouble than you first thought.*

They walked briskly to Luke's car, Luke keeping one arm around Georgia. On the drive back to her apartment, Georgia couldn't help checking the side mirror every couple of minutes.

'It's okay,' said Luke, one hand on the steering wheel and the other reaching out to hold her hand. 'She's not following us. That's not her car behind us.'

'Good.'

Georgia didn't even realise how tightly she'd been clenching her shoulders until they finally stepped inside her apartment and Luke placed his hands on her shoulders and gently pushed them down. 'You'll hurt yourself doing that,' he said. 'Sit down, I'll get you a drink. You want tea or a proper drink?'

'Proper drink, please. There's a bottle of bourbon above the fridge.'

Georgia settled onto the couch, pulling the throw rug over her knees, and Luke brought over two bourbon and Cokes. He sat down next to her and rubbed her shoulders again. Georgia picked up her glass and took a large sip.

'Listen,' he said, 'I'm going to fix this. I'll let her know that she's crossed a line and that if she doesn't stop, I'll be going to the police.'

'But how would that work? I mean, if you go to the police, the only thing you could really ask for is a restraining order, right? Is one creepy note at dinner enough for that? Plus, what happens when you tell them where you live? *This woman is hassling me, but we still live together.* They'll laugh in your face.'

'I know, I know. You're right. I need to find a way to move out.'

Georgia hesitated for a moment. There *was* one way he could escape from Cadence. But surely it was too soon, wasn't it? Then again, it didn't have to be permanent.

'Luke … I know we're in no way at this stage yet, but do you want to stay here for a while? Like, even if it's only temporary?'

'That is incredibly kind of you, but I honestly didn't mean to make you feel like you have to offer.'

'You're not making me. And anyway, I'm not suggesting you *officially* move in, I just think that this might be the only solution.'

Georgia paused. She was worried he was going to think she was overreacting, that he'd be frightened away because she was moving too fast. First, the invite to the family wedding, now this. But if he stayed there with Cadence, how was any of this ever going to end? As long as Luke's ex still had him in her life, she was going to keep fighting to take him back. And what if she fought hard enough that she won?

Luke stared back at her. 'You know what?' he said. 'That would be an absolute godsend, but only if you're sure.'

'I'm sure. I mean, once you can afford it, you'll get your own place anyway, right?'

'Absolutely.'

'You think that'll make her stop?'

'I think it will help. I think it will make her properly realise that there's nothing between us anymore. That there hasn't been for a long time.'

Georgia nodded. Anything that got this woman off their backs was going to be a good thing. An idea crossed her mind then.

'Hey, can I see a photo of her? If she's following us and leaving notes on my car and stuff … I want to be able to recognise her if I ever see her.'

'Of course.' Luke reached for his phone and opened up the photo album then started scrolling through the images. 'I don't have many,' he said, 'but there should be something here.'

Eventually he stopped on one and showed it to Georgia. 'This is her. Is she familiar at all? Have you seen her around?'

Georgia frowned. It wasn't a great angle. Cadence was side-on and her hair was partially obscuring her face. 'I don't think so. Do you have any other photos? Something that shows her face front-on?'

Luke took his phone back and kept searching. 'She's one of those girls who gets self-conscious if you try to take her photo, so I don't really have many good ones. She's the type that has to have her makeup and hair absolutely perfect before she'll even leave the house, so if you try to take a nice candid snap she'll be grabbing the phone off you and deleting it, claiming it's the worst shot ever. Sorry, I'm getting off-track. Here, is this one any better?' He offered the phone to Georgia and she took a good, long look.

The woman in the photo had strawberry-blonde hair, huge blue eyes and petite, pretty features. She thought for a moment about the overt difference in both looks and personality between Cadence and herself. Short blonde hair versus long, curly brown hair. Wears makeup versus struggles to choose an appropriate shade of lipstick. Did Luke have a type? And if so, was Cadence his type, or was she?

'Hey, are you okay?' Luke asked.

Georgia realised she was still staring at the photo. 'Sorry,' she said. 'I was just noticing … she's, umm, she's very pretty. And ah, very different from me.' She handed the phone back and added, 'I don't think I've ever seen her around though. But at least I've got a good image of her in my mind now so I can keep an eye out.'

'Georgia,' said Luke, 'I know I used to date her, but can I be honest with you? I'm not the least bit attracted to her anymore. I *never* loved the fact that she always had to do the whole hair and makeup thing before we could go out. On top of that, her personality …' He paused, looking torn. 'I don't want to sound like I'm being an arsehole, but she was kind of stuck-up. You know how I said she's an artist? Well, I was never really a big fan of her art. She went to this crazily expensive art school and it was like she believed that just because she had the best training available, that made her talented. But the fact is, her art wasn't selling … but you could never suggest that she might consider a part-time job because you'd get your head bitten off. Add to all that the way she's acting now, and well, like I said, I'm not the least bit attracted to her. Trust me.'

Georgia couldn't help but feel pleased to hear all of this. Her own inability to choose a suitable shade of lipstick suddenly felt like a positive attribute rather than a failed life skill.

'So,' said Georgia, 'the thing is, if I ever do see her … what am I supposed to do? Confront her? Tell her to leave me alone? Or ignore her? Or run?' She was joking with the last suggestion, but at the same time there was a part of her wondering if she really did need to be afraid of this woman.

'If you see her — although hopefully you won't — just call me, okay?' Luke put an arm around her and pulled her in close.

CHAPTER SEVEN

Georgia leaned on the counter of the nurses station while Rick sat behind the desk, directing a visitor to a patient's room. The visitor moved off and Rick glanced up at Georgia. 'Your favourite patient is back again,' he told her.

'Jerry? Yeah, I know. He's making a name for himself.'

'Pretty sure he's already made a name for himself. You have too much of a soft spot for that old bloke. We don't have enough beds to have him here every month.'

'I know but … it's Jerry. He's a sweetheart.'

Amber approached from the other direction and joined them at the counter. 'What are you two slackers doing?'

'Not slacking off. Just … pausing,' said Georgia.

A shout in the distance stopped their conversation.

'What was that?' said Georgia.

'Coming from maternity,' said Rick. 'Just someone in labour.'

'No, it's not,' Amber said, her voice sharp. 'That's a different sound. That does not sound like someone giving birth.'

'How can you tell?' argued Rick.

But Amber had already moved away from the counter and started striding in the direction of the shout. A second later there was a different shout, clearly a man's voice, and then a shrill scream and a crash as though something had been knocked over.

'Shit, she's right,' said Georgia.

Rick dashed around from behind the desk and they both hurried after Amber, who'd started running towards the commotion.

When they pushed through the double doors into the maternity ward, it took Georgia a moment to take in what was going on. A tall man dressed in striped pyjamas was facing away from them, and opposite him two nurses and a doctor were spread out across the hall, all of them holding their hands up in a non-threatening manner. A rounds cart lay on its side, its contents scattered across the floor.

'What —' Georgia began, trying to figure out why they all looked so afraid of the man. Then he turned and Georgia realised he was holding a large knife. She gasped. It wasn't as if this kind of thing hadn't happened here before. Working in a public hospital in Western Sydney meant incidents as if this were par for the course. Last month a teenager in the throes of drug withdrawal had punched a paramedic down in Emergency. Another time, a sixty-year-old woman suffering from hyperactive delirium flip-kicked a nurse with surprising dexterity for a woman her age. But none of these had happened on one of Georgia's shifts and she was horrified to realise she had no idea what she was supposed to do. That was when she noticed Amber slowly moving towards the man.

'Mate,' said Amber, her voice loud and clear, not a hint of a wobble to it. 'You need to put that knife down.'

It all happened in a flash. The man lurched at Amber, she swung one arm out knocking the knife out of his hand, sidestepped him, and then used his own momentum to tackle him down to the floor. One of the other nurses stepped forward along with Rick to help restrain him, and at the same time, two security guards arrived.

The whole thing was over as fast as it had started, and Georgia was starkly aware of the fact that her only contribution to the entire incident was to stand and stare, while Amber had been a bloody hero. So why was Georgia the one feeling like she could easily have a panic attack right now? She did the only thing she could think to do — turned and fled.

*

Georgia saw the paper well before she reached her car. It was fluttering in the wind, fighting against the constraints of the windscreen wiper. One big gust and it might have been whipped away and she wouldn't have known it was ever there. Her stomach clenched and her pace quickened. She didn't need this right now, not after what had happened in the maternity ward. Not after the way she'd run away from the scene like a frightened child. In the end, her panic had subsided as quickly as it had risen up and she'd covered her quick departure by pretending she'd disappeared in order to get more help.

So, this means Cadence knows where I work.

That shouldn't have surprised her though. Cadence had somehow found her car out the front of her parents' house, so why wouldn't she be able to find it in the staff carpark at the hospital? Social media. That was the problem. Everyone could find out everything about you in the space of a few bloody clicks. Thank God her home address wasn't public knowledge.

A thought occurred to Georgia then. Had she struggled to cope with that situation at work just now *because* of Cadence? Probably. With everything that had been going on, it was no wonder she was feeling more anxious than usual.

Bloody Cadence.

She reached the car and snatched up the note. For a moment, she considered tearing it to shreds without even reading it. Then Cadence wouldn't have the satisfaction of having affected her. That would take away her power, wouldn't it? But curiosity was making the paper burn in her hand and she opened it all in a rush, reading the words with her body braced for impact.

You know you're not going to be able to keep him, right?

He's MINE, bitch.

Georgia's entire body was trembling. How dare she? How dare she treat her this way? She looked around, wondering if Cadence was still here, watching to see how she'd reacted to the note. Now she wished she had ripped it up without reading it. Her shoulders and back ached from the tension. She hopped into the car and phoned Luke.

'Hey gorgeous,' he answered.

'Hi.'

'What's wrong?'

Her tone had already given her away.

'I just found another note on my car from Cadence.'

'Are you okay? What did it say?'

'That I won't be able to keep you. That I'm a bitch.' There was a wobble to Georgia's voice that she hated.

'I'm so sorry. Where are you? I'm coming to see you.'

'No, it's okay, I'm leaving the hospital now. I'm all right.'

'You're not, I can hear it in your voice. I'll meet you at your place. We can go out, stay in, whatever you want.'

Georgia felt a wave of relief that he was insisting. The truth was, she did need him, very much. 'Okay.' She hung up and took a moment to steady her breathing before starting the car and pulling out.

*

They walked hand in hand to a cafe up on the main road. The first thing Luke had done when he'd arrived at her place was hug her warmly for a good few minutes. When he looked at the note his cheeks flared red. 'She's wrong. You know that, right?'

Even though Georgia had been tempted to suggest they head to a pub for a few strong drinks, she'd decided to go with the more sensible option of coffee and a triple-choc brownie, considering it was a Wednesday night and she couldn't let Cadence turn her into an alcoholic.

They arrived and Georgia picked a comfy couch in the corner while Luke ordered.

'God, I hope she stops when you move out,' Georgia said when Luke joined her, placing their table number between them.

'So, you're still okay with me moving in with you?'

'Of course I am! I wouldn't have offered if I wasn't.'

'I know, but I was worried that it might have been a spur of the moment thing. Or that she might start to scare you off. I hate that she's treating you this way.' His voice was filled with despair and Georgia looked up at him and saw that his shoulders were slumped. She was furious with Cadence for making such a positive, happy guy look so down-trodden. She was determined to make it stop.

'Yes, she is scaring me ... a bit ... but she's *not* scaring me away from you, not in the slightest. Let's move you in as soon as we get back from Marcus's wedding.'

'Sounds good to me.'

'Can I tell you something?'

'Sure.'

'I think ... no actually, I *know*, I almost had a panic attack today.'

'Really? Because of Cadence's note? God, I'm livid with her.'

'No, not because of the note, because of this thing that happened at work. A patient lost it; he had a knife and was threatening people with it. Amber took him down.'

'That sounds awful. I'm so sorry. Anyone would feel like panicking in a situation like that.'

'Not just panicking, though. I mean almost having a full-blown panic attack. It's something that used to happen to me a few years back. I went through a really long period of mental health problems — depression, anxiety, that kind of thing.' Georgia was talking with her head down, her gaze fixed on the table. She didn't often share her history with guys she was dating. There was still such a stigma around mental health, as if once a person knew you had a propensity to depression, then they had to be careful around you. As though saying the wrong thing might set you off. As though a bad day meant you were having an episode rather than just simply *having a bad day*. Sometimes she'd even got the feeling that people thought her depression might rub off on them, as though it was contagious and if they were around her too much she'd bring them down.

The last boyfriend she'd shared her story with was Will. She still wondered if that was the reason he'd broken up with her, despite his assurances that the timing, so soon after she'd told him, was nothing but coincidence.

She stopped talking and looked up, prepared to see that look in Luke's eyes too — the combination of sympathy and apprehension. But instead she saw something else. It was a look of complete and utter understanding. He was nodding his head, and he reached across the table to take hold of her hands. 'I went through something similar,' he said.

'You did?'

'Remember how I told you about my weight problems and you asked me if it affected my relationship with my parents? Well, you were spot-on. I did resent them for the way they dealt with it. In fact, for a long time, I hated them. I felt … somehow lesser. Like they couldn't accept me for who I was. Like they couldn't really love me until I lost the weight. Especially because it often felt like it wasn't really about the health problems for them, but instead it was about looks. I didn't fit in with the image they wanted to portray to the world. Having a fat son didn't suit their idea of a nice, middle-class family.' Luke paused for a moment and Georgia saw his face twist. He was struggling with whether or not to continue. She squeezed his hands and he took a breath and continued. 'We had a professional family photo done once and I overheard my mum on the phone, asking the company if they could airbrush me so I looked a bit slimmer.'

Georgia felt a rush of goose pimples on her arms and she shivered. How could anyone do that to their own child? When she spoke, she had to steady her voice. 'That's horrible, Luke. Really awful.'

'That was the first time I cut myself.'

Georgia stayed quiet, giving him the space and time to keep talking.

'I took my dad's razor into my room and I sliced at the skin on my legs.' He stared at Georgia. 'Then I bandaged myself up and kept it hidden under my jeans until it healed — even though it was the middle of summer and I was boiling hot.' He stopped, looking shocked. 'I've never told anyone that. No one.'

Georgia stared back him. 'Luke,' she whispered, 'I'm so, so sorry.'

He nodded. 'It's okay,' he said. 'I'm glad I've finally been able to tell someone.'

Georgia paused, trying to decide if this was the moment she was going to tell someone her truth as well. She closed her eyes. Saw a bathroom sink. Saw the small white pill bottle. Saw her shaking hands gripping the edge of the basin. Saw her reflection in the mirror. Pale skin. Mascara lines down her cheeks.

She opened her eyes and looked at Luke. 'I tried to commit suicide … twice.'

CHAPTER EIGHT

The first time Georgia self-harmed was on her twenty-first birthday. Prior to that, she'd always believed that the only people who deliberately hurt themselves were teenagers chasing attention. But something had been building and building in Georgia's world. A sense of pointlessness. An all-consuming loneliness.

It started when she finished high school and noticed an obvious difference between herself and her friends. They all knew what they wanted to do next. Amanda was going to study criminology at Sydney Uni. Rebecca was going to TAFE to become a graphic designer. Heather's plan was to get an entry-level office job in an IT company. Casey was going to take a gap year to travel around Europe and then come home and enrol in a law degree.

Georgia very clearly remembered wondering, *but wait, when did you all decide?* It was like she'd missed some important decision-making meeting that all her friends had attended and no one had warned her that the *rest of her life* depended on this. It was embarrassing! How could she simply not know what she wanted from her life?

She enrolled in an Arts degree at Western Sydney University because she felt that doing something was better than doing nothing, but she still didn't know what she really wanted. She moved into on-campus accommodation with an infuriatingly driven roommate named Cynthia who somehow managed to be simultaneously always studying while also attending every single university event or party *and* holding down a part-time job in the uni bookshop *and* sticking to a strict daily exercise regime. It was exhausting just watching her get through each day. And somehow, each day that Cynthia achieved more and more, Georgia felt herself achieving less and less, slipping seamlessly into the role of Cynthia's polar opposite.

She didn't fit in at the parties thrown by the other uni students because she still wasn't sure what she wanted out of life. She was drifting away from her high school friends because they'd all gone their separate ways, and when they did try to catch up, Georgia felt like the loser of the group, so she started declining invites. Her parents went off travelling around Eastern Europe, Marcus moved down to Melbourne, and Georgia felt very much alone.

Leading up to her twenty-first birthday, some of her friends sent messages, asking her what she was going to do to celebrate it, but she pretended she didn't care about her birthday, that she wasn't fussed on having any kind of party. She turned off her phone and spent the evening sitting on her bed in the dark, torturing herself with nasty thoughts.

You're worthless.

You're never going to figure out what to do with your life.

You're a spectacular loser.

You lost all of your friends.

You're alone.

Because you don't deserve friends anymore.

Around and around the thoughts went, chasing the tail of the thought before. She started off pinching at the skin under her arms. *You idiot, you moron, you loser, you deserve this, you deserve this pain.*

No, you deserve more, this pain isn't enough for you.

She looked around the room, searching for a way to punish herself. Then she stood up and walked very carefully and purposefully towards the door. She opened it. She put her right hand on the doorjamb, closed her eyes, and then with her other hand, she swung hard and fast to close the door on her fingers. At the last second, she pulled back slightly, afraid of the pain.

This only caused her to berate herself more. *You can't even do this properly, can you? Again, Georgia, do it again. Do it properly. Don't hold back, slam it hard. As hard as you can.*

She did it three times before she was satisfied that she'd been appropriately punished. The tears were streaming down her face and her hand was shaking uncontrollably. She climbed back onto her bed and continued to sit in the darkness and the silence, her hand throbbing in her lap.

In the morning, she turned on her phone and listened to her messages. Marcus had sung happy birthday into the phone and told her not to worry about phoning back because she must be out partying hard with her mates. Her other brothers had left similar messages. There was no message from her parents. They'd warned her there would be times while they were travelling that they wouldn't have much access to a phone. Cynthia noticed Georgia's bruised fingers and told her she ought to put some ice on that.

Throughout the rest of her degree, she continued to self-harm. They were always small, innocuous things that could easily be construed as accidents. Dropping something heavy on her toe. Purposely smashing her knee into a piece of furniture. She scraped through her degree with marks that never lifted above a Pass. It was easy to hide her depression from her family because they were never around. And when Marcus called for a chat, she became adept at putting on a perky, bubbly voice and pretending that life was busy and full.

The first time she attempted to kill herself, no one even knew she'd tried. It was the day after she graduated from university. While she'd been at uni, at least she could pretend she was headed towards something. But now she was done, she had no idea what was meant to come next. She had an Arts degree with a major in English lit. What kind of job was she supposed to get? Where was she going to live? No more campus living, and she couldn't move back home because her parents were still travelling and renting out the family home.

She tried to fling herself off a cliff at the beach. But just like that first time she tried to slam the door on her fingers, at the last second she panicked and changed her mind. So instead of launching herself out into the sky, she did a sort of half-jump and ended up tumbling several metres down some rocks and landing on a ledge with scrapes and bruises. Then she had to climb her way back up.

It was a turning point though.

Stop this, she told herself as she scrunched up her suicide note and drove away from the beach. *Enough. Something isn't right with you. Pull it together. Fix yourself.*

And for a while, she did manage to pull herself together — to an extent. She found a job — it might not have been an actual *career*, but it was something to pay the bills and take her through the days from nine to five; she found an apartment with a friendly girl called Lena who had *fifteen* body piercings and six tattoos, and she stopped telling herself she was worthless, even though she still didn't really know what she wanted out of life. She started to see her old friends again.

But the darkness was always there, hovering beneath the surface. And every now and then it would manifest through the smallest of acts. Taking something hot out of the oven and, when it started to burn her hand through the tea towel, holding on for a few more seconds rather than putting it straight down on the bench. Balling up her fists and letting her fingernails dig into the palm of hands, not because she was angry about something, but because she suddenly desired the comfort that those old feelings of pain used to bring.

Later, she understood that she should have *told* someone. She shouldn't have tried to fix it on her own. She should have asked for help, seen a doctor, allowed her family or her friends to support her. Because then maybe she wouldn't have relapsed so hard.

But she didn't realise that at the time.

And perhaps the relapse wouldn't have happened at all, if not for the incident.

CHAPTER NINE

Georgia adjusted the seat down, sat on it, hopped off and adjusted it back up again.

'Hip height,' said Rick.

'I think I have it.' She climbed back onto the stationary bike and tested her feet in the pedals. That would do. She couldn't believe how refreshed she was feeling today after having opened up to Luke yesterday. She felt like a weight had been lifted off her shoulders. The way the two of them had shared their stories had definitely brought them closer than ever. Admittedly, she hadn't told him absolutely everything; she couldn't quite bring herself to go right into the details of the darkest parts of her history. But she'd shared so much more than she'd ever shared with any other boyfriend. And it felt good.

'Did you hear about the reason that patient lost it?' Rick asked. 'Apparently it was a psychotic episode. Potentially relating to a mistake with his meds.'

'Jesus, tell me I didn't give him his meds yesterday.'

'Wouldn't have been you. They're already talking to Victor. And there's a chance it was Dr H prescribing incorrectly anyway.'

'Where did he get the knife?'

'Good question. They're still investigating that.'

Georgia pedalled the bike slowly as they chatted. Maybe Rick was right, maybe she would enjoy this class. All you had to do was sit and move your legs, much less coordination than the Pilates reformer class.

'I still can't believe Amber took him down like that. And I just stood there. I didn't move. I didn't do a thing.'

'That's not something you need to feel bad about. You were taking a beat to assess the situation. And you know what? Amber could have been seriously injured. Yes, it all worked out in the end, but part of that was sheer luck. You didn't do anything wrong.'

The instructor hopped on his bike up the front of the class, and Rick and Georgia both turned their attention to him while he greeted everyone and called out instructions for set-up.

Five minutes in and Georgia had severely changed her opinion of this class. No, it did not involve just sitting here and moving your legs. It involved flicking levers back and forth for speed or power or strength; it involved jumping up and pumping your legs hard while you 'climbed a hill'; it involved twisting a dial to increase the resistance, *once, twice, again, again, a quarter turn, another quarter turn, sit back down, go faster, your watts should be at 300! Your RPM should be above 100. Turn it again, stand back up, turn it again!*

The sweat was dripping down her face, her butt was hurting from the seat, her legs felt like lead. Why oh why did she keep trusting Rick?

At the end of the class, when she climbed off her bike, her legs very nearly gave way under her.

'Oh look,' said Rick. 'Now as well as having a string cheese core, you have jelly legs.'

'Don't push me, Rick, seriously, do not push me.'

*

She was on her way to her car in the gym parking lot when she felt that same hot rash creep up the back of her neck, exactly the way it had when she'd found the first note on her car. Someone was watching her. She was certain of it.

She's here again. There's going to be another note. She stopped still and considered turning back around to find Rick, maybe asking him to walk her to her car. But then she shook her head and forced herself to continue on. *Don't let her get to you in this way. You're stronger than that.* When she reached her car, her eyes scanned the windscreen, her body braced.

Nothing. There was nothing there.

*

'Did bloody Rick tell you about the spin class he made me do yesterday?'

Amber laughed. 'Yeah, I heard. Also heard you could barely walk afterwards.'

They were sitting on upturned milk crates out the back of the hospital, and Georgia was watching Amber smoke a cigarette and feeling slightly wistful for the days when she used to smoke. It wasn't really the nicotine that she missed — she'd never been a heavy smoker — but more the social aspect of it. Several of the nurses snuck out here for a cigarette throughout their shift. Officially, you weren't supposed to smoke anywhere in or around the hospital, but most of the security guards smoked themselves, so they turned a blind eye to the little smokers' area.

'I almost fell down the stairs on the way out of the gym! Next time I'm making you come with us.'

'Good luck with that.'

'Hey, how are you feeling since the whole … drama with the knife?'

'Umm, not great to be honest.'

'Oh really? Why?' Georgia was surprised; if she'd acted the way Amber had, she'd be feeling on top of the world right now.

'Denise took me to task over it.'

'What? Why?'

'Apparently my actions were reckless. I should have stayed right back, kept my distance and waited for security.'

'Ah.'

'To be honest, maybe she's right. You know what I keep thinking? I have a daughter. I've finally got Violet back in my life and there I am risking myself when there was no need. I should have been thinking of her.'

Georgia hesitated. *Finally got Violet back in my life?* That was the first time Amber had revealed anything more than the basic terms of her custody arrangements. So, for a while she hadn't had any access to her daughter? Amber seemed to realise what she'd said; she'd obviously got carried away without meaning to. Now she looked uncomfortable.

'You know what?' said Georgia. 'I don't think you were risking yourself needlessly at all. You acted on instinct, and your instinct was to protect others by trying to get him to stop. And a protective instinct is a bloody great thing for a mother to have.'

Amber smiled. 'Thank you.'

'Anyway, what about me?' Georgia continued. 'All I did was freeze. Fat lot of good that did.'

'Yeah, well, it was the smarter move, according to Denise.'

'All right, I have something to take your mind off things. Luke's about to meet my entire family in one fell swoop. We're flying to Melbourne this weekend for my brother's wedding.'

'Family wedding. Moving in. Tomorrow you'll tell me you're engaged.'

'Ha. Don't even joke, and him moving in is *temporary*, remember?'

'Sure, sure. Four big brothers; how do you reckon Luke's going to fare?'

'He should be fine. My brothers used to be more over-protective when we were younger, but now that they have their own families, they don't do the whole "intimidating big brother" schtick anymore.'

'I would have loved to grow up with four big brothers. It sounds like so much fun.'

'Sometimes it was. Sometimes it was awful. Do you know what a house with four boys smells like? Like there's a small dead animal somewhere but you can never quite figure out where. Which once there was, because Troy tried to do a science experiment on a dead rat he found in the gutter.'

'Yeah, okay, maybe I'm seeing the benefits of growing up as an only child.'

*

Luke snaked his arms around her waist and guided her hand to the spoon to help her stir the curry on the stove.

'Now,' he said, 'the first thing you need to know about cooking a green curry is that regular stirring is essential. The second thing you need to know is that I'm completely full of it, I know nothing about cooking green curry and this is just an excuse to feel you up.'

Georgia laughed and elbowed him in the stomach. 'I knew you were bullshitting when you said I needed to add more fish sauce.'

'You did not! You went ahead and added it. Anyway, to be fair, it was an educated guess.'

'This dinner is going to be terrible, isn't it? Neither of us knows what we're doing.'

'Look, there's a good chance it's not going to taste like an actual green curry, but who cares, it'll be unique,' Luke said with a grin. 'Hey, meant to tell you, I've booked the truck to move my stuff for the weekend after Melbourne.'

'I can't wait. The sooner you're away from Cadence the better.'

'And I told her that I was moving out.'

'How did that go?'

'Pretty much as well as can be expected. First, she tried to guilt me, saying that she'd end up out on the street because she wouldn't be able to afford the rent on her own, so obviously I told her I wasn't leaving her in the lurch and I'd keep paying my share until our lease is up. For a second I thought she was okay, but then she started crying and begging me not to move. It was horrible.'

Georgia felt a strange mix of sympathy for Cadence and satisfaction that she was hurting, considering what she'd been doing to Georgia these last couple of weeks.

'How did you handle that?'

'Basically, I told her if she really still cared about me then she'd stop stalking you … then she switched from tears to rage and I legged it the hell out of there.'

'Wow. Do you think she needs professional help? She sounds seriously unstable.'

'Yeah, I agree. I have tried to bring up the idea of her going to talk to someone before, but she's shut me down. Maybe I'll try one more time before I move. Because once I'm out of there, I'm cutting ties. I feel terrible about it, but I have no choice. I can't take her anymore.'

'Agreed. Here, taste this.' Georgia held a spoonful of the curry sauce out to Luke and he leaned in. She cringed at the expression on his face. 'Oh my God, it's really bad, isn't it?'

'No, it's, umm, it's super flavoursome.' His voice had risen several octaves though and Georgia laughed.

'You're a terrible liar.'

'I am not; flavoursome is the exact right description.'

Georgia tasted it herself. 'Holy shit, that's the worst thing I've ever tasted.' She lurched to the sink and rinsed her mouth out under the tap.

'Yes, but you can't argue that it isn't flavoursome, can you? I just didn't specify which flavours, that's all.'

They binned the curry and ordered in. When they sat down on the couch with a glass of wine each to wait for their dinner, Georgia heard her phone beep with an email. She pulled it out of her pocket and looked at the sender: Cade.s8758@gmail.com. For some reason, it didn't even click that Cade could be short for Cadence, so she opened it up, thinking it would probably be junk mail. When she saw the photos in the body of the email, her chest constricted. They were of her and Rick leaving the gym after the spin class the previous day. One was of the two of them standing together and laughing. Another was of Rick giving her a hug goodbye; one where she'd obviously leaned back in to hear him say something. They were taken from a distance and out of context, which made it seem like there was something more intimate going on between the two of them. The graininess of the images seemed to make them seem sordid somehow. She immediately remembered that feeling she'd experienced while she was walking to her car, the sense that she was being watched. Clearly she'd been right.

Below the photos was a message.

You fucking slut, you think you can steal my boyfriend and then cheat on him? How do you think he's going to feel when I show these photos to him?

She felt Luke's hand touching her arm before she even heard him speak. 'Georgia? What's wrong? What is it?'

She looked up. 'Cadence took photos of me,' she whispered. Oh God, what was he going to think when he saw them? They looked so wrong.

'What the hell?' He reached for the phone and Georgia held it back.

'Wait, let me explain …' she began.

He frowned. 'What do you mean? Why would you have to explain?'

'It's just that … these photos, they're not what they look like. She's got it all wrong.'

He gently extricated the phone from her grip. 'Trust me. Whatever it is, it's going to be okay,' he said.

She watched his face as he looked at the email. Even though she knew there was nothing at all to hide from him, a part of her was still afraid. Would he think there was something more going on?

'It's not what it looks like,' she tried again.

Luke looked up at her. 'You know what it looks like to me? It looks like you're leaving the gym with a mate and my psycho ex is trying to turn it into something it's not, and I've seriously had enough.' He handed the phone back, stood up and ran his hands through his hair. 'I can't believe this. She's completely violated you. This has to stop. She cannot get away with this.'

Georgia felt a wave of relief. 'So, what do we do?' she asked.

'Go to the cops? Report her?'

'But you haven't moved out yet.'

'I know, but I'm about to. Besides, at this stage I'm thinking the restraining order would be more for you than me, wouldn't it? You're the one she's taking photos of. I'm terrified of what she's doing to you, of what else she might be capable of. We need to make her stop, and so far, she won't listen to me.'

'I guess. It's just that a restraining order feels so serious … It makes it all so … real. Is this actually happening? Is she properly stalking me? It's so surreal.'

'I get what you mean. Look, if you want, I can try again to talk to her, to reason with her, and we can wait until after the move before we take this to the cops … It's up to you.'

'Okay. Let me think about it.'

The buzzer for the front door went and Georgia jumped.

'It's okay, babe, it'll be the food.' He gave her hand a squeeze and then went to get their delivery.

*

Georgia looked in the rear-view mirror for what must have been the fifteenth time. When her eyes slid back down, she had to slam her foot down hard on the brake as the car in front slowed for a red light.

She needed to concentrate. But was that the same red car that had been behind her on Quakers Hill Parkway? Or a different one? She couldn't be sure. The light was still red so she risked another look in the rear-view mirror as the offending car rolled up behind her.

It was a woman driving. Blonde hair. Giant dark sunglasses. Could it be Cadence? But reconciling the photo she'd seen of her with the tiny reflection in her rear-view mirror was impossible. The light went green and Georgia crossed the intersection. She changed lanes and checked the mirror. The car behind changed lanes too. But that didn't necessarily mean anything, as this lane would be ending up ahead.

At Windsor Road, she turned right. So did the red car.

At Showground Road, she turned left. So did the red car.

Her breathing rate increased. She changed lanes. So did the red car. She changed back. So did the red car.

Okay, she's following me, she's absolutely, without a doubt, following me.

What was Georgia supposed to do now? Drive straight to a police station? Go running inside shouting for help? She was overreacting. This was silly, anyone could be taking the same route as she was. These were all main roads.

Georgia decided to make an unexpected turn off onto a quieter street up ahead. If the red car followed, then she would call that proof. She indicated late, took the turn a little faster than she would have liked, then looked behind her. No one. The red car was gone.

She pulled over and calmed her breathing. Then she slammed her hands against the steering wheel. For fuck's sake, she didn't have time for this. She was supposed to be going home, grabbing the bag she'd packed the previous evening before her night shift and then heading straight to the airport to meet Luke. Fuck Cadence. Fuck her for making her feel this way. If she didn't have to get down to Melbourne for her brother's wedding, maybe she'd go and confront her right now, tell her she couldn't take it anymore. Tell her that it was time for her to let go of Luke, that she had to move on.

But the truth was, it was only the adrenalin talking. She couldn't do that. Could she?

THE ELEVATOR

Georgia's lungs burned, she was gasping for air. 'H-hey,' she said. 'Can you ... please, can you just let me out of here?' She was trying to keep her voice as calm as possible; maybe if she pretended that this was no big deal then Cadence would snap out of it.

CHAPTER TEN

Georgia placed her hand on Luke's knee and he instantly stopped jiggling it up and down.

'Sorry, didn't realise I was doing it again.'

'Are you sure you're okay?'

They were seated by the window at Gate 27. Their flight to Melbourne was due to board in the next ten minutes.

'Yeah, I'll be fine.'

'You should have said something sooner. We could have road-tripped it instead.'

Luke shrugged. 'No one wants to drive twelve hours when the trip can be done in ninety minutes.'

'I feel so bad though.'

Luke put a hand over Georgia's, which was still placed on his knee. 'Seriously, you shouldn't feel bad.'

Georgia couldn't help but feel impressed that he was still trying to reassure her, despite the fact that he was shaking with nerves right now.

'So, you never fly for work?'

'All on the road. They have other reps interstate so I've only ever needed to travel within New South Wales.'

'Did something happen … to make you afraid? Or you've always been bothered by planes?'

'Nothing happened. Just a grown man with an irrational fear.'

A message came over the PA system. 'Attention all passengers travelling with Virgin on flight VA565 to Melbourne. We'll commence boarding shortly. Please familiarise yourself with your row number.'

Luke's knee began to dance again under Georgia's hand and she squeezed it.

'Honestly, I'm giving you an out right now. I can go to this wedding on my own if you like. I'm serious — I don't want to force you into this.'

Luke's leg fell still again and he looked up at Georgia and gave her a crooked smile. 'And be forever known as the boyfriend who chickened out on meeting your family because I'm too afraid to fly? It's okay, I can do this.'

Georgia leaned in, kissed him then pulled back. 'Okay, just tell me if you need anything at all.'

'You're so fucking sweet.'

'Don't you forget it.'

Luke's phone lit up on the seat next to him and Georgia saw him glance at it and then groan.

'Cadence?' Her voice became terse. She hadn't told Luke about the incident on her way home from work this morning yet. As soon as she'd met Luke at the airport she'd realised something was up with him, and when she'd found out it was a fear of flying, she'd immediately put all thoughts of Cadence out of her mind to focus on making sure Luke felt okay. But here she was, interfering with their lives yet again. God, she wished Cadence would leave them alone. Enough was enough; why was it so hard for this woman to accept that her relationship with Luke was over? What was it going to take?

'Yep. It's her.'

'What does it say?'

He put on a funny announcer-style voice. 'Today, Cadence will be playing the part of the victim.' He sighed. 'The same old stuff — how could I do this to her, how could I hurt her this way. I'm so sick of it.'

'That reminds me, what colour is her car?'

'Why? What happened?'

'This morning, driving home from the hospital, I thought she might have been following me.'

'Shit, really?'

'No, no, I mean, yes, I was worried about being followed, but in the end, I don't think it was her. I was being paranoid. It was just this red car I thought had been behind me for a while, but then I wasn't even sure if I was imagining it.'

'So, it was red?' He looked worried.

'I take that to mean she does drive a red car?'

'Yes. Did you catch the make? Or the number plate?

'I'm not really sure. Hatchback … maybe a Toyota, but don't quote me on that. I didn't get the number plate.'

Luke winced. 'Could you see the driver?'

'I got a bit of a look when we were both stopped at a light.'

'And did it look like her? I mean, I know you've only seen a couple of photos, but ... if you had to guess?'

'Hard to say. She had big sunnies on. But she was blonde.'

'Jesus Christ. I mean, I don't know, I guess blonde chicks driving red cars can't be that rare ... but she does drive a hatchback. Maybe it's a complete coincidence?'

But he was shaking even more now and Georgia realised this news had really freaked him out. Maybe she should have waited until after the flight to tell him.

'I feel awful,' he added. 'I'm so sorry.'

'You don't need to be sorry, this isn't your fault. She's the one with the problem. Anyway, it probably wasn't even her.'

They waited to board until the very end of the line was trickling through the door and the flight attendant gave Georgia a knowing smile as she scanned their tickets. Luke's dead-white face and iron-fisted grip on his ticket was a total giveaway.

'Is he okay?' she asked.

Luke's mouth was clamped shut but he nodded, and Georgia smiled back. 'We'll be fine.'

'It'll be over before you know it.'

The first time Georgia had flown down to Melbourne was when Marcus was moving there. She'd offered to go with him and help him find a place. The two of them had traded scary movie titles with aeroplane-based plots as they boarded.

Snakes on a Plane.

Castaway.

Red Eye.

Flightplan.

Black Hawk Down.

That one doesn't count, helicopter, not a plane. Plus, it's a war movie. I win.

She couldn't remember why they'd started doing it, but Georgia had thought it was funny at the time. Now she felt guilty. What if someone nearby had a fear of flying and their conversation had made them even more terrified? She certainly wouldn't be offering to play that game with Luke right now. She imagined what it would have been like if Marcus were with them. He was a great brother, but he wasn't particularly sensitive. He'd be giving Luke hell. He'd probably start shaking in his seat and pretending the plane was going down. His idea of a hilarious prank. She hoped her brother was going to treat Luke well when they arrived. He used to be quite adept at chasing her boyfriends away when he wanted to. A skill she'd taken advantage of when she was younger and had wanted to call it quits with a guy without having to break up with him herself. This time, though, she really wanted him to behave. Provided they made it through this flight, of course.

*

At Melbourne Airport, Georgia suggested Luke go into the bathroom and take a few minutes to wash his face and recover before they walked out of the arrivals gate and met Marcus. He'd actually coped really well, although he'd gripped her hand for almost the entire flight and his face was still a little grey. She leaned against the wall and checked her phone while she waited, their carry-on bags by her feet.

There was a text message waiting for her from Amber.

Hospital boring without you. Hurry up and come back. Take photos of your hot brothers for me.

Georgia tapped out a reply. *AMBER! FFS, they're all taken!! Hey, turns out Luke terrified of flying. I feel awful.*

Seriously? See this is why you should have taken me to the wedding instead.

'Who are you texting?'

Her head snapped up. 'Shit, you scared me.'

Luke laughed. 'Sorry, didn't mean to sneak up on you. I'm all good now.'

'It was Amber. Hassling me again about my supposed "hot brothers".' Georgia slipped her phone into her back pocket and realised she maybe shouldn't have told Amber that Luke had a fear of flying without checking if he minded people knowing first.

'I thought Amber was gay.'

'Bi. Or actually I think she calls it sexually fluid.'

'Ah. So, I just turned my phone back on too. Want to place a bet on how many voicemails and messages Cadence left me while it was off?'

'Two hundred and forty-six.'

'Ha. Take away the two hundred and you'd be close enough.'

Georgia took a steadying breath before replying. As angry as Cadence was making her, she didn't want to take it out on Luke. 'Unbelievable.' She reached down to pick up their luggage but Luke beat her to it.

'Here, let me take both bags. You carried everything off the plane. My turn.'

Georgia decided not to argue. As much as she wasn't normally the type to let guys hold doors open or carry heavy things for her, she guessed that he really wanted to do it, maybe even to feel more masculine again, not that he should have felt any less masculine for being afraid of flying.

When they made it out of the terminal, she spotted Marcus right away. It helped that he was a foot taller than almost everyone else in the airport.

'Why didn't you tell me your brother was that big?' Luke asked as they made their way towards Marcus.

'Not intimidated, are you?'

'Ha. Only in the sense of fuck yes.'

Georgia laughed. 'Don't stress, you'll be fine.'

They reached Marcus and he gave Georgia a bone-crushing hug before shaking Luke's hand.

'Good to see she's got you waiting on her hand and foot, mate. Can't carry your own bags, Georgie?'

'Shut up. He's being a gentleman.'

'Mate, you start doing that kind of shit and you'll end up doing it for the rest of your life. Trust me.'

Luke laughed. 'All good. I owed her.'

Marcus took one of the bags and they followed him towards the exit.

'Yeah? Why's that?'

'Because I have an irrational fear of flying and she put up with me quaking in my seat on the plane.'

Georgia felt a pang of pride at his honesty and stopped worrying about the fact that she'd mentioned it to Amber. He didn't need it to stay a secret; he was more mature than that. Impressive.

'My fiancée is the same, mate. I'll see if she's got a Valium or something for you to take on the way back.'

'Really?' Georgia interrupted. 'I didn't know Bianca was scared of flying.'

'Yep, we're totally fucked for the honeymoon to Europe, ay?'

'Jesus,' said Luke. 'Best of luck with that, mate.'

*

They pulled into the driveway of the townhouse Marcus and Bianca had bought together in West Footscray. Georgia hadn't actually seen it yet. Last time she'd come down to Melbourne, Marcus had still been living in the same bachelor pad Georgia had helped him find in St Kilda.

'Nice place,' she said. 'How the hell did you guys afford this?'

'Bianca,' Marcus said immediately. 'She's kicking arse at her law firm.'

Georgia knew that even if Bianca was bringing in a big salary, Marcus was also being modest about his own career. He'd worked hard since moving to Melbourne and was now head chef at a two-hat restaurant in the middle of the city. He and Bianca were the ultimate power couple.

They climbed out of the car and Georgia wrapped her arms around herself as an icy wind whipped through them. 'How do you live down here? It's always so bloody cold.'

'Georgia,' said Marcus, 'it's winter, it's cold everywhere. Come on, we have a fireplace inside.'

'Who else is here?'

'Everyone. Yours was the last flight in. Smart move actually, Bianca's put them all to work on the bonbonnières.'

Luke and Marcus carried the bags and they headed up to the front door, which was thrown open by Bianca as they stepped up to it. Georgia felt strange meeting the woman her brother was about to marry the day before it was going to happen.

'Um, hi,' Georgia said, holding out a hand. Bianca whacked it out of the way, stepped forward and threw her arms around Georgia.

'Oh yeah,' said Marcus from behind her, 'don't think I warned you — she's a hugger.'

Bianca ignored Marcus and held on to Georgia for just that bit longer than was comfortable, only releasing her when Marcus called out. 'Hey hon, any chance we could get in with the bags?'

'I can't tell you how great it is to finally meet you,' Bianca said, backing up as the three of them trooped inside. She turned her attention to Luke. 'And the boyfriend!' she shrieked. She threw her arms around Luke as well, delivering another ten-second too-long hug while Luke gave Georgia a bemused look over her shoulder. Eventually he was released. 'Okay,' Bianca said, 'the others are all through here on bonbonnière duty. We're going to Marcus's restaurant for dinner at seven. Follow me!'

Marcus grinned at Georgia. 'She's a force,' he said quietly. But Georgia could see the look in his eyes. In all the years he'd been with different girlfriends, he'd definitely never looked this content. She was happy for him. Maybe she and Luke could have the same thing down the track, if only Cadence would leave them alone.

CHAPTER ELEVEN

It was one of those restaurants where the kitchen was centre stage and opened right up so you could see bursts of flames every now and then, along with the chefs hurrying about, shouting out instructions at one another. Floor-to-ceiling glass windows showcased a view of the Yarra River, and quiet drum and bass music thrummed through the room. The wait staff all looked like models and they swept about the restaurant somehow looking simultaneously serene and urgently busy.

When they arrived, Marcus headed over to the kitchen to do complicated handshakes involving fist bumps and high-fives with several of the staff before returning to join them at the long table. Bianca's close family and bridesmaids were already there, plus Marcus's groomsmen.

Georgia leaned towards Luke as they followed the rest of her family towards their chairs. 'How are you doing so far?'

She had the sense he was a bit shell-shocked. Back at the townhouse, Bianca had led them through to the living room and Luke had been introduced to Georgia's parents, her three other brothers and their three wives all at once in a flurry of handshakes and back slaps and hugs and kissed cheeks. At least most of the nieces and nephews weren't there. They'd stayed behind in Sydney with babysitters, and only baby Emma had come down for the wedding.

'I'm coping. Your family is great,' said Luke. 'So, your brother is head chef here? Nice place.'

'Yeah, I haven't been down since he started here. It's pretty cool, hey? I kind of don't feel I dressed well enough.' Georgia was wearing a chunky jumper and jeans but she felt as though she ought to be in a slinky dress.

'You look gorgeous,' he replied, flicking his eyes over her body and making her feel warm inside.

They squeezed their way behind some chairs to reach their places, smiling and nodding at the various faces as they went.

A guy with dark curly hair sitting opposite them stood and leaned across the table. 'What? I don't warrant a kiss from Marcus's baby sister?'

'Grant! I didn't even see you there.' Georgia leaned over the table to let him kiss her cheek.

'Highly offended, babe. I'm sitting right across from you.'

'Unfair, I only just got here.'

Georgia sensed Luke watching, so she sat back down and introduced him. 'Luke, this is Grant, Marcus's best man. He's flown down from Sydney too.'

'How's it going?' said Luke, reaching across to shake Grant's hand.

'Not bad. It'll be better when we get past the speeches tomorrow though.'

'You'll be right,' said Georgia. 'A bit of liquid courage should see you through.'

'Oy,' said Marcus, who was a couple of seats up. 'No one's giving Grant a drink until *after* the speeches.'

'Well, you can drink tonight at least,' said Georgia, reaching for a bottle of white wine and waving it at Grant. 'Calm your nerves?'

'Yes please, fill 'er up.'

Georgia poured drinks for Grant, Luke and herself. 'Any other Sydney boys down here?' she asked.

'Just me for now. I'm the only one who scored a jersey for the bridal party. But a few more from the old group arrive first thing in the morning for the wedding.'

'You met the other groomsmen yet?' asked Georgia.

'Briefly. They both work with your bro. That's them down the end on your side.' He turned his attention to Luke, and Georgia guiltily realised she'd been excluding him from the conversation. 'How long have you two been dating?'

She bit her lip. She knew Grant would be surprised that she'd bring Luke along to a family wedding so soon.

'Coming up on about two months,' said Luke.

It was a bit of rounding up but Georgia was glad — it sounded better than six weeks.

'So, you went to school with Marcus?' Luke asked.

'Yeah. Known him since kindy days.'

'Back when he used to steal your jam sandwiches,' Georgia added.

'You know he only told me that was him a few years back? We used to plan missions to figure out who it was and the whole time the bastard was chowing down on them behind the toilet block every day.'

Georgia almost spat out her wine. 'Are you serious? You didn't know all that time? It was because Mum always made us eat Vegemite and Marcus hated it. She said jam was too sweet for school lunches.'

'Your mum was a classic. She was tough on everyone. I remember she made me eat meatloaf when I came for dinner one night. Then my mum found out and was like, right, if you can eat it for Mrs F, then you can eat it for me. I was devastated.'

'Yeah, she really didn't help us make friends.'

Susan overheard them from the other side of the table and leaned across Troy. 'I did not,' she said. 'I would never have forced you to eat something you didn't like.'

Troy's mouth dropped open. 'You must be having a laugh, Mum.'

'No,' she said firmly. 'That goes against all of my core values as a Buddhist.'

'Only problem is you weren't a Buddhist back then, were you?' Georgia argued.

'I still don't recall making you eat Vegemite. It's full of salt. Could someone pass me the wine?'

'I don't think Buddhists drink, Mum.'

'Hush, Troy, no one likes a know-it-all.'

Grant made eye contact with Georgia and winked before passing the wine bottle to Susan. 'Here you go Mrs F, enjoy.'

'You been involved with much of the wedding prep being in the wedding party? Or is it too hard being up in Sydney?' Georgia asked him.

'Not heaps. I mean I flew down a few weeks back for the tux fittings and the buck's night, which was a cracker of a night, by the way, but that was it. From what I saw though, all the wedding prep seemed like utter chaos. Think I'll elope when it's my time.'

'Yeah, I'm sure your parents would let you do that.'

Grant came from a huge Italian family. He was the apple of his mother's eye — there was no way she'd ever forgive him if he eloped.

Georgia realised that once again she'd got caught up chatting with Grant and excluded Luke from the conversation. She put a hand on his knee under the table and gave it a gentle squeeze while racking her brain trying to think of a talking point he could be included in. She was saved when Marcus started tapping his fork against a glass to make a toast.

*

'I can't believe you still smoke Winnie Blues. Haven't you given up yet?' Georgia folded her arms around herself, trying to keep warm as she wandered over to where Grant was smoking out the front of the restaurant.

'Tried to, probably about five or six times, but the old Winnies keep calling me back. What's your excuse for being out here?'

'Fresh air. It's hot and loud in there. And between you, Luke and the waiter, my wineglass has been topped up so many times, my head's started spinning. Food's great though. I'm impressed.'

'Beautiful food. Luke seems like a nice bloke.'

'Yeah, I reckon he's one of the good ones. I'm happy.'

'I'm really glad for you.'

'How about you? Seeing anyone at the moment?'

'Few irons in the fire. No one serious enough to invite along tomorrow.'

'You have irons in the fire? How romantic.'

'Screw you; it's an expression. So, you two must be pretty serious if Luke's meeting the whole family?'

'I guess. I mean, the timing of the wedding just worked out that way.' Georgia hesitated. What if she'd tried to push things along too quickly by inviting him to this wedding ... not to mention asking him to move in? But it was the right choice, wasn't it? The only way to protect their relationship from Cadence. 'It is pretty early for him to meet everyone, isn't it?' she asked.

'Look, it's early days, but if it feels right, then why not? Fingers crossed you make it through the honeymoon period.'

'I reckon we'll be fine.' *As long as Cadence leaves us alone.* 'Fuck it, give me a drag of that cigarette, will you?'

'Little Georgia Fitz. Surely you don't smoke anymore, do you?'

'No. But there's no harm in the odd drag here and there. Hand it over.'

Grant continued to withhold the cigarette. 'Do you remember what happened last time I got caught sharing a cigarette with you?'

'Oh my God, I was fifteen! And it's not my fault Marcus punched you. I never asked him to play the part of my protector.'

Grant stared at her for a moment and then passed the cigarette across. They were quiet as she dragged it in, inhaled and then passed it back.

'You know that's not the real reason he punched me, don't you?'

'What are you talking about? Yes, it was. I remember him walking around the corner of the house and catching us. The look on his face!'

A voice spoke from behind them. 'Catching you what?'

Georgia turned to see Luke approaching and he put an arm around her shoulders. 'You cold out here, babe?'

Georgia noticed a tiny intonation on the word *babe* that didn't seem quite right. 'Freezing, actually. But I was feeling claustrophobic in there. Sorry, didn't mean to ditch you with my family.'

'It's fine. I'm holding my own.' He grinned. 'So, who caught you doing what?'

'Marcus caught Grant letting me smoke one of his cigarettes when I was fifteen. He lost it. They got into a fight. I ran for it.'

'Ah. Classic big brother move.'

'Yep, they're always happy to pick on you, but if they think someone else is doing the wrong thing by you — bam, they're in for it,' Georgia said. 'All right, enough fresh air for me. You want to go back inside?'

'Sure.'

'See you two shortly,' said Grant as he continued to puff on his cigarette.

Luke kept his arm around her waist as they headed back in, and Georgia noticed he was holding her closer than usual. She gave him a sideways look. 'You weren't getting jealous of me chatting with Grant out there, were you?'

'Of course not. Why? Should I be?'

'Ha. Not in the least.'

'Okay, maybe a little. But only because the guy has history with you.'

'What history? We were never a thing.'

'I just mean he's known you most of your life. If I'm jealous of anything, it's that. Plus, the fact that he calls you babe … I'm just glad I braved the flight to join you here.'

Ah, that explained it.

'I am too. And don't worry about him calling me babe. It's not like that at all. Marcus always used to refer to me as the baby, and it caught on with his mates as well. Babe is just a progression from baby.'

CHAPTER TWELVE

It felt like the wedding reception had descended into more of a twenty-first birthday party, now that all the formalities were done with. The lights in the marquee had been turned down low and the music had been turned up loud. The atmosphere meant Georgia couldn't help cutting loose herself — especially with all the free-flowing Prosecco. She wasn't usually a sparkling wine girl but, like the previous evening, her glass kept getting topped up and it was going straight to her head, making her feel giggly and light. Her new sister-in-law's three bridesmaids had pulled her onto the dance floor and the four of them were dancing to Beyoncé.

'When Queen Bee plays, you bow down to your queen,' the tallest of the three had informed her.

The ceremony had been beautiful. They'd had a garden wedding under the winter sun, and Georgia had shed a tear as she watched Marcus's face light up when Bianca walked down the aisle towards him. Susan had completed her seven Hindu blessings and they were actually really lovely sentiments. The seventh one had been Georgia's favourite: *May this couple always be the best of friends.*

The song changed and Georgia took the opportunity to escape from the dance floor. She scanned the room looking for Luke and did a double-take when she eventually spotted him in a darkened corner. Was he … holding a baby?

She headed over to him and as she got closer, realised he was cradling her niece, Emma.

'Hey, stranger. Where you been?' he asked as she approached.

'Trapped on the dance floor with a gaggle of bridesmaids. I feel like gaggle is the correct collective noun for bridesmaids, right?'

'Sounds legit.'

She sat down next to him and tried not to look too closely at the way he was gently rocking her sleeping niece. Her ovaries might explode. Even though they were a long way off that stage of their relationship, she couldn't help flashing forward, picturing him holding a miniature version of himself. 'So how did you end up on baby duty?'

'Your sister-in-law, umm, it's Chloe, right? I accidentally made eye contact with her. Next thing, she's made a beeline for me and she just handed the baby over. She did double-check that I was your boyfriend and not some random before she took off for the dance floor.'

'Ha. Poor Chloe. I can find Troy, if you want? Remind him he has a baby daughter he should be looking after.'

'Nah, I'm good. Happy to chill here for a bit.'

'You're looking pretty natural with her there. I've,

umm …' She paused as her voice dried up and she had to cough to clear her throat before continuing. 'I've never asked you about your thoughts on kids. Are you … do you …' Oh God, why was she getting all flustered about this?

Luke smiled at her. 'I'd love to be a dad one day.'

She felt the relief slide over her. 'That's nice.'

'How about you? Plans to be a mum down the track?'

She nodded. 'Yeah, I'd like to.'

'That's equally nice.'

Marcus appeared next to them and pulled up a chair. 'Aww. Look at the cute little family,' he said.

'You're the one who just got married.'

'Yeah, I know. Bianca's mum has already started doing the whole "nudge nudge wink wink, when are you two going to have a baby" thing with us. So, I'm using you two as an outlet.'

'Oh great,' said Georgia, at the same time as Luke said, 'Bring it on.'

Marcus raised his eyebrows at Georgia and she looked away, simultaneously embarrassed and delighted.

Aaron and Troy came and joined them. 'Guess what?' Troy said, 'Mum's wasted. And I mean *proper* scuttered.'

'She is *not*,' said Georgia. 'She told me she wasn't going to drink tonight because the Prosecco's not organic.'

'Yeah, well, she's currently trying to teach Pete how to waltz but it looks more like an excuse to get him to hold her up. It's only a matter of time until she's sick.'

'Nice introduction to our family for Bianca,' said Georgia. She accidently slurred a bit on the word 'introduction' and Aaron, Troy and Marcus all zeroed in on it at once.

'Littlest Fitz is scuttered too!'

'Cut it out, I'm fine!'

Pete seemed to have escaped from Susan because he suddenly appeared next to them, followed closely by their dad. 'Quick! The baby! I need the baby. She can't make me keep dancing if I'm holding the baby.'

Luke allowed Emma to be scooped out of his arms by Pete, who then took a seat, holding the baby close to his chest like she was a shield.

'Shit,' said Graham, 'I was coming to ask for the baby too.'

'You guys are terrible,' said Georgia, standing up and pulling Luke up by the hand. She swayed a little. Annoyingly, her brothers were right, she was fairly tipsy. She'd thought sitting down would stop the light-headedness, but instead she was worse. 'Come on, let's go outside for a bit. I need some fresh air.'

'Sure,' said Luke, while her brothers all made knowing faces at her.

They weaved their way through the marquee, Georgia grabbing her small silver clutch on the way past their table. They headed out into the gardens where they found a small bench seat between fairy-light-covered hedges. Georgia leaned back and sighed.

'You okay?' Luke placed his hand on the back of her neck and stroked her skin with his fingertips.

'Yeah, just ... over-indulged a little.' She opened her clutch to look for some chewing gum and noticed a message on her phone. She pulled it out and opened it. Unknown number.

You think blocking my number is going to make me go away? I miss one date and you treat me like a fucking nobody. So, who's the evil bitch here? You are, you fucking whore.

'Oh my God.' Georgia's hands were shaking as she handed the phone to Luke. 'Look at this. Look at this horrible message.'

'What the hell?' said Luke as he read it. 'Who is this prick?' His voice sounded dangerously low, and for a moment Georgia was afraid he was going to be upset with her for not having told him sooner. She rushed to explain. 'It's this guy. This absolute dickhead. Remember how on the night we met I was stood up by a Tinder date?'

'Yeah, of course.'

'He texted me, like a week later or something, asking me to give him another chance. I ignored him and he got really nasty.'

Luke's voice softened. 'No way, that must have been awful for you. Why on earth didn't you tell me sooner?'

She shrugged. 'Because it kind of paled in comparison to your Cadence issues. And anyway, I blocked his number so I thought that was the end of it.'

'And now he's using a different number to contact you. What an arsehole. Listen, if anything like this ever happens again, you need to know I'm here for you, okay? You should never have to deal with crap like this on your own. I'm going to let him have it,' he added, going back into the message and starting to tap out a reply.

'No, no, don't do that. I don't want to give him the satisfaction of a response. I just want to ignore it.'

'Are you sure?' Luke was still holding the phone. 'Maybe I should call the guy? See if I can scare him off for you.'

'Honestly, I think it's better to leave it.'

His shoulders relaxed and he nodded, passing the phone back. 'Okay, but any hint of him trying to contact you again and you let me know.'

'Deal. Listen, can I ask for the biggest favour in the world?'

'Glass of water?'

'No. Cigarette.'

'What for? You don't smoke!'

'I know I don't, but sometimes I get random cravings, and just one cigarette would really relax me right now. That message shook me up. You could try Grant, or I'm pretty sure Bianca's mum smokes.'

'If it's something you really need, then I'll see what I can do. But can I be honest? I don't think you should let that absolute dickhead be the reason you take up smoking again, okay? You're stronger than that.'

Luke stood and disappeared back inside, and Georgia couldn't help feeling like she'd disappointed him. He had a good point: she shouldn't lapse into old habits because of one nasty message. She leaned back and looked up at the stars.

'What are you doing out here all alone?'

Georgia brought her eyes back down from the stars and fixed them on Grant.

'Getting some air. Drank too much.'

'It's a wedding, that's what you're supposed to do.' He sat down next to her and pulled out a pack of cigarettes and a lighter from inside his jacket.

Maybe she could smoke one quickly before Luke came back? It was just one, after all. It wasn't like she was actually going to start smoking full-time again. 'If you don't take two smokes out of that pack and give one to me, I'll throat-punch you, just by the way.'

'Message received.' Grant handed her a cigarette, lit it for her and then lit his own.

'You all right?'

'Yeah, why?'

'Oh, I don't know, talk of throat punches and whatnot, thought something might be up.'

'Nah, I'm good. Just pissed and thinking about stuff, that's all.'

'Is it the typical "sister at her brother's wedding" stuff?'

'And what the hell would the typical "sister at her brother's wedding stuff" be? And if you say jealous sister wants to get married, I really will throat-punch you.'

Grant touched a hand to his throat. 'Jesus, stop talking about throat punches, it's getting hard to swallow. No, idiot, I mean the emotional, "my big brother is all grown up" stuff.'

'Ah, fair enough. No, it's way more selfish than that. Just some horrible boy problems. Don't worry about it.'

'What's Luke done? You need me and Marcus to take him out back and beat him up for you?'

'No! It's not Luke! Luke's great. It's this other idiot. This Tinder date I was supposed to have before I met him. This guy won't stop messaging me now. Anyway, as if you'd ever beat anyone up. You and Marcus were all talk when you used to threaten my boyfriends in school.'

'I know. Remember when we tried to have a go at that wanker in Year Seven after he made you cry?'

'Yes! You ended up asking him to join your footy team.'

'Our intentions were good. So, what's the deal with this guy texting you?'

'It's nothing really. He's just being a troll.'

A shadow appeared across Grant's face and Georgia turned around to see Luke holding two glasses of water. 'Oh, you found a cigarette.'

Dammit, he definitely sounded disappointed. Georgia wished she'd stopped herself.

'I was coming back to tell you I hadn't been able to track one down yet,' he continued. 'It's way harder to find someone who smokes than it was in the nineties. Everyone's so health-conscious now.'

'Tell me about it. Smokers are a dying group — pun intended,' Grant said as he stood and put out his cigarette. 'All right, there's a bridesmaid in there who already told me she wants to share an Uber home with me. Better get back before she changes her mind.'

Luke took Grant's seat and Georgia stubbed out her cigarette as well, even though it wasn't quite finished. 'Thanks for the water,' she said. 'Don't tell Grant I wasted one of his smokes. A couple of drags was more than enough. You were right, I don't want to start smoking again.'

'Your secret is safe with me. I'm glad you don't want to take it up.'

Georgia leaned in to Luke and he wrapped an arm around

her shoulders. 'Hey, you had any more calls or messages from Cadence this weekend? I keep forgetting to ask.'

'A few. I've been deleting them and not responding though.'

'You know, I've never had an ex try to get me back after we split up.'

'You sound like you think that's a bad thing.'

'I just mean that as much as she's being awful, it shows how much you must mean to her — the fact that she won't give up.' Georgia shivered involuntarily. Was Cadence ever going to give up? She pressed herself into Luke.

'Does it? Or does it show that she's deluded?'

As if on cue they both felt the buzzing of Luke's phone through his jacket.

'Maybe *I* should answer it.' Georgia made to reach for his pocket but he pressed his hand over the top of hers. 'No way. I'm not subjecting you to her ranting. Ignore it, it'll stop.'

Georgia looked back up at the stars again. Luke leaned in and kissed her cheek. The music floating out into the garden switched from a fast dance track to a slower song. 'Only You' by Yazoo. Luke stood and pulled Georgia to her feet, then he wrapped his arms around her and they swayed slowly together.

She found herself wishing she could somehow press pause on this moment. She didn't want to go back to Sydney and reality tomorrow. She didn't want to keep looking over her shoulder, wondering if Cadence was somewhere, lurking, waiting to pounce, waiting to ruin the most perfect relationship she'd had in a very long time. She was going to do whatever it took to protect it.

THE ELEVATOR

Cadence swung around to face her. She ran her hands through her hair and then her fingers tightened and she was pulling at it, pulling and pulling. She took a step towards Georgia and Georgia slid sideways along the back wall of the elevator, crumpling into the corner.

CHAPTER THIRTEEN

Georgia took a moment to lean against the side of the flatbed truck and drink from her water bottle. Her hair was frizzing from the light rain. It had been such a dry winter that Luke hadn't actually seen her how frizzy her hair could get yet. She imagined him returning from inside her building, taking one look at her and saying, 'I'm sorry, it's over. I had no idea your head could look like that.'

She tried to smooth it down but it was a losing battle. Besides, Luke was going to see her at all of her worst stages now that he was moving in. Arriving home from nightshift — bleary-eyed and smelling of Betadine and latex. Early evening bedhead — when he arrived home from work she'd be waking up from a day sleep with a drool-stained pillow and stale coffee breath (she always wound down from nightshift with a decaf on her way home). No more presenting her best self only — he was going to see it all.

But then again, she was going to see it all from him as well, wasn't she? The good, the bad, the ugly. She couldn't really imagine him looking anything but drop-dead gorgeous though. Even with his hair flattened from sleep and pillow creases on his face he looked irritatingly handsome.

Luke reappeared from the front door of her building and grinned at her. 'Slacking off on the job,' he said as he walked right up to her, placed one hand on her hip and then leaned in and kissed her, pushing her back against the ute.

'Kissing in the rain,' she said as he eventually broke away. 'Tick that one off.'

He raised his eyebrows. 'What do you mean?'

'I mean that's the first time we've kissed in the rain.'

'It is not, is it?'

'Yep, it is. This is the first time it's rained in ages. And I'm not slacking off, thank you very much. I just lugged your bloody bedside table up three flights of stairs. I deserve a breather.'

Luke had only brought a few pieces of furniture over to her place, saying he was happy to leave most of it with Cadence and start fresh once he got his own place. But with no elevator in her building, it was still hard work getting it up to her apartment.

He reached both hands around and squeezed her butt. 'Ah yes,' he said, 'I can feel the difference in your glutes from all those stairs already.'

'Shut up!'

He leaned back and looked at her. 'Check out this curl,' he said, touching her hair, 'right in the middle of your forehead.'

'There was a little girl, who had a little curl …' Georgia recited.

'I love it, you're fucking adorable.'

'First of all, it's not a curl, it's pure frizz, and second of all, it's hideous.'

'I respectfully disagree. I love your hair like this. Hey, let's go out. We can celebrate the fact that we're getting Cadence off our backs.'

'Sounds like a plan. What was she like as you left today? How did she cope with you taking all of your stuff?'

Georgia hadn't gone with Luke to collect his things from his apartment; they'd both agreed that her meeting Cadence would be a bad idea.

He twisted his mouth and Georgia sensed he was trying to come up with a diplomatic way to answer the question.

'It's okay,' she said. 'You can tell me if she was bad.'

'Okay, she was bad.'

'What did she say?'

'There was a lot of yelling and screaming. There were some tears. She even threw a vase against the wall. Not sure if my head was the target and she's not a great shot or if she was only trying to be dramatic.'

'Far out, that is full on.'

'Yep, it wasn't much fun.'

'Don't suppose you asked her … do you know if it was her behind me last week when I was driving home from work?'

'Yeah. I mean, I didn't come right out and accuse her, because I thought she'd shut down, but I tried to hint at it and see if I could maybe catch her out.'

'And what do you think?'

'Honestly, I'm still not a hundred per cent sure. When I tried to talk about you she got tight-lipped. But there was something about the look on her face when I mentioned your name, this sort of smug expression. It bothered me. But look, hopefully me moving out is going to be the end of it all and you'll never have to stress about a red car behind you again. That said, let's both keep an eye out for the next little while. I don't want her anywhere near you.'

Or near you, Georgia thought. She wondered if this really was going to be the turning point with Cadence. Would moving out actually make her stop? Or would she step up her game instead?

*

They walked to a local pub, huddled together under an oversized umbrella. The rain had increased to a steady downpour. Georgia had showered and slicked her hair back into a tight ponytail — no need for him to *continue* to see how frizzy her hair could get in adverse weather. Luke had joined her in the shower and kissed her under the running water. 'Now this we've definitely already done before,' he'd whispered in her ear. Shower sex was his favourite. But she'd used all of her self-restraint and pulled back before they could get too carried away.

'I'm starving. If we start now we'll never make it to the pub.'

At the pub, they took a booth and ordered beers and a couple of chicken schnitzels. While they waited for their meals, Luke reached across the table to hold her hands. 'Right,' he said, 'here's your chance. Any house rules you want to impose on me before it's too late?'

'Isn't it already too late? You're in. Your workout gear is taking up half my living room and your nerdy Transformers collection is taking up most of my shelves.'

He gave her a mock look of shock. 'Nerdy? That collection'll be worth millions one day.'

'Doubt it. There's a Megan Fox action figure in there. You can hardly call that a classic collector's item.'

'Are you insulting my Megs, woman?'

'Oh, so she's *your* Megs, is she? So why aren't you shacking up at her place instead of mine?'

'You're hotter.'

'Excellent answer.'

Their Coronas appeared on the table in front of them, each with a wedge of lime stuffed into the top of the bottle. They pushed the limes inside then clinked the beers together.

'Cheers to being Cadence-free,' said Luke.

Maybe he was right. Maybe they really were about to be free of her.

'Cheers. Here's to sex on tap,' she replied, winking at him.

*

The two of them were smashed. That hadn't been the plan. It was supposed to be a couple of beers and dinner and then home for an early night after a long day of work and moving. But after the beers they'd decided to share a bottle of wine over their schnitzels, and then after the wine they thought they'd follow it up with some spirits. Next thing, they'd somehow made friends with a trio of German tourists up at the bar and the five of them were all doing shots to celebrate Luke moving in with her. It helped that their new-found friends were insisting on shouting the rounds.

'Another round!' Georgia shouted, slapping her hand down on the bar. 'On them!' She was a loud drunk. Always had been.

Luke laughed. 'Georgia, you have to wait for them to offer.'

'They don't mind, do you, boys?'

'Of course not,' said Jake. Or was it Nick? Georgia couldn't be sure; she kept getting those two mixed up. 'It's a celebration. You two are becoming *verschmolzen*.' He laced his fingers together to indicate the two of them becoming one.

Georgia leaned in and said in a mock whisper, 'No, no, boys, we'll be doing that when we get home.'

One drink later, Georgia was washing her hands in the bathroom when she noticed a blonde woman standing at the next sink, checking her eyeliner in the mirror. Was it her imagination, or was the woman looking sideways at her as she checked her makeup? Georgia's eyes were blurry from too much vodka. She couldn't properly make out the woman's features. She closed her eyes and tried to picture the photos Luke had showed her of Cadence. Was it possible? She didn't know. She couldn't think, couldn't concentrate. She opened her eyes and her gaze met the other woman's in the mirror. The woman winked.

Georgia stepped backwards and stumbled a little.

'Are you okay?' asked the woman.

'Fine,' Georgia mumbled, turning and hurrying out of the bathroom and back towards the bar.

As soon as Luke saw her face, his expression changed. 'What's wrong?'

'Nothing,' she said. 'It's probably nothing. Just this woman in the bathroom, I thought …'

Luke jumped up and pulled Georgia towards him. 'Shit! It's not, is it?'

'I don't know! I mean I'm probably being paranoid. It was just that she kept looking sideways at me, but maybe I was imagining it. And then she winked, but it could be that she was being friendly. Women do that. Women are friendly and chatty in the ladies' bathrooms.' She knew she was babbling, but the combination of drunkenness and fear wasn't doing her any favours.

Luke looked past Georgia in the direction of the bathrooms. 'Did she come out after you? Do you see her anywhere?'

Georgia turned around to look. 'I don't know, I can't see her.'

'Do you think it was Cadence? Did you recognise her from the photos?'

'Not sure. I mean, she had long blonde hair. I couldn't focus on her face properly. She was tall, I guess, although maybe she was wearing heels? I don't know how else to describe her. She was pretty, and that's one thing I do remember from her picture — she was pretty.'

'I guess you could describe Cadence as tall, especially with heels on. But I don't know. Surely she can't be here. Do you want me to go into the ladies' and check?'

'No, no, that's crazy. You'll get yourself into trouble. Let's just go home.'

'Okay, going home is probably a good idea. I don't want her anywhere near you. I can't believe this, I can't believe she cornered you in the bathroom. That absolute psycho.'

The fear in Luke's voice was making Georgia feel nervous. 'It might not have been her,' she said in a small voice.

'Yeah, well, considering everything else she's done, it wouldn't surprise me. Come on, let's get out of here.'

They said goodbye to the German tourists and headed back out into the cold, wet night.

*

Sunday morning Georgia slept late and woke to find Luke lying next to her, propped up on one elbow, watching as she opened her eyes. The sun was across her face and she squinted back at him. 'Creepy,' she said.

'Not creepy, sweet. Romantic.'

'My mouth is like sandpaper.'

'Not surprised. You drank like a fish last night.'

'So did you.'

'Yeah, but I hydrated more between drinks than you did. Every time I tried to get you to have water you told me water was for pussies.'

Georgia yawned. 'I'm so charming, right?'

'Absolutely. Here,' he rolled away and pushed the hanging curtain aside so he could reach a glass of water from his bedside, 'drink this. Or is water still for pussies?'

'Water is liquid gold,' she replied, sitting up and taking the glass. 'Thank you.' She took a long sip. 'Hey, I keep meaning to ask you — do you totally hate sleeping in this ridiculously over-the-top bed?'

'No way. This bed is awesome.' He sat up cross-legged with a straight back. 'Check me out, I feel like a sultan in this bed. Or like an Arabian prince or something. We need to buy ourselves some silk sheets for it.'

Georgia laughed. 'Silk sheets, going on the shopping list.' She took another big gulp of water. 'Do you think I was being overly paranoid last night?'

'Not at all.' He reached out for his phone. 'Here,' he said, 'do you want to look at her photo again, refresh your memory, see if you think it really was her?'

Georgia was about to accept, but then she changed her mind. Wasn't this exactly what Cadence wanted? To constantly interfere in their relationship? To always be on their minds? Georgia didn't want to look at her face again. She wanted to think about other things, to start moving forward, away from Cadence. 'No. I want to forget about it.'

'Okay, well hopefully it wasn't her, but I'm not liking the way she's made you feel. You shouldn't have to be afraid that my idiotic ex is following you. I really am sorry.'

'It's okay. You don't need to apologise.'

He climbed out of bed and pulled a T-shirt over his head. 'Come out to the kitchen when you're ready. I'm making pancakes and bacon before I go for my run. Killer hangover cure.'

'I knew there was a reason I let you move in.'

Georgia rolled over and picked up her own phone from her bedside. There was a message from a number she didn't recognise. Oh God, not again, not another one. She opened it up and read it.

It was a pleasure to meet you last night.

But you're even uglier up close.

She almost dropped the phone. So much for moving forward. She climbed out of bed and strode straight out to the kitchen where she held up the screen for Luke to see. 'It was her,' she said. 'It was Cadence in the bathroom last night.'

'Shit, I'm going to kill her,' he said, snatching the phone and looking at the message. 'She must have got your number off my phone when I was still living with her.'

'And this means she followed us again last night. Maybe she followed you back here when you drove the truck over?'

'Maybe. Dammit, I didn't want her to know where you lived. I'm so sorry. You don't deserve to be copping any of this shit.'

'It's all right, this isn't your fault. She already knows where I work and she left me that note at my parents' house. It's no surprise she found out where my apartment is.'

'Well, it feels like it is my fault. I'll call her now, tell her to back the fuck off. I hate the fact that I'm away for work for the next two nights. I don't feel at all comfortable leaving you alone with this going on. I'm worried you won't be safe.'

Georgia gave him a wry smile. 'I can look after myself. You forget that until yesterday I lived alone. I'll be fine.'

CHAPTER FOURTEEN

Georgia was surprised to find that the apartment felt empty when she arrived home from work. Even though Luke had only just moved in, it already felt as though he was meant to be there. Maybe it was the sight of all his things around the place. His weights bench squeezed in beside the couch. His grey shirt on the back of a dining room chair. His collectibles crowding the shelf. And maybe, if she was entirely honest with herself, she didn't love being alone because of Cadence.

Come on Georgia, she scolded herself, *shake it off. You're not a scaredy cat.*

She was starving, so she dumped her bag and went straight to the fridge to see what she might be able to cook. As soon as she opened the door she smiled. On the middle shelf were two Tupperware containers with Post-it notes attached.

The first one said, *Having seen you cook, I don't get how you survived this long. Put this in the microwave for 2 mins. Miss you.*

She opened the lid to find a chicken stir-fry with brown rice. The note on the second container read, *This one is dessert. Dessert comes after dinner. X*

She laughed and pulled her phone out of her back pocket to text him.

Just discovered my dinner. Don't deserve you. Xx

She put the food in the microwave and then dialled her brother's number while she waited for it.

'Hey Georgie Porgie, what's up?' Marcus answered with his usual greeting.

'Not much, how's married life?'

'So far it's exactly the same as pre-married life.'

'Fair enough. When do you guys head off to Europe?'

'Day after tomorrow. We had to wait for Bianca to wrap up a case at work before we could go. What's happening with you?'

'Not much.' Georgia rested the phone between her ear and her shoulder while she crouched down to open the microwave and pull her dinner out.

'Your voice just went squeaky. What's going on?'

'Okay, okay.' She spooned the food out of the container and onto a dinner plate. 'I haven't told anyone this yet because I know you'll all think it's too soon, but … Luke moved in over the weekend.'

Marcus made a spluttering noise like he was spitting out a drink but she suspected he was faking it to be dramatic. 'Jesus, are you serious? I mean, I know you brought him to the wedding, but didn't you guys only just meet?'

'Oi! You're the one family member who's not supposed to judge me. Oh, and don't tell Mum. She doesn't know yet.'

'Yeah, yeah. Just be careful, okay? I might come up and visit after we get back from the honeymoon. Suss him out properly.'

'Okay, sounds good — as long as you're nice. Anyway, I've gotta go, my dinner's getting cold in front of me.'

'No worries, take care, Little Fitz. Talk soon.'

She hung up the phone and was about to sit down to eat when she heard the sound of a sharp crack against her glass balcony door.

'What the hell was that?' she murmured to herself. She strode over to the door and then stopped with her fingers on the handle. *You're not a scaredy cat*, she reminded herself. She opened the door and stepped out onto the balcony. A small rock was on the ground by her feet. Had someone thrown that up here? She picked it up, stepped forward to the balustrade and looked out at the street. It all seemed quiet and still. She turned back to the door to check the glass for damage. There were a few small scratches, but it was too hard to tell if they were all old. She took one more look at the rock in her hand then tossed it over the balcony into the bushes below.

When she went back inside to her dinner, she locked the door behind her, drew the curtains and switched on the television, turning the volume up loud.

*

Georgia dragged one of the chairs over closer to the hospital bed and sat down. She knew full-well that she didn't have the time right now, but she couldn't help it. She was feeling a weird mixture of happiness to see her favourite patient again, guilt that she felt happy to see him when it meant he was unwell, and concern that he was back.

'So,' she said, 'I hear you took the express route here last night.'

Jerry looked sheepish. 'I didn't ask Eileen to call an ambo, she did that on her own.'

'She was worried about you.'

'Yes, well, maybe I was carrying on a bit.'

'Actually, she says you *weren't* carrying on and that was what worried her more. Not like you to go quiet if something's wrong.'

Jerry looked sideways and Georgia was surprised to realise that he was having trouble meeting her eyes.

'What's going on?' she asked. 'You don't seem like yourself.'

He kept looking past her, his gaze fixed on the abstract artwork on the opposite wall. When he spoke there was a tremor to his voice that she'd never heard before. 'My mother used to have this sixth sense when it came to death,' he said. 'My old man died when I was a young fella. He worked on the rail and there was an accident. You know what my mum said? She said, "I knew it." She said, "I told him not to go in today after that dream I had last night." Scared the bejeezus out of me.'

'Oh, Jerry,' Georgia tried to interrupt, but he held his hand up.

'Happened again and again throughout her life. Night before her best friend passed she had another dream. Night before my uncle died? Dream.'

Georgia nodded, letting him speak, despite the fact that she was confident Jerry's mum had stretched the truth about these so-called prophetic dreams.

'Night before she kicked the bucket herself she called me to say, "Jerry, that's it. I'm gone." She'd had the dream. She knew. She was right: next day I got the news, she was gone. Last night I had a dream. Saw my mum, my old man, my uncles, aunts. The whole lot of 'em, all giving me this friendly wave, like, *come on over.* And I was thinking, *Well, Jesus, you don't have to all look so happy about it.*' He finally made eye contact with Georgia. 'That's it,' he said. 'I'm a goner.'

Georgia stood and took hold of his hand. 'Jerry,' she said, 'to use your own words, respectfully, that's the biggest load of bullshit I've ever heard. A dream is nothing more than neurons firing in your brain during REM. You are not a goner, you're going to be perfectly fine and we'll have you back out of here and home with Eileen in no time. That's a promise.'

Jerry cracked a smile. 'Look at you getting all school-marm with me.'

'Yes, well, sometimes you have to be firm about these things.'

In fact, maybe I ought to use the same attitude on some of my own problems with Cadence, she thought to herself. *Get firm with her, tell her to stay out of lives. If only it were that simple.*

She returned her focus to Jerry and an idea occurred to her. 'Actually, hang on one sec, I'm going to get something for you,' she said, letting go of his hand and striding from the room.

She came back five minutes later and handed him a small yellow stone. 'Okay,' she said. 'First of all, do not breathe a word of this to the other nurses or doctors, because the idea of using healing crystals goes very much against my medical training. However, this is a citrine crystal. It's something this amazing nurse, Kathy, gave to me a long time ago when I was … going through a difficult time. In fact, Kathy was the reason I decided to even become a nurse. When she gave it to me, she said it was a pocket-sized piece of sunshine to carry with me always. Although I wouldn't tell her this, these days it mostly just lives in my locker. Anyway, if you can believe that dreams are prophecies, then you can believe that crystals have healing powers. This is supposed to fill you with positivity, okay? So, cut out this negative "I'm a goner" talk and believe in a different outcome. Got it?'

Jerry stared down at the stone sitting in the palm of his weathered hand, then his fingers closed around it. 'All right,' he said. 'I'll give it a go.'

*

The line at the bar was at least five people deep.

'See, this is why we should go somewhere else once in a while,' Georgia said to Ally, one of the other nurses who'd come to help her carry back the round of drinks. She had to shout to be heard over the music.

'I know. I hate trying to get to the front when it's this busy, everyone's always pushing in on you. So, where's this boyfriend we all keep hearing about?' Ally asked as they took a step closer towards the bar. 'I thought maybe we'd get to meet him tonight?'

'I would have loved to have brought him along to meet everyone. But he's away for work.'

'What does he do?'

150

'He's a sales rep, travels all over the state.'

A few people moved to the side in front of them and they took the opportunity to sneak further towards the front of the queue. 'Is that hard?' Ally asked. 'Or good because you get lots of space?'

'Probably a bit of both. Spot at the bar, grab it.'

Ally darted forward and squeezed her way between two tall women to claim her place at the bar. She was already a petite girl, but she was also wearing flats so she looked like a schoolgirl next to the other women. She twisted back around. 'What's our order again?'

Georgia relayed the order from the table and waited while Ally got the attention of a bartender. A few minutes later they carried the drinks back to their table to find half their group missing.

'Where's everyone gone?' Georgia asked.

'Outside to smoke,' said Victor.

'Someone text them,' said Ally. 'Tell them if they don't hurry up we'll drink their cocktails.'

Rick and Amber appeared next to them. 'Who's drinking my cocktail, bitches?' Amber asked.

'Us,' said Ally, 'because you ditched us to go outside and smoke.'

Amber reached out for her drink. 'Don't even think about it. You know how much I need this after today's shift.'

'Why? What did I miss today?' Georgia asked.

'Just a really shitty situation helping a patient to the bathroom. And when I say a shitty situation, I do mean that literally.'

'Delightful,' said Rick.

Amber shrugged. 'Hazard of the job.'

'Do you ever think it's weird that more of us smoke than not?' asked Ally. 'With everything we see, I don't get why we're not the healthiest people in the world.'

'Nope,' said Amber firmly, 'with everything we see, we need alcohol and cigarettes to survive.'

'True that,' said Rick, leaning across to high-five Amber.

'Mmm, would we call this a high-five-able moment?' Georgia felt her phone start vibrating in her back pocket. ''Scuse me,' she said, turning away to pull it out and take a look. It was Luke. She smiled and answered it, pressing her finger to her other ear to try and block out the noise. 'Hey! How's Inverell?'

'It's fine, but listen, I need to ask you something. What are you wearing tonight?'

Georgia frowned, suspecting she must have misheard him. He sounded worried, but why would he be worried about what she was wearing? She moved away from her friends.

'What?' she said.

'I know it's a weird question, but what are you wearing? Or more specifically what colour?'

His tone was starting to worry her. She pushed through the crowd and found a door that led to the quieter outdoor area. 'Green,' she said as she walked. 'A green top and dark jeans.'

'Fuck,' came back the response.

'What? What's wrong?'

'Are you with your friends?'

'I was. I've just walked outside to talk to you.'

'Okay, listen carefully, I need you to go straight back to them. I don't want you on your own.'

'Luke! What's going on?'

'I'm so sorry, Georgia. It's Cadence. She's there. She's watching you.'

Georgia's head snapped up. 'You're kidding me. How do you know?'

'She messaged me. Said something about the way you looked in your green top. I was hoping she was bluffing, trying to get a rise out of me. That's why I wanted to check what you're wearing. Tell me you're walking back to your friends now. I'm staying on the phone until I know you're with them.'

'Okay, I'm going back inside now.'

Georgia moved quickly, pushing her way back through the crowd yet again. The faces around her had taken on a new feel. Earlier there was a sense of festivity and fun. The drunken dancing people around her had seemed friendly and jovial. Now they were too drunk, too close, invading her personal space. Someone pinched her bum as she moved past them and she swung around, her heart beating fast. A middle-aged guy grinned at her; she glared back at him and pushed on. A girl elbowed her, and Georgia let out an audible gasp. The girl gave her a look and said loudly, 'Overreact much?' before turning back to her friends. She was brunette. Not Cadence.

Georgia was still holding the phone to her ear.

'Georgia,' Luke's voice came through, tinny and small, 'are you okay? Who was that?'

'Just some girl. I'm fine.'

Finally, she arrived at the table where her friends were. Rick caught her eye and immediately stood. 'What's wrong?' he asked.

She held up a finger to Rick and spoke to Luke, 'I'm here,' she said. 'I'm with my friends.'

'Good. Can one of them go home with you when you leave tonight? I still don't believe Cadence would ever actually do anything to hurt you, but I'm not taking any chances. I feel terrible about this. I'll be home tomorrow afternoon and we'll get this sorted out, okay? We'll go to the police and take out a restraining order if we have to.'

'Okay, I will. Luke, what exactly did she say? In her message?'

There was a pause. 'It's not very nice,' he said eventually.

'Please tell me. I want to know.'

'She said green's not your colour, and that … um, that it's a really slutty top.'

Georgia stayed silent and Luke filled the space. 'Please don't let it get to you. It's not true, none of it. I bet you look fucking stunning tonight.'

'Okay, it's all right, I'm fine. Listen, I've gotta go, my friends are all looking at me wondering what's up.'

'All right. Call me later when you're home, okay?'

'I will.'

There was another pause and then Luke said all in a rush, 'Georgia, I love you.'

It was the first time either of them had said it and Georgia was temporarily filled with pure bliss. She turned away from her friends and spoke quietly. 'I love you too,' she said. 'Bye.'

'Bye, take care.'

Georgia hung up and turned back to her friends. Amber and Rick were both looking at her expectantly.

'What's going on?' Amber asked.

'That was Luke. Apparently his ex is here tonight … watching me. She texted him about me.'

'What?' Amber looked horrified. 'What do you mean? What did she say?'

'She said I look like a slut.'

Rick looked around. 'You mean she's here now? Where? I'm gonna have a go at her.'

Georgia looked around too. 'I don't know. I mean, I've seen a couple of pictures of her but I don't know if I'd recognise her. She's blonde, that's about all I can tell you.'

'Well, that's about sixty per cent of the women here,' said Amber, scanning the room as well. 'What about that one over there?' she asked, pointing.

Georgia slapped her hand down. 'Amber! Don't point!' She took a look at the woman Amber had singled out. 'I don't think so. Maybe she's not even here anymore. Maybe she sent the message and then left.'

'Do you want to stay and finish your drink or do you want to get out of here?' Rick asked.

'I kind of want to go.'

'That's fair enough,' said Amber, 'even though it sucks. That bitch has completely ruined your night. How do you think she even knew you were here? Do you think she followed you?'

'Probably. I hate to ask this, but could one of you come home with me? I don't really want to go alone.'

'Of course,' Rick said immediately. 'There's no way we'd let you leave here on your own.'

'Yeah, I'll come too,' Amber said. 'I don't feel like lining up for half an hour for my next drink anyway.'

In the cab on the way back to her place, Amber and Rick chatted animatedly about Cadence while Georgia fell silent. She realised that from their perspective it made for an exciting drama — a strange woman watching them at the bar, sending nasty messages, disappearing into the night. If it had been happening to someone else, Georgia probably would have got caught up in the excitement of it herself. But right now, she just felt flat. The comment about her outfit being slutty had stung, and even though she'd always loved this green top, she found herself self-consciously tugging at it now, trying to hide her cleavage. She hated that Cadence had managed to get inside her head. And she was sick of that word haunting her.

She opened Facebook on her phone to try to take her mind off everything and checked her notifications. There was a friend request from an old schoolmate she thought she was already friends with. She accepted it, figuring she must have been mistaken.

She scrolled through her newsfeed and saw the photo that Ally had taken earlier of them all. She zoomed in on the picture and examined her top. The very edge of her black lacy bra could be seen. Maybe she did look slutty.

Amber glanced over. 'Hang on,' she said, snatching the phone from Georgia. 'This is it. This is how she knew where you were.'

'What?'

'Look, Ally tagged you in this photo and she checked us into the Bella Vista Hotel.'

'Okay, but I'm not friends with Cadence on Facebook. How would she have seen it?'

'Ally's got it set to public. Anyone can see it. If this girl is stalking you and Luke, then I'm guessing she knows your full name somehow. I reckon she's searched your name on Facebook, this photo's popped up and, bang, she knows where you are.'

'You realise this means she might not even have been there tonight,' Rick put in. 'Maybe she pretended she was there when she messaged Luke, but all she actually did was look at your photo and describe you from that.'

'Maybe,' said Georgia.

She wasn't sure if she felt better or worse about the possibility of Cadence having tricked her. On the one hand, it was less serious if she hadn't followed her physically. On the other hand, Georgia felt humiliated at the idea that this woman had chased her away with a simple message.

They arrived back at Georgia's apartment, and Rick and Amber came in for a drink.

'Hard stuff is above the fridge,' said Georgia as Rick headed into the kitchen. 'Deja vu,' she added. 'This is exactly what I did with Luke when Cadence sent him the note at that restaurant. She's going to turn me into an alcoholic.'

'I can make it a weak one if you like?' Rick offered.

'Fuck that,' said Amber. 'Girl needs a strong drink. Something to put her to sleep.'

Georgia shrugged. 'Yeah, screw it. Strong sounds good. Actually, do either of you have a cigarette I could steal?'

'Since when do you smoke?' Rick asked.

'I don't. I mean, I used to, long time ago. And I had, like, half a cigarette at my brother's wedding, and I don't know … suddenly I just feel like one.'

Amber was already reaching into her handbag. 'Here you go,' she said. 'I'll have one with you.'

'Me too,' said Rick, bringing the drinks around from the kitchen. The three of them went out onto her balcony. Georgia brought a blanket from the couch out with them and they huddled together on her bench seat with the blanket across their knees, drinking quietly and listening to the night-time sounds of suburbia.

'What's that rustling?' Amber asked. 'Coming from the trees over there?'

'Fruit bats,' Georgia said firmly.

'Oh,' said Amber, sounding disappointed.

'Amber! Were you hoping that my boyfriend's ex was hiding in a bloody tree, watching us?'

'No! I was just making sure.'

CHAPTER FIFTEEN

Georgia woke early from a restless night, glad to feel the sunshine streaming in through the window. Daylight. Everything felt so much better in the daylight. The more Georgia thought about it, the more confident she felt that Cadence had been bluffing about being there last night. Luke's old apartment with Cadence was in Artarmon. How could she have had time to get from Artarmon to Bella Vista after seeing that picture on Facebook? Why would she bother? She wasn't a threat, she was a nuisance, that was all. Georgia needed to stop letting this woman stress her out, stop letting her control her life. She needed to see this woman for what she was — a jealous ex who couldn't let go, instead of a boogieman who scared her out of a fun night with her friends.

Georgia rolled over and picked up her phone to check for messages. There was a new Facebook private message showing up in her notifications. She clicked through to it, stifling a yawn. It was from her old school friend Rachael Carver.

It was cute how you just accepted my friend request without bothering to check that I am who I say I am.

Georgia sat up straight. She continued reading.

Tell me something, Georgia, is there anything missing from your apartment?

She was breathing hard. Her heart thudded against her ribcage. She looked around the room, her eyes roving as though she would immediately see some obvious omission from her bedroom. Everything looked normal, everything looked the same. She held still, torn between the desire to race out of her bedroom and check the rest of the apartment and the paralysing fear that told her not to move a muscle.

You can't stay here in bed, Georgia, she told herself firmly. *Move.*

She threw back the covers in one swift movement, then slammed her feet down on the floor, making as much noise as she could.

'I'm not afraid of you,' she said out loud, but her voice didn't come out as strong as she'd intended. She strode out of her bedroom, banging the door against the wall as she went, stomping her feet and ignoring the desperate flutters of her heart inside her chest.

She stopped in the middle of the living room and spun around in circles, eyes darting, searching, checking. Did anything look different? Was anything gone? Was there anyone *here*?

'I'm not afraid!' she said again, louder this time. 'I'm not afraid of you! You can't scare me.' But on the last word her voice almost tipped from a shout to a sob. Out of the corner of her eye she saw movement. A guttural scream left her throat but at the same time she realised it was an Indian myna bird, landing on her balcony.

She let all of her fear and rage and anguish out on the bird, running to the balcony door and banging her fists against the glass. 'GET OUT OF HERE! GO AWAY YOU STUPID, HORRIBLE BIRD!'

The bird flew away and then the tears came properly. *I'm not brave*, she thought, *I'm not. I'm fucking terrified.*

She sat on the floor of her living room and cried for a good ten minutes before she decided it was time to stop. *Enough*, she thought. *Georgia, that is enough.*

She picked herself up and walked through her apartment again, but this time she checked it meticulously. She opened cupboards and drawers in the kitchen. She scanned each shelf in the living room. The coffee table, the couch, the dining table. She went into the bathroom, looked in the shower, opened the cabinets. Then back into the bedroom, where she opened bedside drawers and searched through her cupboard. Nothing seemed different. Nothing was missing. Cadence was messing with her. Playing with her mind.

She picked up her phone and was about to call Marcus to tell him all about it, but then remembered he was in Europe. She couldn't bother him with this while he was on his honeymoon. It was going to be difficult not chatting with him or messaging him for two weeks. They usually flicked one another a text at least once every few days. She went back onto Facebook and looked at her friends list. There were two Rachael Carvers. How could she have been so stupid not to realise that when the new request had come through from Rachael? It was a fake account using a stolen photo.

She went into the message again. The logical part of her brain told her she shouldn't respond. *That's what Cadence wants*, she thought. *She wants to get a reaction out of you, a rise. She was bluffing again in order to screw with you.*

But Georgia couldn't help it. She was too filled with rage to simply let it go. She typed out a reply, her fingers banging against the screen.

Fuck you. Your little game didn't work so give it up.

As soon as she'd sent the message, she reported the offending account to Facebook as fake and then blocked it as well.

Taking action had given her courage. She wanted to do more. She wanted to put an end to this, once and for all. What if she could stop being the one on the back foot? What if she could stop being the victim in all of this? What if she could confront this woman, face to face? After all, most of Cadence's stalking had been from a distance, through handwritten notes and messages. Chances were, she wouldn't be able to keep it up if it came to the crunch. Wasn't that why online trolls said such horrendous things? Because it wasn't straight to another person's face. That was what Cadence was — a nasty troll, nothing more.

The problem was how to find her. If she called Luke and asked for the address, he'd want her to wait until he got home. He'd want to do it with her. Georgia couldn't wait. She needed to do this now before she backed out. She just needed to figure out how.

*

Georgia stood on the footpath, looking up at the building in one of the side streets up the hill from Artarmon train station. It was a lot more rundown than she was expecting and she checked the number again, making sure she had the right one. Definitely number 428. This was it. She wasn't sure what exactly it was she'd been expecting. Why she'd had an idea that the building might be nicer than this.

The front door was propped open with an old Yellow Pages book, so she didn't have to worry about trying to get Cadence to buzz her in. She pulled open the heavy door and headed inside. There was a small lift with a brown door and she jabbed at the button and waited for the door to slide open. Inside, she chose the fifth floor and willed it to take her there slowly. Earlier, she'd been filled with confidence about what she planned to do, but the drive here had given her too much thinking time and now she was having doubts. What if she was wrong in her assessment of Cadence? What if she really was *more* than just talk?

She'd felt so clever when she'd figured out where Cadence lived. She'd found the receipt from when Luke had hired the truck for the move. The address on the top was Luke's old apartment.

The lift was ignoring her pleas to move slowly and it juddered to a stop on the fifth floor much faster than she would have liked. The door opened and she stepped forward, but then hesitated. Maybe this was a mistake. Maybe she shouldn't do this.

Come on, Georgia, move. Do it, you can do it.

I can't. I can't do this.

The door started to close. She hadn't even noticed she'd been holding her breath until she found herself breathing out slowly. She realised she'd been on the verge of a panic attack, just like that day at the hospital. This was the right choice. Go back home, regroup, tell Luke what happened, take action from there. What had she been thinking, coming here?

The door was almost closed when an arm was thrust through the crack, causing it to jolt to a stop and then slowly shudder its way open again. Georgia stepped back.

Whoever it is, just don't let it be Cadence, don't let it be Cadence. Please, please, don't let it be Cadence.

A woman stepped in, her eyes down, her face blotched with angry patches. Blonde hair partly obscured her contorted features. But Georgia could still recognise her.

Cadence.

Georgia took another step back, until she was almost pressed against the back wall of the lift. Cadence hadn't seen her yet, she was facing the doors. Georgia's breathing rate increased, she was trying to keep quiet but her chest was heaving and she knew that Cadence was going to hear the sound of her ragged breathing. That she was going to turn around, going to see who it was. And then what? What would she do? What would happen? She should never have come here.

Fourth floor.

Third floor.

Hurry up, hurry up.

Second floor.

Just get me the hell out of here.

Cadence suddenly lurched towards the control panel and slammed her hand against the large red stop button. Georgia's head snapped up. What was she doing? What was about to happen? How far was she willing to go? Cadence stayed where she was, facing away from Georgia, breathing hard, her forehead resting against the elevator wall.

Georgia's lungs burned, she was gasping for air. 'H-hey,' she said. 'Can you ... please, can you just let me out of here?' She was trying to keep her voice as calm as possible; maybe if she pretended that this was no big deal then Cadence would snap out of it.

Cadence swung around to face her. She ran her hands through her hair and then her fingers tightened and she was pulling at it, pulling and pulling. She took a step towards Georgia and Georgia slid sideways along the back wall of the elevator, crumpling into the corner. She held her hands up defensively.

But Cadence stopped still. 'I don't,' she began. She paused. She let go of her hair and looked down at her feet. 'I didn't mean to ...' she said.

Georgia didn't care what she did or didn't mean. She just wanted to get away from her. Coming here had been a horrible mistake. 'Please,' she said again, 'please let me out of here.'

Cadence swung back around and jabbed at the buttons again. Georgia's pulse raced. The elevator made a clunking noise and then shuddered back into action.

First floor.

Ground floor.

The door opened slowly. God, it was slow, excruciatingly slow. Georgia could barely breathe. *Let me out, let me out, let me out. Who knows what she's capable of? Who knows what's going through her mind right now?*

Cadence turned side-on. She looked straight at Georgia. 'Just go,' she said.

Georgia was shocked. What had changed her mind? Why was she letting her go?

The door finished opening and Georgia lurched past Cadence and out into the foyer of the building.

She didn't stop running until she reached her car.

CHAPTER SIXTEEN

Luke was sitting on the couch with his head in his hands. Georgia had decided not to call or text him about the events of the past twenty-four hours; instead she'd waited until he arrived home. He was already worried when he walked in the door, asking if she was okay after the message from Cadence the previous evening.

She'd given him a look and said, 'Oh, there's a lot more now.' Then she'd proceeded to tell him everything.

His face had taken on a more and more tortured expression as she described each moment, and now she couldn't tell what he was thinking.

'Luke,' she said quietly, 'are you annoyed that I went to see her?'

He lifted his face out of his hands and looked at her. 'Annoyed?' he asked. 'How could I be annoyed with you? I feel awful. All of this, every single thing that's happened is my fault. I hate this. I hate that you've had to go through it.'

Georgia shook her head. 'It's not your fault,' she said firmly. 'This is her fault and her fault alone.'

'But still, just the thought of you here alone this morning, reading that horrible message, not knowing if you were safe in your own home. I'm so sorry.' Her pulled her towards him and she rested her head on his shoulder.

'Listen,' he said. 'I need to make you an offer. If you … if you don't want to be with me anymore … if it's too much to take, all of this shit with Cadence, I won't blame you. If you need an out, as much as I want to be with you, your safety is more important to me.'

Georgia shook her head. 'No way. I'm not letting her win. I don't want to lose you.'

'Thank God,' Luke said with a relieved smile. 'Here's what I'm going to do, tomorrow I'll go and see her myself. I don't know, maybe I can appeal to the part of her that once cared for me. And then I'll go to the police as well, find out if everything she's done is enough to warrant a restraining order and see what I have to do to put it into place. This is going to end, I promise you.'

*

Georgia had already showered and was picking out some nice underwear when she heard Luke's key in the front door. She clipped on her bra and headed out to the living room to meet him.

Things were definitely improving. When Luke had confronted Cadence the other day, he told Georgia she'd completely broken down and confessed to hassling Georgia in an attempt to scare her away from Luke. But the threat

168

of a restraining order had snapped her out of it and she'd promised to back off.

Tonight, they were going out to a bar in Parramatta so that Luke could finally meet Georgia's nursing friends.

'Hey there, sexy. I'm liking this new way of greeting me.' Luke dropped his bag on the couch, placed his hands on her waist and kissed her on the cheek.

'Thought it might make a nice change from you finding me waking up from a day sleep with a bird's nest on my head. Now get changed, we're leaving in ten.'

She made to pull away and head back into the bedroom, but Luke caught her hand and pulled her back. 'Wait, don't tell me you're about to cover up that gorgeous body.'

'Yep, 'fraid so. Sexy times later. Come on, move it.'

She headed back into the bedroom and started looking through her wardrobe for something to wear. Her hand fell on the green top she'd worn last week when Cadence sent that nasty message. She gave an involuntary shiver, then yanked it off the hanger and stuffed it to the back of the wardrobe. She heard a ding from her phone, and walked over to check it where it was sitting on the bed, assuming it would be Amber or Rick.

It wasn't.

It was a Facebook private message from another old school friend.

Not again.

Her entire body clenched as she opened it up and read it:

Fool you twice. Shame on you.

You still haven't figured out what's missing, have you?

She dropped the phone onto the bed just as Luke walked into the room.

'Hey,' he said, his voice bright. Then he stopped. 'Babe, what's wrong?'

'It's a message. Another message. She's doing it again!'

Luke took quick steps across the room and snatched up the phone to look at the screen. 'She promised,' he said. 'She fucking promised.' He wrapped his arms around Georgia. 'You're okay,' he said, 'I'm right here with you. Nothing bad is ever going to happen.'

They sat down on the bed together and Luke rubbed circles on her back. 'Try to slow your breathing,' he said gently.

Georgia was sucking the air in and out again as she had the other day, without even realising it. She was almost hyperventilating. She tried to calm down. Tried to focus on drawing the air in through the nose and out through the mouth.

Luke looked at the phone again. 'Phoebe James,' he read out. 'Who is that meant to be?'

'Another old schoolmate.' *Breathe in.* 'I'm sure I accepted that friend request ages ago.' *Breathe out.* 'I'm an idiot. Obviously, I need to go right through the whole list and clean it out.' She realised that tears were starting to well up and she tried hard to stop them from falling. *Pull it together, Georgia.*

'You're not an idiot. And we'll do that together, okay?' He kissed her forehead and continued to rub rhythmic circles on her back. And then his hand stopped mid-circle. 'Georgia?' he said, his voice strained.

'What's wrong?'

'Remember when you lost your keys?'

'At the movies?'

'Yeah, when you thought they'd fallen out of your bag or something.'

'Yes.'

'What if it was her?'

'What? How?'

'Well, she followed us to the Persian restaurant. What if she also followed us to the movies? It's dark in there. She could have sat right behind us without us even knowing. What if she stole them from under your seat?'

'But … but I got my keys back.'

'Two days later. That would have been enough time for her to make a copy.'

Georgia's skin turned cold. 'Jesus.' She grabbed the phone back off Luke and re-read the message.

You still haven't figured out what's missing, have you?

'Then she *has* been in here. She's been in here and she's taken something. But I checked! That day the first message came through, I looked.'

'Maybe we should have another look around, together this time.'

'You mean now?'

'The sooner the better. We need to know what she's taken.'

Georgia nodded. 'In that case I think I should cancel our plans.'

'Shit,' said Luke. 'I feel awful about this, you look so sad. I don't want you to have another night ruined.'

171

'Me neither,' Georgia said with a shrug. 'But to be honest, I don't even feel like going out tonight anymore.'

'All right, let's check through this place. I can't believe I fell for her act the other day. I can't believe I let her trick me into thinking she was sorry, that she was going to stop. No more warnings now, we have to go straight to the police.'

'I agree.'

They scoured the apartment to within an inch of its life. Every now and then, Luke would tap on a shelf or a tabletop and ask, 'What about here? Anything used to sit here? Anything missing?' But each time Georgia would shake her head.

They were almost done when Luke called her into the bedroom. He was standing in front of her tallboy. 'At the back here,' he said when she walked in. 'There's a circle shape in the dust, like something used to be sitting there. Do you know what it was?'

Georgia stared at all the various ornaments and things sitting up on top of her tallboy. She was about to say there was nothing missing. That one of the candles had probably been moved and that's why there was a circular shape in the dust, but then Luke put a hand on her shoulder and spoke gently. 'Close your eyes and think. Try and picture it. What used to sit here?'

Georgia closed her eyes. She let the image of the tallboy float across her mind. She saw the three photo frames in different shapes and colours. In one was a photo of her and Marcus in a canoe on a holiday up the coast, the canoe tipping sideways, the two of them about to tumble out into the lake. In another was a black and white shot of her parents on their wedding day. Her mother's long hair was braided over her shoulder, the same way Georgia liked to wear her own hair sometimes. Her dad's grin exploding out of the photo. And in the third was a terrible photo of all of her nieces and nephews on a picnic rug at a park — Gertie in tears, Joshua facing the wrong way, Hattie in the middle of shoving Max — but she loved it anyway.

Behind the photos was a collection of various things. A ballerina ornament her grandmother had given her when she was a small girl. A Jemima Puddle-Duck toy she hadn't been able to bring herself to throw away. Several different candles: the green one that was supposed to smell like a rainforest but instead smelled like marijuana; the fat white one — vanilla and cinnamon; the two matching gold pineapple-shaped ones. What else? What else sat up there?

Her eyes flew open. 'My happiness jar,' she said.

'Your what?'

'It was an idea that I got from … a friend. You get a jar and decorate it. Then every time you feel grateful for something, or happy about something, you write that thing down on a scrap of paper and put it in the jar. At the end of the year, you open up the jar and get these reminders of everything you've felt grateful for throughout the year. But I haven't thought about it for ages … not since …'

'Since what?'

'It's a bit embarrassing … Since the night I met you. I wrote myself a note about the fact that I'd met someone. But I haven't done another one since then.'

Luke smiled at her. 'Don't be embarrassed, it's nice that you wrote that.'

'But why would she take that?'

He rubbed the back of his neck with his hand. 'I don't know,' he said, shaking his head. 'But this is the only thing we've come across. I guess she must have thought it was important to you. Probably thought you'd notice it was gone straightaway. But her plan backfired because you didn't even realise it was gone.'

'It didn't completely backfire though.' Georgia shivered. 'Because now that I know she has it, I can't bloody stand the thought of her reading through all those personal thoughts. Those were for me, for my eyes only, not for some obsessed stalker to find out my innermost thoughts. She doesn't deserve to know those things about me … she has no right.'

Luke hugged her. 'I know,' he said. 'She absolutely does not have any right to know a bloody single thing about you. She has no right to have ever even looked at you. You don't deserve any of this.'

He guided her by the hand out to the living room, where they sat together on the couch. 'I'll organise a locksmith for tomorrow and I'll talk to the police as well. I'm so sorry, I should never have fallen for her act when I went to see her the other day. This is on me. I should have realised she was just saying whatever she needed to, to stop me from going to the cops. I'm an idiot.'

'No. You're not an idiot, you're lovely and kind and trusting, and that's not a bad thing.'

'Thank you, but I still feel like a moron.' He drew her into his arms. 'What do you want for dinner? I can cook you something? Or order in?'

Georgia shrugged. 'I don't really feel all that hungry.' She snuggled closer into him. 'I just want you to keep holding me. And never let go.'

'Easy,' he said. 'I can do that in my sleep. No, I mean I could literally hug you all night long while I sleep.'

She laughed and tipped her head back to kiss him. He kissed her back, long and slow. Their tongues entwined and suddenly Georgia felt all of the emotion and drama from the last few weeks coursing through her body. She kissed him harder, grabbing at his shirt, pulling him closer and closer still. Tears started to slide down her face, the salty taste intermingling with their kisses.

Luke pulled back, worried. 'Are you okay?'

'Don't stop,' she replied, climbing on top of him and kissing him again. 'I want you,' she whispered, 'I want you so much.' He pulled off her shirt and kissed his way down her neck to her breasts, reached around her back and unclipped her bra. She pressed her body against his.

They didn't make it from the couch to the bedroom.

CHAPTER SEVENTEEN

Jerry was sitting on the edge of his bed, looking out of place dressed in normal clothes rather than pyjamas. He looked sheepish as he pulled the yellow stone out of his pocket and held it out to Georgia. 'Ah, here you are, love. I think it's done its job.'

Georgia guessed he was feeling embarrassed about his dramatic talk of prophetic dreams now that he was being checked out of the hospital again, having been given a clean bill of health. Anxiety had been the diagnosis for his unexplained pain. When there was nothing physical to be found, it seemed to be the best explanation.

'Why don't you hang onto it for a tiny bit longer?' Georgia suggested. 'Eileen's exchanged details with me, so I can come visit some time and get it back then.'

Jerry hesitated. He gave Georgia a look, as though he was searching her face for something. 'But what if you need it?'

Georgia sat down beside him. 'I'm fine,' she said. 'Don't need it at all at the moment.'

'Really?' he said. 'Because it looks to me like something's taken a bit of the spark out of your eyes lately.'

Georgia sighed. 'Maybe you're right ... a bit. But it's nothing I can't handle. A jealous ex-girlfriend of Luke's has been hassling me, making it hard for me to go out and have fun when I'm off work. I guess I didn't realise how much I need that time for myself. This job ... it can really drain you.'

'So,' said Jerry, 'take the stone, carry around some of this sunshine for yourself.'

Georgia shook her head. 'Nope,' she said. 'And I'll tell you why. The reason that nurse Kathy first gave it to me was because I was suffering from depression. I was in a dark place, Jerry, a really, really dark place. But right now, I'm not headed back there. Whereas you? You, I'm worried about. I know you don't like the fact that Dr Kouzeleas has diagnosed you with anxiety. Eileen told me you called it a load of mumbo jumbo hogshit. I'm here to tell you it's *not*. Mental health problems are very real. I need you to take this seriously, okay? For Eileen and me.'

Jerry didn't look convinced, but he dropped the stone back into his pocket. 'All right. I'll keep it for now. But only so there's a reason for us to meet again. Maybe we can have you round for a barbie one weekend.'

'Sounds like a plan,' said Georgia, giving him a hug.

Once she'd said goodbye to Jerry, she snuck outside for a break, telling herself it was for the fresh air and that she was *not* going to ask anyone for a spare cigarette. She was sitting on one of the milk crates when a message came through on her phone. She hated that her immediate reaction was one of fear. Who was it this time? She was relieved to see it was a message from her dad. It was written in all caps, although she didn't think he'd intended for it to come across as shouting.

G, YOUR MUM AND I HAD A CHAT. WE WOULD LIKE TO PAY FOR YOU TO FLY TO BALI WITH US FOR A LITTLE MEDITATIVE GETAWAY SATURDAY AFTER NEXT. LOVE, DAD.

The offer took her completely by surprise. Her parents were well-off but they'd always been very firm in their belief that their kids should start paying their own way as soon as they had the capacity to work.

Her initial reaction was excitement — who wouldn't be excited at the idea of a free trip to Bali? She would have to get someone to cover one or two of her shifts, but it should be doable. It was followed by apprehension though. What exactly did a 'meditative getaway' mean? And why did they think that was something she needed?

On top of that was the fact they obviously weren't extending the same invitation to Luke — not that she would expect them to. They didn't know he'd moved in. And even if they did invite him along, he was terrified of flying. After seeing what he was like on a short flight to Melbourne, there was no way he'd cope with a trip to Bali. Would it be wrong to take off overseas and leave him behind? Would he be offended? Especially considering the situation with Cadence. Was it harsh to say, 'Right, I'm taking off and leaving you here to deal with all of this shit'?

Once again, she wouldn't mind chatting to Marcus, but she hadn't heard from him once since he'd gone off on his honeymoon, which was perfectly understandable — who'd want to talk to their sister while they're honeymooning? But she was finding it really difficult not being able to shoot him a text any time of day.

A shadow appeared in front of her and she looked up to see Amber. Her hair was platinum blonde now and she'd had a blunt fringe cut across her forehead.

'Hey honey,' Amber said as she sat down beside her, and Georgia released a huge sigh. 'That was dramatic, what's up?'

'Nothing really. Hey, can I have a cigarette?'

'Bad girl,' said Amber. But she passed one over anyway and they both lit up and sat smoking in silence for a few minutes.

Another shadow crossed their feet and they looked up to see Rick standing in front of them.

'You a proper smoker now, Georgia?'

'Nope. Another one-off.'

'You know that several one-offs very quickly become a pattern and stop being a one-off, right?'

'No lectures, thank you. Sit down, you're blocking our sun.'

Rick sat down on Georgia's other side and lit up one of his own cigarettes. 'Well, you two are very lively,' he said sarcastically. 'What's the matter with you both?'

'Nothing,' said Amber. 'We're enjoying some peace.'

Georgia's phone started ringing and she gave Amber a guilty look for ruining the peace. She stood and walked away from Amber and Rick as she answered Luke's call.

'Hey,' she said.

'Hi, babe. Um, listen, I hate to do this over the phone, but I've got some bad news.'

'Oh no, what is it?'

'I came home from work early, ready to meet the locksmith and … we were too late — we've had a break-in.'

Georgia clapped a hand to her mouth. 'A break-in? What do you mean? You mean like a proper …'

'Yeah, a proper break-in. As in, the place has been trashed, things knocked over, broken …'

'Was it her? Was it Cadence?'

'Look, I guess we won't know for sure until the police do their thing but, yeah, I'd say it must have been. The lock wasn't smashed, so whoever did it let themselves in with a key.'

'No! No, no, no. I can't believe she'd take it this far. What did she steal?'

'Honestly, it's hard to tell. The place is such a mess.'

Georgia started breathing hard and fast again. In and out. In and out. In … in … in …

She caught herself and breathed back out. *Slow down, Georgia, take it easy.* But she couldn't stop the thoughts. How long ago was it that she lost her keys at the movies? How many weeks? How many times had Cadence simply let herself into her home while she was out? And what about while she was home? Had she ever done it while she was there? While she was sleeping? Her breathing quickened again. *In, out, in, in, out, in, in, in, out, in, in, in, in, in …*

'Georgia,' Luke's voice came sharp and urgent. 'Are you okay? You don't sound okay? Georgia!'

Next thing she knew, there were people gathered around her. Rick was taking her by the arm and leading her back over to the milk crates to sit down. Amber was taking the phone off her. She could hear her speaking to Luke, asking what had happened, reassuring him that yes, Georgia was okay, but that she was hyperventilating and they were taking care of her.

Ah yes, that's what I'm doing. I'm hyperventilating. I'm a nurse, I know this.

But why am I hyperventilating? Surely this is an overreaction to hearing you've had a break-in.

'Georgia,' said Rick, 'I want you to listen to my voice and we're going to breathe together and slow things down, okay? Let's go in through the nose ... two ... three ... four ... and out through the mouth ... two ... three ... four ...'

Georgia zeroed in on Rick's voice, glad to have something to focus on. Something else to fill her mind so that she wasn't thinking about Cadence being inside her apartment. She began to follow his instructions.

Eventually, her breathing returned to normal and Amber handed her the phone back.

'What happened?' Rick asked.

'There was a break-in at Georgia's place,' said Amber. 'Luke said it looks like it was Cadence, his ex. Apparently, she got a copy of Georgia's key somehow.'

'What? How the hell could she —' Rick stopped at the look on Georgia's face. 'Sorry,' he said. 'Not meaning to get you worked up again.'

Georgia shook her head. 'It's okay,' she said. She took in a deep breath. 'I'm feeling ...' — another deep breath —

'much … better.' Although in truth she was still feeling a little short of breath and light-headed.

'This bitch has to be stopped,' said Amber.

'Couldn't agree more,' said Rick.

*

Georgia arrived home to find Luke already working to tidy up what he could.

'Shouldn't we leave it all exactly as it is for the police?' she asked.

'They've just left,' said Luke. 'Sorry, I thought Amber would have told you that I already had them on the way when I called you.'

He put down the broken pot plant he'd been holding and picked his way through the mess to reach her and pull her into a hug. 'I was so worried when you started breathing like that over the phone.'

'It was silly. I was overreacting.'

'No, you weren't. Who the hell wouldn't have a panic attack after everything you've been through?'

'I guess.' Georgia pulled back and looked around her little apartment. There was something about the way her things had been deliberately destroyed that felt vindictive. Personal. Pages were ripped out of novels. Cushion covers were slashed. There was broken glass from shattered photo frames. Dirt from pot plants was stomped into the carpet. The intent was to inflict pain upon her. And even worse, it looked like Cadence had had *fun* while she was at it.

'What did the police say?'

'Well, obviously I gave them the full rundown on everything Cadence has been doing — the notes on your windscreen, the photos she emailed. Oh, and I accessed your iMessage through your laptop so I could give them all the messages. I hope that's okay?'

'Of course.'

'And I did mention the nasty messages from Brett as well, just in case — I figured it was better that they knew absolutely everything. They agreed that Cadence is the most likely candidate. They think our idea that she stole your keys at the movies and made a copy is a fair assessment. But they'll look into Brett too, seeing as he's been hassling you.'

'Okay, that all sounds good. So, what will happen with Cadence?'

'They'll give her a visit, question her. They said we definitely have grounds for getting a restraining order against her, so we'll get that underway now too. Enough is enough. This needs to end now.'

The clean-up took them most of the night. In the end, the only thing missing was some of Georgia's underwear, which felt so creepy that Georgia almost wished something valuable had been stolen instead. What was Cadence going to do with it? Wear it? Surely not!

It wasn't until they were going to bed that Georgia remembered her parents' offer to take her to Bali. But she didn't want to bring it up with Luke right now. Maybe tomorrow would be a better time.

CHAPTER EIGHTEEN

It was no one's fault when Georgia had to cancel on Amber and Rick yet again. Well, actually, Georgia supposed she could blame Barbara's Pizza Shop for using dodgy prawns on their half-marinara half-vegetarian pizza. It was just unfortunate that Georgia had guaranteed her mates she wouldn't bail on them this time. Not to mention the fact that she'd been looking forward to finally introducing Luke to them all. They might start to think he was a figment of her imagination.

'I could take a photo of you vomiting into the toilet and send it to Amber if you like.' Luke handed her a cool face washer and Georgia sat back against the tiled wall and wiped her mouth.

'That's disgusting.'

'Taking a photo, or what you just threw up?'

'Both. Why aren't you sick? Not fair.'

'I didn't eat any of the seafood slices.'

'Lucky bastard.'

'Look, if you want, I'll go out to the kitchen and eat one right now.'

'Ha. Oh God, I'm gonna be sick again.' Georgia went back onto her hands and knees and reached out to grab hold of the toilet bowl. 'Go away please! Don't watch me!'

'I'm not leaving you.'

She felt his hand rub circles on her back. She threw up again, and as much as she hated the idea of him watching her like this, she had to applaud his dedication.

Half an hour later, when she was sure there couldn't possibly be anything left in her stomach to throw up, Luke helped her undress and put her under a hot shower. He waited while she rinsed off and then, when she was done, he wrapped a towel around her and guided her through to the bedroom.

'I'm not an invalid,' she complained when he started to dry her body for her.

'You're weak,' he said. 'Let me help you.'

He helped her dress in her pyjamas, put her under the covers and then kissed her forehead. 'Hey, listen, before you drift off to sleep, there's something I've been wanting to ask you about ... Well, actually, I need to make a confession.'

'A confession? What for?'

'You know how I said I logged into your messages so I could give all that info to the police?'

'Yeah.'

'Well, I accidentally saw the message from your dad. The offer to take you to Bali. I was waiting for you to say something about it, but I have a feeling you don't want to ... because of me, because of my fear of flying ... am I right?'

Georgia bit her lip. 'Umm ... maybe ... I mean, I guess. It's only that I feel bad —'

Luke cut her off. 'You absolutely do not need to feel bad. You should go on this trip. It sounds awesome. And it also sounds like the exact thing you need right now. I really want you to go.'

'Really?'

'Hundred per cent. Now sleep,' he said. 'I'll call Amber and make sure she knows you're proper sick and not bailing on her for no good reason.'

'Thank you,' she murmured, already feeling sleep beginning to drag her down. 'You're so fucking sweet. Best boyfriend ever.'

'I know I am. Night.'

*

On Wednesday morning when Georgia woke up and got ready for work, it would have seemed unfathomable that by that evening she would pretty much be out of a job. Of course at the time, she had no idea there was any chance of such a thing ever happening. All she did know was that she'd woken up with a killer headache and a sore stomach after the food poisoning the previous evening.

And maybe that was part of the problem. Maybe if she hadn't still been feeling sick and groggy she would have noticed something.

But instead, at midday she was being called in to see her boss, and that's when everything went sideways.

Georgia had always got along quite well with Denise, so it was disconcerting to see her looking so stern when she was summoned into her office. She'd been told to bring her bag with her.

'I was told you needed to see me?'

'Yes, take a seat, Georgia.'

'Is everything all right?'

'Hopefully it will be, but a serious allegation has been made against you. Some medication has been reported stolen and your name has been put forward —'

'What? That's ridiculous! I would never —'

'I know,' Denise cut in. 'And I don't like this at all, but the … informant was quite adamant, and I have to follow up. Listen, legally, I can't ask to search your bag, not without going through the proper channels first, but I'm hoping you'll agree to show me and then we can get this all cleared up.'

Georgia was already lifting her bag onto Denise's desk. 'Of course,' she said. 'You can look through all of it. I have nothing to hide in here.' She upended the bag, shaking the contents out.

She saw it before Denise did. Three small rectangular boxes. 'Those aren't mine,' she said quickly. 'I didn't put those in there.'

Denise reached across to pick one up. 'Endone,' she said. She picked up the other two. 'And Ritalin.' She looked across at Georgia and there was blatant disappointment in her eyes. 'These are all Schedule 8 drugs. Georgia, this is really serious.'

'No, no, you don't understand. Those aren't mine. I don't know how they got in there.'

'It doesn't look good.'

'But if I knew they were in there why on earth would I tip everything straight out for you to see it?'

Denise shrugged. 'The fact is, these are the drugs that went missing and now here they are in your bag. Like I said, it doesn't look good.'

'Denise, you know me. You know I would never do this. And anyway, how would I have done it? You need two people to sign them out of the Pyxis machine.'

'These were taken from the surplus supply in the storage cupboard.'

'Even better then — I don't have access to that room. I can't have stolen them.'

'Okay, listen, we're going to have to find a way to sort this out. To be frank, I've never had to deal with anything like this before. The worst I've had was when someone was stealing Panadeine, and that was a slap on the wrist and we put the episode behind us. But with Schedule 8 drugs involved, it's a lot more serious. I want to believe you, Georgia, I do, but the evidence is pretty damning. I think it's better if you go home today. I'll take you off the roster for the rest of this week and I'll call you once I find out what happens next.'

Georgia started gathering her things back up from Denise's desk, her hands shaking as she tried to suppress tears. She stopped and looked back across at Denise. 'Who was it?' she asked.

'I'm sorry?'

'Who was it that said they saw me stealing the meds?'

'I can't say.'

'But … but that's not fair. Whoever it is, they lied. And they must have been the one to put the drugs in my bag as well. Maybe if I can talk to them, I can find out why they're doing this to me.'

'I'm sorry, but I promised them full confidentiality.'

Georgia finished packing up her bag. The three boxes of pills remained on Denise's desk. On the way home, she bought herself a packet of cigarettes and a lighter.

CHAPTER NINETEEN

Georgia had thought she was out of tears by the time Luke arrived home. But as soon as she recounted the story of what had happened, a fresh flood started up. He was the first person she'd told. There was a missed call on her phone from Rick, so she assumed he'd somehow heard — no doubt the rumour about a nurse being accused of stealing drugs was already flying around the hospital — but she hadn't been able to bring herself to call him back. What if he believed the rumour? What if he was calling to have a go at her? She hadn't heard from Amber but she knew it was her weekend with Violet.

Marcus was the one person she wanted to talk to. She'd decided this was enough of a reason to disturb him on his holiday. So, she'd sent him a text message, asking if they could please talk. But so far there'd been no response. She was trying hard to understand — it was his honeymoon, he had every right to ignore her if he wanted to. But she was just a tiny bit hurt.

She didn't want to tell her parents or anyone else in her family; she felt too embarrassed about the whole thing. What if they thought she was guilty? What if her parents thought it was like last time? What if they thought she was having ... problems again?

Luke sat on the couch next to her, an arm around her shoulders as he tried to console her.

'This is ridiculous,' he said for what was probably the third time. 'Haven't you been working there for two years? Why would they think you'd suddenly start stealing pills now? Surely they know you well enough.'

'I know. But the problem is they were in my bag.'

Luke slapped a hand against his own knee in frustration. 'But how was someone able to put them in there? Don't you keep your bags in lockers?'

'We do, but the lockers are so old that half are broken, and most of the keys have gone missing. They've never bothered to replace them over the years, and it's never mattered because the staff room is locked so it's only other staff that go in there.'

'Do you have any idea who'd want to set you up?'

'No! There's no one. I've never had any issues with any other nurses, and as far as I know no one's ever had a problem with me.' Georgia stood up and started pacing. 'I don't get it, I don't get it at all.' She stopped at Luke's workout bench, mindlessly picking up one of his dumbbells and swapping it from hand to hand.

Luke stood and walked over to her. He carefully took the weight out of her hand and put it down. 'I know that right now everything seems awful, but listen, it's all going to work out, I know it is. There must be cameras they can check, right? Something to prove you didn't do this and to figure out who the hell did. Because obviously someone does have something against you. Those tablets didn't appear in your bag on their own.'

'Maybe. I'm not sure. I can't remember if they have cameras in the storage room.' She looked up at Luke. 'You really think someone at the hospital hates me that much?'

'I don't know, but there has to be some kind of motivation behind it. It's not like it's a funny prank. It's a serious sabotage of your career. You're sure you can't think of anyone?'

Georgia stared down at her feet. Faces flashed through her mind. Nurses, doctors, colleagues, friends. Surely one of her friends couldn't have done this to her? Could they?

She shook her head. 'I really don't know.'

'And what about your trip to Bali? Do you think this will all get sorted out in time for you to still go?'

She hadn't even thought about that. But there was no way she could go traipsing off overseas in the middle of this. She sat back down, put her head in her hands and started crying again. 'I can't go,' she said through the tears. 'I'm going to have to call Mum and tell her what happened, and it's going to be so embarrassing and they're going to be so ashamed of me.'

'What? No way. How can they be ashamed of you? You didn't do anything wrong. Oh babe, please don't cry. I'm telling you, this is all going to work out. I'm sure of it.'

*

The following morning, Denise called and told Georgia there would be an automatic two-week suspension without pay and that an investigation would take place immediately.

'Listen,' she said, 'one way or another, we'll get to the bottom of this. I promise you, we'll sort out the truth.'

But there was a slight edge to her voice, and Georgia couldn't help feeling that Denise might have already made up her mind about what the truth was.

She sent a message to her parents.

Hey Mum and Dad, thank you so much for the generous offer but I can't come on the holiday to Bali. It's impossible for me to get the time off work. Thanks again though.

She hated lying to them. She had planned to call and tell them the truth, but after speaking to Denise, she couldn't do it. Five minutes after she sent the message, her mum tried to call, but Georgia declined it and turned off her phone.

She spent the day sitting in front of Netflix, switching from one show to another, wrapped up in a quilt, pretending to herself that she was off work because she was sick with a cold. In fact, she told herself that so many times that eventually she started to feel like her nose actually was blocked and her throat was scratchy. Every now and then, she shuffled out onto her balcony to smoke a cigarette, but she didn't enjoy it. As the day finally edged towards evening, she turned her phone back on and discovered voicemails from Amber, Rick and her mum. She deleted them all without listening to them. She wasn't ready to talk to her mum. And as much as she wanted the reassurance of her friends, there was a tiny part of her deep inside that had begun to question: who could she trust?

When Luke arrived home, she told him she was coming down with a cold, so he made her chicken soup and then ran her a hot bath, and didn't comment on the fact that she wasn't sneezing or coughing or feverish. She was grateful.

CHAPTER TWENTY

If she had been asked, Georgia would have said things couldn't get any worse. But she was wrong. The call came through the following morning, just after Luke had left for work. She almost didn't answer it, but at the last minute she thought it could be about the investigation, so she picked it up.

The sound of the shaking voice on the other end broke her heart in an instant.

Eileen.

Georgia knew. She knew right away and the tears came even as she asked the question, and prayed and hoped that she was wrong. 'Eileen, what's happened?'

'He's gone.'

Georgia stopped telling herself she was sick and pulled herself together, showered, dressed and drove straight around to the address Eileen had given her the last time Jerry left the hospital. It was a weatherboard house painted pale blue with neat square garden beds out the front. A slightly rusted metal railing bordered the concrete stairs up to the front door. As Georgia looked up at the house, she found herself imagining

Jerry out here painting the walls blue. She saw him kneeling in the garden, trimming his roses. For all she knew, maybe it was Eileen who did all the gardening. Maybe they hired someone to paint the outside of the house. But it was nice to imagine. She wished she'd had the chance to come around for that barbeque that Jerry had suggested.

When she reached the front door, and raised her fist ready to knock, she hesitated for a moment. Who else might be here? Was she going to be intruding on this family's grief? But Eileen had asked her to come. She couldn't let her down. She knocked and waited. After thirty seconds, she heard the sound of someone shuffling towards the door, which seemed wrong. Eileen didn't shuffle. Eileen strode. Eileen walked with purpose, with a bounce in her step.

When the door finally opened, Georgia couldn't stop her face from reacting. It was like a punch to the gut, the sight of Eileen. Her lightly greying blonde hair that was usually perfectly set was tousled and tangled. The face that was normally made up with a spot of blush — never overdone, always the perfect amount — looked pale and slumped. For a moment Georgia even thought the woman in front of her could have had a stroke. She was ready to spring into nurse-mode, to start assessing her symptoms, but then Eileen spoke and she realised that wasn't the case at all. She was simply suffering from a huge loss.

'Darling,' she said, 'thank you for coming.'

Georgia stepped through the door and immediately embraced her. She wanted to convey just how sorry she felt with this one hug, but at the same time it felt like she was hugging a bundle of twigs and that Eileen's bones might snap, so she let go and stepped back.

'I'm sorry,' she said, 'I'm so, so sorry, Eileen. I can't imagine how you must be feeling right now.'

'Oh, I'll be okay,' said Eileen, in a voice that told Georgia she most certainly would not be okay. 'Come through. Can I make you a cup of something?'

'Please, no, let me get it.'

Eileen shuffled ahead of her and into a sitting room, where she eased herself down onto an armchair. 'Oh well … yes please, love, that would be nice. The kitchen is through there.' She gestured towards a doorway and Georgia hesitated.

'Is there … is anyone else here with you?'

Eileen shook her head. 'No, it's only me.'

On the last two words, her voice became so small and so very sad that Georgia almost burst into tears right there. She sounded like a very small child who'd misplaced her best friend in the school playground.

Georgia managed to hold back the emotion and nodded and hurried through the doorway. The kitchen reminded her of her own grandmother's kitchen, back before she'd sold her home and moved into a 'lifestyle resort' up in Queensland. Orange laminate benchtops and yellow glass cabinet doors.

She flicked on the kettle and allowed a small sob to sneak out, doing everything she could to keep it as quiet as possible. But that poor woman, all alone and clearly broken. Jerry was her everything. How could this have happened? Dr Kouzeleas had sent him home with assurances that there was nothing, absolutely nothing physically wrong with him, so what had gone wrong?

Georgia searched out the mugs and the teabags. When the tea was made, she carried the two cups back out to the sitting room and found Eileen staring intently at a blank corner of the ceiling.

'Eileen?' She spoke softly so as not to startle her, but Eileen still jumped.

'Love!' she said. 'I almost forgot you were here.'

Georgia placed the two cups of tea down on a coffee table.

'See that cabinet there,' said Eileen, pointing. 'There's a bottle of whiskey on the top shelf. Could you add a small nip to my cuppa for me?'

'Of course.'

Georgia added a generous splash to Eileen's cup, hopeful that it might help to jolt her out of this strange demeanour that was so unlike the woman she'd come to know so well.

'Eileen,' she said when she was sitting, 'what on earth happened? I don't understand. Jerry was fine when he left the hospital last week.'

Eileen nodded. 'Yes, he was, wasn't he? And he was fine the next day and the day after that, and then his stomach started to give him trouble again and he …' She stopped and Georgia saw that she was trying to compose herself before she could continue.

'… and he didn't want to front up to the hospital again after all those times he'd cried wolf.' The tears started to fall now and Georgia bit down hard on the inside of her cheek as she tried to stop herself from crying too.

'He never cried wolf,' Georgia murmured, wishing desperately that she could change the outcome of this story, but Eileen waved her hand at her.

'It's okay, I convinced him we should go and we did. Dr Harris saw him. I think he was a bit cross to see us back, to be honest. He diagnosed Jerry with gallbladder inflammation. He was given antibiotics and sent back home, but … it kept getting worse. The problem was, Jerry tried to hide it. Tried to be brave. He said …' Eileen let a small sob escape. 'When I found out how bad it was … he said he didn't want to embarrass me by going back to the hospital for another false alarm.'

The tears were sliding down Georgia's face now. She couldn't help it. 'Oh Jerry,' she whispered.

'It turned out his gallbladder was ruptured and Dr Harris had missed it.'

'Sepsis?' Georgia asked quietly.

'Yes. The paramedics said he was already in septic shock by the time they arrived. They took him back to the hospital, but they couldn't save him. Every organ had shut down, they said. His heart …' her voice broke, 'his heart was failing.'

Georgia felt sick. 'I should have *been* there,' she said, fighting to stop the flow of tears. Patients died, it was part of the job. But there were certain times when it just felt too hard.

Eileen shook her head. 'They all did their best.'

'Yes but … the first time, if I was there the first time, when Dr Harris sent you back home, maybe I could have done something, I could have said something.'

Now it was Eileen reaching for her hand. 'You mustn't think like that.'

But Georgia couldn't be sure there wasn't a hint of resentment in her voice. She had a feeling that deep down, Eileen agreed. She agreed that if Georgia had been there she could have done something. She could have stopped Dr Harris from sending them away. She could have suggested more tests. What would Eileen think if she knew that the reason Georgia wasn't there was because she'd been suspended, accused of stealing drugs?

Georgia stayed until a next-door neighbour let herself in and promised Georgia she would take good care of Eileen.

As she was saying goodbye, Eileen suddenly pulled away. 'Hold on, I have something for you,' she said.

Georgia waited at the front door and after a minute, Eileen returned and pressed the citrine stone into her hand.

'He was holding this, you know? When he … when he … left. He had it right there in his hand and his fingers kept turning it over and over …' Her voice petered away.

Georgia found that she couldn't speak. Instead she gave Eileen another hug and turned and quickly walked away.

In her car, she sobbed. But after a solid five minutes of crying, she realised something. She wasn't just sad, she was angry. She was furious. Because if she'd been at the hospital as she should have, there was every chance that Jerry would still be alive. And the only reason she wasn't there was because someone had set her up.

And who was the most likely person to set her up?

Cadence.

Who else had it in for her bad enough that they'd want to destroy her life? Who else had proven she was crazy enough, determined enough to do something like this?

Enough.

She'd stalked her and she'd frightened her.

She'd broken into her home.

And now not even the police had made her stop.

Fuck it. Georgia was going to go and see her again, and this time she wasn't going to run away: she was going to stand her ground and make her stop.

*

This time she made it all the way up to Cadence's apartment. There was no panicking in the lift, no backing away into a corner. She stormed down the hallway and when she reached the door, she only paused to take one deep breath before she lifted her fist and pounded against it.

There was silence for a moment, and then the sound of movement from inside, then silence again.

Georgia waited. Nothing.

She banged the side of her fist against the door again, then called out. 'Cadence, I know you're in there. Open up. NOW.'

Another scurrying of movement, then a voice, smaller than expected. She'd assumed that Cadence would start shouting back at her, maybe scream abuse, maybe tell her to fuck off. Instead the voice called out, 'Who is it, please?'

Georgia almost laughed at the sweet, polite voice. 'Who is it? You're fucking joking, right? Who the fuck do you think it is? Let me in. I want to talk with you.'

'Umm, I'm sorry, I don't know who you are and I ... I don't really want to let you in. Maybe you have the wrong apartment?'

'Cadence! I know it's you! And I also know you told Luke you were going to stop, but you haven't, have you? So now you need to let me in and we need to sort this shit out.'

There was another pause. When Cadence spoke again, it sounded as though she was closer, right there on the other side of the door.

'You know Luke?' she asked.

Now Georgia did laugh. 'Um, yeah, I know Luke. Just open the door so we can stop shouting through the bloody thing.'

'Luke's not home right now.'

'Very funny. Of course he's not. *Open. The. Door.*'

She heard the sound of the key turning in the lock and then the door began to open slowly. As soon as it was ajar, Georgia placed her palm against it and pushed hard, forcing it all the way open before striding inside, shoving past Cadence as she did. Cadence stumbled backwards, a bewildered look on her face. And something else ... fear? Did Cadence look afraid of her? Well, she bloody well should. Georgia was about to come down hard on this horrible woman. She probably knew her time was up. No more hiding behind nasty notes or messages. She was going to have to face Georgia and accept responsibility for everything she'd been doing.

Still … it put Georgia slightly on the wrong foot. This wasn't at all what she was expecting. She'd thought Cadence would be ready for a fight, ready to yell and swear and tell her to give her boyfriend back. She'd thought she might even get physical. That she might lunge at her, try to hurt her, pull her hair, something like that. Georgia had been imagining how it all might go on the drive over here. Planning how she would block any kind of physical attack from Cadence if she came at her. She vaguely remembered a few moves from a self-defence video she'd seen on YouTube once. Besides, she was fuelled with anger, adrenalin was going to see her through this time.

Another thing — Cadence was smaller than she remembered. In the lift that day, it had felt as though she was looming over her. But instead she was quite petite with limp blonde hair that rested on her shoulders. She wasn't the perfectly made-up Barbie doll she'd imagined.

Her eyes were sharp though, and they flittered across Georgia as though they were taking each and every part of her in. It made Georgia want to pull her coat tighter around herself. She was waiting for Cadence to stop playing dumb and admit that she knew exactly who Georgia was. But for some reason she was still staring blankly at her as though she was a complete stranger.

Georgia looked around at the apartment. It was a similar size to her own, but a lot older. The mottled brown carpet was coarse and hardwearing. The walls were yellowed and the features were distinctively seventies. The furniture had a bit of a seventies feel to it as well, but in a cooler way. There was a large brown leather couch that took up half the room, with a shag-pile rug in front of it and a funky wicker armchair in the corner.

She realised that Cadence was still staring at her, waiting for her to speak first.

'Cadence, I *know* that you know who I am, and I'm here to tell you enough is enough. This has to stop.'

'But ... but I honestly don't know who you are.'

Was she being deliberately obtuse? Or did she think she needed to play this game because she didn't want to get herself into trouble by making any kind of admission?

'Cadence, *seriously*, you can drop the act. I know you've been stalking us ever since we got together, but you've taken it too far now. A man is dead.'

Cadence's mouth dropped open. 'What? What are you ... who? Who's dead? What do you mean?'

'One of my patients at the hospital. If I'd been there, I could have done something ... I could have helped, I could have ...' Shit. The tears were threatening to come back.

Georgia looked up at the ceiling and took in a deep breath. *You will not cry in front of her, you will not, you will not. You're not sad, you're angry. You're furious. Pull it together.*

She locked eyes with Cadence. 'Look, the point is, if you hadn't set me up with those drugs, I would have been there and things would be different.'

Cadence was shaking her head. 'But I genuinely don't know you! I don't! Did I meet you through Luke at some point? I mean, you do look a tiny bit familiar but ...' Cadence suddenly snapped her fingers. 'That's where I've seen you! You were in the lift with me, I was meant to be going downstairs to check the mail, but I … I had an … an episode. I'm so sorry, I didn't mean to frighten you that day, but I think maybe it was a bad reaction to these tablets I'm on. I suddenly couldn't bring myself to go downstairs and I panicked.'

'What? That's not what happened. You weren't scared, you were … God, I don't know, you were deranged, you were trying to intimidate me. But that's not the point. The point is, that's not how you know me. You know me because I'm Luke's girlfriend. You know this. And ever since you broke up with Luke you've been making his life hell, and mine as well.'

Now Cadence's face was more perplexed than ever. 'What do you mean you're Luke's girlfriend? Wait, do you have the wrong place? Are you talking about a different Luke? This doesn't make any sense.'

'Of course I'm in the right place,' said Georgia, feeling frustrated. 'You're Cadence, yes? And Luke Kauffman is your ex-boyfriend.'

'Yes, I'm Cadence. But Luke isn't my ex. He's still very much my boyfriend.'

CHAPTER TWENTY-ONE

Georgia was stunned into silence. But then she composed herself and spoke again, keeping her voice gentle, her words careful. *Remember who you're dealing with here, Georgia. She's clearly got issues.* The best thing to do was to treat her like she was a child. Like a toddler who'd had her favourite toy taken away.

'*No*, you and Luke broke up six months ago. Don't worry, we didn't get together until after that. You'd already split when I met him. But it's definitely over between you. That's why he moved out.'

Cadence took a step back away from Georgia. 'Look, I don't know who you are. But can you please stop saying that? That's an awful thing to say. To come into my home and tell me my boyfriend isn't my boyfriend. Why are you doing this?'

Georgia was completely bewildered. What was the point in Cadence playing this ridiculous game?

'Why am I doing this? Oh, that's bloody rich. Considering every little thing you've done to me. All the abusive notes. The emails, the Facebook messages. Jesus, Cadence, *you broke into my home.* And tell me something, if Luke is still your boyfriend, then why did he move out of here? Where did he go?'

'Stop it! Stop making up all this weird horrible stuff! He hasn't moved out! He took some of our stuff, yes, but that wasn't because he moved out. That was because he's getting our new place set up. He can't have moved out, he was here *this morning*!'

Georgia started to back up herself now. Cadence was raising her voice and wringing her hands together. She looked like she was really panicking. And there was something else. Something about the way she spoke. She was so ... *emphatic.*

Was she so deluded that she'd created an entirely different reality for herself? One in which she and Luke had never actually broken up. One that she really believed?

Georgia had to reconsider her game plan here. Maybe she'd done the wrong thing by coming. Maybe she should have trusted that the police would eventually sort all this out. It looked like Cadence needed professional help. She needed to see a doctor, a psychologist. And what about the tablets she mentioned before? The ones she claimed had messed her up in the lift that day? Maybe she was self-medicating. Georgia remembered the man at the hospital, the one with the knife who was experiencing drug-induced psychosis from being incorrectly medicated. And the violent woman who was suffering from hyperactive delirium. People can find extraordinary strength when they're not themselves.

Georgia shouldn't be here.

Cadence might be dangerous.

As if on cue, Cadence lunged at her. She put her hands on Georgia's shoulders and started shoving and shoving her towards the door.

'GET OUT!' she screamed, 'Get out, get out, get out. Leave me alone you horrible, evil woman. Leave me the hell alone.'

Georgia didn't fight back. She was too stunned. She allowed herself to be pushed backwards until she'd stumbled right out into the hallway, and next thing the door had been slammed in her face.

She took a few more steps backwards until she was leaning against the opposite wall, and then she slid down to the floor and held still, breathing hard.

From the other side of Cadence's door, she could hear crying.

CHAPTER TWENTY-TWO

That night, Georgia had her first ever fight with Luke. She didn't tell him that she'd been to see Cadence again. She was too shocked at the way Cadence had reacted. Did Luke realise just how deluded she was? That she was pretty much living in an alternate reality? And how much damage had Georgia caused by trying to force Cadence to face the truth? She was confused and scared and she couldn't bring herself to admit to Luke how reckless she'd been. The police had advised getting a restraining order and not responding to any of her messages. And what had she done? The complete opposite. She knew she'd have to tell him eventually, but not now, not while she was still trying to understand it all herself.

So, when Luke suggested they go out so she could try to cut loose a bit, she agreed. It was funny, both Amber and Rick had sent her texts asking her to meet them. Rick wanted her to come to the Bella Vista for drinks with all the others and tell her side of the story.

None of them believe you would have stolen drugs, he wrote in his message. *Don't worry, the truth will get sorted out for sure.*

Amber said she didn't care where they met, she just wanted to talk — face to face. But Georgia kept on ignoring their texts. She wasn't ready to see any of them. Especially not when there was this horrible niggling feeling that someone among them wasn't the friend she'd thought they were. Cadence might have been behind the set-up, but someone who worked with her had to be involved; she couldn't have stolen those drugs on her own.

However, the chance to drown her feelings with Luke was appealing. They'd walked up to the main road and were having drinks at the Hillside Tavern when everything began to tip sideways. She was drinking fast. She knew that. It was because she wanted to numb the pain of the last few days. There were times when you intend on having a few drinks, and somehow you get carried away and unexpectedly find yourself remarkably tipsy. And then there were other times — times like tonight — where you have one goal, and that goal is to write yourself off. She wanted to be drunk, she wanted to be drunk enough that she could bury her head in the sand and forget everything that was going on. But apparently life had other plans for her.

When she saw Luke pull his phone out of his pocket to look at a message, she didn't even need to ask who it was from.

'It's her again,' she said.

He nodded and stood up. 'Yeah, um, we kinda need to get the hell out of here.'

'What? Why?'

'Because she's here. She's watching us.'

Georgia closed her eyes and breathed slowly out of her nose. She knew it. She knew that bloody innocent act that Cadence had played with her was all utter bullshit. She couldn't believe she'd almost started to feel sorry for her. She opened her eyes and looked back at Luke. 'Sit down,' she said.

'Huh?'

'I said sit down. I'm not going anywhere. She doesn't get to control our lives anymore. This isn't happening.'

Luke hovered above her. 'Ah ... I don't know if that's such a good idea.'

'She's probably bluffing. She's probably sitting at home *pretending* to be here watching us. I'm not letting her chase us away. I'm having a good time and I'm staying.'

'Small problem with that — she definitely isn't bluffing. I could tell from her message.'

'Why? What did it say?'

'It said that I look really sexy in my blue shirt ... It said ... um, it said that by tonight my blue shirt would be on her bedroom floor, and then ...' He trailed off, looking nervous.

'And then what? What the fuck else did that bitch say?'

'Babe, seriously, the rest of the message is the worst part, that's why I want us to get out of here. She sounds deranged, dangerous.'

'For fuck's sake, Luke, just be honest with me. Tell me what it says.'

'Okay, okay. It says if she sees you touch me one more time she's going to come over here and scratch your eyes out.'

Now Georgia did stand up. She spun around on the spot and almost fell over. 'Where is she? Can you see her? Fucking hell, Luke, help me look!'

'Georgia, calm down, please!'

'Calm down? You want me to calm down? You have got to be joking. She's talking about scratching my eyes out and you think *I* need to calm down.'

'I know! I know. But I don't want you to get hurt. I want to protect you, Georgia.'

'But you're not, are you? If you were protecting me, you'd be storming over to her right now and telling her to back the fuck off. You'd be telling her that you love me. Me and only me. You'd tell her that she means nothing to you, absolutely nothing.'

She knew she was screaming, knew that people were staring, that a baby-faced barman who'd served them earlier was now headed towards them, a concerned look on his face. But she didn't care, she couldn't take it anymore.

'Okay, I will tell her that, I'll tell her all of those things, but right now you're not the only one who's had enough of her. I have too. I think we just need to leave.'

He put his hand on the small of her back, ready to guide her out, but Georgia pushed his arm away.

'No! She said if she saw us touch she'd come over and scratch my eyes out and you just touched me. So, where is she?' She whipped around again, searching for her enemy. 'Where are you, Cadence?' she screamed. 'Come at me, bitch!'

The bartender stepped up to them. 'Is everything okay here, guys?' he asked.

'Yes,' said Luke, at the same time as Georgia shouted, 'No, it's not!'

'Um, I think I might have to ask you two to take this outside.'

It seemed absurd to Georgia that this child was playing the part of the mature adult, asking them to 'take it outside'.

'It's okay,' said Luke. 'We're leaving.'

'No! We're not! Not until we find her. Not until we tell her this is not okay!' She knew what the bartender must be thinking. Jealous girlfriend doesn't like the fact that there's some other woman in her boyfriend's life. She wanted to explain, she wanted to tell him, *It's not me! I'm not the crazy one! It's her!*

But she knew how she sounded. She was drunk and she was shouting in the middle of a bar, and now a bouncer was heading this way, and he was big and he had that no-nonsense look that bouncers always had, and she knew she'd lost.

She pulled away from both Luke and the bartender. 'It's fine! I'm fine! I'm *going*!'

She hated the fact that half the people in there were all staring at her as she left.

Luke followed her. As soon as they were out in the fresh air, she wheeled around to face him. 'Why do you let her win? Why do you let her do this to us? You said she was going to stop!'

He nodded. 'You're right,' he said. 'You're absolutely right. This has been going on long enough. I'm not certain if the police have served her with the restraining order yet or not, but either way, I know they went to talk to her about the break-in, so it's unbelievable that she still hasn't let up. I'm so sorry.'

His refusal to get drawn in by her angry accusations and argue back was starting to take some of the wind out of Georgia's sails. She took in a deep breath and when she let it out, she tried to release some of the anger at the same time.

'But …' she said, her voice smaller now, 'why did we have to leave?'

'To be honest, I was being selfish. I know you wanted me to confront her but I didn't want to have to see her. I'm tired and I'm stressed and I don't know the right way to deal with all of this. But I couldn't bring myself to face her. She's trying to ruin my life — *our* life. And I'm at the end of my rope. I don't know how to fix this and I hate that. I just needed to get out of there. I'm sorry.'

'Oh.' Georgia felt a flood of guilt wash over her. What if the reason Cadence had followed them tonight was to get back at her for going to her apartment? What if Georgia had been the one to set her off again?

'I'm sorry too,' Georgia said.

Luke took her hand and they started walking towards home.

CHAPTER TWENTY-THREE

The following morning Georgia wanted to start the day on a better note. She woke up early, before Luke, and forced herself to get out of bed. She snuck out to the kitchen to make him some breakfast. After checking through the pantry and fridge to see what ingredients she had to work with, she decided to go with French toast with berries. An impressively gourmet-looking but easy to make breakfast feast.

I will not get sucked back down into the darkness. I will not give in. I will not go back to that place. I can't, I can't, I can't.

She was frying the egg-dipped bread when Luke emerged from the bedroom, one hand massaging the back of his neck as he shuffled towards her and yawned. He kissed the back of her neck. 'What's all this?'

'French toast,' she said proudly.

'Ah.'

'Ah?' she said. 'That's all I get? Ah? I thought you'd be way more impressed.'

'Oh, no, no, I'm totally impressed. Sorry, babe, it's only that ...'

He trailed off and Georgia stared at him, waiting for him to continue. 'Only what?' she prompted.

'It's nothing. Seriously, nothing. This is awesome.' He gave her another kiss and she turned her attention back to the bread, flipping it over before it could burn. 'But what were you going to say?'

'Nothing.'

'Luke! Tell me.'

'Okay, you don't remember me mentioning ... the thing about French toast?'

'What thing about French toast?'

'How it was something Cadence always used to make.'

Georgia spun around again. 'No! You never said that! I would have remembered.'

He shook his head. 'You're probably right, maybe I never did say it. It's stupid anyway. Just because she used to make it doesn't mean anything. I can't let the woman put me off it for life. Please forget I said anything.'

'Oh, but now I feel bad. This was supposed to be a nice surprise for you to take your mind *off* Cadence after last night. I'm sorry.'

'No, *I'm* sorry. I shouldn't have even mentioned it. I'm being childish.'

Georgia made a snap decision and picked up the pan, tipping the contents into the bin. 'You know what, let's just go out for breakfast and both stop apologising.'

*

They wandered through the shops after breakfast, window shopping. They went into a clothing store, where Georgia tried on a bright pink beanie and Luke insisted on buying it for her because he said she looked like a cute little elf in it. They left the centre and walked out through the piazza, where they discovered the main street had been closed for a food festival with live music.

'I didn't know there was something on here this weekend,' said Georgia as they found a spot in the sun where they could sit down to watch a band playing folk music.

'They're good,' said Luke, putting an arm around her and letting her lean back into him and rest her head on his chest.

'Mmm, I could fall asleep sitting here in the sun listening to them.'

Georgia was actually starting to let her eyelids droop when she spotted the familiar face, watching the live music just five or ten metres away. Her hair was different, longer and lighter. But the face was unmistakable. Georgia jolted forward, wide awake now.

'What's wrong?'

'Over there,' she said, pointing. 'That's Lena, my old flatmate.'

'Oh, is it?' He looked at her and frowned. 'You seem upset to see her.'

'Umm, yeah, well ... she's not really someone I want to run into.'

'How come?'

'We just ... we used to be friends, but then ... there was this thing that happened. It's hard to explain.'

'You want to go? We can head home, if you like?'

Georgia hesitated. 'Does that make me a hypocrite? I was going on about you letting Cadence chase us out of the place last night, now I'm doing the exact same thing.'

'Not at all. They're two completely different things. Come on,' he said, standing up and pulling Georgia to her feet, 'let's go.'

'Thank you.'

They were moving through the crowd when Lena somehow appeared right in front of them. She locked eyes with Georgia and threw her arms open wide. 'I thought that was you!' she exclaimed, and Georgia was alarmed to realise that she was coming in for a big hug.

Oh God, why on earth does she want to hug me?

There was no way out of it though, she had to hug her back and pretend she was delighted to see her.

'I'm so, so glad to run into you,' Lena said when they'd pulled apart again. 'It's been *such* a long time.'

'Yeah, it has.' Georgia really didn't know what else to say, but at that point Lena finally turned to look at Luke and did a double-take. 'Oh! Hey!' she said.

'You two know each other?' Georgia asked, frowning.

'Well, yeah, I mean, of course —' Lena began.

But Luke was already pulling on Georgia's hand and starting to walk away. 'Yeah, sure, great to run into you but we have to go.'

Lena's face changed from excited to a sort of hurt, bewildered look. 'O-okay,' she said, her voice faltering. 'Bye …'

Georgia let Luke pull her through the crowd and she waited until they were clear of the noise to ask him what was going on. Something wasn't right. She'd never seen him so brusque with anyone.

'You know Lena?' she asked, as they slowed their pace.

'Nah, not really. Not properly.'

'But ... but *how* do you know her?'

'Just from, like ... friends of friends or whatever. Like I said, I don't know her properly at all.'

'She seemed like she knew you well.'

'Yeah well, she also wanted to hug you when you clearly weren't into it. Seems like she's one of those people who go totally over the top with people she barely knows.'

'Why didn't you say you knew her, when I pointed her out?'

'I didn't even realise, to be honest. I didn't recognise her until she was right in front of us.'

'It's weird though, right, that you knew the girl who used to be my flatmate?'

'I guess, a bit. Although not that weird — sometimes it seems like everyone in the Hills area knows everyone else.'

'I suppose.'

CHAPTER TWENTY-FOUR

Sliding across the ice was more exhilarating than Georgia remembered. She hadn't been ice skating since she was a teenager. In fact, she'd thought Luke was joking when he suggested they go to the ice rink to take her mind off things that night, but he was completely serious.

It was nice to discover that she was actually quite good at ice skating; she could go quite fast. *Say yes to things, Georgia. That's how you stave off the darkness. You say yes to things.*

Unfortunately, her insistence that she needed to say yes to things wasn't extending to anyone else in her life right now. She was still ignoring Amber, Rick and her parents. The messages and voicemails were piling up. *Say yes to Luke.* He's the only one that truly understands everything you're going through right now. He's the one that loves you.

I'll deal with the others later. They'll understand.

Meanwhile, Marcus still hadn't replied to her messages — even though she'd sent him two more saying that she really needed to talk.

They stopped for a break and Luke eyed her up and down.

'What?' she asked. 'What's that look for?'

'Nothing … it's just, you look really fucking hot right now.'

'I do not.' She laughed. She was wearing the pink beanie he'd bought for her.

'No, I'm serious. Watching you skate is the sexiest thing ever. You're good at this.'

'Thank you,' she said, noting that an inner glow she hadn't felt in ages was creeping back in. It felt as if they'd stopped having these kinds of moments. These wonderful, 'we're still in the early stages of our relationship and everything is fresh and bright and magical' moments. Cadence had taken that away from them.

'You know the only problem?' Luke asked.

'What's that?'

'My plan was to have you slipping all over the place so I could be the manly man, holding you up, and instead, you skate better than me.'

'Ha. If you like I can hold you up instead?'

'Yes please, my lady. Actually, how's this?' He wrapped his arms around her waist from behind and they pushed off from the side to start skating around the rink again, Georgia leading.

'Can you believe everything we've already had to endure through our relationship? Cadence trying to break us up. Even that dick Brett trying to get me to date him.'

'I know. We're like Romeo and Juliet — star-crossed lovers.'

'Jack and Rose! There was room on that door for Jack, you know.'

'Yes! Or Ross and Rachel.'

'Actually, I think we've gone off track and started naming random couples that aren't actually star-crossed lovers,' Georgia mused.

'Good point. Okay, I have one. Florentino and Fermina,' Luke said.

'Who the hell are Florentino and Fermina?'

'They're the couple in *Love in the Time of Cholera*,' Luke replied.

'Ah.' Georgia had never read it. Although, something was twinging at the corner of her mind. Where had she heard of that book only recently?

Luke squeezed her a little tighter. He kissed the top of her head and they glided smoothly across the ice. 'Don't worry,' he said. 'No one has succeeded in breaking us up. We're stronger than ever.'

CHAPTER TWENTY-FIVE

Georgia was waiting on a park bench the following morning. After Luke had kissed her goodbye and headed off to work, she'd been lying in bed, wondering whether she'd leave the apartment today or just curl up on the couch again. There had been no further information from Denise about the investigation. When the message came through Facebook from Lena, Georgia was going to decline. Their history was so difficult, she wasn't sure if she wanted to talk to her. Besides, she wasn't even seeing her best friends at the moment. But then the last line of Lena's message piqued her curiosity.

Hey stranger, the message had begun. *It was really good to run into you the other day but I wished we'd been able to chat properly. I get why you didn't want to talk with me — but I do often wonder how you are and I miss being friends with you. Although I'm not altogether sure how you'll be feeling about me now after realising that Luke and I know one another!!*

Lena had gone on to suggest that they catch up and Georgia had found herself agreeing and suggesting they do so right away. *I'm not altogether sure how you'll be feeling about me now after realising that Luke and I know one another!!* What did that mean? Luke said he barely knew her. The curiosity had overcome her apprehension.

Georgia thought it was strange that Lena had suggested meeting in a park. It made her think of clandestine meetings between spies with turned up trench-coat collars and black umbrellas. But when Lena arrived Georgia discovered she had two small girls, who immediately made a beeline for the swings.

Lena gave her yet another great big hug as she sat down next to her and Georgia hugged her back awkwardly.

'Wow,' Georgia said as she managed to pull back. 'I can't believe you have two kids now.'

'Georgia!' Lena exclaimed. 'They aren't mine! I nanny for their parents.' She paused for a moment. 'Wait, let me guess, even though we're friends on Facebook you have me hidden from your feed so you have no idea what's going on in my life?'

'Oh, I don't really use Facebook that much ...' Georgia could feel her cheeks flaming. She absolutely had Lena hidden from her feed.

'It's fine,' said Lena. 'I understand.' She pointed at her two charges. 'The little one on the swings is Eliza-Jane and the one hiding in the sandpit is Darcie.'

Georgia smiled at the two small girls even though they weren't really paying them any attention. 'Cute,' she said, because she really didn't know what else to say.

'Yeah, they're good kids. So, listen,' Lena said, getting straight to the point. 'There are a couple of things I wanted to talk to you about. First, our history. You and I … we used to get along really well. You were such a great flatmate. And I know why you backed right away from me after your … your breakdown. You were embarrassed, right? Ashamed?'

Georgia twisted her hands together and stared down at her feet. She didn't like reliving that part of her life. 'I don't know,' she said, her voice small. 'I guess it was something like that.'

'Okay, so here's the thing. You don't *need* to feel that way. Honestly. Everything that happened, it wasn't your fault. And I miss you. Seriously. I don't have a lot of mates. When we flatted together, you were pretty much my best friend. I don't know, I kind of feel like us running into each other was sort of serendipitous. Like, it's a chance for us to be friends again.'

Georgia was still looking down at her feet. 'Maybe,' she mumbled.

'You're not convinced, are you? Now I'm embarrassed. Admitting I have hardly any friends and almost begging you to be friends with me again. Sorry, maybe this was stupid.'

Georgia realised there was a real note of vulnerability in Lena's voice and she finally looked up and made eye contact with her. Georgia was being mean and there was no need for it. 'No,' she said, 'It's not stupid. I'm the one who needs to say sorry. You're right, we were good friends.'

'Then is it the other thing holding you back from being friends with me? The thing with Luke?'

'I don't actually know what you mean by that.'

'You don't? That was the second thing I wanted to talk with you about, my history with him.'

'What history?'

'He didn't tell you?'

'No. He said he knew you from around, like, as friends of friends or something. Is there more to it than that?'

'Sorry, I assumed he would have said. Now I don't know if I'm doing the right thing by telling you. I've totally fucked up. Maybe you should ask him.'

'Lena, please. Could you just tell me?'

She winced. 'I really don't know if I should.'

'*Please.*'

'Okay. We met about six months ago. We literally bumped into one another — as in, properly knocked into one another at this bar. I'd just been stood up and I was getting up to leave when he walked into me and spilled his drink on me. We got to talking and, well, you know how it is … one thing led to another and we ended up having a one-night stand.'

Georgia stared back at her, completely shocked. Lena rushed to reassure her.

'It was before you two got together though — I'm certain of it. He was definitely single when we met, and anyway, we didn't really have a connection. So, it was nothing more than a one-night thing. Is that weird? That I slept with your boyfriend before you met him? It is, isn't it? You probably definitely don't want to be friends again with me now, do you?'

'Ah, no, it's not that, it's just …' Georgia's head was spinning. She was trying to make sense of everything that Lena had said. She'd slept with Luke? Before Georgia met him? But how was that even possible? Luke was with Cadence right before they met. And why would he lie to Georgia about the way he knew Lena? Unless … had he cheated on Cadence? Maybe he was too ashamed to admit it to Georgia.

She was still untangling everything Lena had said, working her way back through the story.

'You want to know something really funny?' said Lena, seemingly oblivious to Georgia's confusion. 'The night we had that one-night stand, we actually talked about you.'

'What? What do you mean? You said it was before Luke and I got together.'

'Yes, absolutely it was, I don't mean *he* talked about you, I mean *I* did. Somehow, we got talking about old flatmates and I ended up telling him about you — not by name, of course! Like, I wasn't sharing all these intimate details about you or anything like that. It was more that he was telling me about his old flatmates, and then I was talking about mine and saying how I missed you, and then he asked questions, I guess, and —' She stopped short. 'Georgia, are you okay? Your face has gone all white. Is something … is there something wrong?'

Georgia swallowed. Her breathing was starting to become shallow again. 'He asked questions about me? What kind of questions?'

'What? No, no, it's not like he knew that it was *you* we were talking about. I mean this is all just some sort of weird coincidence.'

Georgia clenched her hands on the seat beneath her. 'Please, what did he ask?'

'Well … I don't know, it's hard to remember. I guess I told him you went through this really hard time emotionally and he just sort of … asked about it. But it was no big deal — we were chatting, that's all, making conversation.'

Georgia leaned forward and sucked in a big mouthful of air.

Lena put a hand on her arm, 'Georgia! Are you okay?'

'Help … help me breathe … just … talk me through it.' She didn't even know what exactly it was that had brought this panic attack on. All she knew was that something was very wrong here. Something wasn't adding up.

'Okay, okay, sure. In … that's it, yes, breathe in, hold it … Should you hold it? Or not hold it? Oh shit, I don't know what I'm doing.'

'Count …' said Georgia. 'Just count … for me …'

'Right, got it. Okay. One … two … three … four … Now breathe out, yeah?'

Georgia tried to ignore the clearly panicked tone in Lena's voice and focused on the count instead. In, two, three, four. Out, two, three, four. She was calming down. Quicker than last time. She was gaining control again. The clenched fist on her lungs was unfurling. She leaned right back on the seat and looked up at the wide blue sky above. A few more deep, slow breaths and she was almost back to normal. She stayed still for another good few minutes, just staring at the sky and breathing.

Finally, she looked at Lena, 'Sorry,' she said, 'That keeps happening to me lately.'

'That's okay. Don't be sorry. But what's going on? I don't understand.'

'I don't know,' said Georgia. 'But I'm going to find out.'
She paused, as something clicked into place. 'Lena, what was
the name of the date who stood you up — the night you met
Luke?'

'I think it was Brett.'

CHAPTER TWENTY-SIX

For the third time, Georgia looked up at the old building on Francis Road in Artarmon. She couldn't tell if she was more or less nervous than the last time she'd visited, but either way it was a different feeling. She was frightened, but this time it wasn't Cadence she was frightened of. It was whatever she was about to find out. There was something strange about the way she and Luke had met, something … wrong. And the more she struggled to piece it all together, the more she felt like Cadence might have the answer. She was just hoping that she somehow had it all wrong. The idea that her perfect relationship with Luke might not be everything she'd believed terrified her.

Once again, the front door was propped open; the Yellow Pages was gone, but there was a folded mat wedged in the door to stop it from latching. Georgia pushed it open and headed inside. At the sight of the lift she remembered how terrified she'd been, riding down to the ground floor with Cadence in there with her. Thinking that at any moment she might turn around and attack her. Then she remembered Cadence's explanation. *I had an episode. I was frightened.*

She stopped still for a moment and closed her eyes, pictured the way Cadence had looked that day. Was it possible she was telling the truth? Was she really having some sort of breakdown rather than trying to intimidate Georgia?

She stepped into the lift and pressed number 5. It rose slowly with lots of clanks and bangs — enough to make her wonder if it was entirely safe. Finally, it juddered to a stop on the fifth floor. She walked down the hall to Cadence's door, took in one more deep breath, and knocked.

'Who is it?' came the voice from inside. Once again, she sounded nervous and timid.

'Cadence? This is Georgia again.' She paused. There was no response from inside. 'Listen,' she called out, 'I know you probably don't want to let me in after last time and I understand, I do. But we seriously need to talk. So … could I come in? Please?'

There was more silence and Georgia waited. Then the door opened slowly inwards and Cadence stood, her head down, her hair covering her face. She had her arms wrapped around herself protectively. She looked up, her hair shifted to the side and Georgia gasped.

'What happened to your face?'

There was a dark purple and black bruise around Cadence's left eye. She immediately dropped her head back down. 'It's … it's nothing,' she said. 'An accident.'

'It doesn't look like nothing, it looks pretty bad.'

'Please, can you just tell me why you're here?'

'Oh okay, right. This is going to sound like the stupidest question in the world, and I don't even know why I'm asking this because it's not like I have any reason to believe that you'd answer me truthfully, but … fuck it. Have you been stalking me?'

Cadence looked up again and stared her right in the eye. 'No,' she said. 'I still don't even know who you are.'

A wave of pins and needles swept across Georgia's skin. Cadence was telling the truth. It was written all over her face. Georgia's heart plunged and she swayed on the spot. Luke had been lying to her. How could she have got everything so wrong? She tasted bile in the back of her throat and her body felt hot. Too hot.

'I'm sorry,' she said. 'I just need … I need a minute.' She walked past Cadence and straight over to her couch where she sat down and put her head in her hands, trying to make sense of it all, trying to process this news. She breathed in and out slowly. *Luke is not the perfect guy you thought he was. Luke lied. Luke orchestrated your chance meeting with him. But why? Why would he possibly do any of this?*

'Excuse me!' Cadence said.

But Georgia ignored her. After a few moments, she became aware of Cadence sitting down next to her.

'All right,' Cadence said. 'Now it's my turn. Why do you keep coming here? Why did you ask me if I've been stalking you?'

'Because … oh God, how do I even explain all of this? Because, I think it's possible that Luke has been lying to the both of us.' She fought against the tears that were threatening to spill. She couldn't fall apart. Not here, not in front of Cadence. And not until she properly understood everything.

'But how do you even *know* Luke?'

Georgia lifted her head out of her hands and looked back at Cadence. 'I know him because he's my boyfriend.'

'Please, not this again. Are you going to start shouting at me and telling me we broke up? Because if you are then you can just leave right now. I can't take that again. Not after ...' She trailed off and Georgia quickly shook her head.

'No, no, I promise, I'm not going to shout. Let me stay. We have to talk, we have to figure out what's going on. Here's the truth. I met Luke a few months ago at a bar in Castle Hill. He told me he was single, but that he'd just had a really bad break-up ... with you. He said that you weren't over him, but that you still lived together.'

She saw the look on Cadence's face, knew that she was doubting her story, so Georgia opened the photo album on her phone and passed it across. 'Here,' she said, 'see for yourself. There are lots of snaps on there of the two of us together.'

Georgia felt cruel, especially as she watched Cadence's face change as she went through the photos. It was like she was crushing this girl's heart with her bare hands.

'But, these could have been taken any time,' Cadence said. 'Maybe you used to know him, maybe these are old.'

'Look at the dates of the photos. When you click into it, it shows you.'

Cadence passed the phone back. It seemed as if she couldn't bring herself to keep looking.

Georgia ploughed on with her story. 'Then I started getting these nasty notes left on my car, messages sent to my phone — messages from you. At least, I believed they were from you. I don't know, I don't even understand how he could have done it, how he could have tricked me, but he did. I truly believed you were stalking me. He moved in with me but the stalking got worse instead of better. There was a break-in, my keys were stolen — he said he thought you took them from under my seat at the movies.'

Cadence was shaking her head. 'No! I would never, I —'

Georgia held her hand up. 'It's okay,' she said, 'let me finish. I lost my job because someone framed me at work, and I guess … I guess I was hitting rock bottom — a place I've been before, if I'm honest. But then something weird happened. We ran into my old flatmate and Luke seemed to know her. So, I spoke with her this morning, and it turns out he lied to me about how he knew her.' Georgia stopped and locked eyes with Cadence, making sure she had her full attention before continuing on. 'Cadence, I think … I think he arranged it so that he could meet me. I think there's more to the way we got together. I think neither you nor I can trust him.'

Cadence stood up and backed away. 'No,' she said. 'There's no way. None of this is even possible! You're telling me that for the last three months of our relationship, he's somehow been in a simultaneous relationship with you? How would he even manage that?'

'Okay, tell me something, where did he tell you he was over the weekend? This weekend just past?'

'He was away for work. He has to travel a lot for work.'

'Cadence, I'm really sorry, but no, he was with me on the weekend. We went out to the Hillside Tavern on Friday night.'

234

Cadence shook her head. 'No! No way! He messaged me from Adelaide. He even made a joke about how quiet the nightlife was there.' Cadence snatched up her own phone, opened up the messaging app and thrust it in Georgia's face. 'See! Right there, that's the message he sent me.'

Georgia glanced at the message but she didn't want to keep looking at it. The idea of him sending secret fake messages to Cadence while he was with her made her feel sick. Not to mention the lies he must have sent to her when he was actually with Cadence.

She tried to keep her face deadpan, her voice steady. 'He lied to you. He wasn't in Adelaide. Actually, he told me he hated flying and he only ever travels within the state for work.'

'Luke isn't afraid of flying! He has to go overseas for his job all the time!'

'Jesus. Why would he make something like that up?' Georgia thought of how scared he'd been as they waited to board their flight to Melbourne. Was that all an act? How could he? She'd been so worried for him. Or was it real and he'd he been lying to Cadence about flying for work?

She hated this. She hated that she was having to untangle all his lies. She still couldn't reconcile the idea of Luke — her amazing boyfriend who she'd shared so much with — being a *cheat*.

'Here's the other thing,' Georgia said. 'He also told me that you were there watching us when we were at the Hillside. That you were stalking us.'

'I wasn't at the Hillside on Friday! I was right here at home. There's no way I could have been there because I can't …'

'Can't what?'

'Nothing, never mind. Just trust me, I wasn't there.'

'He let me believe you were following me home from work once as well. I kept looking at this red hatchback in my mirror —'

Cadence cut her off. 'I don't drive,' she said. 'I don't have a red hatchback. I don't even own a car.'

'Fucking hell.' Georgia thought back to all the times she'd believed Cadence had been stalking her. The note at the Persian restaurant — he must have slipped it to the waiter and asked for it to be delivered to their table. The phone call from Luke when she'd been at the Bella Vista Hotel. But Cadence was there, wasn't she? She'd known that Georgia was wearing her green top. But no. Luke had asked what colour she was wearing *first*. Then there was the blonde woman in the bathroom who winked at her — she really was just a stranger being friendly. She didn't look anything *like* Cadence. Georgia had frightened herself and then Luke had gone along with it seamlessly. Time after time, Cadence had been an invisible presence and Georgia had filled in the blanks.

'Listen,' Georgia said, 'I'm still coming to terms with all of this myself. I came here hoping that maybe there was going to be an explanation for the weird things going on with him. I don't know what, I don't know how you could have explained any of it away. Or maybe I came here because I knew … I knew that if he'd lied about the other stuff then maybe he'd lied about you as well. But I needed to find out for sure. The thing I don't get though, is why he's doing this. Why would he pretend he'd broken up with you and that you were stalking us? What's the point? What did he have to gain?'

'I don't know!' Cadence's hands were shaking and Georgia was worried she was about to kick her out, but instead she walked over to a shelf and took down a small pill bottle. Her hands were shaking so much she was having trouble opening it.

'Do you need help?' Georgia offered.

Cadence tried one more time to open it and then relented.

'Okay, thanks.' She passed her the bottle and then disappeared into the kitchen. Georgia glanced at the label. 'Nature's Choice Serenity tablets'. She used to take these back when she was going through her darker times, before she was properly medicated.

Cadence returned with a glass of water, and Georgia watched her tip two tablets out onto her hand. She frowned. 'Those don't look right.'

'Excuse me?'

'I used to take Serenity,' said Georgia. 'They were small round white tablets, not big yellow ones. Those aren't Serenity.'

'Yes, they are,' said Cadence. 'Maybe they changed since you last took them.'

'Maybe.'

'Okay.' Cadence seemed to calm down a little having taken the tablets, likely a placebo effect as they wouldn't have had time to do anything for her that fast. 'I think we need to talk to Luke, the both of us together, see if he can explain.'

'I don't know if that's a good idea. This isn't some small misunderstanding that he can explain away. This is serious. He's been living a double life. And he's been terrifying me into thinking I was being stalked these past two months. Why is he doing this to us?'

'I don't know if I can act like I never met you. I want to give him the chance to tell me his side.'

'His side? Cadence, there is no "his side"; he's a liar and a cheat.' She paused. 'Wait, do you still not believe me? Do you still think I'm the one who's crazy here?'

Her eyes slid away from Georgia. 'Well, it's not that … I …' she stammered.

'Cadence! I showed you proof, I showed you the photos! I'm telling you, he's playing us, he's playing the both of us. I mean, shit, I don't know, maybe he's even dangerous. I think he trashed my apartment just to stage that break-in.'

'He did what? No, that's not right. That doesn't sound like Luke; he'd never do something like that. He could never be dangerous.'

Georgia felt like grabbing Cadence by the shoulders and shaking her. She was clearly in denial. Her world was crashing down around her and she was trying to prop it back up with sticks and Blu-Tack. But there was no way Georgia could leave here until she convinced Cadence she was telling the truth. Or else the first thing Cadence would do was call Luke and tell him everything, and then Georgia might never find out exactly what he was up to: Why had he sought her out and faked their chance meeting at The Crooked Tailor? Why had he quizzed Lena about her past? Why was he systematically tearing her life apart?

'Cadence, what happened to your eye?'

'I told you, it's nothing. It was an accident.'

'What kind of an accident?'

'He didn't mean to … He was upset and when he swung out … He wasn't meaning to actually hit me.'

Georgia knew what the answer was going to be, but it was still a shock. 'Luke did that to you? This is bad, this is really, really bad. He *is* dangerous. We can't "talk this out". We need to go to the police.'

Thinking about the police made Georgia remember the restraining order, the police report from the break-in. Had he somehow faked all of that as well? It was possible. She'd never actually spoken to any of the cops herself. They were already gone when she'd arrived home after the break-in. Later, he'd asked her to write the letter for the restraining order, then he'd offered to drop it into the station on his way to work. None of it was real, was it?

'Has he hurt you before?' Georgia asked.

Cadence shook her head. 'No, never. I told you, this was an accident.'

'Okay,' Georgia said. She knew if she kept pushing Cadence on this, she might end up shutting her out. 'Can I show you some of the messages I've been getting? Here, I took photos of the ones that were left on my car. Luke said they were from you.'

Georgia held out her phone once again.

Cadence read one out loud. '*You know you're not going to be able to keep him, right? He's mine, bitch.*' She looked up at Georgia. 'Luke said I wrote that? I would never! I don't even … I mean, I don't talk that way. That doesn't even sound like me.'

Georgia took the phone back and went into her email. 'And this,' she said, passing it back across, 'look at this email.'

Cadence's eyes widened. 'This is my email address. How is this possible? I didn't send this. I didn't take these photos.'

'Cadence, it's possible because Luke did it. He must have been the one to send it. He must have followed me, taken those photos himself.' Georgia shivered, it was a horrible thought.

'*You fucking slut, you think you can steal my boyfriend and then cheat on him?*' Cadence read out. 'I've never called anyone a slut in my entire life.'

'Cadence, I know. That's what I've been trying to tell you. I know now it wasn't you. But you have to believe me when I tell you that Luke isn't who he says he is. Oh my God,' Georgia said suddenly. 'That word —*slut*— that's what Brett kept calling me as well.'

'What? Who? Who's Brett? There's someone else involved?'

'Brett must be Luke. He must have used a fake profile to meet me, and then to taunt me as well.' Georgia felt sick. How could he say those things to her while simultaneously telling her he *loved* her? Was he some sort of sociopath?

'This is too much,' said Cadence. 'You come into my home and you tell me all these things. You tell me my boyfriend's left me, that I've been stalking you, that I can't trust him … Well, what if I can't trust you?'

'Take a look in the goddamned mirror. That's how you know you can trust me, because I'm not the one who did that to you, he is. *He* did that, *he* hurt you.'

They stood staring at one another and Georgia knew this was make or break. Either Cadence was about to break down and accept the truth, or she was about to dig her heels in and push Georgia away.

But she didn't get the chance to decide. Because that's when they heard it. The sound of keys jangling outside the apartment door.

Georgia's breath caught in her throat. 'Is that him? Is that Luke?' she hissed.

He was supposed to be away in Armidale right now. But of course he wasn't. Of course, every time he told her he was travelling for work he was actually with Cadence. And now he was here and she was trapped.

Cadence nodded, her eyes wide, but with maybe, just maybe a hint of relief in them. In her mind, she was about to get the reassuring explanation she wanted.

'Cadence, please,' Georgia whispered, 'I need to hide. I don't want him to know I'm here.'

Cadence looked unsure and Georgia pleaded with her eyes. She saw her face change, give in, and next thing, Cadence was pushing her towards the leather couch.

'Back there,' she whispered, 'behind the couch, under the window. That's all there's time for.'

Georgia didn't think it was the greatest hiding spot; she would have preferred to be in a wardrobe or somewhere she'd be properly out of sight. But Cadence was right, there was no time, the key was in the lock. Georgia dove behind the couch and curled herself up in a ball, desperate to make herself as small as possible. Then she did her best to slow down her breathing so she couldn't be heard.

She heard the door open. Footsteps. Cadence's voice, saying 'Hello'.

And then she heard it: Luke's voice. Her own boyfriend lovingly greeting someone else: 'Hi, babe!'

She waited. She held her breath.

Was Cadence going to turn on her?

PART TWO

Cadence

CHAPTER TWENTY-SEVEN

I wouldn't say that the start of our relationship was especially romantic. Certainly it was no epic love story. It was messy from day one. And there were warning signs from the very beginning, too. Red flags that should have made me stop and ask questions. But I was caught up in it all and I pushed those red flags aside. Six months later, when Georgia turned up at my door, I knew right away that something wasn't right. I argued with her anyway. I didn't want to believe that it was all about to come crashing down around me. Plus, it seemed so implausible. Not only was he supposed to have left me, but he'd started an entire relationship with someone new? All while the two of us were still very much together. Impossible. How could he achieve that? Who would have the time? But you clear your mind — you need to clear it up first — and you start back-tracking, and you realise — of course it's possible. And more and more you realise you knew it all along.

I'll start at the beginning though. Explain it so you can understand how I could have let all of this happen.

When Luke first spoke to me in the middle of the cereal aisle in the grocery store, I assumed he thought I worked there. My first thought was, *Oh God, did I dress in the same colour as the staff again?* I looked down at my top and saw that it was green. The staff in Coles wear white shirts. Maybe he thought we were in Woolies? They wear green. I was so caught up in this thought process that I didn't even hear what he actually said and my autopilot response was to smile and nod and hope I'd catch on. Obviously, this was wrong though, because he got this bemused expression on his face and I knew I had to come clean.

'Sorry, can you say that again?'

This time I would listen and obviously it would be something like, 'Can you tell me which aisle the chicken stock is in?' And I would have to decide whether to save him the embarrassment of having mistaken me for someone who worked there and just send him to aisle 6, or come clean yet again and admit that I was another customer but that it was okay because it happened surprisingly often.

But then he said something that came completely from left field.

'Your shoes are awesome. Where did you get them?'

I had to look down at my feet to see which ones I was wearing. They were my rainbow Converse and, well, once I realised, three thoughts went through my head in quick succession.

One: Yes, I know, they are brilliant, aren't they?

Two: He probably wants to know where I got them so he can buy a pair for his girlfriend.

Three: Oh fuck, no he doesn't. He's being sarcastic. He's making fun of me because I'm a thirty-eight-year-old in rainbow shoes and I look like a twelve-year-old.

Because all of these thoughts went through my mind so quickly, I got confused and reverted back to my original theory: He thinks I work here. He needs my help to find something.

'I don't work here,' I blurted out in response.

He cocked his head on the side and I swear to God his eyes actually twinkled at me. I haven't mentioned yet how good-looking he was, have I? That was part of it. Part of the reason I was so goddamned flustered. Extraordinarily good-looking guys don't usually just come up to me and start chatting. He had blond hair that flopped into his pale grey-green eyes (did I notice the colour of his eyes right then? I'm not sure actually; maybe I didn't know the colour until later, but it feels like I did). You could tell by the way his T-shirt sat that he was muscular, but not *too* muscular, if you know what I mean. Broad-chested, nice shoulders.

'I know,' he said. 'I was just wondering about your shoes.'

At this point I was feeling completely humiliated.

'Sorry,' I said. 'They're from an online store, PixieButter. com.' I was back to assuming he didn't really want to know where to buy them, back to assuming his admiration of my shoes was sarcasm.

'Okay, confession, I don't really want to know where they're from.'

Bingo. I knew it.

'It was a lousy pick-up line, but I didn't know how else to start up a conversation with someone in the middle of the supermarket.'

A pick-up line? I had to replay his words in my head. It seemed so unlikely that he'd be trying to pick me up. Not only unlikely, unfathomable. Impossible. He was ridiculously hot. This entire thing was ridiculous. Someone was playing a practical joke on me. And what was I supposed to say to that? I had no idea, so I didn't say anything at all. I stayed quiet.

'I'm really sorry,' he continued. 'I'm Luke.'

He waited and I realised I was supposed to reciprocate. 'Oh, I'm Cadence.'

What now? That was when I became acutely aware of the contents of my shopping trolley. First off, I should note that I've always had mild anxiety. Back then it wasn't nearly as bad as it is now though. But at the time, I'd been reading up on natural remedies to help with anxiety, and my trolley was full of bizarre items from the health food section with names I couldn't even pronounce — amaranth and acai berries and cordyceps mushroom powder. Luke seemed to become aware of the things in my trolley at the same time. Or maybe it was my fault that he noticed them. He followed my line of sight and locked on to one of the items.

'Maca root. Is that stuff good?' he asked.

'Umm, I don't actually know. I haven't tried it before.'

'How about the propolis? I've heard good things.'

'I don't know about that one either.'

He grinned at me. 'New health kick?'

I felt like a complete moron. He was going to think I was one of those people who jumped in and out of fads all the time. Atkins diet one week. Paleo the next. Sugar-free the one after.

The thing was, each time I expected him to scoff and walk away, each time I thought we were about to reach the moment where he'd realise he was bored with making fun of me — he didn't. He *kept* chatting to me. And slowly, I had to come to a conclusion. He actually wasn't making fun of me at all. He was being perfectly nice.

He put down his basket and placed one hand casually on the end of my trolley to lean on it, and he told me how he'd heard that amaranth was a great substitute for rice and even better for you than quinoa. He said the chia seeds were really good sprinkled over smoothies and he warned me that the cordyceps mushroom had a very bitter flavour. He said he worked as a pharmaceutical rep for a company that was in the process of branching out into more natural remedies, which was how he knew so much about several of the products I was buying.

He was so friendly that eventually my shoulders stopped clenching, and I stopped waiting for the other shoe to drop and relaxed into the conversation.

We chatted for a good fifteen minutes, shifting out of the way when shoppers needed to grab a box of Nutri-Grain or a packet of muesli. He even reached up to the top shelf to pass a box of honey wheets down to a little old lady with a walker, and I couldn't help letting my eyes stray to the strip of his lower back that was exposed when his T-shirt rode up.

As the conversation was drawing to an end, he asked for my number, and even though a voice inside was still questioning how he could possibly have any interest whatsoever in me, there was no way I was going to refuse. I gave him my number and I finished my shopping and went through the checkout in a daze.

By the time I was home, the dreamlike daze had lifted and I was back to thinking he couldn't possibly be interested in someone like me, and preparing myself for the fact that I would never hear from him again.

That's why his first text message was such a shock.

Hey Cadence, loved meeting you this arvo and really keen to see you again. Maybe over a coffee tomorrow? But if I'm being too forward, just say the word and I'll back off — sorry, never hit on anyone in the aisle of a supermarket before!! Uncharted territory!

I was thrilled. And of course I didn't want him to back off.

I rushed to reassure him.

Yes! I'd love to have a coffee. And you're definitely not being too forward! Where would you like to meet tomorrow and what time suits?

I hit send and then immediately worried that I sounded far too needy. *When? Where?* Slow down! He was the one who'd suggested the date, I should have waited for him to offer the details instead of demanding them. I knew I'd made a mistake when I watched the little dots appear to show he was composing a reply, but then they disappeared again and nothing came through. I waited. I stared at the screen and I waited. Then I locked my phone, put it down, walked around my living room — two laps — went back to it, picked it up and checked. Still no reply. I opened up the message screen and as I watched, the speech bubble with the dots appeared again. I held my breath. I waited. Nothing. They vanished again and still there was no reply.

I shook my phone in frustration. What was he thinking right now? Had I come on far too strong? Or should I have put more reassurance into my message? Should I have reiterated that I was definitely interested? Apologised for coming across a little withdrawn when we spoke? Explained that it was only because I was shocked that someone like him would ever want to talk to someone like me.

Somehow, I stopped myself from texting all those things and coming across as the most desperate woman alive. I turned on the television instead and kept myself distracted.

He didn't write again until four hours later. Just before midnight, as I was climbing into bed and berating myself for somehow completely destroying my one and only chance with the hottest guy I'd ever laid eyes on.

10 am at the Proper Coffee Pot cafe. Can't wait to see you.

Relief flooded my entire body. I hadn't screwed it up. He still wanted to see me. I ignored the tiny twinge at the back of my mind. The voice that said he didn't actually check if the location or time suited me. He didn't apologise for disappearing from the conversation and then texting so late at night. I was too excited to let that voice push through. I immediately googled the cafe and then my mood plummeted yet again. It was part of a chain and there were two within close proximity. Which one were we supposed to meet at?

I wrote back quickly.

Sounds great. Just double-checking, which Proper Coffee Pot did you want to meet up at?

I considered adding a kiss on the end of my message, but decided that was too much. We'd only just met. I added a smiley face emoji instead. I wanted to make sure my tone was friendly, and didn't come across as annoyed at not knowing which cafe. This time it showed as 'read' but no little dots came up. I waited and waited but still no reply. Eventually I fell asleep.

In the morning when I woke, the first thing I did was check my phone for a response from Luke. Nothing, no notification whatsoever. It was 8 am. I had two hours before I was meant to meet him. Should I send another text? Chase him up? I decided to hold out a bit longer, give him the chance to respond.

He didn't reply until nine thirty, right as I was starting to panic.

Sorry babe! Didn't see this until just now. The one near the supermarket where we met, obviously! Lol!

I felt like an idiot. But instead of baulking at how he'd laughed at me for not knowing, I was weak at the knees at the fact that he'd called me 'babe'. It was familiar so fast and I loved it. And anyway, of course it would be the one near Coles. That made the most sense. I should have known.

Here's the other thing you need to understand. At that stage, I'd been alone for *so* long. And I don't just mean single, I mean alone. That's why him being so familiar with me sent me all a-flutter. I work alone. I have no family. I don't have many friends.

Let me explain. My parents had me quite late in their lives. They'd pretty much given up on being parents when it happened, 'change of life' baby the 'experts' like to call it. Mum was forty-eight and Dad was fifty-three. They were ecstatic. They'd tried and tried for years and then all of a sudden, bam: baby. But Mum always had trouble fitting in with the other school mums in the playground. Not only was she older, but she was a career woman as well. Ran her own company, which she'd built from the ground up. And look, I don't blame her for this, but I could see the relationships being formed between the kids whose mums were best buddies. The extra playdates they had while their mums shared a bottle of wine, the sleepovers, the family barbeques, even camping trips over the school holidays.

And maybe it was me as well. I was an only child and I was used to enjoying my own company. I was used to going out to expensive restaurants with Mum and Dad and discussing politics or the stock market or seventeenth-century literature or art, in the same way other kids discussed Pokémon or handball with their parents. I never quite felt like I fitted in.

I know they both felt guilty when they got sick — one after the other — and then passed away just over two years ago. Before she died, my mum tried to apologise to me for not being one of the young mothers bouncing about in active wear, but I shut that talk right down. 'You can't be serious,' I said. 'You two have been the most amazing parents I could ever have dreamed of. You gave me more cultural experiences before I was five than most people get to have in their entire lives, you helped me find my love of art, and you taught me how to do my taxes and how to change a tyre and how to make a martini with a twist. I wouldn't change a single thing about you.'

And not only were they the most wonderful parents, they also left me with a safety net after they were gone. Well, more specifically, my mother did, when she transferred her company shares into my name. It's a safety net that I've never been able to bring myself to touch though.

As for my own work, as I mentioned, my mother helped me find my love of art, so I became an artist, and it's a solitary pursuit that I adore. But it is lonely. And often thankless. I can go from one month where I sell a piece a week and I feel like the biggest success in the world, to six months in a row where I don't sell a single thing and I'm convinced I'm an utter failure. As for friends, there were some connections that I formed in school, but I guess having such a solitary career has accidentally spilled out into the other parts of my life. I didn't mean for it to happen, but it did.

Anyway, despite all of the anxiety over Luke's slow replies and stressing over not knowing where to go, the date itself was utter magic. He was even more gorgeous than I'd remembered. He refused to let me pay for my coffee, and when I said I didn't want anything to eat (I was too nervous to eat), he insisted on ordering some scones with jam and cream because apparently they were too good not to at least try.

We stayed in the cafe for a full four hours. Around us the people who'd come in for morning tea cleared out and a new wave of people came in for lunch, and then they left as well. And we talked nonstop the entire time. For me, with my anxiety, being able to talk so easily for so long to a complete stranger was completely unheard of. I was nervous when he asked me what I did for a living. People can be so sceptical when you tell them you're an artist, and it can sound pretentious. And of course, then there's the follow-up questions: What kind of art? Can you actually make any money doing that? And they always want to see something right away. Do you have any pics on your phone of your work? And you know they're ready to judge it. My art is pretty subjective. When people paint lifelike portraits or realistic landscapes, it's easy to judge whether or not they're any good. But mine is very abstract, and most people don't know what to make of it.

My voice croaked when I answered his question. But his reply surprised me.

'Why do you say it like that?' he asked.

'What do you mean? Like what?'

'You sound so worried. Like you're almost apologising for your career. Being an artist is awesome. I wish I was artistic. Tell me about your art.'

Something about the way he spoke, and the way he tuned right into my insecurities, put me at ease and I was able to chat effortlessly about my work.

When we finally left, he walked me to the train station and kissed me on the cheek and suggested that next time we make it dinner.

CHAPTER TWENTY-EIGHT

I guess from there you could call it a whirlwind romance. Or maybe whirlwind is too tame. Maybe it was a hurricane. Or a roller-coaster, because of all the ups and downs. The problem was, the ups were so high, they made you want to ignore the dips. And the dips? They were so innocuous that sometimes you weren't even sure they'd happened at all. To start with, they were only ever in text messages. Face to face, we were always perfect. That's why the messages seemed so difficult to understand. Maybe I was misunderstanding his tone? Maybe he'd misunderstood my tone and that's why he was sounding so strange?

Like the one that came through after we went out to dinner for the first time. He picked me up and drove us there. Once again, the date itself was incredible — easy conversation, amazing food, and he still wouldn't let me pay or even split the bill. 'Next time, babe,' he reassured me as he handed over his credit card.

And when he dropped me home, we shared our first kiss and it was fireworks-unicorns-and-rainbows level amazing.

You know how sometimes you can kiss someone for the first time and it can be just that little bit awkward? One of you opens your mouth a tiny bit too wide or someone uses their tongue too soon or your teeth bump or you lean in the wrong way. But other times, you seem to fit together and it just works. For us, it just worked.

But then the message came through a little after midnight as I was about to fall asleep, my mind still on the kiss.

Thanks for an amazing night. I have to ask you this though, and don't hate me for asking, it's only that I've been hurt before. Please tell me you're not only after me for my money.

I was flummoxed. First of all, what money? Was there a secret fortune that I was supposed to know about? He seemed comfortable enough; he drove a nice car but I didn't think it was anything especially luxurious. And yes, he'd paid for our first two dates, but that was only because he'd insisted. I'd offered to contribute. I suppose he must have assumed that as an artist I'd be pretty hard-up. I might have been well set up for my future, but I definitely didn't live that way.

Once again, I rushed to reassure him: *Absolutely not in any way after you for money or anything like that. I like you for YOU! Next time, dinner is on me!*

I hit send and then cringed. Was it presumptuous of me to assume we'd be having dinner again when we hadn't actually made any plans for the next date yet? But surely we would be, the night had gone so incredibly well. Then I replayed our entire night in agonising detail, trying to pinpoint any moment where I might have led him to believe I was some sort of gold digger. Was it an expensive bottle of wine that we'd drunk? Who picked it? Him or me? It was him, wasn't it? Wait, *was* it? Actually, we chose it together, but he seemed happy with the one we'd landed on. What about the main I chose? It was pasta — linguine with prawns. That couldn't have been too pricey, could it? Should I have said no to dessert because we'd already had entrees? Three courses! Greedy, right? An hour later, I was still lying in bed, wide awake, wondering once again if I'd ruined everything when my phone lit up with another message.

Ha ha! Okay, deal. Thursday night suit?

Once again, I was flooded with relief. Everything was okay, he still liked me, he still wanted to see me again.

That's how it continued on. One magical date after another. It was the fastest I'd ever progressed in a relationship. Within three weeks we'd said we loved one another. He said the words first, but I'd already been dying to say them so I said them back in an instant. It was the perfect moment. On the same night, a text came through after we'd gone our separate ways: *Tell me the truth, did you only say I love you because I said it first? Because don't say it if you don't mean it. Don't fuck with my heart, okay?*

Again, I raced to reassure him. *Absolutely not. I meant every word — I even wanted to say it before you did!!! The only reason I waited was because I was scared you would think it was too soon. Please believe me, I really have fallen completely in love with you.*

The response came straight back. *Ok, I'm still scared that you might just be messing with me. I've never fallen for anyone as fast as I have with you. There's just something about you, you're special. Don't hurt me.*

I couldn't understand how someone as attractive and seemingly as confident and charming as him could ever have those kinds of doubts. Didn't he see what I saw when he looked in the mirror? And at the same time, how could he think I was something so special? I'm nice-looking, that's how I'd describe myself — just *nice*-looking. Nothing exceptional, not striking, not drop-dead gorgeous. I'm friendly enough, but I don't have one of those big personalities people gravitate to — I'm not the life of the party, I don't tell crazy stories that make people fall about laughing. There's nothing special about me. So what was he seeing in me?

I put it down to pure luck. I was lucky to have captured his interest, and if I lost him, I'd never have anyone nearly as amazing look my way, which meant I couldn't mess this up. Which meant I needed to be more careful! Obviously, I was doing something wrong to make him worry so often. Something about the way I'd said the words 'I love you' had made it seem like I wasn't being genuine, or perhaps it was the way I'd kissed him after we spoke the words.

Or, was it because we hadn't actually slept together yet? Was that the reason he had his doubts? Was it strange that we'd told each other we loved one another before we'd had sex? Or was it better this way? We were building up our emotional connection before the relationship became sexual.

The thing is, I'd been ready to sleep with him for the previous two weeks. I don't usually move that fast, but with him … I'd never wanted someone the way I wanted him. And I wanted every part of him.

Maybe he didn't know. Maybe I hadn't made my desires clear enough and that was why he was getting worried. But to be honest, if anyone should have been worried, it should have been me! I'd invited him back to my place three times now after different dates, and each time he'd turned me down. So at that stage, I was torn. If I kept pushing, kept asking him, would he get annoyed? Would it seem like I was being too pushy? But here he was in his messages worrying that I was going to break his heart, so if I pulled back, surely that would make him even more paranoid?

I'm not sure if that was the catalyst for my anxiety to increase; it's hard to remember exactly when things started to get bad. I guess I can't really pinpoint it because it was such a gradual thing. But I do know that the stress of not knowing how to keep Luke reassured was affecting me. I was so scared of letting him down. And at the same time, so scared that any day he would realise the truth that I already knew: I was nothing special. Certainly not as special as he said I was. And nowhere near good enough for someone like him. I lived in fear of that day coming. Obviously that was out of my control, but what was in my control was keeping him reassured that I did love him. That I could never ever break his heart. That of course I wasn't messing with him. That I wasn't after his money — although I still didn't really know what money he was talking about.

One week after we said we loved each other, we finally slept together.

The way it happened was a tiny bit strange. Luke was dropping me home and I was trying to decide if it would be too pushy for me to invite him in once again, when he smiled at me and said, 'All right, are you finally going to let me see inside this apartment of yours?'

I was taken aback. What did he mean 'let him'? I'd asked him so many times! But I was too happy that he wanted to come in so I didn't bother pointing that out. Instead I just said, yes, of course. He parked the car and we walked in with his hand on the small of my back, shepherding me just ahead of him. In the lift, he took me by surprise by suddenly pushing me up against the wall to kiss me, hard. It was the most aggressive he'd ever been and it was an incredible turn-on. Just as the lift was about to reach my floor, he spun away from me and hit the emergency stop button. Then he turned back to me and whispered, 'I have to have you right now.'

'Luke! We're almost there!'

'I know but I can't wait any longer.'

I laughed at him. 'But here? We can't do it in here!'

'Why not?'

'Because, that emergency button is busted. As soon as someone presses the button to call the lift, it'll move again. We might get caught.'

'Couldn't care less. I need you now.'

He stepped towards me and the look in his eyes was making my insides melt.

'There's another problem,' I said.

'What's that?' he asked as he placed his hands on my waist and guided me back up against the wall again.

'If no one calls the lift we're going to be stuck here forever. The emergency phone line doesn't work. There's no way to get it to go again.'

Luke smiled at me. 'Stuck in here forever with you? Sounds good to me.'

He started kissing me again and I stopped caring about someone catching us half naked or even about the two of us being trapped here all night. All I could think about was how much I wanted him. As it was, we didn't need to worry about either thing happening. He'd barely slipped a hand under my top when the lift started back up again and we quickly pulled apart and turned to face the doors.

Five seconds later, the lift reached my floor, and we stepped out to see a middle-aged couple waiting. I knew my face was flushed and my hair was probably slightly messed up, but I didn't care. We stepped past them, and as they disappeared into the lift, we stumbled down the hall to my door, stopping every few steps to kiss again, spinning in circles as he pushed me up against one wall and then the next.

The sex itself was without a doubt the best I'd ever had in my entire life. I might have thought I was hooked on him before that, but once we slept together, I knew irrevocably that I'd found my soul mate, that if he ever left me I'd be crushed beyond repair. That no one else would ever be enough for me.

From then on, I was terrified. One wrong move and I'd lose him. I couldn't let that happen. I had to be perfect for him. I had to be this special person that he, for some godforsaken reason, already thought I was.

So of course, that night while I lay in his arms, when he suggested that he move in with me, I said yes immediately — even though I was surprised that he'd want to move into my shoddy old apartment. I'd never seen his place; he always picked me up or else we met up at the place we were going to on our dates. But the way he spoke about his home, it sounded really nice. Just the odd comment he dropped here and there — the mention of hardwood floors in a restaurant that he said were similar to his, or a casual comment about his view of the Harbour Bridge from his living room. I wanted to ask him why, if we were to live together, it would be at my place and not his, but I also knew a question like that might make him doubt my intentions. Like I said, I needed to be the perfect girlfriend, and I was not going to come across as a gold digger, not when he was so afraid of me being after him for his money.

Thankfully, he offered an explanation himself. He'd been thinking about renovating his place for a while and this was the perfect opportunity. He'd move in with me while he got it done up, then the two of us could move back into his place and I could cancel the lease on mine. I hadn't even realised he owned his own place, but I didn't comment in case it came across the wrong way.

'I'll make a deal with you,' he'd said then. 'I can't chip in on your rent while I'm living here because the renos on my place are going to have me tapped out, but when you move in with me, my place will be your place. *Mi casa es su casa*, babe. You won't have to help out with the mortgage. Sound fair?'

'No, no! I can't let you do that. I'll pay you rent when we move into your place.'

'Look, we'll work it out when the time comes, okay? But trust me, we'll make sure it's fair.'

I see how it sounds *now*. Of course, I do, I'm not a complete idiot. But at the time I was utterly blinded. He moved in within a few days and convinced me it would be better if I didn't see his place at all until it was completely renovated. *Save it for the big reveal, babe.*

CHAPTER TWENTY-NINE

It was after he moved in that things started to change. As I'd said, we already had our ups and downs with his paranoid text messages, but something different started to happen. He started having to travel for his work. He'd be gone anywhere between two and four days at a time, sometimes even longer. And when he was away, contact was sporadic. One minute I'd get a text telling me how much he missed me, how he ached to touch me, how he couldn't stand to be apart from me for a second longer. The next he'd go two days without even responding to a single one of my texts or answering my calls. And then when I finally did hear from him again, he'd send me a simple: *Hey, how's your day going, babe?* Completely ignoring any of the previous messages I'd sent him. And I'd think: *What? What do you mean how's my day going? Where the hell have you been?* But I wouldn't ask, because the one time I did try to comment on his absence his response had been swift and sharp: *I'm under a lot of pressure from work. Don't need it from home as well.*

I sent him a flurry of apology messages and promised never to nag him again. When he arrived home two days later, he had a bunch of flowers for me and he kissed the top of my head and squeezed me so tight that for a second I thought he was going to crack one of my ribs, and then he *cried*. He actually cried into my hair. 'I'm so sorry I was short with you, I hated the way I spoke to you in that message, I hate to be that guy.'

I squeezed him back just as tight. 'No, no, no, you don't need to be sorry; I'm the one who needs to be sorry.'

He continued as though I hadn't spoken. 'You have to understand though, when you hassle me for not replying to one of your messages right away, it makes me afraid that you're going to get upset with me and leave me, okay? That's the only reason I lashed out, because I was scared of losing you.'

'Never,' I whispered back. 'You will never, ever lose me.'

Another time, we made plans to meet at a bar near his office for drinks on a Friday night. We were supposed to meet at five-thirty. I'd been working on a new piece that day and it was finally starting to come together. It was going to be included in an exhibition in a few weeks' time, which was a big deal for me. So I was relieved that I was getting it to work after having felt uninspired and stressed out recently. But at four-thirty I stopped work, showered, changed and dashed out to meet Luke. I made it to the bar just on five-thirty, ordered a drink, picked a table and sat down to wait.

Twenty minutes passed and I was on my second drink and checking my phone frequently. No word from Luke. I wanted to send him a quick text, just to make sure I hadn't got the time or the place wrong. But I didn't want him to think I was nagging, so I held off.

By ten past six, I was getting worried when a message came through.

I'll be there at 7.

I was annoyed. He was going to be an hour and a half late and he was only letting me know now! I could have kept working myself. Time in the zone with my art was precious. I checked myself though. He'd obviously got caught up at work. Maybe an unexpected meeting. Maybe he'd only had a second to dash out that quick message and that's why it was so abrupt. He'd explain it all when he arrived. And in the meantime, I figured I'd have something to eat and another drink.

I've never been much of a drinker. The first time I tried alcohol at a party when I was sixteen, I just didn't get it. Around me guys and girls were getting sillier and louder with every sip while I took one mouthful of beer and almost spat it straight back out. 'How can you drink this stuff?' I remember asking one of the girls as she stumbled past me.

'Close your eyes and think of England,' she slurred back at me, while her friend cackled back at her and shouted, 'That's for sex, you idiot!'

Anyway, I was drinking cocktails and eating bruschetta and playing Words with Friends on my phone, and I was pleasantly buzzed by the time Luke finally turned up at quarter past seven.

He kissed me on the forehead and then sat down opposite me. 'Eating without me, babe?'

I didn't let the slight edge to his tone bother me. 'Just some bread while I was waiting.'

He reached for the plate and pulled it towards himself. 'I'm starving,' he said, picking up a piece. 'I did an epic workout at the gym just now.'

It took me a second to catch on. 'You were at the gym?'

He swallowed his mouthful. 'Yeah, went there straight from work. You need a drink?'

I shook my head and watched him walk away to the bar. Inside, two voices were warring in my head.

That's rude. That's actually really, really rude. Instead of meeting me when he was meant to, he went to the gym. That's not okay.

Yes, but he's been under a lot of stress at work and the gym relaxes him.

So? It was rude!

I had to say something. I knew I had to. It didn't matter how much I loved him, or how afraid I was of losing him, I didn't deserve to be treated that way.

But then he came back with his drink, sat down opposite, reached out for my hands, looked me in the eye and spoke gently. 'Hey, I'm so sorry I kept you waiting tonight. I got held up at work with that dickhead Trent bailing me up about a new account. And I know I should have skipped the gym and come straight here to you, but I had all this pent-up anger after talking to Trent, and trust me, you wouldn't have wanted to see me right then. I thought it was better if I fixed my mood before I saw you. I'd hate to take any of my work stresses out on you.'

I nodded. 'It's okay,' I said.

'No, it's not. I shouldn't have left you waiting for so long. It was rude.'

The clenched-up fist that had been holding onto my stomach released its grip and I smiled back at Luke. He did care about me.

The next day though, I was back to struggling with my work. I was hungover after drinking all those cocktails and I couldn't focus like I had the day before. I was chatting with Luke on the phone about the trouble I was having and he told me he had an idea of how he could help me.

That was the night he first gave me the tablets. He said they were a natural remedy for my anxiety. They were called 'Vit-a-Peace' — made up of magnolia and phellodendron. All natural ingredients. Apparently, they'd help settle my nerves a bit, which would help me to get back into my work. Plus, he joked, then I wouldn't add to his stress when he was away by texting or calling him too often.

'It'll help you sleep better as well,' he said. 'Stop you from tossing and turning all night and keeping me up.'

He said it with a bit of a laugh, but I felt instant guilt. It was the first I'd heard I was keeping him up at night, I'd always thought I slept quite well! But I was happy to take them if it meant it was going to make him happier too.

When my anxiety got worse instead of better, I didn't put two and two together. Again, it might seem ridiculous that I couldn't see what was right in front of me, but you have to understand I had no reason not to trust him. I had no reason to ever suspect those tablets might not be what he said they were.

The worse it got, the more tablets I took. I developed strange habits that I'd never experienced before. My skin wouldn't stop itching no matter how hard I scratched at it, usually on my forearms. And the scratching would drive Luke to distraction, so I'd try my best to resist when he was around. At that stage I was still able to leave the apartment — although going out was getting more and more stressful — and I'd go to the chemist and try every type of cream and ointment to stop the itching, but nothing worked.

Sometimes I had blurred vision as well. And I was losing weight. Eventually I had to tell Luke the tablets were no good, that they weren't working for me. I didn't want him to think I was being ungrateful, or that I wasn't willing to keep trying to fix my anxiety issues. He didn't see how it was possible, as the tablets were all natural and only mild, but he was understanding. 'Of course,' he said, 'Don't worry, we can try something else.'

The next day he came home with new tablets called 'Serenity'. 'Still all natural, but these are stronger,' he said. 'They should help you get your anxiety back under control. I can't believe you're even functioning at the moment with how badly you're sleeping.'

Again, I was confused. I couldn't recall waking up through the night; I still thought I was sleeping fine. But Luke assured me that I was constantly sitting up in the middle of the night or mumbling in my sleep or even gasping for breath. 'Have you had a history of sleep apnoea?' he asked. I didn't think I did.

I wondered if I should see a GP, get an actual prescription rather than continuing to try the natural ones. But Luke said he'd had an old girlfriend on the kinds of meds a doctor would end up giving me, and he'd hated the way she was always so doped up that she didn't even seem to feel anything. Never happy, never sad, never angry, just coasting down the middle, he said. He felt like he could slap her across the face and she wouldn't even react. I did think it was an odd thing to say — why would he think about slapping her? But I agreed with him. I didn't want to end up like some sort of dazed zombie. I said I'd keep going with the natural tablets and that I'd try harder to get myself under control.

He kept promising that things would be different when his apartment was ready as well. 'We'll be happier there,' he said. 'This place is draughty and musty, and the smell of your oil paints is practically in the walls and the carpet. I don't know how you've been able to stand it all this time. I've been struggling to cope living here from the day I moved in.'

That one took me by surprise. And if I'm honest, it hurt a little bit. I know my apartment is old and shabby, but it's always felt like my cosy bohemian home to me. I'd always been happy here. That said, the idea of moving into a beautifully renovated apartment in Double Bay definitely appealed, and I was excited when he came home one night and said the builders had told him it should be done within two weeks.

The problem was, within that next two weeks, things got a lot worse. I was trying so hard. Taking two tablets in the morning and two at night, just as Luke instructed. Forcing myself to leave the apartment and get out into the world.

Doing everything I could to ignore the voices in my head telling me I would do something embarrassing if I went out; that I would make some monumental mistake, and that mistake would lead to me losing Luke. That's what it came down to. All my fears, all my insecurities came down to the one utter truth, the voices in my head saying: *You will lose him. If you make one wrong step, one wrong move, you will lose him. Something will go very, very wrong.*

And then something did go very, very wrong. My worst fears came true — I hurt Luke. I almost lost him. Of course, it was all a huge misunderstanding. At this stage, we weren't going out very much but we had a rare dinner out together after I'd forced myself to pull it together. *Snap out of it, Cadence,* I'd told myself. I was scared that if all we ever did was stay in, he'd get bored and leave.

I made the booking and I let him know well in advance that we had dinner plans. I agonised over what to wear and I spent the afternoon scratching my arms to pieces as I imagined all the things that might go wrong, all the ways I could humiliate myself or Luke by doing or saying the wrong thing. What if I ordered something off the menu and mispronounced it? Something silly like quinoa or sriracha. And then what if the waitress looked down her nose at me and giggled at Luke behind my back and next thing, Luke's run off with the beautiful anxiety-free waitress who knows how to pronounce sriracha and I'm left all alone in the world again.

To be honest, at first, I thought the dinner had gone well. It wasn't until we were on our way back home that I found out it hadn't, not at all.

Like that time in Grade Five at school when I ran late for band practice and the teacher said, 'Thank you for joining us, Cadence.' I'd beamed at her and replied, 'You're welcome!' Then she'd scowled and said, 'I didn't actually *mean* thank you, you silly girl.' It was like a slap across the face.

On this night, it was the waiter. I'd flirted with him. Of course I hadn't meant to, but once I saw it through Luke's eyes, I understood why he was upset. And knowing how scared he was of losing me, how paranoid he was, how low his self-esteem was, I should have been more careful. I thought I was just being friendly. He was one of those jovial waiters who put you at ease right away, and it was just what I needed when I was feeling so nervous about the night out.

At the end of the meal I tried to pay, but Luke snatched the bill away from me. 'I've got this,' he said.

Back in the car, he gripped the steering wheel tight enough that his knuckles turned white. I put my hand on his shoulder. 'What's wrong? Are you feeling okay?'

'I can't believe you did that.'

'Did what?'

'Acted like that, right in front of me.'

'Like what?' I was entirely clueless.

'Like a dumb slut throwing yourself at our waiter all night.' It was just like when the band teacher had called me a silly girl: a slap to the face.

'I wasn't flirting!' My voice tumbled, tripped over itself as I rushed to reassure him. 'No way, not even a little bit! I wasn't interested in him, I could never! Not when I have you, how could I, I mean, why would ...'

'Shut up.'

My mouth snapped closed. We drove home in silence and my eyes prickled with tears that I forced back. I didn't want to annoy Luke by crying. I swallowed down the hard lump that had formed in my throat and stayed quiet and still.

We made it all the way home, through the foyer and into the lift in complete silence. I was desperate to speak up, desperate to reassure him again, to convince him that I had no interest whatsoever in that waiter. We were halfway to the fifth floor when he stepped forward and slammed his hand against the emergency stop button. I was bewildered. Why would he do that when he knew we'd be stuck here until someone else came along?

When he turned away from the control panel and looked at me, at first I was afraid of him. For just a second I thought, *he's going to hit me*. But then the look in his eyes changed and the feeling passed and I couldn't believe I'd ever considered that possibility. Instead he stepped forward, put his hands on my upper arms and squeezed them hard as he looked into my eyes and spoke.

'You can't do that to me, babe,' he said. 'You can't make me feel that way. I've always told you how afraid I am of you messing with me, and tonight you made all my worst fears come true.' I opened my mouth to speak but he silenced me with a look. 'I'm serious,' he said and his fingers dug harder into my flesh. 'Don't ever, ever do that to me again.'

I nodded, but didn't speak because I didn't want to say the wrong thing. And then he kissed me. It took me by surprise because it didn't feel like that's where our conversation was heading at all. I almost didn't kiss him back because I was so blindsided, but then I pulled myself together and responded, otherwise he would have had another reason to be upset with me. I thought in a second we'd stop kissing and start trying to figure out how we were going to get out of the lift, but then he was pushing me back, pressing me up against the wall, reaching under my top, kissing me harder and harder.

I managed to break my lips away and speak. 'Luke, wait,' I began.

But he took hold of my chin, turned my face back and continued to kiss me. His entire body was pushed up against mine, but it was completely different to that first time we'd been in this lift together four months ago when he'd pushed me up against the wall. That time we'd both been fuelled by passion, and probably wine as well. But now I wasn't in the mood. Two minutes prior he'd been so upset with me. In the car on the way home, all I'd wanted to do was cry. There was no way I could get my mind focused on sex right now.

I managed to turn my face away again. 'Luke,' I said, 'should we ... could we maybe wait?'

'No,' he whispered in my ear. 'Want you now.'

It was a command, not a request, and I knew if I argued he'd be hurt again. I had upset him. I was going to have to do this for him to make it up to him. *Close your eyes and think of England.*

'O-okay,' I stuttered. I closed my eyes and tried to relax into it. Tried to forget about the possibility of the lift suddenly moving and the two of us getting caught by some elderly neighbour or a parent with young children. Tried to forget about the fact that only minutes ago I'd been afraid that he was actually capable of hurting me. And to be honest, he was hurting me a little now. My shoulder blades were smarting. He pushed me harder and harder against the wall, and when he reached down and started to hitch up my skirt he scratched the skin on my thighs.

He's just being passionate, the voice inside my head told me. *Extra passionate because tonight you scared him into thinking he could lose you. You can't blame him for that.*

But another voice whispered back, *But why can't he tell that you don't want this right now?* I couldn't understand why he wasn't reacting to the cues my body was giving him. And I couldn't help but wonder, if I told him no, if I tried to be firm, if I said, I don't want to do this right now, would he listen? Would he stop? I wasn't so sure that he would.

The truth was, I didn't want to test that theory. I didn't want to know the answer. So, I let him yank my underwear to the side and fuck me up against the wall of the lift, and it was rough and it felt loveless. It felt like angry sex. It felt like he was making a point: I own you. You're mine.

Afterwards, all I wanted to do was cry. But I didn't because I couldn't be sure how he might react if I did. So instead I bit down hard on my lip in order to squash down those feelings and I hugged him and pretended I was fine.

Eventually someone must have pressed the button to call the lift and it juddered back into life. When Luke beamed at me and took my hand, I smiled back as though everything was fine.

That night in bed, he made a suggestion. 'Until your

anxiety gets better, I think you should pull out of the Collins Street exhibition. Working on your piece is putting a major strain on you. You need to cut out the source of your stress.'

I chewed on my lip and lay very still. 'Umm,' I said, 'I … I can't, that's the only income I have coming up.'

'Don't worry about money, I'll cover your rent while you take the time to get better.'

'That's really sweet of you, but you don't need to do that. I'm okay to keep working.'

'I know you probably are, but this is something I want you to do for me. Seriously, you need to take the time to actually rest so you can get a handle on your mental health. I honestly don't think tonight would have happened if you'd been back to your old self.'

I felt a sting of shame when he said that.

'But how could you afford to cover my rent? You're trying to pay for all your renovations at the moment.'

'That was something I was going to talk with you about tonight, you know, before everything went wrong. I have some good news.'

'Oh yeah?'

'Yep. The renos are all done, babe. We're going to move in to my place asap.'

'Really? That's brilliant news!'

Only it didn't turn out that way. A couple of days later, Luke told me he was going to move in first and get everything set up ready for me. And then, after he'd moved a whole heap of our stuff out, he suggested I may as well see out the end of my lease.

'There's no point wasting money by breaking it early,' he said, 'and there's only two months to go. That'll give me heaps of time to make sure my place is absolutely perfect before you move in.' He said he'd have it filled with a beautiful mix of old and new, of the familiar and the strange. He said we'd be happy there.

The other thing he said was that this would give me exactly two months to get better. 'It'll be good for you to have a deadline,' he said. 'This is your motivation to work hard to get back to your old self. By the time my place is ready for you, you'll be strong enough to leave your apartment and live somewhere new without this big change triggering a breakdown. If you were to move right now, it might be too much for you — it could tip you over the edge.'

In the meantime, he said he'd still come back and sleep at my place all the time — when he wasn't away travelling for work, of course. But from the point when Luke moved out, I only deteriorated more and more. I wasn't working on my art, even though I desperately wanted to, even though I craved it. Instead I told myself that I'd made Luke a promise. He was right — I needed to take a break in order to get better.

To start with, I only left the apartment for essentials — basic groceries, that kind of thing. But each time I went out, it got harder and harder. I would imagine that people around me were whispering, pointing. I was dizzy and confused. Once I stepped out onto the road in front of a bus. The sound of the horn shook me awake and when I realised what I'd done, I was horrified. The look of anger on the driver's face only made it worse. I'd ruined his day. I'd almost ruined his life! Imagine. Having to live with my death, all because I'd been stupid and confused enough to step right out in front of him without checking.

Before I knew it, I'd confined myself to the inside of my building. The furthest I ever got was downstairs to check the mail slots in the foyer. I thought Luke would tell me that wasn't okay. I thought he'd push me to keep leaving the apartment, but instead he did the opposite. He told me it was probably for the best that I was staying inside.

'Keep taking the tablets,' he said. 'Keep resting. You're going to get better. Soon you'll move into the new place with me and everything will be different.'

I missed some of my things. I understood why he had to take them, and I knew that our new place was going to be beautiful, that he was getting it just right for us. But in the meantime, I missed them. I missed the bedside table made of beech timber with the green and blue handles. Sometimes I'd fall asleep with my fingers caressing the smooth wood, tracing the circular handles. Green, blue. Green, blue. It would lull me off to safety. Once it was gone, there were nights I'd close my eyes and reach out for it and find nothing but empty space.

And I missed my oval glass dining table. It was always cool to the touch. Sometimes I'd rest my cheek against it if I was feeling flushed and it would calm me in an instant. The blood would stop pounding against my temples. My breathing would slow. I could hear the ocean, as though I was holding a shell to my ear. In and out. In and out.

With the table gone, I'd sit on the couch to eat my meals, the plate perched on my knees. If I felt that rising heat climbing up from my chest, to my neck, to my chin … I'd try alternatives — the tiles in the bathroom. I would get down on belly and press my face to the floor. Or, the laminate benchtop in the kitchen — but nothing had the same effect as the table once did.

I'd spend entire days just sitting in the very centre of the bed, my knees drawn up to my chest, my arms wrapped around my legs. Every now and then I'd notice that my teeth were chattering as though I was freezing cold, when instead I was hot. Hot enough that I could feel sweat trickling down my back. Each time I'd notice, I'd force my mouth to hold still, sucking in my cheeks and biting down on the insides. But then my mind would take me somewhere else, and my teeth would start to chatter again and the cycle would repeat.

I was beginning to wonder if I'd lost the ability to function as a normal human being in the world. And I wasn't really quite sure when that had happened.

Obviously, Luke moving out was the beginning of the end for us. I just didn't know it. Not until a strange girl knocked on my apartment door and told me my boyfriend wasn't my boyfriend anymore.

CHAPTER THIRTY

The first time I met Georgia — well, not met her exactly, more saw her in the lift — I was a mess. I'd tried to tell myself that enough was enough. That I couldn't keep hiding inside, that I needed to see the sunshine. So, I took extra tablets. Luke had said they were all natural so I couldn't see any harm in it; maybe they'd give me the extra boost I needed to push myself out the door.

Instead, they had the opposite effect. At first, I didn't even notice there was someone else in the lift with me, I was so focused on myself. But within seconds of getting into the elevator, I panicked. I couldn't go outside. I couldn't leave the sanctuary of my own home. As the elevator descended it felt as though ants were crawling all over my skin. I slammed my hand against the stop button, and that's when I realised there was someone else in there with me. I was mortified! But I was also in the throes of some sort of weird reaction to those tablets and I couldn't calm myself down enough to explain. Thank God the lift had been fixed a couple of weeks prior, otherwise I would never have been able to get it moving again.

And then one week later she turns up at my door. I didn't recognise her at first. And she's shouting at me! Saying all these awful strange things about Luke, making accusations. None of it made any sense, and in the end I was afraid of her. Why on earth had I let her in? So, I got physical with her. I pushed her out of my apartment and out of my life, and the plan was to never think of her again. Unfortunately, though, Luke didn't allow that.

When he came home from his business trip, that's when the accident happened.

You see, I shouldn't have lied to him. I should have called him right away and told him that a crazy woman had turned up at my door saying things about him.

'But … but how did you know she was here?' I'd asked.

That only made him angrier. How dare I question him that way. That wasn't the point, Cadence! The point was, I should have told him, immediately.

I chanced another question. 'Luke, who was she? The things she was saying … she said that … she said she was your girlfriend.'

That's when he swung out. He didn't mean it, he was lashing out in anger and he caught the side of my face by accident. As soon as it happened he had me in his arms and he was apologising and crying and holding me and swearing that it would never, ever happen again.

And then three nights later, she came back for a third visit.

But this time, she showed me things. Photos. Messages. Emails. And the look on her face when she saw my bruise —

the shock and the fear, all mixed up with sympathy. And something else as well. I couldn't put my finger on it right away, but eventually I realised what it was. It was judgement. She was judging me for the way I was excusing what Luke had done.

To be honest, it was the judgement that got to me the most. There she was, shoving her phone in my face, telling me all these stories — half of which I could hardly follow because I was struggling to keep up — but the entire time, something was happening in the back of my mind. A small argument was taking place.

She's right you know: it's not okay that he hit you.

Yes of course — if he did it on purpose. But this was an accident.

But how exactly was this an accident? He swung out. His fist connected with your cheekbone. If he didn't intend on hitting you, then what was he doing?

Well, he was angry, he was upset, he was lashing out.

Lashing out at you.

No! Not intentionally.

Yes. Yes, intentionally.

But he loves me! He would never want to hurt me.

And yet he did. Think about the lift, think about the way he forced himself on you, think about the way you felt.

I don't want to think about that! I don't need to, it's over, it's in the past.

Think about what your mother would say if she could see you now. Think about the rage and the anguish that would swell inside her if she saw the bruise on your face. Tell me something — if a man ever hurt her, what would she do?

She would leave. She would never let him touch her again.

Well then, Cadence, what are you going to do?

When Luke arrived home, I have to admit I was torn. A part of me wanted to immediately give Georgia up. 'There's an insane woman behind our couch,' I wanted to hiss at him, while gesticulating wildly in her direction. And then let him deal with it. 'She's escaped from a mental institution!' he would say. 'Of course none of what she says is true; of course I'm not cheating on you.'

But as much as I wanted him to reassure me, as much as I wanted him to tell me it was all lies, I knew that this time, it wouldn't work. Georgia had proof, and what she'd said made sense. His being supposedly away so much for work gave him the perfect alibi to live a double life. I felt like a fool for believing his story about renovating his apartment, and I considered demanding that he show it to me right now. *Take me there,* I wanted to say, *take me there and show me that it's real, show me that you haven't been lying to me, day after day after day.*

But, deep down, I knew that was impossible. And maybe I'd known it from the moment he moved out. Maybe I'd known from the first day he gave me the tablets. Or the time he left me waiting while he went to the gym. Or the time he screwed me in the lift when he knew I didn't want it.

Or maybe I'd known from that first day we met.

I said it, didn't I? I said it made no sense that he would ever be interested in someone like me. I was right, wasn't I? The thing I didn't understand was why he had pretended. What was the point? And that scared me.

Right now, though, I had to deal with the problem at hand. I needed to distract Luke so that Georgia could escape from our apartment without being seen.

Luke kicked off his shoes and yanked off his tie. He came over and kissed me on the top of the head and looked down to see the bottle of Serenity tablets in my hand. 'You been feeling worse than usual today?' he asked.

'A little, I guess. Bit of a stressful day.' I pushed the bottle into my pocket.

'Really, how come?'

'Umm, I've just been trying some ideas for a new piece and I couldn't get anything to work, that's all.'

Luke's forehead creased. 'Uh, I thought we agreed you weren't going to work at the moment.'

'Yeah, I know. I wanted to play around with some art for fun, that's all.'

'All right, but I want you to take it easy. I mean, the fact that just trying to come up with ideas stressed you out proves that you really shouldn't be doing any art right now.'

'Okay, I won't. So how come you're home early today?'

Luke shrugged. 'Closed on a few big clients these last few days, figured I deserved an early mark.'

'That's great! Maybe we should go out? Celebrate?'

Luke tipped his head to the side and stared at me. 'Cadence, what the fuck? You can't go out. You know this. You haven't left the apartment in weeks, you're not well enough.'

I shook my head and tried to laugh it off. 'Oh yeah, of course, sorry. I got excited, that's all … confused. Well … I should cook for you then, right? Why don't you take a shower? I can have a look and see what we have.'

'That sounds more sensible.'

He headed for the bedroom and I wondered if I should make my move to get Georgia out now or wait until I heard the water running so that I knew he was actually in the shower. I moved slowly and silently across the room, keeping my back to the couch and my eyes on the bedroom door in case he suddenly reappeared. I crept around to the end of the couch and chanced a look back at where Georgia was crouched down hiding. When I saw her face, it hit me. She'd still been hoping for none of this to be true too. Like me, she wanted it to all be some ridiculous misunderstanding. But obviously listening to our conversation had cemented it for her. There were tears running down her face as she silently cried.

She made eye contact with me, and in that moment I knew — she and I were in this together. I wasn't going to say a word to Luke tonight. I wasn't going to accuse him of anything and I wasn't going to try to catch him out. I was going to play along and pretend I was still completely in the dark. I needed time so I could speak to Georgia again and figure out a game plan.

I held up one finger to her and mouthed 'wait'. She nodded.

'Can you bring me a fresh towel?' Luke called from the ensuite. 'You did do the washing, didn't you?'

'Yep,' I called back, trying to keep my voice level, even though I'd jumped a mile when I'd heard him call out. 'One second.'

I grabbed a clean towel, took it in to him, waited at the ensuite door until I heard the water turn on and the shower screen door close, then I ran back out to the living room.

'Now,' I said to Georgia. 'Come out now, quickly.' I reached behind the couch to pull her up and she grabbed hold of my hand. 'Come on,' I said, 'I don't know how much time we have.'

We were hurrying towards the door when Georgia stopped still. 'Cadence!' she said, her voice high with alarm.

'What?'

'Look, my purse. I left my purse on the coffee table. Do you think he saw it?'

I snatched it up and shoved into her hands. 'Fuck,' I said, 'I don't know, I have no idea … but he didn't act like he'd seen anything. Come on, you just have to go. We'll have to assume he didn't see it.'

'What do we do next?' Georgia asked as I shepherded her towards the door.

'We both pretend we don't know anything for now. And as soon as possible, we meet up and we figure out what the hell is going on. Hang on, give me a sec.'

I left Georgia at the door and dashed back to the kitchen bench where I kept a notepad and a pen. I scribbled down my number and then raced back and thrust the piece of paper at her. 'Text me tomorrow, but not until after 9 am, got it?'

'Got it.'

I pushed her out the door and closed it behind her, my heart beating so fast it felt like it was pulsing through the walls. I listened. The sound of the shower had stopped already. That had to be the fastest shower he'd even taken. Why so fast? Maybe he had seen the purse? I moved away from the door and positioned myself in front of the open fridge, pretending I was examining the contents to find something for dinner, just as Luke appeared from the bedroom. His hair wet, a towel tied around his waist.

'You say something, Cade?' he asked.

I turned around and did my best to look confused. 'What? Me? No, I didn't say anything.'

'Oh, I thought I heard you talking.'

I pursed my lips and shook my head. 'Nope. So, what do you feel like for dinner?'

PART THREE

Georgia and Cadence

CHAPTER THIRTY-ONE

Georgia

When she stepped out onto the street she let go of the chest full of air she'd been holding all the way down in the lift. A part of her wanted to giggle at the absurdity of it all. Here she was, running from her boyfriend's ex-girlfriend's apartment so that her boyfriend didn't catch her because apparently, the ex-girlfriend wasn't an ex at all.

But it wasn't funny, it was awful. And the more Georgia thought about it, the more the gravity of the situation crept up on her, forcing her to stop and lean one hand against a wall for support as she tried to calm her thoughts. *I'm not doing that again, I'm not going to have another panic attack and I'm not going to hyperventilate. I'm going to keep my shit together and get to my car and drive myself home and pour myself a drink.*

As she walked to her car, she silently thanked the parking gods for the lack of spots available out the front of Cadence's building when she'd arrived earlier, meaning she'd had to park around the corner. What would have happened if Luke had seen her car right there? Although there was still the chance he'd seen her purse on the coffee table, wasn't there? But surely he would have reacted if he had, said something to Cadence, right?

In the car, she turned the radio right down and spoke out loud to herself as she drove towards the turn-off for the Lane Cove Tunnel. 'What next, Georgia? What do I do now? Do I go to the police? Do I wait? Do I call someone? Rick? Amber? Mum and Dad?'

She kept her speed at about fifteen kilometres under the limit; she felt as though she couldn't trust herself to drive any faster, not while her heart was still thudding as if she'd sprinted around an oval.

Her heart didn't settle until she'd reached the M2, and it was then that she heard the ding from her phone sitting in the centre console. She chanced a quick glance at the screen. She wasn't going to pick it up, she absolutely wasn't. She knew full-well how dangerous, how distracting it was to use your phone while driving.

But the words jumped out at her.

It was from Luke, and she could see the preview of the message on her locked screen:

I know your secret …

Her heart skipped a beat. He knew. He knew she'd been at Cadence's place tonight.

There was nowhere on the motorway to pull over. Her windpipe seemed to contract and her breathing became laboured. She reached for the phone. Just a quick look. Just to see what the rest of the message said. She fumbled and the phone slipped from her hand and dropped between her legs. She looked down to see where it had gone. When she looked up again, she realised her mistake too late.

The car only clipped the barrier in the centre of the motorway, and maybe it would have been okay, but in her panic she over-corrected, wrenching the steering wheel back the other way. The sudden turn was enough to cause the car to lose its grip on the road. And in that moment, she couldn't understand why the world had started tumbling. It wasn't until just before she hit her head and blacked out that she realised.

Oh, the world isn't tumbling, I am.

I fucked up.

CHAPTER THIRTY-TWO

Cadence

I'd barely touched my dinner. That didn't seem to really concern Luke though; he cleared my plate away without asking if I was done.

'I've just got to make some work calls,' he said, 'so I might hole myself up in the bedroom for a bit, if that's okay?'

'Of course,' I said. 'I'll stay out here and give you some privacy.'

I wondered what he was actually doing. Calling Georgia? A thought occurred to me then. What if there were others? What if he was cheating with more than one woman? Was that all this was to him? Some kind of conquest to bed as many women as possible? To string us along just because he could? Or was there more to it than that? At this point, anything seemed possible.

As Luke picked up his computer and his phone and headed for the bedroom, I pushed my hands into my pockets and my fingers touched the bottle of tablets I'd shoved in there earlier. I remembered Georgia's comments as I'd taken the Serenity pills.

Those aren't Serenity.

She'd said it with absolute certainty. I reached into my pocket and pulled out the jar, then unscrewed the lid and poured a few into my hand. I went to my computer, which was set up on a desk in the corner of the living room, and tapped the keys to wake it up. I copied the name of the medication from the bottle into Google and hit image search. The screen filled with various pictures — some packets, some bottles, and some of the actual pills. None of them looked like the large oval-shaped pills I was holding in my hand. I sat still for a minute, my hands shaking, and then I felt a rage swell up inside of me and slammed my hands down on the desk, sending the pills flying everywhere.

'You all right out there?' Luke called from the bedroom, a note of irritation in his voice.

I swallowed then called back, 'Yep, fine, sorry.' I didn't bother trying to come up with an explanation. I had no idea what I would say, I couldn't think clearly. Thankfully, he didn't pursue it.

I stood up and strode into the kitchen, yanked open the door of the small cupboard above the microwave where I kept all my medications, and grabbed out the other packets and bottles of tablets Luke had been giving me over the course of our relationship. The Vit-a-Peace that was supposed to be a fully natural remedy. The multivitamins. I took them back to the computer and did more searches.

More lies. Not one of the images I found matched up with the corresponding tablets Luke had given me. I picked up one of the tablets and tried putting a description of it into the search engine to see if I could figure out what the hell I'd been taking: *Large, white oval tablet, shiny coating.* There were hundreds of results and none of them seemed to match the ones I'd been taking. It was too generic. I tried another one. *Square tablet with rounded edges. Pink.* I added the numbers that were imprinted on the side: *54 883.*

A website appeared in the search results, called 'pill identifier'. I clicked through to the site and filled in the drop-down boxes.

One result: methadone.

Methadone? He'd been giving me methadone? Wasn't that for people trying to come off serious drug addiction? I opened another tab on my browser and searched 'Methadone tablets side effects'. A list appeared. Common side effects included anxiety, nervousness, restlessness, weakness … the list went on. More serious side effects were hallucinations, dizziness and confusion.

I tried entering the details of another one into the pill identifier site.

Shape: Round

Colour: Blue

Scoring: one line

Markings: A 51

Fourteen results. I scrolled through them and spotted an image that matched the tablet. Oxycodone. A narcotic pain reliever. Side effects included dizziness, sleeplessness, itching. *Do not stop taking this drug suddenly without talking to your doctor.*

My hands were shaking. I didn't know if I wanted to cry or scream. What had he done to me? What had I been putting into my body? And how much? How close had I been to overdosing when I blindly took as many tablets as he told me to, believing they were perfectly safe? I thought back to that day I'd stepped out in front of that bus. I thought of the weeks I'd spent trapped inside my own home, afraid to go out because my anxiety was crippling me. How dare he? Was any of it real? I'd always had issues with anxiety, before I'd even met Luke, but it had never been like this before. I thought back to all those times he'd convinced me I was sleeping badly and it had seemed so odd because I thought I was sleeping fine. It was because I really was sleeping fine, wasn't it?

And *why*? What was Luke's motivation here for giving me these tablets? For lying to me? For keeping me on the hook while he went off and started a new life with a new woman?

I remembered the time in the lift when I'd been afraid he was going to hurt me. I'd convinced myself he would never be capable, but then he did, didn't he? He'd swung out and he'd hit me. If I confronted him about all of this, if I forced his hand, how was he going to react? How bad might it get?

So, what to do next? It wasn't like I could run away, this was my home. If there was a chance he could be dangerous, then I needed to be smart about this, I needed to be careful. I wouldn't flush the tablets away, I'd pretend to keep taking them. But at the same time, I was going to need to figure out what the hell was actually going on. I needed to know what he wanted from me, I needed to know what his endgame was.

I needed to know why he'd made me fall so deeply in love with him only to break my heart.

And in the meantime, I had to talk to someone — a doctor. I needed to find out what damage had been caused by this concoction of tablets he'd been feeding me. And whether I could stop or if I had to wean myself off them.

Which meant tomorrow I was going to have to pull myself together and leave the apartment. That was going to be easier said than done. And who could I see to ask these kinds of questions without being questioned myself? I didn't really have a regular GP; if I needed to see a doctor, I just went to the medical centre and asked for the first available.

Actually, maybe what I needed was a chemist. That would be less official than a doctor's appointment, right? And they should know their medications, shouldn't they? There was an old school friend I'd stayed connected with through Facebook who worked as a chemist in St Leonards. I decided to send her a message right now, asking if I could come and see her tomorrow, before I backed out.

Hey Michelle, I know this is out of the blue, but I was hoping I might be able to ask a favour of you? Could I come and talk to you for some advice about some medication I'm on?

I was relieved when the messaged showed up as 'read' immediately. That meant hopefully I could get this all arranged before Luke came back out of the bedroom.

Michelle responded with the obligatory platitudes:

Cadence! How are you? How long has it been? Etc. etc. But then she got to the point.

Of course you can come and talk with me! I work 8 till 6 Monday to Thursday and 10 till 4 on Sundays. Although honestly, I'm sure any pharmacist could assist you. Or else your GP, of course.

I came back quickly: *Can I come and see you tomorrow?* I knew she was going to think it was weird, but I needed to be locked in.

Her response came back within a minute or two: *Yeah, tomorrow works. Listen, why don't you come by around 12 pm and I'll take a break so we can grab a coffee together. Will be good to see you.*

Now I had no excuses. I absolutely had to leave the building tomorrow.

*

'Come and sit with me,' said Luke. 'There's some stuff I need to talk with you about.'

It was later that night and I was feeling weirdly wired. Obviously, I hadn't taken any more of the tablets since the two I took earlier when Georgia was here, before I knew that they weren't harmless vitamins. I wondered if they were the reason I was feeling wide-eyed and jittery.

Luke took me by the hand and guided me to the couch. He had his laptop tucked under one arm. He sat down and I moved to the other end of the couch, wanting to be as far away from him as possible. Then I panicked as I realised that would probably seem suspicious, and I quickly shifted along to sit beside him.

Luke opened up his laptop and tapped at the keys. 'Here's the thing,' he said. 'I know I told you we'd be right with money while you took some time off, and that I was back on top of things now that the renos are all done. But it turns out I fucked up a bit with my budgeting. Here, take a look at this.' He turned the screen towards me so I could see a spreadsheet with figures and dates and a list of bills like rent, electricity and groceries.

'I know you might not be able to cope with the extra stress right now, but I thought it was important to be honest with you. We're in a bit of trouble. See, look here.' He pointed at a cell in the spreadsheet with a red minus figure. 'Right there, we go under after these bills are paid. Now I've actually got some savings that could cover it, but they're tied up in term deposits at the moment and I can't access them for four more weeks. So, we just need to sort something out to get through until then.'

'Okay,' I said, wondering where he was going with this. He couldn't want money from me, he knew I didn't have any right now. He was the one who'd pushed me into giving up the Collins Street exhibition. 'Well, like I said, I'm definitely improving, so I can get back to work —'

He cut me off. 'No way. You have to focus on getting better. But I was thinking, maybe there's some things we could sell.'

His eyes strayed to my art equipment that was stacked in a corner of the room: my custom-made oversized easel, my canvases and Mijello paints. My heart jumped. He wouldn't ask that of me, would he?

My voice stuttered as I responded, 'I–I don't know if I have anything worth selling.'

He chuckled. 'It's okay, babe. I'm not going to ask you to sell your gear. I know how precious it is to you.'

For the first time, I could hear the patronising tone in his voice. Had that always been there? How had I never noticed it before?

'No, I was thinking more about any assets the both of us might have. I don't know about you, but I picked up some shares from an old job that I reckon I can sell for a bit of extra cash.'

My stomach dropped. He knew. Somehow, he knew about my safety net. About the small fortune I had set aside for later on in life. The shares I kept a careful eye on, while simultaneously trying to pretend they weren't there because I didn't want to ever become complacent with my work, or get too excited about how much they were worth and sell them and squander the money on something frivolous.

Or at least that's what I told myself. The truth was, the real reason I hadn't been able to bring myself to sell them was because they were my connection to my mother. To the company she'd created from the ground up.

But then again … how could he know? No one knew about those shares.

They were already worth quite a bit when my mum signed them over to me, but last year, something had happened. Her company had merged with someone else's. The value of the shares went up, *a lot.*

I spoke carefully. 'Umm, I don't think I have anything like that.'

'Are you sure? You might have picked some up somewhere along the line. Some companies include shares as part of their salary package, for instance.'

I wrinkled my nose as I pretended I was thinking hard. *Think Cadence, think.* Does he know? Or was this some sort of wild coincidence? But that seemed unlikely. Should I continue to play dumb, or fess up to the fact that I did indeed own shares? The problem was, if he really did know and I lied, then he was also going to know I was onto him, wasn't he?

He was giving me a funny look now. I was waiting too long. And maybe he could see it in my eyes. I made a decision.

'Yeah, actually, now that you say it, I do remember getting some shares transferred over from my parents a while back. But they weren't worth a lot so I didn't really pay them much attention. I'd have to really search to find out how to even access them now.'

He shrugged. 'Hey, could be worth checking out. When you first received the shares you probably would have been set up with some kind of trading account. Do you have a standard password you usually use?'

'Not really. I use lots of different passwords.'

'That's okay, don't stress. Why don't you let me look into it for you? I don't want you to have the extra worry right now of trying to track down some old login. Just tell me some of the passwords you've used in the past.'

'Okay, sure,' I said. 'Umm, sometimes I use the name of the dog I had when I was little. His name was Cactus.'

'Cute. Right, Cactus — what else?'

'And I use Mercury, because, I don't really know why. I like it, that's all. But with the number 3 instead of the letter E. And I've also used 55Larkin, because I once lived at 55 Larkin Place.'

Somehow, the lies tumbled easily from my lips. Obviously, I wasn't going to give him the real password for my ASX account. I never had a dog when I was young, my dad had allergies. But I always thought if I did have one I'd name him Cactus. No idea why. And I wasn't stupid enough to use one of my addresses as a password.

Even as I knew there was no way any of what I was saying would allow him to access to my shares, my fingers were still twitching to grab hold of my computer and log in to my ASX account and do something with my shares. Hide them away from him somehow. Stop him from finding them.

I went to bed that night still feeling hyped. After we'd finished discussing our finances, Luke had yawned and said how tired he was after dealing with all that money stuff. I headed to bed with him, wondering how I was going to cope lying next to him all night long. There was no way I could sleep right now. I lay facing the other direction, slowed my breathing and pretended I was drifting off, but in reality I was wide awake. So, I was well aware when Luke quietly climbed out of bed about forty-five minutes later. I shut my eyes and held still, listening as his footsteps left the room. I waited to hear if he headed for the bathroom, but he went down the hall to the living room. I sat up in bed and strained to listen, wondering what he was up to. On his computer, I guessed, trying out my passwords. Could I sneak out after him and see exactly what he was doing? But what if he caught me?

The curiosity was burning inside of me though. I needed to know. I pulled back the covers slowly and placed my feet onto the floor. Then, ever so carefully, I stood and began to creep from the room and down the hall. At the entrance to the living room, I stayed close to the wall, terrified that the sound of my heart hammering in my chest would give me away. I peered around the corner, praying he had his back to me.

He did. He was on the couch, bent over a computer, but it wasn't his, it was mine. I fought back the desire to spring him, to force him to come up with an explanation, and instead backed away and crept back down the hall to the bedroom. *Play it safe*, I told myself. Even using my computer, he wasn't going to be able to log in to my ASX account. I wasn't silly enough to have any passwords saved on my computer.

Back in bed I had an idea. Until all of this was over, it would be good if I had a way to keep tabs on him when he wasn't here. I rolled over and looked at his bedside table. He'd left his phone sitting there. I knew the passcode, not because he'd ever told me and not because I'd ever thought I'd need to check up on him, just because I was good at noticing patterns and I'd seen his fingers move around the screen whenever he unlocked his phone. He was quite slow at typing it. Bottom left, top middle twice, middle right, top middle, middle right: 722626. And I'd also worked out that it actually spelled out the word PACMAN, which made sense, because he'd joked once that there would never be a better computer game than Pac-Man. I'd never used it. I'd never needed nor wanted to. But now I did.

Ever so quietly, I sat up, leaned across and picked up his phone. I held my breath as I typed it in. Please be right, please be right.

722626.

The phone unlocked.

Moving quickly, I went into the extras folder and found the Find My Friends app that was standard on iPhones. I opened it up, clicked add, and typed in my number. Next to me, my own phoned dinged with the notification, 'Luke wants to share his location with you.' *Fuck*. Had he heard that from out in the living room? I held still, barely breathing as I waited to see if there was movement from Luke. I couldn't hear anything. I quickly closed the app and locked Luke's phone then put it back where I'd found it. On my own phone, I accepted the invitation and then put it aside.

I stayed awake until I heard him coming back down the hall, and once again I closed my eyes and calmed my breathing. I felt the mattress dip as he climbed into bed next to me and then all of a sudden, his whole body pressed up against my back and I had to physically control myself to stop every inch of my body from clenching in response.

'Babe,' he whispered into my ear. 'Babe, are you awake?'

I kept my eyes shut, my breathing slow. 'Cadence,' he tried again. And then his hand closed on my waist and gave a short, sharp squeeze. I had to react, there was no way I could pretend to sleep through that. I tried to play the part of being roused from a deep sleep and turned my head slightly.

'What's up?' I asked, keeping my voice groggy.

'I can't sleep. I thought maybe we could … you know?' He pushed his groin against my butt suggestively and instantly I felt ill.

'Oh,' I said, thinking fast. How was I going to be able to turn him down without offending him? Or even worse, without him forcing himself onto me like he had in the lift that time. 'I would,' I whispered, 'but it's that time of the month. Sorry.'

'So?' he said, 'I don't care if there's a bit of mess.'

'Umm, it's really heavy right now and I think it would be really uncomfortable for me. I've had bad cramps. Can we try again another night?'

He huffed and all I wanted to do was roll over and slap him. *Get away from me you creep, get your goddamned body away from mine.* I really wasn't sure how long I was going to be able to keep playing along with any of this. What the hell was I going to do?

'Okay, fine. But can you at least give me a blow job then instead?'

Jesus Christ! There was no way I could do that.

'I wish I could, but I think I'm getting a cold sore just inside my mouth. Sorry. Night.' I turned back away again and held my breath as I waited for his response.

Several seconds passed and then the pressure released as he rolled back away from me.

'Well, that's just great,' he said.

'Yeah, sorry.'

'No worries. Night.'

'Night.'

I'm not sure how long it took me to fall asleep, but eventually the tiredness sucked me down and I slept fitfully with mixed dreams of Luke and Georgia and fistfuls of tablets being crammed down my throat.

CHAPTER THIRTY-THREE

Cadence

Despite the lack of sleep, I woke early. I wanted to be on guard and I didn't want to give Luke another opportunity to be alone with my computer. As soon as he left for work I wanted to check on my shares, make sure he hadn't found a way to access them last night. And then I was going to start preparing myself. I had to make sure I could leave the apartment when the time came to go and meet Michelle.

The first hiccup came, though, when Luke sat up in bed and leaned across to kiss my cheek. He stretched his arms out lazily and smiled at me. 'I'm going in late today, been working too much. We can spend the morning together.'

'Oh really?'

'Yeah. I've been leaving you here alone so much, I feel bad.'

I spoke carefully. 'You don't need to feel bad, not at all. I know how busy you've been.'

'Still though, you must have been so lonely being stuck here these last few weeks. I want to make it up to you.'

I was worried that if I kept pushing for him to go to work he'd get suspicious, so I forced my face into a smile. 'Okay, that sounds great.' I couldn't stay in bed with him a moment longer though, so I threw back the covers and climbed out. 'Taking a shower,' I said, praying he wouldn't invite himself along. Thankfully, he didn't.

After I showered and dressed, I headed out to the kitchen, where Luke was rummaging through the cupboards. 'Slim pickings for breakfast,' he said.

I nodded. 'Yeah, we've been low on supplies lately … Obviously I haven't been able to —'

'You don't have to apologise, babe! I know it's not your fault you can't go out shopping at the moment.'

I'm not going to apologise, I thought. But I bit my tongue and nodded.

'I'll find something to eat. Have you taken your tablets yet this morning?'

'Yep.'

'Good. That's the only way you're going to get better.' He pulled a packet of cereal out of the cupboard. 'Bowl of dry Sultana Bran, that'll see me through. Want some?'

'Not really that hungry,' I said.

He didn't seem concerned. 'No worries, babe.'

I wondered if he'd stopped acting like he cared about me a long time ago and I just hadn't noticed because I'd been so blinded. I hated feeling like such a fool.

*

By 11 am I was worried. It was getting closer and closer to the time I'd need to leave if I wanted to still make it to St Leonards in time to meet Michelle, and I had no idea when Luke was going to go to work. I couldn't leave until he was gone. Obviously, it suited him to believe I was still housebound and I didn't want him to know I was gearing myself up to get the hell out of here. I just hoped that when he did leave I was going to be able to follow through.

Finally, at eleven-thirty his phone rang. I watched him as he answered it and then very quickly moved away from me and into the bedroom to continue the call in private.

'Really?' I could hear him saying. 'Oh my God … okay, sure … of course.' Then the door closed and I couldn't hear him anymore. Two minutes later he emerged from the bedroom again.

'Everything okay?' I asked mildly.

'Ah yeah, sure. Just some work stuff. He started gathering things up. 'All right,' he said, 'as much as I'd love to stay here all day with you, someone's gotta make us some money!'

God, I wanted to slap him.

To be honest, once he was out the door, I think it was a good thing that I didn't have any time to spare. Too much time trying to work up the nerve to leave the apartment after all this time being afraid to go out and I might have over-thought it and had a panic attack. Instead I pushed myself into autopilot. *Grab what you need: wallet, keys, phone, the tablets to show Michelle. Put one foot in front of the other. Out the door, close it and lock it behind you. Down the hall. Down the stairs —* I wasn't getting in that lift today, it brought back too many memories. *One floor at a time, count them as you go: fourth floor, third floor, second floor, first floor, ground. Now you're in the lobby. And you've made it this far before. But this time, you're not turning back and you're not slowing down and you're not giving yourself any time for excuses, you're not giving yourself any time to think. Because you can't — if you do, you'll be late, and you can't be late. Through the lobby, all the way up to the front door. Don't think, don't think, don't think. Push on the heavy front door, and there, you've done it. You're out into the street. And the weather is beautiful and God, you've been so stupid to stay stuck inside for so long.*

But then the noise of the traffic and the people chatting as they walked past and the drone of a lawnmower in the park across the street ... I stumbled back, pressed my hands against my ears, closed my eyes and breathed in deeply. *You can handle this, Cadence. Yes, it's noisy and it's startling and it's pushing your heart up into your throat, but it's also everyday sounds that you used to be perfectly fine with. Pull it together.*

I opened my eyes and slowly dropped my hands from my ears. One foot in front of the other, I headed for the train station.

As soon as I found a seat on the train I did the one thing I'd been desperate to do since the moment I'd woken up that morning. I logged into my shares account. Everything looked fine. My shares were still there. The value was still the same. Actually, it looked like they'd gone up a couple of points since I'd last checked. That was good to see. I exhaled slowly. They were safe, they were fine.

It was a short walk from St Leonards station to the chemist where Michelle worked. When I arrived, I hesitated out front.

What was it going to be like, catching up with Michelle after all these years? We'd actually been pretty good friends in high school. Close. But we'd drifted apart soon after school finished. Was it going to be awkward? And what was she going to think when I asked her about these tablets? Would she suspect that I was some kind of junkie? My breathing started to quicken.

I can't do this! What am I doing here? What was I thinking?

I closed my eyes and thought of my apartment. Safe, warm, familiar. I needed to get back there.

'Cadence!' The voice broke through the chaos inside my head and I opened my eyes to see Michelle standing in front of me. 'I can't believe how long it's been.' Over her chemist uniform, she was wearing a bright pink woollen coat that clashed brilliantly with her long red hair.

I tried to slow my breathing, tried to arrange the features on my face so I looked normal, but I could see it in her eyes — she knew something wasn't right.

'Are you okay?' she asked. 'Here, come on, let's go find somewhere to sit.' She took me by the arm and guided me away from the chemist. 'There's a great cafe over here. We'll get you a coffee.'

I let her lead, aware of the fact that I still hadn't spoken a single word. She was going to wonder what the hell she'd got herself into, agreeing to meet up with me. We sat down at a table out the front of the cafe, underneath an outdoor heater.

'Right,' she said. 'I'll go in and order, you wait right here. What can I get for you? Cap? Latte?'

I pushed myself to respond. 'You don't have to —'

She waved her hands at me. 'Don't be silly, it's fine.'

'Okay. Cappuccino, please.'

'Done,' she said. 'I'll grab you something to eat as well. I'll be right back.'

I felt mortified as I waited at the table for her to return. *Pull it together, Cadence! What is wrong with you?*

Michelle returned to the table a few minutes later and sat down opposite me. She put a glass of water and a small plate with a cookie down in front of me. 'Do me a favour and eat some of that now, please. I want to see if we can get some colour back in your face.'

I didn't know what to say so I did as I was told, breaking off small pieces of the cookie and eating it. I realised after a few bites that I was actually ravenous, and before I knew it, the entire cookie was gone.

'Good,' said Michelle. 'Feeling a bit better?'

I nodded. 'I'm so sorry,' I said. 'I didn't mean to do that, I just … I was about to come into the chemist to find you and then I …'

'Don't apologise. It's fine. How long have you been having panic attacks?'

'Umm, I'm not really sure … I don't know if it is a panic attack really. It's sort of complicated.'

Our coffees arrived, along with some more food. One raspberry muffin and one choc chip.

'I wasn't sure what flavour you'd want,' Michelle said. 'Happy to share both?'

'Sounds good.'

'All right, tell me what's going on with you. What's happening with these complicated, possibly but possibly not panic attacks of yours?'

It was like we were straight back in high school. Michelle had always been the motherly type. And there was no preamble with her either: she was straight to the point. I wondered how much I should tell her.

As it turned out, I told her everything. It was something about the way she listened quietly and gently encouraged me. The twenty years since high school melted away and the words tumbled out. I told her about meeting Luke. About the strange way our relationship got started, with his paranoid messages that made me feel like I needed to constantly rush to reassure him, and then how fast it all progressed. I told her about the way he'd started commenting on how I acted, on my sleep, or on the things I said, and made me believe my anxiety was ramping up. About the first day he'd given me tablets.

I hesitated at this point. Would she judge me for blindly taking the pills Luke had given me rather than going to see a doctor for myself? But she didn't look judgemental and I pushed on with my story.

When I explained the part about discovering what the tablets actually were, she let out a small gasp. 'Bloody hell, Cadence.'

That's when I pulled the tablets out of my bag to show her. She took each bottle and tipped the pills onto the table, tutting as she looked at the misleading labels and then at the actual pills.

'You're right,' she said. 'I recognise these ones. They're strong. How many of these were you taking?'

'Two in the morning and two at night.'

'Fuck me. How are you still functioning?'

'Well, I didn't take any last night or this morning. But I'm thinking maybe that was a mistake … I know I probably shouldn't be stopping cold turkey. That's why I think what happened before might not have been so much a panic attack as some kind of withdrawal reaction.'

'Maybe, it's possible. And you're right, stopping cold turkey on some of these is bad. Okay, here's what you need to do. With these ones, go one week with one at night and one in the morning, then one week with only one a day, then a week on half a tablet, then you should be okay to stop.' She picked up a different tablet. 'These you can come off faster. Halve your dose for a week and then stop. These white ones, you know what they are?'

'I'm not sure, there were too many options when I looked online.'

'They're familiar. Give me a sec.' She picked up her phone and started typing.

'Aha!' she said a few minutes later. 'I've got it. I knew they were familiar. They're quetiapine. You can stop those now, they're out of your system within twelve hours.'

'Okay,' I said, 'I'll put those ones straight in the bin.'

'No, you bloody well won't!'

'What?'

'You're taking them to the police, aren't you?'

'Oh. I … I wasn't sure.'

'Cadence, this guy has been drugging you. You need to get the hell away from him and you need to report him. Straightaway. This is serious. This is abuse.'

'But he never … he hasn't …'

'He hasn't what? Hurt you? So where did you get that black eye, sweetie?'

'I … yes, I mean, he did, but that was one time only, and …'

'Cadence, even without the black eye, the guy's been drugging you!'

'But he didn't force me to take them, I took them on my own. I was the idiot who didn't look into it properly.'

Michelle sat back and ran her hands through her hair, breathed in deeply and then leaned forward again. 'Cadence, look at me. This. Is. Abuse. He manipulated you. He led you to believe you were taking vitamins, for Christ's sake. You need to promise me that you're going to go to the police and that you're going to leave him.'

'I'm … I'm definitely going to leave him. I just don't know how to do it. I'm scared.'

'Well then, that's why you're going to get the police involved. And if you want, I can be there with you when you break it off with him. I'll back you up.'

'I couldn't ask you to do that. We haven't even spoken for twenty years.'

Michelle shook her head. 'Doesn't matter. I don't care how long it's been, you're still my mate and I'm here for you. Right, you need a plan in place. When are you going to do this?'

'Okay, well, he's at work right now, but he should be home later tonight, around five-thirty, I think.'

'Okay, later today I'll come over to your place and be with you when you tell him it's over. He claims he has some other apartment, right? In that case we can tell him to pack up his shit and leave right then and there. In the meantime, you need to go and talk to the police. Will you do that today? Now?'

'Umm … maybe … or I might do that in the morning.'

Michelle frowned. 'Cadence, you have to promise me you're going to go to the police.'

'I will,' I said. 'I just need some time to get my thoughts together. Coming out today, it's been hard. I kind of just want to get home. And I know I'll be safe because Luke won't be there.'

'All right, fair enough. How about the other woman — Georgia, wasn't it? Do you have a way to contact her?'

'No, I'm not sure how to reach her. I gave her my number but it was all in a rush, there wasn't time to get her number. I'm a bit worried — I told her to call me this morning and I haven't heard anything.'

'Hopefully she's fine. Maybe she's already broken it off with him. Here, give me your phone. I'll put my number in it for you, then you can text me your address and I'll come round later after work. You're going to get through this, okay?'

'Michelle,' I asked, 'why are you being so nice to me? After all this time, I feel like most people would just say "not my problem".'

Michelle shrugged. 'Because I've always liked you, Cadence. You're a good person. And because women have to stick together.'

CHAPTER THIRTY-FOUR

Georgia

As she woke, the first thing she became aware of was the tube coming out of her nose. She crinkled her nose as though she could shake it away, but it was stuck there.

I know what that is. That's an NG tube. Why is there an NG tube in my nose? Who put that there?

She opened her eyes and saw nothing but blurred shapes. She blinked a few times and the shapes slowly began to take focus. An IV bag hanging from its pole above her. A patient monitor to her right. She was at work. What was she doing at work? She wasn't supposed to come into work at the moment, not until the investigation was finished. And why was she lying down? *Shouldn't lie down on the job, Georgia,* she thought in a silly, stern voice. And she wanted to giggle but she didn't seem to be able to push any sound through her throat. In fact, now that she was paying particular attention to her throat, she was noticing how dry it was. *So* dry. Astoundingly dry. Parched. That was the word for it. She was unequivocally, irrevocably, indisputably parched. She wasn't entirely sure why she was feeling the need to describe it with so many large words.

I'd rather like a glass of water, thanks. If someone could just ...?

She was suddenly so very tired. She closed her eyes and breathed deeply. She'd like a glass of water, but she'd also very much like to sleep. Sleep was about to pull her back down, but she was hearing something in the distance, a voice. It was sort of friendly, but sort of not. Sort of stern and brisk. Her eyelids fluttered open again and someone turned the volume up on the voice.

'Welcome back, Georgia,' the voice was saying. And she was aware of a woman bustling around her, fiddling with the IV drip and peering at the monitor. 'Now, I expect you'll be wondering where you are. You're at North Shore Private, you had a nasty accident but you're going to be absolutely fine. How's the pain right now, Georgia?'

She opened her mouth to answer but once again, no sound would come out.

'That's all right, you can show me with your facial expression. You'll probably find it difficult to speak for a while yet, because the seatbelt pulled right across your windpipe. So, show me: how is the pain? Good? Bad? Muddling through?'

Georgia closed her eyes and focused in on her body, searching for any sources of pain. Her mind ran down through her torso, out through her arms, right to the fingertips. It spun back around and travelled down through her legs, all the way to her toes. Could she feel anything?

She didn't think she could. She opened her eyes and tried to reward the nurse with a happy expression. If she could lift her arms she would give her a thumbs-up. But she was pretty sure her arms weighed about one hundred kilos each and that lifting them would be impossible.

The nurse raised her eyebrows. 'I think that's a happy face. Is that a happy face? Yes, I think that's a happy face. All right, listen, now that you're awake I'm going to give you control of your morphine. I'm going to pop this clicker in your left hand here and when the pain starts to creep up on you, you press the button, okay?'

I know how a PCA pump works, Georgia said crossly. Although wait a second, she didn't say it, did she? She only thought it. *Wait, why am I here again?*

'Now, you might be wondering why you don't have any visitors. We've only just learned that your name is Georgia. Apparently, your purse was thrown from the car and the police didn't find it right away. But, the good news is, now that we have your details we've been able to reach your partner and he's on his way here right now, so you'll probably have plenty of company and a room full of flowers before you know it, okay? So, best thing to do now is close your eyes and get some rest while you can. You have lots of recovering to do.'

The nurse bustled away again and Georgia lay still and felt a warm happy feeling about the fact that Luke was on his way. What was he going to say when her saw her? He must be so worried! And then in an instant, the warm, happy feeling vanished. Because she was remembering. *I was on my way home from Cadence's place.*

I was on my way home from Cadence's place where I'd just found out that everything Luke had told me was lies.

That Cadence hasn't been stalking me. She never followed me at all.

Her car isn't red because she doesn't have a car.

She's not tall and scary. She's short and petite.

And Cadence hasn't been messaging me, either.

And neither has Brett.

Because Brett never really existed.

Because Luke was Brett.

Love in the Time of Cholera.

And he kept calling me a slut. Over and over he called me a slut. Cadence called me a slut. Brett called me a slut. But it wasn't them. It was never them.

And on the way home, Luke sent me a message. What did it say?

It said: I know your secret.

But when I tried to open it, when I tried to read the rest of the message ... that was when the world started tumbling.

And now he's on his way here.

She needed to call that nurse back. She needed to tell her that she couldn't let Luke in to see her. She needed to tell her that it wasn't safe, that she couldn't trust him.

She felt the small plastic shape in her hand. The button under her thumb. Ah, she would press this button right here and that would tell the nurse that she needed her to come back. Georgia clicked the button with her thumb, over and over again. Click, click, click, click, click.

Come on, what's taking her so long?

A pleasant, tingling sensation was enveloping her body and she was drifting off to sleep when she realised: *You moron, that's the pain-control pump, not the button to call the nurse.*

*

The next time she opened her eyes, Luke was holding her hand.

He leaned in close and whispered in her ear. 'What a nasty, nasty accident, you silly girl. I wonder if they've got a toxicology report back on you yet? I'm assuming they took your blood to test for drugs. Come on, you're a nurse, you should know. Will the quetiapine I put in your wine after we went ice skating the other night still show up today? I can't believe you didn't pick up on it, actually. Not the best nurse, are you? Or maybe that's on me. The few times I drugged you I tried to make it enough to fuck you up a little bit, enough so that you'd be a bit dopey and agreeable, but not so much that you'd notice. I guess I nailed it.

'Listen, I don't know if you got the chance to read my message, but I want you to know this: I know what you've been up to. Now, I have to go somewhere for a bit and finish up with something. But I'll be back very, very soon, okay? Don't go talking to anyone about me though, will you? Oh, that's right, you can't talk at the moment, can you?'

Then he kissed the top of her head and left.

Georgia was left frozen in her bed.

CHAPTER THIRTY-FIVE

Cadence

I was pacing. Michelle was right. I needed to talk to the police, I absolutely had to talk to the police. But I was terrified to do it. Michelle might have offered me her unwavering support, but what were the police going to think of me? Would they trust everything I had to say? Would they question Luke? Check for his side of the story? And if so, what if he spun the same bullshit story to them that he'd spun to Georgia? About me as an angry ex who was stalking him.

Once I did this, there would be no turning back. Besides, I wanted to talk to Georgia first. I wanted to check in with her, see if everything was okay. I really thought she would have contacted me by now, but I hadn't heard a word from her and I didn't know how to reach her.

Tonight, Michelle wanted to be there with me when I confronted Luke and broke it off with him. But I wanted to let Georgia know my plans first, to make sure she was prepared for how he might take the news. Presumably she would then break things off with him too.

And how was he going to react? Maybe he wouldn't care. Maybe he'd be happy, thinking he'd be able to go running off to Georgia. Although probably not, if he was still hoping to somehow get hold of my shares.

When I heard the key in the lock, I froze. Luke wasn't due back here until tonight.

The door swung open and Luke stepped inside. He smiled brightly at me. 'What are you doing standing there in the middle of the room?' he asked as he closed the door behind him.

I hesitated. 'Just … just doing a bit of tidying,' I said, picking up a random glass from the coffee table and carrying it into the kitchen. 'What are you doing back already?' I asked.

'Was able to come home early,' he said. 'Happy to see me?'

'Of course.'

He walked across the room and put his laptop bag on the kitchen benchtop, then pulled out his computer and a small white bottle. 'Two things,' he said. 'I have something for you to try. You were super jittery yesterday and these tablets are meant to have amazing calming capabilities.' He unscrewed the lid and shook two tablets into the palm of his hand.

I couldn't help taking an automatic step back. 'But if the ones I'm already on are working …'

'Trust me, it did not look that way to me last night. These are brand new and my company is having amazing success with them. Most people would have to pay a fortune for them, but I've managed to get you a couple of months' worth. Trust me, you're going to want to try these.' He stepped towards me, holding out the tablets. 'Unless there's a reason you don't trust me?'

My stomach flipped. He was calling my bluff. He *had* seen Georgia's purse here and he was backing me into a corner. I either refused the tablets and showed my hand or I took the tablets and kept playing the game. No wonder he'd felt the need to make the move on my shares last night.

But those tablets could be absolutely anything. I couldn't risk taking them.

'Of course I trust you,' I said carefully, eyeing the tablets. 'But I've already taken my usual dose this morning, so I better not try them until later.'

He reached for my hand, lifted it up, unfurled my fingers and placed the tablets in it. 'Nope. You're all good. I checked into it. These don't interact with the ones you've been on. You can take them now.' He turned away and grabbed a glass out of the cupboard, filled it with water from the tap, then handed it to me and grinned.

'Take them, babe. For me,' he said.

It was over. He had me. I stared him in the eye. 'No,' I said. 'I'm not taking these.'

He sighed. 'She came here again, didn't she? Georgia?'

'Yes, she did, and she told me everything.'

'All right, stay calm. The last thing we need is for you to have an anxiety attack. Sit down with me and let me explain it all for you.'

I laughed, I couldn't help it. 'Explain? You're joking, right? You can't *explain*.'

'Absolutely I can. And if you stop getting yourself worked up it will all become very clear in a minute. Please, sit down with me.'

There was something in his tone that told me I needed to at least indulge him. Right now, he was still playing the part of loving boyfriend who thought he could bring me around. But if I pushed him, what might happen?

I sat down with him. He put his hand on my knee, and there was a level of pressure in his grip that suggested I shouldn't try and pull my leg away. I resisted the urge and breathed deeply.

'Let me guess,' he began, 'she told you she's my girlfriend, right? That I'm cheating on you with her?'

I nodded.

'Cadence, it's utter bullshit. This girl is a freak.'

'Okay, so if she's not your girlfriend, how do you know her?'

'She's a client. Works at one of the hospitals I sell to. She's a nurse; Georgia Fitzpatrick is her full name. Look her up if you want. You'll see that it's true. And I'm not even supposed to deal direct with her, but she developed this crush on me. I swear I thought it was harmless at first. She struck up a friendship with me. That's it, that's all we are, or were anyway — just friends. But she got obsessed with me.'

'She had photos.' I kept my tone neutral. I didn't want to sound too accusatory, I didn't want him to turn on me. I just wanted to get through this conversation and then get away from him.

'I told you, babe, we *did* become friends, but that was

before I realised she had a crush on me it. We're not even that anymore, obviously. But that's the only reason she has photos of me. Reps and hospital staff go out together all the time. It's networking. The only reason I tolerated her was because of our working relationship. But she's crossed a line now. Like I said, I always knew she had a crush on me, but I never thought she'd do something like this. I'm so sorry you had to go through all that. I wish I was here when she came around.'

'How did you know?'

'Know what?'

'That she came here.'

He hesitated. 'Have a look up there at that shelf. You see that ornament, the black owl? It's a security camera. That's how I knew.'

'You've been spying on me?'

'Spying! No, you're my girlfriend and you've been going through a tough time. I've been keeping an eye on you, making sure you're safe. That's all.'

I wondered if I would have fallen for this if it wasn't for the fact that I knew about the tablets, if it wasn't for the fact that I'd been to see Michelle. I thought about the alarm on her face, the conviction as she leaned across to me and said *Cadence, this is abuse.*

Maybe I would have been naïve enough to fall for his excuses.

But not anymore.

'All right,' I said. 'I believe you.' I went to pull my leg away, about to stand up.

He caught my arm and stopped me. 'Hang on,' he said, 'there's still some other stuff we need to talk about.'

'Could we maybe do it later? I actually need to ... be somewhere.'

'Be somewhere?' He gave me an incredulous look. 'Where on earth could you possibly need to go? You can't leave the apartment at the moment.'

'Funny thing, like I said, those tablets you've been giving me have really made a huge change. My anxiety has been right down. So, I can go out ... and I need to meet a friend.'

'Who?' His voice was sharp.

'An old schoolmate.' Michelle was the only person I could think of.

He smiled. 'That's great, so great to hear. But I really need to sort this stuff out before you go anywhere, okay?'

He was still holding onto my arm.

'Okay, what is it?'

'You know how I was talking with you about money the other day? I actually really need you to give me the right password for your account with your shares. You see, I tried all the passwords you suggested, but none of them worked. But when I checked your computer last night, I saw that you've visited the ASX website quite recently, which means that you *do* know your password.'

I knew there was no point pretending or trying to play dumb. I just needed to find a way to stall him for a little bit longer.

I hesitated. 'I will,' I said. 'I definitely will ... but I don't feel comfortable giving it to you right now, not with everything that's been happening. Can we do this another time? Later tonight?'

He shook his head. 'We can't. With you being home sick, not working, you've seriously bled me dry. I'm going to need access to those shares.'

The anger flared up inside of me. I couldn't play this game anymore. I couldn't keep pretending and I couldn't keep stalling. I wrenched my arm out of his grip and stood up.

'I've bled you dry?' I exclaimed. 'Are you for real? You've been living in my place and you haven't been paying rent! You don't pay for groceries, you don't pay for anything!'

He jumped up as well. 'Don't you dare speak to me that way. I paid for date after date for you.' He stepped in close, held a pointed finger in my face. 'You owe me.'

I hit his hand away and matched his tone. 'I don't owe you a damn thing. What are you going to do? Are you going to hit me again? Are you going to say it's an accident? Because this time I'm not going to let you get away with it. This time if you touch me I'll go straight to the police.'

Next thing he was holding me by the shoulders and shaking me. 'You see what's happened? You're *not* well. You're *not* okay. You need help! You need to take these new tablets and stop fighting me. You need to do as you're told.'

I struggled against him but he was stronger. 'Luke! Let go of me, you're hurting me. Let go.'

'JUST GIVE ME YOUR FUCKING PASSWORD.'

That's when I heard someone banging against the front door, followed by a voice. 'Hey! What's going on? Open up!'

I recognised the voice. It was Michelle; she must have decided to come and check up on me even though she wasn't meant to be here until tonight. The distraction made Luke loosen his grip and I wrenched myself away from him.

'It's over,' I whispered. 'We are *done*.' I moved quickly towards the front door and unlocked it to let Michelle in.

She burst through the opening. 'Are you okay?' she asked. 'I heard yelling.'

I nodded. 'I'm fine.' But my voice was shaky.

Michelle looked over at Luke. 'You need to get the fuck out of here,' she told him. 'Get out and stay away from my friend.' She shifted her position so that she was standing in front of me.

Luke looked from Michelle to me. He locked eyes with me. 'It's not over,' he said. 'Not by a long shot.' He grabbed his laptop bag and strode out of the apartment.

Michelle hugged me. 'Don't listen to him,' she said. 'It bloody well is over. I'm taking you straight to the police.'

CHAPTER THIRTY-SIX

Georgia

It was a different nurse doing her obs this time, and Georgia kept trying to make meaningful eye contact with her. *I need to talk. I need to tell someone. You can't let him back in here. You can't let Luke in to see me again.* But the nurse was too focused on the task at hand. Georgia tried to clear her throat, tried to push her voice to work the way it was supposed to. But all that came out was a weird wheezing noise.

'Careful,' said the nurse, 'you need to rest that throat of yours. Don't worry, you'll be back chatting away in no time.'

Georgia tried to shake her head and was rewarded with a searing pain through her skull. She'd stopped pressing the button for the morphine, despite the fact that pain had started presenting itself in all sorts of places. Both of her knees were throbbing, there was a sharp pain in her abdomen, and it felt like someone was plunging a screwdriver into the side of her neck, over and over and over.

'I see you're not managing your pain anymore. You know there's no need to be a hero. Earlier you were clicking that thing like a demon. You know we can see how often you press it, right?'

Yes, of course I know how it works because I'm a nurse, you idiot, but the problem is I can't press it anymore. I can't because I need to stay clear-headed. I need to stay awake, and for fuck's sake, could you please stop and listen to me because there's something I need to say!

But the nurse was already finishing up and leaving, ignoring the pleas Georgia had been making with her eyes.

Jesus, if that was me, I'd take the time to actually see my patient. I'd realise there was something important she needed to say and I'd figure out a way to help her communicate.

Georgia turned her head slowly, slowly to the side, trying her best to ignore the rolling waves of pain that coursed through her head as her brain protested against the terrible, terrible idea of moving even an inch. *Hold still*, it begged, *I'm not done healing you.*

She couldn't hold still. There was no bloody time. She looked at the small cupboard on caster wheels to her left, where a few of her personal belongings had been placed. She could see her scarf, folded neatly. Her sunglasses, somehow undamaged. Then: there, that's what she'd been looking for, her phone. She reached an arm out and yet again the pain shot through her body. Oh God, her shoulder. Was it dislocated? No, because they would have popped it back in if it was. Still, it bloody hurt. She pushed through it. *Just get the phone. Just reach out and grab it.*

When she finally closed her fingers around the small cool shape, she knew immediately that there was a problem. She could feel the roughness of the screen. It wasn't meant to be rough. It was meant to be smooth.

She picked it up and brought it up to her face to see. The whole screen was smashed. With shaking fingers, she pushed on the home button to turn it on. Why was it responding so slowly? *Wake up little phone! Don't be dead.* The screen finally lit up. At the same time, she heard footsteps and she almost cried with relief. Thank God, that nurse had come back and this time, Georgia would make her pay attention. She would make her realise that she needed to communicate.

She lifted her eyes and saw him. Luke, standing above her bed. The strangest expression on his face. A weird sort of half smile on his lips. But his eyes, his eyes looked like hard glass marbles. He was angry. No, he wasn't angry, he was furious. He grabbed a chair and pulled it up to the bed, then sat down, placed his elbows on the bed and clasped his hands together, staring at her with that manic gaze.

'Georgia,' he said. 'Georgia, Georgia, Georgia.' He snatched the phone back out of her hand and put it on the table.

Her body was rigid. If another nurse could just come in, if someone could come and check on her, then she wouldn't need her goddamned voice, she'd bloody well make them understand. She'd throw her entire body about like she was having a fit if needed, whatever it took to get their attention.

'You really fucked everything up for me, didn't you? You couldn't leave it alone. And you know what really pisses me off? I was almost done. I was about to finish it with the both of you. But you had to go and see Cadence and make her doubt me. A few more days and I would have got what I wanted from her. She would have just handed it over, because that's how much she trusted me. Instead she's refusing. Instead she's breaking up with me. Fucking hell, that insecure little bitch breaking up with me. And it's all your fault.'

Georgia's eyes flittered around the room like a wild bird trapped in a classroom. Could she reach the button above the bed to call the nurses? If she made a move for it would she get to it fast enough before he stopped her? She was so weak right now, he wasn't going to let her do anything he didn't want her to do. And still, at the same time, a part of her wanted to simply take him by the hand and say, 'Why? But why are you acting this way? What happened? What changed?'

'With her it was all about the money,' he said then. 'I mean, yeah, revenge as well, but it wasn't really her fault, was it? But with you, it was different. With you, it was way more personal. It was pure revenge. You fucked up my life so I was going to fuck up yours too. Remember the night we met? When I said you looked familiar?'

Georgia was completely confused now. Revenge? Revenge for what? What was he on about?

'I was testing the waters. I had to make sure you didn't know who I was because otherwise the entire thing would have been a waste of time.' He gave a small chuckle. 'Anyway, you didn't, did you? You didn't twig, you dumb bitch. Even funnier was when I made that joke, you remember? I said imagine if I'd already hit on you and you'd shot me down. And you put on your best flirty little voice and batted your fucking eyelashes and said, "But I'm pretty sure I wouldn't have".' He put on a horrible mocking imitation of her voice. Then he rolled his eyes and placed a hand square on her chest, his fingers close to the base of her throat, pressing down on her with the heel of his hand. 'But you already fucking had, hadn't you?'

She tried to shake her head. *No! No, I didn't. I've never shot you down! I didn't even know you!*

'You still don't know who I am, do you? My name isn't Luke Kauffman, you fucking idiot. But you're too dumb to figure out who I really am, aren't you?' His hand was still heavy on her chest.

She couldn't understand. Why was he saying these things? Why was he claiming she'd turned him down in the past? He didn't look familiar at all, so how could she possibly have shot him down without even knowing it? And why come after her with a fake name? Why go through all of this just to get back at her for allegedly refusing to date him at some point in the past? She racked her brain, trying desperately to figure out who he could be. She thought of ex-boyfriends. She thought of guys she'd swiped left on Tinder. She thought of friends who'd suggested setting her up with their single mates. She pictured faces, names. But nothing was jumping out at her. Nothing seemed familiar. Nothing seemed significant enough to warrant this kind of reaction.

And then she remembered.

The incident. It couldn't be, could it?

CHAPTER THIRTY-SEVEN

Georgia

She was thirty when she took the admin job at KB and Thomas Net. She was still trying to figure out what she wanted to be when she grew up. In truth, she was starting to think she might never figure it out. Not like Marcus, who knew right away that he wanted to be a chef. Or Aaron, who'd always been great with numbers, so becoming an accountant was an easy choice. Even Troy, who struggled throughout high school, still found his calling, falling into a successful career as a personal trainer and starting a business together with Pete.

Over the years since that night after graduation, the darkness had continued to court her, almost always skirting around the edges. Sometimes it would take hold for a day here or a week there. Sometimes it would seem as if it had vanished altogether, but she knew better. She offered it her respect and she continued to keep its existence as her secret. No need to ask for help; she had a handle on it.

She quite liked the people at KB. They were friendly, the work was easy enough, and on Fridays they always went out for drinks at the Monkey and Squirrel. There was still a nagging feeling though. *Where are you going to go from here? What's going to be left when you're dead and gone? What will you have to show for your life? What's the point? What's the point in it all?*

One Friday at KB work drinks, she had far too many. One by one, each of her colleagues called it a night until it was just her and Kev, the manager of the administration department, which made him her direct superior. So, flirting with him was probably a bit inappropriate. But she didn't care, because he was cute, and she'd had several Fruit Tingle cocktails, and she was pretty sure he was flirting back, and so what if he was her boss? They were both adults.

They teamed up to play a game of pool against two randoms in the pub. Kev was a crack shot. He sunk ball after ball. It was incredibly sexy to watch. When it was Georgia's turn, he'd pretty much won the game for them. All she had to do was sink the black ball, which was lined up for an easy shot. She took aim and sunk the white, losing the game. Kev groaned and grabbed her around the waist, pretending to shake her with frustration. She giggled and tipped her head back to look up at him.

'Sorry,' she said, looking him right in the eyes and then flicking her gaze to his lips.

He leaned down and whispered in her ear, 'Did you know that you have a fuck-me mouth?'

It sent a shot right through her body, that line. The boldness of it! The dirtiness! Not to mention the fact that as her boss he felt like forbidden fruit. She was the one who kissed him first. She couldn't help herself.

She never actually slept with Kev. They spent a good hour making out in a corner of the pub and his hand definitely crept underneath her top more than once during their make-out session, but that was the end of it.

'Maybe don't mention this to anyone at work,' Kev suggested as he put her into a cab. 'It might not go down to well with, ah … my own bosses.'

Georgia promised she wouldn't tell a soul. What she didn't expect, though, was for Kev to be the one to start spreading rumours.

The first hint that he'd told other people was when Georgia was chosen for the employee of the month award, which was really just a silly, fun thing they did in the office for a bit of a laugh — all you actually got was a Freddo Frog and a laminated certificate. But one of the other girls on the admin team made a comment about 'special circumstances' and 'playing favourites'. Slowly, the girls who she used to get along with quite well started freezing her out. It all felt very high school.

And then the first email came through. It was from the marketing manager who worked out of the city office. Sam Burton. It started out innocent enough.

Hey Georgia,

I hear you're doing a great job there in the Ryde office. There's been some talk that you might have a bit of an aptitude for marketing. Have you ever thought about where you want to go next in your career? There's lots of opportunities here at KB for someone like you.

Cheers,

Sam

She'd been so excited when she received that first email. People were talking about her as someone with potential. Maybe this was it. Maybe this was what was going to be her thing. A little embarrassing to be discovering that at thirty, but still!

She wasn't entirely sure why anyone would be talking about her having an 'aptitude for marketing'. Maybe it was the funny sign she'd made for the printer when everyone kept forgetting to refill the paper after they used it. Whatever it was, his words made it easier for her to weather the nasty comments from the other girls in the admin team. Who cared what they thought if there were people in management who believed she had potential?

She wrote back to Sam to say thank you so much and sure, she was interested in pursuing a career in marketing. Over the next few weeks, they kept emailing back and forth. The tone of the emails changed so gradually that she didn't even realise it was happening at first. One minute it was the odd friendly joke here and there, that, looking back, could have been construed as flirtatious, but at the time, didn't seem like anything more than an innocent laugh. The next minute, he'd taken it that one step too far. And Georgia didn't know how to deal with it. He was a superior. She didn't want to offend him by saying she didn't feel all that comfortable with the types of emails he'd started sending her. Besides, had she somehow led him to this point, in the way she'd responded to his previous emails? Was this all her fault?

In the end, she decided the best way to deal with it was by being honest. This was a workplace, he'd respect her for being professional.

Hey Sam,

I'm so sorry, and I absolutely know you didn't mean anything by that last joke you sent through, but I thought I should let you know that I did find it a little inappropriate. Is that okay? Sorry!!! Like I said, I know you didn't mean anything bad by sending it!

Cheers,

Georgia

She was terrified as she waited for him to reply. Would he get offended? Annoyed? She was hoping he'd come back with a friendly, *Oh no! Sorry! I didn't mean to upset you! No worries, I'll pull right back on those sorts of jokes.*

Instead, though, his email back was like a punch to the gut.

Really? It said. *I thought a slut like you would love it.*

Georgia closed the email right away, terrified someone would walk past her desk and read it over her shoulder. She didn't write back because she didn't know what to say. She didn't need to though, because Sam wrote again anyway.

Gone quiet now, have you? From what I heard, you weren't very quiet when you were with Kev. I heard you're a screamer.

The implication was clear. People in the office must have thought she'd actually slept with Kev, rather than just kissed him. Had he spread that rumour himself? Or told someone what happened and then other people had taken it upon themselves to expand on it for the fun of sharing some juicy office gossip?

Now what should she do? Tell someone? Take this to management? Make a formal complaint? But what would they think of her knowing that she had kissed Kev? Would they say, well, you brought this on yourself, didn't you? After all, the rumours were obviously all over the company, so everyone must know.

She decided to do nothing. And the emails kept right on coming.

Come on, he wrote, *when am I going to get my turn with you? If you can give it up for Kev then you're obviously keen to have a go with anyone.*

And then: *If you keep ignoring me, then I might have to let management know that you fucked up on a simple job I sent your way. I'd say they'll have to give you an official warning. Don't expect to keep your job much longer after that.*

She wrote back then. *Hi Sam, I think maybe things have got a bit out of hand. I'm really sorry if I led you on or gave you the wrong impression. And the rumours about Kev aren't actually true. So, please, could we let this go?*

He wasn't interested in letting it go.

Sure, he replied. *I'll stop sending you these emails if you come out with me and give me the same happy ending that Kev got. But if you don't give me what I want you can consider your job as good as gone.*

Between the emails and the nasty looks and comments from the girls at work, Georgia felt like KB had become an awful, hostile place. If she got fired, how would she pay her rent? And once again, her parents were on the other side of the world, so she couldn't move back home.

But surely she couldn't stay here, not if Sam wasn't going to stop. On top of that was the humiliation at realising that he'd lied about people seeing some special talent for marketing in her. She didn't have any special talents. She had nothing going for her. She was an idiot who should never have flirted with and kissed her boss. Sam would never have targeted her if she hadn't done that — it was all her own fault. Sam was right, she was a slut. And if she tried to complain about him, even with the emails as proof of his harassment, he was worth way more to the company than she was. So they'd probably give him a slap on the wrist and keep him on, while she'd be pushed out the door. That was the way it worked, wasn't it?

Eventually, she crumbled. She typed up a letter of resignation and took it into Tina Sutton, the managing director of KB and Thomas. The plan was to hand it in and walk away, but Tina stopped her.

'Why are you quitting?' she asked.

Georgia shook her head, too ashamed to tell Tina the truth. 'I just don't think I fit in here anymore.'

Tina stared at her. 'I had noticed a change in you,' she said. 'You used to seem a lot brighter, happier, but these last few weeks you've looked really down. I'd wondered if perhaps there was something going on in your personal life.'

Georgia was completely taken aback. She'd assumed Tina would never have even noticed someone like her, at the opposite end of the food chain.

'But maybe it's something here that's been bothering you?' Tina continued. 'I'd really like to know.'

Still Georgia couldn't bring herself to tell her the truth.

Even worse, the kindness in Tina's voice was making her want to cry. How embarrassing! She couldn't break down in front of the managing director. She clenched her jaw to stop herself from letting out a sob and then said quietly, 'I don't ... I can't ...'

Tina continued to eyeball her. When she spoke again, her words were careful, measured. 'Has someone here been bothering you, Georgia? Maybe a male superior?'

Georgia was stunned. Did Tina somehow know?

'If you look at my work emails you can see for yourself,' she blurted. Then she turned and fled.

She was supposed to give two weeks' notice but there was no way she would show her face at KB again. She couldn't believe that she was going to have to start over yet again with a new job. The humiliation stung.

And then she humiliated herself at home as well. She was still living with Lena then. They got along well, they were friends, but not super close — Georgia usually kept her at arm's length.

But that night she got drunk on shot after shot of vodka and told Lena she'd lost her job. They were sitting on the couch together and Lena leaned in to give her a hug. Somehow, Georgia got confused. She'd never kissed a woman before, but was Lena ... hitting on her? Well, maybe it was exactly what she needed, a different kind of comfort. She went in for the kiss and Lena recoiled, horrified. The embarrassment when Lena leaped up from the couch and exclaimed, 'You think I'm gay? What? Just because I have lots of piercings and tattoos?'

Georgia tried to explain that she was confused, upset ... but Lena stormed out and Georgia was left alone.

She invited the darkness back in.

She finished the bottle of vodka alone and cried for hours. She ended up in the bathroom, arms wrapped around the bowl of the toilet as she threw up over and over. When she opened the cabinet in the bathroom, she was looking for painkillers. She saw the jar of pills. Lena's sleeping tablets.

The idea of falling into a deep, dreamless sleep seemed like heaven. She could escape from the world, from all of her problems. From the complete humiliation. From Sam's revolting emails that made her skin crawl. From her fear that maybe he would find out her personal email address and keep emailing her here at home.

She picked up the bottle and looked at the label through blurred eyes.

The question was, did she want to wake up again? She thought back to that night that she'd wanted to jump. She thought about how she'd failed.

She tipped her head back and poured the pills into her mouth.

Maybe I'll wake, maybe I won't.

Maybe I don't deserve to wake.

Lena was the one who called the ambulance. Georgia remembered waking up in the hospital and wondering what it had been like for Lena to find her like that. How frightening it must have been.

The truth was, though, she was relieved to be awake. In the in-between stage, after she'd swallowed the tablets but before she'd passed out, the regrets had come marching across her body like an army of ants. *What have you done?* they hissed as they marched. *What have you done?*

Marcus arrived from Melbourne, furious with her. He sat by her bed and demanded she tell him right now. 'Was it a mistake?' he asked. 'Did you overdose on those tablets accidentally? Or did you do it on purpose?'

She shrugged. 'I don't really know,' she lied.

She never told him the full story behind her breakdown though. She was still ashamed. She begged him not to tell their other brothers. She couldn't stand the thought of them all thinking of her differently. Of their wives giving her looks of pity at the next family gathering.

'Fine,' he said, 'but I can't keep this from Mum and Dad.'

'At least wait until they get home from their latest trip,' she said. 'I don't want to ruin it for them.'

Marcus wasn't happy about it, but in the end he had no choice but to agree. It was too hard to reach them anyway. Once again, they were exploring remote parts of the world with limited access to wi-fi or phone signals. He made her promise that in the meantime, she would get professional help. She was transferred across to the mental health ward for assessment and that's where Kathy came in. Where the other nurses would briskly check her vitals and then walk away, Kathy took the time to talk with Georgia. She leaned against her bed and asked her about her life. About her interests. About past boyfriends and annoying flatmates, and about family and about fears.

Surprisingly, it was Kathy who was the person Georgia told about Sam, instead of the psychologist she was supposed to open up to. Kathy was so angry. 'You can report him to the police,' she said. 'He shouldn't get away with it.'

But Georgia had already received a voicemail from Tina telling her that Sam had been fired and that she was welcome to come back to work if she wished. She decided that knowing he'd been fired was enough. And she didn't want to go back to KB. She wanted to find her true passion.

When Georgia was ready to leave the mental health unit, Kathy presented her with two things: the citrine stone, so she could carry happiness with her always, and an empty jar, which she told her to decorate and fill with positive thoughts as often as she could.

By the time she moved back in with her parents, Georgia knew what she wanted to do. She wanted to become a nurse. She wanted to help people in the same way Kathy had helped her. She enrolled in a new degree, picked up a part-time job, and eventually she moved back out of her parents' place and rented an apartment on her own.

Her parents didn't travel again for a good few years, not until Georgia slapped a holiday brochure for Istanbul down on the table in front of them and said, '*Go*, please. I promise I won't do anything stupid while you're gone.' The trapped look in their eyes was too much to handle.

*

Now as Georgia stared up at Luke, it all clicked into place. He was Sam Burton. The guy that had terrorised her with email after email. The man who thought she owed him something because if she was willing to make out with one boss, surely she'd be willing to make out with another.

She would never have recognised his face because she never actually met him in person. But he'd been worried that she'd know what he looked like, probably in case she'd ever seen his photo on the company website or something like that. She hadn't, though; she'd never looked him up because she hadn't wanted to know what he looked like. She hadn't wanted to put a face to the name.

Why was he out for revenge now? After all this time had passed? Why wait so long to make his move? Not to mention the fact that while he might have been fired, he'd sure as hell ruined her life more than she'd ruined his.

He stood up now, leaning over her, and put his other hand on her shoulder. The shoulder that was already filled with pain. Then he pressed down harder, with the full weight of his body, pushing and pushing. The pain was excruciating. Georgia tried to cry out but all that escaped from her lips was the tiniest squeak. Tears streamed down her cheeks.

'You want to know what I had in mind for you?' he said. 'I was going to take you straight back to that place you'd already been. You remember? You remember when you were going to give it all up? When you were going to throw your stupid, worthless life away? But you failed, didn't you? Well I was going to take you back there. I was going to give you a second chance. A second chance to take a fistful of tablets and make it all end. I took away your job and I was taking away your friends, and I was making you think your life was in ruins. Your brother's been ignoring you, hasn't he? Ignoring all your messages. But you were too dumb to notice that's because I blocked his number on your phone. I couldn't have him telling you to go and get professional help again.

'I wasn't going to actually do it to you, you know? I'm not a fucking murderer. I'm not a *monster*! I was going to let you do it yourself. You know, lead a horse to water and all that. The problem, though, is that the jig is up, isn't it? And I didn't get what I wanted. None of it.

'And now I'm angry. Like, really fucking angry. And I want to *get* something out of this. Something for my time. So, I was thinking, if originally I was going to *talk* you into ending it, then maybe doing it *for* you isn't all that different anyway.'

Georgia's eyes were wide with terror. Her hands scrabbled at Luke's arms, trying to get the horrible weight off her chest. She tried once again to scream out but her vocal cords failed her — all that would come out was a hoarse grunt.

'What do you think? Should we use your phone to send a suicide note to your brother? It won't be the first time he's got news like that, will it? Maybe I'll send one for you, after.'

He kept one hand heavy on her chest, holding her down, and reached into his pocket with the other.

CHAPTER THIRTY-EIGHT

Cadence

Michelle was chatting nonstop and I had the feeling it was because she was a bit in shock about what had happened with Luke, or maybe about what could have happened — had he turned violent rather than seemingly accepting defeat and leaving. She was driving us to the police station, and while I knew it was the right thing to do, I was still worried about Georgia.

'The thing is,' I said, interrupting her monologue about the self-defence classes she'd done at her local RSL last year, which meant she could definitely have 'taken him down' had he tried anything, 'if he's gone straight to Georgia, if there's a chance he could hurt her ... then I don't know if the police would act in time.'

'I'm all for warning this other girl,' said Michelle, 'but you said you don't know how to reach her. So I don't see that we have any other option.'

I looked down at the phone in my hands, willing it to ring, willing Georgia to contact me like we'd planned. What was going on? Why had she gone silent since our meeting? Had she somehow fallen back under his spell? Had he found a way to explain it all away and make her believe I was the stalking ex she'd first thought I was?

As I looked at my phone I realised something. I couldn't find Georgia, but I could track Luke. I went straight into the Find My Friends app and clicked on Luke, then waited for his location to load.

North Shore Private Hospital.

He'd said Georgia was a nurse, hadn't he? That must be where she worked, so he had gone straight to her. Was she safe? It was a public place, surely he couldn't do anything to hurt her there. But what if he could? What if he already had? I made a snap decision.

'Turn left up here,' I told Michelle.

'No, that's the wrong way.'

'I know, but take the turn. I've figured out where Georgia is and I need to make sure she's okay. Please, trust me on this. I promise we'll go straight to the police, right after.'

Michelle glanced at me with a look that said, *Okay fine, but I'm doing this under protest*, then pulled hard on the steering wheel for the sudden turn.

As we approached the main reception desk on the ground floor of the hospital, a middle-aged man with a pencil moustache looked up at us with a friendly smile.

'Hi, I'm hoping you can help me find someone?' I said. 'Her name is Georgia Fitzpatrick.'

He tapped away at a computer. 'Fitzpatrick … Georgia. Here she is. She's in room 203 … although visiting hours are almost over.'

I stared back at him. 'Visiting hours? But … isn't she a nurse?'

The receptionist frowned. 'No, she's a patient.'

Michelle tugged on my arm. 'Cadence,' she said, 'what if he did something to her already? You said you were afraid he would. What if that's why she's here as a patient?'

The man's smile was gone now. He frowned at us. 'Is everything okay?' he asked.

'No,' I said. 'I don't think it is. Long story short, there's a guy here somewhere, his name is Luke and he was my boyfriend and he was abusive. And I think he was the one who put that patient, Georgia, in the hospital. And maybe he's here because he's going to hurt her again.'

'Wait right here.' He picked up the phone on his desk and punched in a few numbers. Then he spoke rapidly into the phone. 'We have a potential code black, room 203 …'

I nudged Michelle. *Let's go*, I mouthed at her.

She nodded. We slipped away from the desk while the receptionist was distracted on the phone, and then we made a run for the lifts.

CHAPTER THIRTY-NINE

Georgia

Georgia had never wished more to be in a public room surrounded by other patients instead of in the privacy of her own single room. She felt the same pure helplessness she'd experienced in those moments after she'd taken those sleeping tablets all those years ago. The same helplessness she'd felt when Sam had been sending her those vile emails.

He leaned right down so his forearm was across her neck, making it harder and harder for her to breathe, and then with the other hand, he pulled a syringe out of his pocket.

'I've been doing some research. It's remarkable the information you can find on the internet when you know the right place to look. If I inject this into your drip, you'll be dead within minutes. And the best part is that it can easily look like human error. As though some dumb nurse like you fucked up.'

He climbed up onto the bed and used his knee to pin her down while he reached for the IV tube. Georgia shook her head wildly, scrabbling against him. He unscrewed one of the lines from the IV bag and started screwing in his own vial. As she watched the new liquid spread through the bag, the door flung open, and from her peripheral vision she could see two shapes striding into the room.

'Get the fuck off her,' a voice shouted.

Luke's knee slipped and Georgia's hand flew up to grab at the IV. She twisted it and squeezed it in her hand, holding it tight to stop the flow. At the same time, someone launched themselves at Luke, making him tip sideways and then tumble away from the bed. Georgia realised it was Cadence, and saw her arms flying everywhere as she pummelled Luke over and over.

Another woman rushed over to Georgia's side. 'Are you okay?' she asked, 'Are you hurt? What did he do to you?' The woman saw the tube in Georgia's hand. 'Did he do something to that?'

Georgia nodded. With her other hand, she reached for the line where it connected with the cannula in her vein and tried to disconnect it. The woman understood and helped her remove it, careful to leave the cannula in place. With a breath of relief, Georgia let go of the tube, allowing it to drop to the floor.

They both turned as they heard a shout from the other side of the bed and Georgia saw Cadence rolling to the side as Luke managed to shove her roughly away, clamber to his feet and run from the room. A moment later, more people were pouring into the room — a security guard followed by two nurses.

'He just ran out!' Cadence was getting to her feet and pointing after Luke. 'Him! You have to go after him!' The security guard realised and turned back, while the two nurses went straight for Georgia.

*

The police officers were having trouble taking statements with Georgia unable to speak. She could see that Cadence was trying her best to explain the whole situation from beginning to end, but clearly there were gaps she couldn't fill. The security guard hadn't been able to catch Luke, but the police were hopeful he wouldn't have got far.

It was also clear that Cadence was nervous about telling the police she had willingly taken the tablets Luke had been giving her for the last few months. She looked embarrassed, and Georgia desperately wished she could reassure her. It was when Cadence started spelling Luke's surname that Georgia realised she hadn't communicated to anyone yet the most important piece of information. She started banging her hand on the side of her mattress to get their attention and everyone looked over at her.

She opened her mouth and tried to croak out the word 'Sam'.

'Sorry,' said one of the police officers, 'I can't quite get that.'

She shook her head and reached out for his notepad. He stepped forward and handed it to her.

Sam Burton, she scrawled across the page, in shaky handwriting as everything still hurt.

'Sam Burton,' the officer read out. 'Who's Sam Burton?'

Cadence stepped forward. 'I know that name,' she said. 'I definitely know it.' She looked at Georgia. 'Are you saying that's Luke's real name?'

Georgia reached for the notepad again. *Think so.*

Cadence looked at the police. 'Oh my God,' she said. 'If she's right, then that makes sense. That's why he knew about my shares. Sam Burton worked for my mother's company. My mum fired him after he sent these awful emails to one of the girls who worked there.'

Georgia hit the palm of hand against the mattress again, signalling Cadence. *Me.* She mouthed at Cadence.

'It was you?' Cadence asked. 'He sent the emails to you?'

Georgia nodded.

Cadence's mouth dropped open.

PART FOUR

One Week Later

CHAPTER FORTY

Cadence

It felt strange to be standing in Georgia's apartment, looking at pieces of my own furniture that Luke had taken under the pretence of setting up our new home. I still wasn't entirely sure why I was here. Of course, I'd visited Georgia while she'd been in hospital. When her throat was better, we'd discussed Sam at length and speculated about where he might be. The police hadn't been able to track him down yet. He'd ditched his phone, so the Find My Friends app had been no help this time.

But to be honest, I'd thought that that was where my relationship with Georgia would end. The only thing we had in common was the fact that we'd been targeted by a misogynistic arsehole who held both my mother and Georgia responsible for ruining his life. I do know that my mum made it very difficult for Sam to get another job after she fired him. She made sure it was spread throughout the industry that he would be a liability to anyone who hired him. And he just missed out on getting his ten-year bonus when he was fired, a package that included KB shares.

It must have been the news that KB's shares had skyrocketed when it merged with CarterCOM that triggered him into coming after us for revenge — and for my shares — all these years later. He couldn't go after my mother, because she was already dead. So he targeted me instead. He obviously thought he deserved those shares he'd missed out on, that if Georgia hadn't turned him in to my mother, he'd be sitting on a decent sum of money right now.

I wondered if Georgia thought we ought to stay friends. But I really didn't think I could. As much as I was tired of living my life in such a solitary way — I was keen to keep in touch with Michelle much more often now — Georgia would always be a reminder of this awful thing that happened, and I just didn't think I could be her friend.

For some reason, though, it felt wrong to decline outright when she sent me the message, so I'd agreed to the invite, telling myself I would explain once I was there that I couldn't make this a long-term friendship.

'Wine or beer?' Georgia asked as I wandered over to my own dining setting and touched my fingers to the tabletop. 'Or something else ... Sorry, you don't have to have a *drink-drink*, I just assumed ...'

I smiled at her. 'I'd love a glass of wine.'

Georgia moved slowly around the kitchen to pour our wines, still limping a bit from her injuries. I looked around, checking for other familiar ornaments or pieces of furniture. 'Did Luke — sorry, Sam, I still can't get used to calling him that. Did Sam bring the bedside table here? The one with the blue and green handles?'

'Yes,' Georgia called back. 'It's part of the reason I invited you tonight. I figured that a lot of the stuff he'd brought here might be yours. I'll sort out a delivery truck or something to send the heavy stuff back to your place, but I thought I should also see if there are any small things he took that you might be missing right now.'

'Thank you,' I said, 'I really appreciate that.'

I glanced around the apartment, looking more closely this time, and my eyes fell upon my collection of Transformers figures, sitting on one of Georgia's shelves. I walked over and picked up one. Why would he even take these? They weren't worth anything! They were cheap toys I started collecting as a joke after an old boyfriend gave me one that he'd found in the bottom of a cereal box. I'd grown fond of them though. So it was yet another kick in the gut that he'd gathered them up, pretending to be taking them to our new home, and instead had brought them here.

Georgia came back with the two glasses of wine and saw me holding the toy. 'Don't tell me those are yours?'

I gave an embarrassed shrug. 'Yep. I know they're silly but —'

'They're not silly. They're cute. And he's an absolute bastard.'

'I don't even get why I he took them.'

'I do. Because he has no personality of his own and he was trying to make himself seem interesting … endearing. I'll find a box so you can take them home tonight.'

'Okay. Thank you.'

Georgia handed me one of the glasses of wine. 'The other reason I wanted you here is so that I could thank you. Not only did you and your friend Michelle come in that night at the exact right moment, you also spent all that time visiting me. You didn't have to do that.'

I smiled. 'We had a lot to talk about.'

'I hope you don't mind, but there's a few others coming tonight. My friends Rick and Amber, my brother Marcus, because he's up from Melbourne at the moment, and his mate Grant.'

'That's fine, I don't mind.'

'Hey, can I ask you a really weird question?' said Georgia.

'Sure.'

'Did you used to make French toast for Luke all the time?'

'French toast? No. Why?'

Georgia nodded. 'That's what I thought you might say.'

CHAPTER FORTY-ONE

Georgia

Several pizza boxes with half-eaten pizzas sat open on the middle of the dining room table. Cadence was sitting on the couch, chatting with Rick, while Marcus, Grant and Georgia stood in a circle by the table. Georgia checked her watch.

'We keeping you from something, Georgie?' Marcus asked.

'Sorry, no. I just thought Amber would be here by now.'

As soon as she could after the accident, Georgia had contacted both Rick and Amber, wanting to apologise for freezing them out since the suspension at work. Amber had burst into tears over the phone once Georgia told her all about the car accident and about who Luke was, which was highly unusual for her — Georgia didn't think she'd ever known Amber to cry. But only Rick had been able to visit while she'd been in hospital, so it felt like she hadn't seen Amber in forever.

Marcus and her parents had turned up at the hospital as soon as the police had finished talking with her. Apparently, he'd changed his flight home from Europe to fly into Sydney instead of Melbourne, because he was so worried about the fact that she kept messaging him saying that she needed to talk, but then ignored all of his replies. He'd called their parents, who'd said she wasn't responding to any of their calls either, and they'd driven over to her apartment only to find it empty. They all started to think the worst — that she'd relapsed and tried to hurt herself — when the police phoned them to let them know what was going on.

'I still can't believe I chatted with that prick at the wedding,' said Grant, taking a sip of his wine and shaking his head.

'I let the guy stay at my house,' said Marcus.

'Can you two stop it?' said Georgia. 'I let the fucker move in. I win.'

She was trying to come across as sort of cool and funny and tough about it, as though the whole thing was just sliding off her back. But in truth, she was working as hard as ever to battle off the darkness. This time she wasn't doing it alone though. A counsellor had come to talk with her while she was in the hospital, and Georgia had also set up weekly appointments with her old psychologist. She was determined not to return to that place she'd been at four years ago. It wasn't going to be easy though. The knowledge that she'd allowed the man who'd taunted and harassed her to the point of complete and utter self-destruction back into her life was keeping her up most nights. She would lie awake and replay moment after intimate moment in excruciating detail. The slow and sensual kisses. The nights spent snuggled together on the couch. The deep conversations about everything she'd been through. The sex! Oh God, the sex that she had *enjoyed*. It was impossible not to hate herself for having loved it. When Sam had been sending her those emails, she'd pictured him as a slimy old man, the type of guy she'd *never* fall for. A man who'd never get what he wanted from her. Yet somehow, he'd done it. He'd played the part of the perfect guy, right down to being her knight in shining armour, rescuing her in that bar on the night they first met. And she'd fallen for the entire act.

Often, she would berate herself for being so clueless. For not somehow *knowing* him. For not somehow picking up on some sign, some hint that he wasn't real. But then she'd recite the words the counsellor had said to her: *It's not your fault, it's not your fault, it's not your fault.* And that would make her laugh because she was pretty sure the counsellor was just copying that scene from *Good Will Hunting.* And then she'd get mad. Because, yes, that was true, it wasn't her fault. It was Sam's fault. And it wasn't fair! He had no right to get revenge on her because *he* was the one who'd done the wrong thing in the first goddamned place. How dare he! How dare he blame her for ruining his life, how dare he think she somehow owed him something. And then she would cycle round to replaying all those intimate moments over and over again.

It was going to be a long road.

'Still, though,' said Grant, 'you should have called me as soon as you knew something was up. I live just two suburbs over and it was always Marcus's and my job to beat up any guys who weren't treating you right.'

'We've had this conversation — you two were terrible at that job. And also, this isn't the 1950s and I'm not a fucking damsel who needs men to rescue her, thank you very much.'

Act tough and you'll feel tough, Georgia. Fake it 'til you make it … Ah, screw it, ask for help when you need it.

'Fair point,' said Grant, looking sheepish. 'But listen, Georgia, I know I'm Marcus's mate, and that you and I don't exactly hang out, but you *can* call me if you ever need anything. Or you know, we could always just —'

He was cut off as Rick called out from the couch, 'Georgia, I think your phone is ringing.'

She patted her pocket. 'No, it's not,' she said. 'My phone is right here.'

'I'm sure I can hear a mobile phone.'

Georgia strained her ears. 'It's coming from the bedroom,' she said with a frown. 'Did someone dump their stuff on the bed?'

Her guests all shook their heads and Georgia headed to the bedroom to track down the source of the sound. It stopped ringing just as she walked in, but she was pretty sure it was coming from the other side of the bed. She skirted around and opened the drawers in Luke's bedside cabinet. The top one was filled with underwear and socks, and as she saw the Bonds waistband on his boxers, she felt an odd sense of longing for the old Luke, the one she'd fallen for so easily … It was followed almost immediately by a rush of revulsion, both for him and for herself. *How could there be any part of you that misses him, Georgia?*

She sifted through the clothes and found a stash of things: a phone, a small brown bottle, a zip-lock bag full of white tablets, and her missing happiness jar.

She pulled them all out, amazed at how much effort he'd put into terrorising her by making her think Cadence had broken in and stolen this jar. Then she smiled. He must have been so frustrated when she didn't notice it missing, when he had to carefully lead her to the conclusion that it was gone. The fucking idiot. Then she thought about the way he must have used the information inside this jar in order to get an insight into her mind, her fears, her insecurities. How he used all that to help control her.

She stopped smiling and felt a wave of despair wash over her. He was never overweight as a child, was he? He never cut himself and he never went through any of the depression or anxiety that he'd described, he'd just used it as a way to get her to open up.

She looked at the bottle and read the label: Syrup of Ipecac. She'd heard of this stuff. Years ago it was used to induce vomiting. She didn't think it was supposed to even exist anymore.

Then she realised why he had it. The night she'd been sick with food poisoning. It had nothing to do with the seafood on the pizza.

She wondered what the tablets were. That night at the hospital he'd said he'd been drugging her on and off — small amounts to make her off-kilter. It was another reason to feel angry with herself. She was a nurse. Why hadn't she noticed? She remembered all the times they'd gone out drinking together and she'd got so drunk so fast. She'd thought it was because she was mixing her spirits. Obviously, they were being mixed with other things as well. It made sense that she hadn't been able to focus on the face of that woman in the bathroom that time, and had so easily believed it might have been Cadence. And that she'd completely lost it when they were at the Hillside.

She put down the bottle and the small bag of pills and looked at the phone. It was a cheap brand and it showed one missed call on the screen. The phone was locked though, so she couldn't see anything more.

'Find it?'

She looked up to see Cadence standing in the doorway.

Georgia waved the phone at her. 'Yep. Guess it makes sense, doesn't it? The guy was leading a double life, he'd need an extra phone.'

'Except that he used the same one to contact both of us. So what was that one for?'

'No idea. I can't get into it, it's locked.'

Cadence walked over closer. 'Try spelling out the word PACMAN, that was his code on his other phone.'

Georgia tapped in the code. 'You were right!'

She went into the messages and Cadence came and sat down on the carpet next to her. They looked at the last text:

You fucking prick. I never would have stolen those drugs for you if I'd known what was going to happen. How did they get in her bag? Tell me what the hell is going on.

'What does that mean?' Cadence asked.

'I think this is about me,' said Georgia. 'I think this is how I lost my job.'

They walked out to the living room, Georgia holding the phone on an open palm as though it were a bomb that could explode at any moment. 'We found it,' she said. 'Luke had a secret phone in his drawer.'

'That fuckwit,' said Marcus, shaking his head.

'There's a message on here,' said Georgia, 'about the drugs that were planted in my bag. I think he had someone helping him or something.'

'Call it,' said Marcus. 'Find out who it is.'

'I don't know,' said Rick, walking over from the couch. 'Shouldn't you let the police know before you do anything else? That phone is evidence, isn't it?'

'Probably … oh fuck it. I'm calling it.' Georgia hit the call button. They all waited. It began to ring. At the same time, they heard the sound of a phone ringing on the other side of the front door. Panicked glances shot around the room.

'Is that … is that this call?' Cadence asked.

'Or a coincidence?' said Georgia.

'Someone open the door!' said Rick.

Marcus and Grant were already moving towards it but Georgia pushed past them. She flung open the door. Standing in front of her, searching through her handbag for her ringing phone, was Amber.

She looked up from her bag. 'Oh, hi,' she said. 'I was just about to knock.'

CHAPTER FORTY-TWO

Amber

Amber saw right through his super smooth act. He was a player for sure. He was saying all the right things, playing the part of the guy who was out to meet his soul mate. Pretending to be interested in everything she had to say. Laughing at her jokes. She even made an absolutely awful joke just to test him out. He failed the test. He laughed when he really shouldn't have given her anything more than a polite snicker. He kept the topic of conversation on her. *Where do you work? What's it like? Do you enjoy being a nurse? Was that what you always wanted to do? What else are you into?*

She let him do it. And she let him shift his body closer and closer. And when he placed one hand on her waist, she didn't brush it away. And when he leaned in for a kiss, she kissed him back. She knew it wasn't going to be any more than a one-night thing, but that was fine, because that's why she went out that night. She went out looking for some fun, looking for someone to fill the void.

No Violet tonight.

No Georgia or Rick — they were both on night shift.

Sometimes she did fine with a night to herself, absolutely fine. But other times, the emptiness in her home made the voices in her head start screaming out for noise. For comfort. For companionship. She longed to ask David to reconsider the terms of their custody arrangement. *Give me just a tiny bit more time with her,* she wanted to say. *Can't you see I'm doing so well? Can't you see how each time you pick her up and take her away, you snap off another piece of my heart and take it with you?* But she knew it had been a push for him to agree to allowing her to have Violet one weekend a fortnight.

She'd fallen for her daughter. Head over heels. In a way she'd never thought possible. Especially not in those early days lying in that bed in the maternity ward after the emergency caesarean. The nurses kept telling her it was normal. They kept trying to press Violet into her arms. But Amber would let her arms drop lifeless by her side and refuse to take hold of her baby. 'Please,' she'd say. 'Just take her away. Just give her to her father.'

If Amber had been her own patient, she would have picked it up in a second. The classic signs of post-natal depression. Veering dangerously close towards post-natal psychosis. And while the maternity nurses *did* pick up on the warning signs, while they did recommend that she see her GP, get a referral for a psychologist, maybe look at medication — Amber ignored them all. She thought she knew better. She wasn't sick. She wasn't suffering from PND. She'd just given birth to a child that she didn't ask for and didn't want, that's all.

To a man who was nothing more to her than a few dates and one broken condom. And she had no family support either, no one to convince her to try. She'd emigrated from the UK at eighteen. She never even let her parents know she was pregnant.

David fought her on it … at first. 'You can't just hand her over and wash your hands of her,' he said. 'This is *your* daughter, she's a part of you. It doesn't work this way. I'm not saying we have to be a family. I get that you don't want to be with me, but surely you want to be with her.'

He'd assumed the custody arrangement would be a 50/50 split. But Amber kept pushing and pushing. *You love her. I don't. You want her. I don't. You can take care of her. I can't.*

Eventually his mother was the one who convinced him to give in. She came around to see Amber with some paperwork she'd had a lawyer draw up.

'We'll take good care of her,' she said, as Amber signed her daughter's life away.

Amber shrugged. 'Okay. Thank you.'

It started with the odd pill here or there that she took when she was out partying with friends. She always made sure she was clean by the time she went into the hospital for her next shift … at first. But then she started taking more. Anything to numb the pain. Anything to make her forget that she had a baby girl out there in the world. A baby girl she'd handed away like she was nothing more than a doll she didn't want anymore.

The pills she took at clubs weren't enough. She started pinching the odd one here and there from work. Oxycodone or Ritalin to give her an extra buzz. She stopped caring about whether they were all out of her system before she did a shift.

It was the grandmother of a patient who first caught her out. A sharp-eyed older woman who she'd mistaken for a clueless old biddy.

'You just put that other tablet into your pocket.'

'What? No, I didn't.'

'Yes, you did. I saw you. You popped three out into your hand but you only gave two to my grandson.'

Amber tried to keep arguing, but the older woman was already charging out of the room to get hold of another nurse. That's when everything came crashing down for Amber. That's when she finally faced the truth about her PND. She got the help she needed, she stopped taking drugs and she eventually got her job back as well. And then when she was properly on the mend, she approached David and begged him to let her take her decision back.

When she transferred to a new hospital in the North West and met Georgia, she was too ashamed to admit that she was the one who'd simply given her daughter away. So she was vague about her past. She let Georgia believe what she wanted about the reasons for her limited access to her daughter.

That night, as she brought the suave, good-looking guy into her home — Sam was his name, not that she cared — she knew that her pleasure would be short-lived. Once they slept together, she'd be alone again. He'd probably creep out in the middle of the night, thinking she'd be none the wiser, thinking she'd wake in the morning and put one dainty hand to her mouth in shock. *Oh, how could he?* she'd cry, *I thought he wanted more than just a one-night stand!*

Ha. *I'm one step ahead of you, buddy. I* want *to wake up and find you gone.*

But she wasn't one step ahead of him. Not at all.

Because when they arrived home, they didn't head straight to the bedroom. Instead he suggested one last drink.

She didn't think to keep a close eye on her glass. In fact, she left him alone with the drinks while she went to the bathroom. After all, why would she think he'd put something in hers? He'd already been invited back. It was clear they were going to have sex, so there was no reason for him to drug her.

But he did. She felt the effects about thirty minutes after she finished her drink, as they were chatting on the couch. She was a nurse. She recognised the symptoms. She knew how much she'd had to drink and she knew it was wrong that her arms had become heavy. That her vision had started to swim.

'Did you …' Her voice came out in a slur, like her mouth had been filled with cotton wool. 'Did you … put something … in my … drink?'

She passed out and didn't wake until the next day. She was in her bed, in her clothes, and none of it made any sense. Had he drugged her last night, or had she miscounted her drinks?

But why do that only to carry her to her bed, fully clothed and never actually touch her? So, what now? Go to the police and report it? But report what exactly? Maybe she was mistaken, maybe she'd drunk way more than she'd realised.

Or maybe he had put something in her drink, but then he'd immediately regretted his actions and backed out. And if she did report it, what if David somehow found out and didn't want her to have Violet anymore? What if he judged her for bringing a strange man into her home, for letting him put something in her drink?

She decided to let it go, but to make sure she was more careful in future.

The following day though, while she was on a break at work, she checked her phone and discovered a message from him.

This is Sam from the other night. I need you to do something for me, the message said. *I need you to get hold of some drugs from your work.*

Amber had stared at the message, entirely confused. Then she wrote back.

You're fucking joking, right? Why the hell would I do that?

Well, I think you'll do it because if you don't, your boss will find out that you're currently at work under the influence of coke.

What are you on about? No, I'm not.

Funny thing is though, if they decide to do a drug test on you, it'll show up in your system. Care to risk that?

She held very still, reading and re-reading the message. Cocaine could stay in your bloodstream for up to two days. He could be telling the truth. If he'd somehow given her some when she passed out the other night — maybe rubbed it into her gums or something — she could be in huge trouble.

While she was thinking, another message came through.

Seriously, you do this one thing and I go away, you never hear from me again. Grab the drugs and meet me at the cafe on Harris Street after you finish your shift and I won't have to contact your boss and tell her that you're high as a kite.

In the end, Amber couldn't see a way out of it. She couldn't risk being found to be working with cocaine in her system, not with her history. And if she lost her job, there was every chance she might lose Violet. Stealing drugs was risky too, but she knew a way she could do it and get away with it. She'd had a lot of practice back when she needed them for herself. Just get it over and done with it, hand them over, don't think about what he wants them for, and forget any of this ever happened.

When she met him at the cafe, he'd had the nerve to place a hand on her waist and lean in like he was going to kiss her on the cheek. She dodged the kiss, resisted the urge to knee him in the balls, shoved the bag into his hands and left.

The next day she called in sick. She wanted to stay away from work for as long as possible to give the cocaine a chance to work its way out of her system. But then Rick called to tell her that Georgia had been suspended for stealing drugs. Her first thought was that she was going to have to turn herself in. She couldn't let Georgia take the blame for the missing drugs. But then Rick said they'd been found in Georgia's bag. She couldn't make sense of it. How did the drugs she'd stolen for Sam end up in Georgia's bag?

She was going to have to talk with Georgia, figure out what was going on. Find out the connection between her and Sam. The problem was, Georgia wouldn't take her calls.

Amber sent texts, left voicemails, but Georgia refused to call her back. It never occurred to her that Georgia's boyfriend Luke might actually *be* Sam.

The guilt was eating away at her. She sent a message to Sam.

You fucking prick. I never would have stolen those drugs for you if I'd known what you were going to do. How did they get in her bag? Tell me what the hell is going on?

But he didn't respond. And then she heard the news that Georgia had been in a car accident. And now Georgia was finally returning her calls, and telling her all about Luke, and how Luke wasn't Luke at all but that his name was Sam, and everything finally made sense for Amber.

She tried to confess then and there on the phone … but she couldn't seem to find a way to say the words. But she knew she was going to have to tell the truth eventually.

CHAPTER FORTY-THREE

Cadence

It took a lot of convincing to get Marcus, Grant and Rick to leave. I could see it in Marcus's eyes — how much he loved his little sister. How desperate he was to protect her. And Rick, he almost looked as though he was more hurt than Georgia as he heard about Amber's part in all of this.

Amber had wanted to talk to Georgia alone, but there were too many cries of protest when she made that suggestion. Everyone else wanted to hear her explanation, so she had to tell her story in front of all five of us.

'I'm so sorry I didn't tell you straightaway,' she said through tears when she was done. 'I'm sorry I let it all get this far. Maybe if I'd gone straight to the police then you never would have got hurt.'

I was impressed by Georgia's reaction. She'd walked straight over to her friend and hugged her. 'You couldn't have predicted any of this,' she'd said. Then she started telling Marcus, Grant and Rick that they needed to go. That this was about the three of us. That we needed to talk and we needed to do it alone.

What I didn't expect was what Georgia said next, once everyone had left.

'I want to make him pay for what he's done to all of us.'

CHAPTER FORTY-FOUR

Georgia

'That's all well and good,' said Cadence. 'Obviously we all want him to answer for what he's done. But how? The police haven't been able to find him yet, what makes you think we can?'

'Because we know him,' said Georgia. 'We know the games he plays. And we can find a way to use that against him.'

'Umm, I hate to say it,' Amber said, 'but isn't the point that we *don't* know him? That he's just spent months being someone else?'

'No ... yes ... maybe, but I still think between the three of us we have a unique insight into the way this guy works. Plus, we have this.' Georgia held up the phone.

'We have to give that straight to the police!' said Cadence.

'We will. But first I want to find out what other messages are on here. And also, who was calling. I saw earlier that they left a voicemail, but I didn't want to say anything until the others left. Here, let's listen to it together.'

Georgia dialled voicemail, put the phone on speaker and held it out. A bubbly sounding voice burst out of the phone.

'Hi Sam! It's Nadia. It's been for-fucking-ever, and I'm in the mood for your body. Call me okay? Mwah!'

'For fuck's sake,' Cadence said when the message finished. 'How many different girls is he juggling?'

'Too many,' said Georgia, thinking of Lena and how she'd been yet another one of his one-night stands. Another one of his victims, used by him to find out more about her past. When all of this was over, she was going to have to let Lena know the full story, and also keep her promise to reignite their friendship. 'But this is a good thing. This girl Nadia is an opportunity to find him.'

'Yeah, but how?' said Cadence. 'She has this number for him and he doesn't have his phone. I don't see how she'd have any more chance of finding him than us.'

'I don't know, but we have to try!'

There was silence for a moment and then Cadence said, 'You know how I knew his password for his phone? Do you think he uses that same password for other things?'

'Maybe,' said Georgia.

'The police took his laptop, right?'

'Right.'

'But did he ever use *your* computer while he was living here?'

'Yep, he did actually.'

Cadence smiled. 'Let's see what we can find.'

*

Two hours later their plan was in place. Nadia had been extremely helpful over the phone once they'd revealed his true colours to her. And his Facebook account under his real name had been fairly easy to find as well.

'I'm still not sure if he's going to fall for it,' said Amber. 'Surely he'll know that we're only trying to draw him out.'

'That's why we're using his own arrogance against him,' said Georgia. 'Trust me. That's his weakness.'

In all honesty, she didn't know if this was going to work. But doing something felt better than sitting back and waiting for the police to track him down. What if they weren't even looking? What if he didn't rank that highly on their list of priorities?

'I wonder how long we'll have to wait to see if it worked?' said Cadence.

As if on cue, Georgia's computer made a dinging noise with a Facebook message. The three of them leaned down and read it together.

When they were done they all looked at one another.

'Nice fucking work, girls,' said Amber.

CHAPTER FORTY-FIVE

Sam

He arrived early and took a table towards the back of the cafe, a corner booth so that he could see her coming first. He liked to watch her walk. *The silly bitch always wear heels that are way too high for her, thinking it made her look sexy, when instead it makes her look like a fucking bimbo. But that doesn't mean I don't enjoy watching her totter along in them. seeing her look so vulnerable, so … inferior, as she tries to look hot for me. It always gives me an instant hard-on.*

He'd missed Nadia while he'd been running his con on Cadence and Georgia. They'd only ever had sex casually after meeting through Tinder, not that long ago. But she was great in bed and she let him get a little rough with her when he was in the mood. He'd been crashing at a mate's place since everything had gone sideways with the girls. Obviously, he did have mates here in Sydney because he wasn't from Perth, like he'd told Georgia. His plan was to take off up north until everything died down with the cops. But one last fuck with Nadia before he left would be nice. It'd cheer him up after everything had gone so far wrong. In fact, maybe this time he'd get even rougher than usual.

He hadn't thought he'd ever hear from her again after he'd left his other phone behind at Georgia's place and lost her number. So he was glad when she contacted him through Facebook and asked him to meet her for a coffee. Not as good as drinks, but still, he knew he could get her into bed. She was easy, always had been.

When the waitress approached his table carrying a plate of food, he immediately shook his head. 'I haven't ordered anything yet.'

She shrugged. 'Whatever, someone ordered it for you.'

He was perplexed as she placed the plate down in front of him. Who'd ordered for him? Why? He looked at the food. French toast with berries. What the fuck?

That's when his phone buzzed with a Facebook message from Nadia. He opened it and read it.

It was cute how you accepted my friend request without actually checking to make sure I am who I say I am.

It all clicked into place. He went to stand, and that's when he saw them. Two police officers making their way through the cafe towards him.

'Just the bloke we've been looking for.'

Cadence

I sold most of my shares. Seeing how easily Sam had isolated me from the world made me want to be a part of it, more than ever. So I bought a small warehouse-style place in Surry Hills. Michelle helped me set it all up. Downstairs was split into a gallery and a work area. Upstairs was my home. I shared the work area with other artists who rented the space from me on a casual month-to-month basis. And we had a gallery to showcase our work, along with pieces from various local artists. Once a month we had a Saturday night exhibition with drinks and finger food, and people got happily tipsy and spent more than they normally would on a new piece of art for their home. It was a decent business model.

I'll admit, my work did take a darker turn. Call it my post-Luke period. Think lots of giant pieces done with wild charcoal strokes and splatters of black ink. But here and there a pop of bright blue or sunny yellow would creep in. A sign that a happier part of me, deep inside, was fighting to come back.

Oh, and I got a dog. A tiny and very fluffy Pomeranian named Cactus.

Georgia

Her parents reissued their offer of a 'healing and rejuvenation trip' to Bali, which thankfully turned out to mean lying on the beach, sipping cocktails and having massages. There was minimal kombucha or yoga. They also suggested that Marcus might like to come along with them, because they knew how good it would be for Georgia to have his company. He accepted. Troy, Aaron and Pete were all curious as to when their parents would be paying for the three of them to visit Bali as well. Once the truth had come out about the stolen drugs, Georgia had been promptly reinstated at work; but when Georgia mentioned the Bali trip, Denise had granted her leave in an instant.

When Georgia asked her mum what had prompted the original offer, Susan had confessed that she didn't really like Luke very much after meeting him at Marcus's wedding.

'You're kidding me?' Georgia said. 'But he was playing the part of the perfect boyfriend at that stage.'

Her mother shrugged. 'What can I say? I could tell there was something not quite right about him. I could see it in his aura. A muddiness. It worried me. I thought maybe I could sneak you away and somehow talk you into breaking up with him. Obviously if I'd known you'd let him *move in* with you I would have pushed a lot more.'

Georgia was confident the muddy aura part was bullshit. Her mother couldn't see auras; she'd probably made that part up after finding out about Luke's true motivations in order to convince herself she knew more than everyone else did.

*

Georgia was still smoking occasionally at that stage, and one night while they were sitting on the balcony, overlooking the ocean, Marcus made a joke about the time he'd caught Grant giving her a cigarette when she was fifteen.

It triggered a memory for Georgia. 'Oh yeah, at your wedding he said that wasn't the reason you hit him that day.'

'Of course, it wasn't,' Marcus said. 'I thought you always knew why I hit him.'

'No.'

'He said you were hot and that he was going to ask you out … so obviously, I hit him.'

'Marcus! What the hell? Why would you hit him for that?'

'Because I was a moronic, immature sixteen-year-old, and I didn't want my best mate to date my little sister. Sorry, but you didn't actually want him to ask you out, did you?'

'Jesus Christ, Marcus, I don't know! Maybe.'

'Shit. I'll fix it.'

Grant phoned her within the hour and they chatted for a good twenty minutes before there was a pause in the conversation and he took a deep breath and asked her out.

Georgia hesitated before responding. 'I want to say yes,' she said. 'A big part of me wants that. But at the same time … I know I'm not ready. I need some more time. Listen, though, if you've waited this long to ask, do you think you could do me a favour?'

'Anything,' he said.

'Ask me again in a couple of months.'

'Deal.'

ACKNOWLEDGEMENTS

My heartfelt gratitude goes out to the following people (diplomatically ordered alphabetically): Susan Badman, Dianne Blacklock, Sheila Crowley, Kati Harrington, Katherine Hassett, Maxine Hitchcock, Kerry Lockwood, Brooke Macdonald, Pippa Masson, Matilda McDonald, Steve Menasse, Bernie Moriarty, Diane Moriarty, Jaclyn Moriarty, Liane Moriarty, Fiona Ostric, Allyson Prowse, Stacy Testa, Sabeeha Toynton, Anna Valdinger, Tess Woods, Belinda Yuille and Kristen Zullo. I'd also like to thank all of the other wonderful people at Curtis Brown, HarperCollins Australia and Michael Joseph UK along with the kind and generous staff at Mini Espresso Bar and Youeni. Every one of you helped to make this book possible — whether it was providing coffee, feedback, support, advice, invaluable edits or answering medical questions. Thank you.

THE FIFTH LETTER

by Nicola Moriarty

Joni, Trina, Deb and Eden. Best friends since the first day of school. Best friends, they liked to say, forever. But now they are in their thirties and real life — husbands, children, work — has got in the way. So, on their annual trip away, Joni has an idea, something to help them reconnect.

Each woman will write an anonymous letter, sharing the things that are *really* going on in their lives.

As the confessions come tumbling out, Joni starts to feel the certainty of their decades-long friendships slip from her fingers. Then she finds a fifth letter, one containing a secret so big that its writer had tried to destroy it. And now Joni is starting to wonder, did she ever really know her friends at all?

'Dramatic, mysterious and compelling ... it's easy to read this book in one sitting' *Vogue*

Available in paperback, ebook and audio

THOSE OTHER WOMEN

by Nicola Moriarty

Poppy's world has tipped sideways: the husband who never wanted children has betrayed her with her broody best friend.

At least Annalise is on her side. Poppy's new friend is determined to celebrate their freedom from kids, so together they create a Facebook group to meet up with like-minded women — and vent just a *little* about smug mums and their privileges at work.

Meanwhile, Frankie would love a night out, away from her darlings — she's not had one in years — and she's sick of being judged by women at the office and stay-at-home mums.

When Poppy and Annalise's group takes off, frustrated members start confronting mums like Frankie in the real world. Cafes become battlegrounds, playgrounds become warzones, and offices have never been so divided.

A rivalry that was once harmless fun is spiralling out of control. Because one of their members is a wolf in sheep's clothing. And she has an agenda of her own …

'I devoured it, loved it and totally escaped into it …
Fun and topical' *Marian Keyes*

Available in paperback, ebook and audio